INTERESTING TIMES

A Novel of Discworld

BOOKS BY TERRY PRATCHETT

The Carpet People
The Dark Side of the Sun
Strata
Truckers
Diggers
Wings
Only You Can Save Mankind
Johnny and the Dead
The Unadulterated Cat (with Gray Jolliffe)
Good Omens (with Neil Gaiman)

THE DISCWORLD SERIES:

The Colour of Magic
The Light Fantastic
Equal Rites
Mort
Sourcery
Wyrd Sisters
Pyramids
Guards! Guards!
Eric (with Josh Kirby)
Moving Pictures
Reaper Man
Witches Abroad
Small Gods
Lords and Ladies
Men at Arms
Soul Music
Interesting Times
Mort: A Discworld Big Comic (with Graham Higgins)
The Streets of Ankh-Morpork (with Stephen Briggs)
The Discworld Companion (with Stephen Briggs)

Terry Pratchett

INTERESTING TIMES

A Novel of Discworld

HarperPrism

HarperPaperbacks
A Division of HarperCollins*Publishers*
10 East 53rd Street, New York, N.Y. 10022-5299

HarperPrism is an imprint of HarperPaperbacks.

HarperCollins®, ⛫ ®, HarperPaperbacks™, and HarperPrism® are trademarks of HarperCollins*Publishers* Inc.

A hardcover edition of this book was published in Great Britain in 1994 by Victor Gollancz Ltd.

Printed in the United States of America

ISBN 0-06-105252-3

There is a curse.

They say:
May You Live in Interesting Times

INTERESTING TIMES

*T*his is where the gods play games with the lives of men, on a board which is *at one and the same time* a simple playing area and the whole world.

And Fate always wins.

Fate always wins. Most of the gods throw dice but Fate plays chess, and you don't find out until too late that he's been using two queens all along.

Fate wins. At least, so it is claimed. Whatever happens, they say afterwards, it must have been Fate.*

Gods can take any form, but the one aspect of themselves they cannot change is their eyes, which show their nature. The eyes of Fate are hardly eyes at all—just dark holes into an infinity speckled with what may be stars or, there again, may be other things.

He blinked them, smiled at his fellow players in the smug way winners do just before they become winners, and said:

"I accuse the High Priest of the Green Robe in the library with the double-handed axe."

And he won.

He beamed at them.

"No one likeh a poor winner," grumbled Offler the Crocodile God, through his fangs.

"It seems that I am favoring myself today," said Fate. "Anyone fancy something else?"

---

*People are always a little confused about this, as they are in the case of miracles. When someone is saved from certain death by a strange concatenation of circumstances, they say that's a miracle. But of course if someone is *killed* by a freak chain of events—the oil spilled just *there,* the safety fence broken just *there*—that must *also* be a miracle. Just because it's not nice doesn't mean it's not miraculous.

The gods shrugged.

"Mad Kings?" said Fate pleasantly. "Star-Crossed Lovers?"

"I think we've lost the rules for that one," said Blind Io, chief of the gods.

"Or Tempest-Wrecked Mariners?"

"You always win," said Io.

"Floods and Droughts?" said Fate. "That's an easy one."

A shadow fell across the gaming table. The gods looked up.

"Ah," said Fate.

"Let a game begin," said the Lady.

There was always an argument about whether the newcomer was a goddess at all. Certainly no one ever got anywhere by worshipping her, and she tended to turn up only where she was least expected, such as now. And people who trusted in her seldom survived. Any temples built to her would surely be struck by lightning. Better to juggle axes on a tightrope than say her name. Just call her the waitress in the Last Chance saloon.

She was generally referred to as the Lady, and her eyes were green; not as the eyes of humans are green, but emerald green from edge to edge. It was said to be her favorite color.

"Ah," said Fate again. "And what game will it be?"

She sat down opposite him. The watching gods looked sidelong at one another. This looked interesting. These two were ancient enemies.

"How about . . ." she paused, ". . . Mighty Empires?"

"Oh, I *hate* that one," said Offler, breaking the sudden silence. "Everyone dief at the end."

"Yes," said Fate, "I believe they do." He nodded at the Lady, and in much the same voice as professional gamblers say "Aces high?" said, "The Fall of Great Houses? Destinies of Nations Hanging by a Thread?"

"Certainly," she said.

"Oh, *good.*" Fate waved a hand across the board. The Discworld appeared.

"And where shall we play?" he said.

"The Counterweight Continent," said the Lady. "Where five noble families have fought one another for centuries."

"Really? Which families are these?" said Io. He had little

involvement with individual humans. He generally looked after thunder and lightning, so from his point of view the only purpose of humanity was to get wet or, in occasional cases, charred.

"The Hongs, the Sungs, the Tangs, the McSweeneys and the Fangs."

"Them? I didn't know they were noble," said Io.

"They're all very rich and have had millions of people butchered or tortured to death merely for reasons of expediency and pride," said the Lady.

The watching gods nodded solemnly. That was certainly noble behavior. That was exactly what they would have done.

"*McFweeneyf?*" said Offler.

"Very old established family," said Fate.

"Oh."

"And they wrestle one another for the Empire," said Fate. "Very good. Which will you be?"

The Lady looked at the history stretched out in front of them.

"The Hongs are the most powerful. Even as we speak, they have taken yet more cities," she said. "I see they are fated to win."

"So, no doubt, you'll pick a weaker family."

Fate waved his hand again. The playing pieces appeared, and started to move around the board as if they had a life of their own, which was of course the case.

"But," he said, "we shall play without dice. I don't trust you with dice. You throw them where I can't see them. We will play with steel, and tactics, and politics, and war."

The Lady nodded.

Fate looked across at his opponent.

"And your move?" he said.

She smiled. "I've already made it."

He looked down. "But I don't see your pieces on the board."

"They're not on the board yet," she said.

She opened her hand.

There was something black and yellow on her palm. She blew on it, and it unfolded its wings.

It was a butterfly.

Fate always wins . . .

At least, when people stick to the rules.

* * *

According to the philosopher Ly Tin Wheedle, chaos is found in greatest abundance wherever order is being sought. It always defeats order, because it is better organized.

This is the butterfly of the storms.

See the wings, slightly more ragged than those of the common fritillary. In reality, thanks to the fractal nature of the universe, this means that those ragged edges are infinite—in the same way that the edge of any rugged coastline, when measured to the ultimate microscopic level, is infinitely long—or, if not infinite, then at least so close to it that Infinity can be seen on a clear day.

And therefore, if their edges are infinitely long, the wings must logically be infinitely big.

They may *look* about the right size for a butterfly's wings, but that's only because human beings have always preferred common sense to logic.

The Quantum Weather Butterfly (*Papilio tempestae*) is an undistinguished yellow color, although the mandelbrot patterns on the wings are of considerable interest. Its outstanding feature is its ability to create weather.

This presumably began as a survival trait, since even an extremely hungry bird would find itself inconvenienced by a nasty localized tornado.* From there it possibly became a secondary sexual characteristic, like the plumage of birds or the throat sacs of certain frogs. Look at *me,* the male says, flapping his wings lazily in the canopy of the rain forest. I may be an undistinguished yellow color but in a fortnight's time, a thousand miles away, Freak Gales Cause Road Chaos.

This is the butterfly of the storms.

It flaps its wings . . .

---

*Usually about six inches across.

This is the Discworld, which goes through space on the back of a giant turtle.

Most worlds do, at some time in their perception. It's a cosmological view the human brain seems pre-programmed to take.

On veldt and plain, in cloud jungle and silent red desert, in swamp and reed marsh, in fact in any place where something goes "plop" off a floating log as you approach, variations on the following take place at a crucial early point in the development of the tribal mythology . . .

"You see dat?"

"What?"

"It just went plop off dat log."

"Yeah? Well?"

"I reckon . . . I reckon . . . like, I *reckon* der world is carried on der back of one of dem."

A moment of silence while this astrophysical hypothesis is considered, and then . . .

"The whole world?"

"Of course, when I say one of dem, I mean a *big* one of dem."

"It'd have to be, yeah."

"Like . . . really big."

"'S funny, but . . . I see what you mean."

"Makes sense, right?"

"Makes sense, yeah. Thing is . . ."

"What?"

"I just hope it never goes plop."

But this *is* the Discworld, which has not only the turtle but also the four giant elephants on which the wide, slowly turning wheel of the world revolves.*

There is the Circle Sea, approximately halfway between the Hub and the Rim. Around it are those countries which, according to History, constitute the civilized world, i.e. a world that can

---

*People wonder how this works, since a terrestrial elephant would be unlikely to bear a revolving load for any length of time without some serious friction burns. But you may as well ask why the axle of a planet doesn't squeak, or where love goes, or what sound yellow makes.

support historians: Ephebe, Tsort, Omnia, Klatch and the sprawling city state of Ankh-Morpork.

This is a story that starts somewhere else, where a man is lying on a raft in a blue lagoon under a sunny sky. His head is resting on his arms. He is happy—in his case, a mental state so rare as to be almost unprecedented. He is whistling an amiable little tune, and dangling his feet in the crystal clear water.

They're pink feet with ten toes that look like little piggy-wiggies.

From the point of view of a shark, skimming over the reef, they look like lunch, dinner and tea.

It was, as always, a matter of protocol. Of discretion. Of careful etiquette. Of, ultimately, alcohol. Or at least the illusion of alcohol.

Lord Vetinari, as supreme ruler of Ankh-Morpork, could in theory summon the Archchancellor of Unseen University to his presence and, indeed, have him executed if he failed to obey.

On the other hand Mustrum Ridcully, as head of the college of wizards, had made it clear in polite but firm ways that *he* could turn *him* into a small amphibian and, indeed, start jumping around the room on a pogo stick.

Alcohol bridged the diplomatic gap nicely. Sometimes Lord Vetinari invited the Archchancellor to the palace for a convivial drink. And of course the Archchancellor went, because it would be *bad manners* not to. And everyone understood the position, and everyone was on their best behavior, and thus civil unrest and slime on the carpet were averted.

It was a beautiful afternoon. Lord Vetinari was sitting in the palace gardens, watching the butterflies with an expression of mild annoyance. He found something very slightly offensive about the way they just fluttered around enjoying themselves in an unprofitable way.

He looked up.

"Ah, Archchancellor," he said. "So good to see you. Do sit down. I trust you are well?"

"Yes indeed," said Mustrum Ridcully. "And yourself? You are in good health?"

"Never better. The weather, I see, has turned out nice again."

"I thought yesterday was particularly fine, certainly."

"Tomorrow, I am told, could well be even better."

"We could certainly do with a fine spell."

"Yes, indeed."

"Yes."

"Ah . . ."

"Certainly."

They watched the butterflies. A butler brought long, cool drinks.

"What is it they actually do with the flowers?" said Lord Vetinari.

"What?"

The Patrician shrugged. "Never mind. It was not at all important. But—since you are here, Archchancellor, having dropped by on your way to something infinitely more important, I am sure, most kind—I wonder if you could tell me: who is the Great Wizard?"

Ridcully considered this.

"The Dean, possibly," he said. "He must be all of twenty stone."

"Somehow I feel that is not perhaps the right answer," said Lord Vetinari. "I suspect from context that 'great' means superior."

"Not the Dean, then," said Ridcully.

Lord Vetinari tried to recollect the faculty of Unseen University. The mental picture that emerged was of a small range of foothills in pointy hats.

"The context does not, I feel, suggest the Dean," he said.

"Er . . . what context would this be?" said Ridcully.

The Patrician picked up his walking stick.

"Come this way," he said. "I suppose you had better see for yourself. It is very vexing."

Ridcully looked around with interest as he followed Lord Vetinari. He did not often have a chance to see the gardens, which had been written up in the "How Not To Do It" section of gardening manuals everywhere.

They had been laid out, and a truer phrase was never used, by the renowned or at least notorious landscape gardener and all round inventor "Bloody Stupid" Johnson, whose absentmindedness and blindness to elementary mathematics made every step a walk with danger. His genius . . . well, as far as Ridcully understood it, his genius was exactly the opposite of whatever kind of genius it was that built earthworks that tapped the secret yet beneficent forces of the leylines.

No one was quite certain what forces Bloody Stupid's designs tapped, but the chiming sundial frequently exploded, the crazy paving had committed suicide and the cast-iron garden furniture was known to have melted on three occasions.

The Patrician led the way through a gate and into something like a dovecot. A creaking wooden stairway led around the inside. A few of Ankh-Morpork's indestructible feral pigeons muttered and sniggered in the shadows.

"What's this?" said Ridcully, as the stairs groaned under him.

The Patrician took a key out of his pocket. "I have always understood that Mr. Johnson originally planned this to be a bee-hive," he said. "However, in the absence of bees ten feet long we have found . . . other uses."

He unlocked a door to a wide, square room with a big unglazed window in each wall. Each rectangle was surrounded by a wooden arrangement to which was affixed a bell on a spring. It was apparent that anything large enough, entering by one of the windows, would cause the bell to ring.

In the center of the room, standing on a table, was the largest bird Ridcully had ever seen. It turned and fixed him with a beady yellow eye.

The Patrician reached into a pocket and took out a jar of anchovies. "This one caught us rather unexpectedly," he said. "It must be almost ten years since a message last arrived. We used to keep a few fresh mackerel on ice."

"Isn't that a Pointless Albatross?" said Ridcully.

"Indeed," said Lord Vetinari. "And a highly trained one. It will return this evening. Six thousand miles on one jar of anchovies and a bottle of fish paste my clerk Drumknott found in the kitchens. Amazing."

"I'm sorry?" said Ridcully. "Return to where?"

Lord Vetinari turned to face him.

"*Not*, let me make it clear, to the Counterweight Continent," he said. "This is *not* one of those birds the Agatean Empire uses for its message services. It is a well-known fact that we have no contact with that mysterious land. And this bird is *not* the first to arrive here for many years, and it did *not* bring a strange and puzzling message. Do I make myself clear?"

"No."

"Good."

"This is not an albatross?"

The Patrician smiled. "Ah, I can see you're getting the hang of it."

Mustrum Ridcully, though possessed of a large and efficient brain, was not at home with duplicity. He looked at the long vicious beak.

"Looks like a bloody albatross to me," he said. "And you just said it was. I said, isn't that a—"

The Patrician waved a hand irritably. "Leaving aside our ornithological studies," he said, "the point is that this bird had, in its message pouch, the following piece of paper—"

"You mean did *not* have the following piece of paper?" said Ridcully, struggling for a grip.

"Ah, yes. Of course, that is what I mean. And this isn't it. Observe."

He handed a single small sheet to the Archchancellor.

"Looks like paintin'," said Ridcully.

"Those are Agatean pictograms," said the Patrician.

"You mean they're *not* Agatean pictograms?"

"Yes, yes, certainly," sighed the Patrician, "I can see you are well alongside the essential business of diplomacy. Now . . . your views, please."

"Looks like slosh, slosh, slosh, slosh, Wizzard," said Ridcully.

"And from that you deduce . . . ?"

"He took Art because he wasn't any good at spelling? I mean, who wrote it? Painted it, I mean?"

"I don't know. The Grand Viziers used to send the occasional message, but I gather there has been some turmoil in recent years. It is unsigned, you notice. However, I cannot ignore it."

"Wizzard, wizzard," said Ridcully, thoughtfully.

"The pictograms mean 'Send Us Instantly The Great'," said Lord Vetinari.

"... wizzard ..." said Ridcully to himself, tapping the paper.

The Patrician tossed an anchovy to the albatross, which swallowed it greedily.

"The Empire has a million men under arms," he said. "Happily, it suits the rulers to pretend that everywhere outside the Empire is a valueless howling waste peopled only by vampires and ghosts. They usually have no interest whatsoever in our affairs. This is fortunate for us, because they are both cunning, rich and powerful. Frankly, I had hoped they had forgotten about us altogether. And now this. I was hoping to be able to dispatch the wretched person and forget about it."

"... wizzard ..." said Ridcully.

"Perhaps you would like a holiday?" said the Patrician, a hint of hope in his voice.

"Me? No. Can't abide foreign food," said Ridcully quickly. He repeated, half to himself, "Wizzard ..."

"The word seems to fascinate you," said Lord Vetinari.

"Seen it spelled like that before," said Ridcully. "Can't remember where."

"I'm sure you *will* remember. And will be in a position to send the Great Wizard, however he is spelled, to the Empire by teatime."

Ridcully's jaw dropped.

"Six thousand miles? By magic? Do you know how hard that is?"

"I cherish my ignorance on the subject," said Lord Vetinari.

"Besides," Ridcully went on, "they're, well ... foreign over there. I thought they had enough wizards of their own."

"I really couldn't say."

"We don't know why they want this wizard?"

"No. But I'm sure there is someone you could spare. There seems to be such a lot of you down there."

"I mean, it could be for some terrible foreign purpose," said Ridcully. For some reason the face of the Dean waddled across his mind, and he brightened up. "They might be happy with *a* great wizard, do you think?" he mused.

"I leave that entirely to you. But by tonight I would like to be able to send back a message saying that the Great Wizzard is duly on his way. And then we can forget about it."

"Of course, it would be very hard to bring the chap back," said Ridcully. He thought of the Dean again. "Practically impossible," he added, in an inappropriately happy way. "I expect we'd try for months and months without succeeding. I expect we'd attempt everything with no luck. Damn it."

"I can see you are agog to rise to this challenge," said the Patrician. "Let me not detain you from rushing back to the University and putting measures in hand."

"But . . . 'wizzard' . . ." Ridcully murmured. "Rings a faint bell, that. Think I've seen it before, somewhere."

The shark didn't think much. Sharks don't. Their thought processes can largely be represented by "=." You see it = you eat it.

But, as it arrowed through the waters of the lagoon, its tiny brain began to receive little packages of selachian existential dread that could only be called doubts.

It knew it was the biggest shark around. All the challengers had fled, or run up against good old "=." Yet its body told it that something was coming up fast behind it.

It turned gracefully, and the first thing it saw was *hundreds* of legs and *thousands* of toes, a whole pork pie factory of piggy-wiggies.

Many things went on at Unseen University and, regrettably, teaching had to be one of them. The faculty had long ago confronted this fact and had perfected various devices for avoiding it. But this was perfectly all right because, to be fair, so had the students.

The system worked quite well and, as happens in such cases, had taken on the status of a tradition. Lectures clearly took place, because they were down there on the timetable in black and white. The fact that no one attended was an irrelevant detail.

It was occasionally maintained that this meant that the lectures did not in fact happen at all, but no one ever attended them to find out if this was true. Anyway, it was argued (by the Reader in Woolly Thinking*) that lectures had taken place *in essence,* so that was all right, too.

And therefore education at the University mostly worked by the age-old method of putting a lot of young people in the vicinity of a lot of books and hoping that something would pass from one to the other, while the actual young people put themselves in the vicinity of inns and taverns for exactly the same reason.

It was the middle of the afternoon. The Chair of Indefinite Studies was giving a lecture in room 3B and therefore his presence asleep in front of the fire in the Uncommon Room was a technicality upon which no diplomatic man would comment.

Ridcully kicked him on the shins.

"Ow!"

"Sorry to interrupt, Chair," said Ridcully, in a very perfunctory way. "Gods help me, I need the Council of Wizards. Where is everybody?"

The Chair of Indefinite Studies rubbed his leg. "I know the Lecturer in Recent Runes is giving a lecture in 3B,"[†] he said. "But I don't know where he *is.* You know, that really hurt—"

"Round everyone up. My study. Ten minutes," said Ridcully. He was a great believer in this approach. A less direct Archchancellor would have wandered around looking for everyone. His policy was to find one person and make their life difficult until everything happened the way he wanted it to.[§]

Nothing in nature had that many feet. True, some things had that many *legs*—damp, wriggling things that live under rocks—but those weren't legs with feet, they were just legs that ended without ceremony.

*Which is like Fuzzy Logic, only less so.

[†]All *virtual* lectures took place in room 3B, a room not locatable on any floor plan of the University and also, it was considered, infinite in size.

[§]A policy adopted by almost all managers and several notable gods.

Something brighter than the shark might have been wary. But "=" swung treacherously into play and shot it forward.

That was its first mistake.

In these circumstances, one mistake = oblivion.

Ridcully was waiting impatiently when, one by one, the senior wizards filed in from serious lecturing in room 3B. Senior wizards needed a lot of lecturing in order to digest their food.

"Everyone here?" he said. "Right. Sit down. Listen carefully. Now . . . Vetinari hasn't had an albatross. It hasn't come all the way from the Counterweight Continent, and there isn't a strange message that we've got to obey, apparently. Follow me so far?"

The senior wizards exchanged glances.

"I think we may be a shade unclear on the detail," said the Dean.

"I was using diplomatic language."

"Could you, perhaps, try to be a little more indiscreet?"

"We've got to send a wizard to the Counterweight Continent," said Ridcully. "And we've got to do it by teatime. Someone's asked for a Great Wizard and it seems we've got to send one. Only they spell it Wizzard—"

"Oook?"

"Yes, Librarian?"

Unseen University's Librarian, who had been dozing with his head on the table, was suddenly sitting bolt upright. Then he pushed back his chair and, arms waving wildly for balance, left the room at a bowlegged run.

"Probably remembered an overdue book," said the Dean. He lowered his voice. "Am I alone in thinking, by the way, that it doesn't add to the status of this University to have an ape on the faculty?"

"Yes," said Ridcully flatly. "You are. We've got the only librarian who can rip off your arm with his leg. People respect that. Only the other day the head of the Thieves' Guild was asking me if we could turn *their* librarian into an ape and, besides, he's the only one of you buggers who stays awake more'n an hour a day. Anyway—"

"Well, I find it embarrassing," said the Dean. "Also, he's not a proper orang-utan. I've been reading a book. It says a dominant male should have huge cheek pads. Has he got huge cheek pads? I don't think so. And—"

"Shut up, Dean," said Ridcully, "or I won't let you go to the Counterweight Continent."

"I don't see what raising a perfectly valid—What?"

"They're asking for the Great Wizzard," said Ridcully. "And I immediately thought of you." *As the only man I know who can sit on two chairs at the same time,* he added silently.

"The Empire?" squeaked the Dean. "Me? But they hate foreigners!"

"So do you. You should get on famously."

"It's six thousand miles!" said the Dean, trying a new tack. "Everyone knows you can't get that far by magic."

"Er. As a matter of fact you can, I think," said a voice from the other end of the table.

They all looked at Ponder Stibbons, the youngest and most depressingly keen member of the faculty. He was holding a complicated mechanism of sliding wooden bars and peering at the other wizards over the top of it.

"Er. Shouldn't be too much of a problem," he added. "People used to think it was, but I'm pretty sure it's all a matter of energy absorption and attention to relative velocities."

The statement was followed with the kind of mystified and suspicious silence that generally succeeded one of his remarks.

"Relative velocities," said Ridcully.

"Yes, Archchancellor." Ponder looked down at his prototype slide rule and waited. He *knew* that Ridcully would feel it necessary to add a comment at this point in order to demonstrate that he'd grasped something.

"My mother could move like lightning when—"

"I mean how fast things are going when compared to other things," Ponder said quickly, but not quite quickly enough. "We should be able to work it out quite easily. Er. On Hex."

"Oh, no," said the Lecturer in Recent Runes, pushing his chair back. "Not that. That's meddling with things you don't understand."

"Well, we *are* wizards," said Ridcully. "We're supposed to meddle with things we don't understand. If we hung around waitin' till we understood things we'd never get anything done."

"Look, I don't mind summoning some demon and asking it," said the Lecturer in Recent Runes. "That's normal. But building some mechanical contrivance to do your thinking for you, that's . . . against Nature. Besides," he added in slightly less foreboding tones, "last time you did a big problem on it the wretched thing broke and we had ants all over the place."

"We've sorted that out," said Ponder. "We—"

"I must admit there was a ram's skull in the middle of it last time I looked," said Ridcully.

"We had to add that to do occult transformations," said Ponder, "but—"

"And cogwheels and springs," the Archchancellor went on.

"Well, the ants aren't very good at differential analysis, so—"

"And that strange wobbly thing with the cuckoo?"

"The unreal time clock," said Ponder. "Yes, we think that's essential for working out—"

"Anyway, it's all quite immaterial, because I certainly have no intention of going anywhere," said the Dean. "Send a student, if you must. We've got a lot of spare ones."

"Good so be would you if, duff plum of helping second A," said the Bursar.

The table fell silent.

"Anyone understand that?" said Ridcully.

The Bursar was not technically insane. He had passed through the rapids of insanity some time previously, and was now sculling around in some peaceful pool on the other side. He was often quite coherent, although not by normal human standards.

"Um, he's going through yesterday again," said the Senior Wrangler. "Backwards, this time."

"We should send the Bursar," said the Dean firmly.

"Certainly not! You probably can't get dried frog pills there—"

"Oook!"

The Librarian re-entered the study at a bandy-legged run, waving something in the air.

It was red, or at least had at some time been red. It might

15

well once have been a pointy hat, but the point had crumpled and most of the brim was burned away. A word had been embroidered on it in sequins. Many had been burned off, but:

WIZZARD

... could just be made out as pale letters on the scorched cloth.

"I *knew* I'd seen it before," said Ridcully. "On a shelf in the Library, right?"

"Oook."

The Archchancellor inspected the remnant.

"Wizzard?" he said. "What kind of sad, hopeless person needs to write WIZZARD on their hat?"

A few bubbles broke the surface of the sea, causing the raft to rock a little. After a while, a couple of pieces of shark skin floated up.

Rincewind sighed and put down his fishing rod. The rest of the shark would be dragged ashore later, he knew it. He couldn't imagine why. It wasn't as if they were good eating. They tasted like old boots soaked in urine.

He picked up a makeshift oar and set out for the beach.

It wasn't a bad little island. Storms seemed to pass it by. So did ships. But there were coconuts, and breadfruit, and some sort of wild fig. Even his experiments in alcohol had been quite successful, although he hadn't been able to walk properly for two days. The lagoon provided prawns and shrimps and oysters and crabs and lobsters, and in the deep green water out beyond the reef big silver fish fought each other for the privilege of biting a piece of bent wire on the end of a bit of string. After six months on the island, in fact, there was only one thing Rincewind lacked. He'd never really thought about it before. Now he thought about it—or, more correctly, *them*—all the time.

It was odd. He'd hardly ever thought about them in Ankh-Morpork, because they were there if ever he wanted them. Now they weren't, and he *craved*.

His raft bumped the white sand at about the same moment as a large canoe rounded the reef and entered the lagoon.

*   *   *

Ridcully was sitting at his desk now, surrounded by his senior wizards. They were trying to tell him things, despite the known danger of trying to tell Ridcully things, which was that he picked up the facts he liked and let the others take a running jump.

"So," he said, "*not* a kind of cheese."

"*No,* Archchancellor," said the Chair of Indefinite Studies. "Rincewind is a kind of wizard."

"Was," said the Lecturer in Recent Runes.

"Not a cheese," said Ridcully, unwilling to let go of a fact.

"No."

"Sounds a sort of name you'd associate with cheese. I mean, a pound of Mature Rincewind, it rolls off the tongue . . ."

"*Godsdammit,* Rincewind is not a cheese!" shouted the Dean, his temper briefly cracking. "Rincewind is not a yogurt or any kind of sour milk derivative! Rincewind is a bloody nuisance! A complete and utter disgrace to wizardry! A fool! A failure! Anyway, he hasn't been seen here since that . . . unpleasantness with the Sourcerer, years ago."

"Really?" said Ridcully, with a certain kind of nasty politeness. "A lot of wizards behaved very badly then, I understand."

"Yes indeed," said the Lecturer in Recent Runes, scowling at the Dean, who bridled.

"I don't know anything about that, Runes. I wasn't Dean at the time."

"No, but you were very senior."

"Perhaps, but it just so happens that at the time I was visiting my aunt, for your information."

"They nearly blew up the whole city!"

"She lives in Quirm."

"*And* Quirm was heavily involved, as I recall."

"—*near* Quirm. *Near* Quirm. Not all that near, actually. Quite a way along the coast—"

"Hah!"

"Anyway, *you* seem to be very well informed, eh, Runes?" said the Dean.

"I—What?—I—was studying hard at the time. Hardly knew what was going on—"

"Half the University was blown down!" The Dean remembered himself and added, "That is, so I heard. Later. After getting back from my aunt's."

"Yes, but I've got a very thick door—"

"And I happen to *know* the Senior Wrangler was here, because—"

"—with that heavy green baize stuff you can hardly hear any—"

"Nap my for time it's think I."

"Will you all shut up right now this minute!"

Ridcully glared at his faculty with the clear, innocent glare of someone who was blessed at birth with no imagination whatsoever, and who had genuinely been hundreds of miles away during the University's recent embarrassing history.

"Right," he said, when they had quietened down. "This Rincewind. Bit of an idiot, yes? You talk, Dean. Everyone else will shut up."

The Dean looked uncertain.

"Well, er . . . I mean, it makes no sense, Archchancellor. He couldn't even do proper magic. What good would he be to anyone? Besides . . . where Rincewind went"—he lowered his voice—*"trouble followed behind."*

Ridcully noticed that the wizards drew a little closer together.

"Sounds all right to me," he said. "Best place for trouble, behind. You certainly don't want it in front."

"You don't understand, Archchancellor," said the Dean. "It followed behind on hundreds of little legs."

The Archchancellor's smile stayed where it was while the rest of his face went solid behind it.

"You been on the Bursar's pills, Dean?"

"I assure you, Mustrum—"

"Then don't talk rubbish."

"Very *well*, Archchancellor. But you do realize, don't you, that it might take years to find him?"

"Er," said Ponder, "if we can work out his thaumic signature, I think Hex could probably do it in a day . . ."

The Dean glared.

"That's not magic!" he snapped. "That's just . . . engineering!"

18

* * *

Rincewind trudged through the shallows and used a sharp rock to hack the top off a coconut that had been cooling in a convenient shady rock pool. He put it to his lips.

A shadow fell across him.

It said, "Er, hello?"

It was possible, if you kept on talking at the Archchancellor for long enough, that some facts might squeeze through.

"So what you're *tellin'* me," said Ridcully, eventually, "is that this Rincewind fella has been chased by just about every army in the world, has been bounced around life like a pea on a drum, and probably is the one wizard who knows anything about the Agatean Empire on account of once being friends with," he glanced at his notes, "'a strange little man in glasses' who came from there and gave him this funny thing with the legs you all keep alluding to. And he can speak the lingo. Am I right so far?"

"Exactly, Archchancellor. Call me an idiot if you like," said the Dean, "but why would anyone want him?"

Ridcully looked down at his notes again. "*You've* decided to go, then?" he said.

"No, of course not—"

"What I don't think you've spotted here, Dean," he said, breaking into a determinedly cheery grin, "is what I might call the common denominator. Chap stays alive. Talented. Find him. And bring him here. Wherever he is. Poor chap could be facing something *dreadful.*"

The coconut stayed where it was, but Rincewind's eyes swivelled madly from side to side.

Three figures stepped into his line of vision. They were obviously female. They were *abundantly* female. They were not wearing a great deal of clothing and seemed to be altogether too fresh-from-the-hairdressers for people who have just been paddling a large war canoe, but this is often the case with beautiful Amazonian warriors.

A thin trickle of coconut milk began to dribble off the end of Rincewind's beard.

The leading woman brushed aside her long blonde hair and gave him a bright smile.

"I know this sounds a little unlikely," she said, "but I and my sisters here represent a hitherto undiscovered tribe whose menfolk were recently destroyed in a deadly but short-lived and highly specific plague. Now we have been searching these islands for a man to enable us to carry on our line."

"How much do you think he weighs?"

Rincewind's eyebrows raised. The woman looked down shyly.

"You may be wondering why we are all blonde and white-skinned when everyone else in the islands around here is dark," she said. "It just seems to be one of those genetic things."

"About 120, 125 pounds. Put another pound or two of junk on the heap. Er. Can you detect . . . you know . . . IT?"

"This is all going to go wrong, Mr. Stibbons, I just know it."

"He's only six hundred miles away and we know where we are, and he's on the right half of the Disc. Anyway, I've worked this out on Hex so nothing can possibly go wrong.

"Yes, but can anyone see . . . that . . . you know . . . with the . . . feet?"

Rincewind's eyebrows waggled. A sort of choking noise came from his throat.

"Can't see . . . it. Will you lot stop huffing on my crystal ball?"

"And, of course, if you were to come with us we could promise you . . . earthly and sensual pleasures such as those of which you may have dreamed . . ."

"All right. On the count of three—"

The coconut dropped away. Rincewind swallowed. There was a hungry, dreamy look in his eyes.

"Can I have them mashed?" he said.

"NOW!"

* * *

First there was the sensation of pressure. The world opened up in front of Rincewind and sucked him into it.

Then it stretched out thin and went *twang*.

Cloud rushed past him, blurred by speed. When he dared open his eyes again it was to see, far ahead of him, a tiny black dot.

It got bigger.

It resolved itself into a tight cloud of objects. There were a couple of heavy saucepans, a large brass candlestick, a few bricks, a chair and a large brass blancmange mold in the shape of a castle.

They hit him one after the other, the blancmange mold making a humorous clang as it bounced off his head, and then whirled away behind him.

The next thing ahead of him was an octagon. A chalked one.

He hit it.

Ridcully stared down.

"A shade less than 125 pounds, I fancy," he said. "All the same . . . well done, gentlemen."

The disheveled scarecrow in the center of the circle staggered to its feet and beat out one or two small fires in its clothing. Then it looked around blearily and said, "Hehehe?"

"He could be a little disorientated," the Archchancellor went on. "More than six hundred miles in two seconds, after all. Don't give him a nasty shock."

"Like sleepwalkers, you mean?" said the Senior Wrangler.

"What do you mean, sleepwalkers?"

"If you wake sleepwalkers, their legs drop off. So my grandmother used to aver."

"And are we *sure* it's Rincewind?" said the Dean.

"Of *course* it's Rincewind," said the Senior Wrangler. "We spent *hours* looking for him."

"It could be some dangerous occult creature," said the Dean stubbornly.

"With that hat?"

It was a pointy hat. In a way. A kind of cargo-cult pointy hat, made out of split bamboo and coconut leaves, in the hope of attracting passing wizardliness. Picked out on it, in seashells held in place with grass, was the word WIZZARD.

Its wearer gazed right through the wizards and, as if driven by some sudden recollection of purpose, lurched abruptly out of the octagon and headed towards the door of the hall.

The wizards followed cautiously.

"I'm not sure I believe her. How many times did she see it happen?"

"I don't know. She never said."

"The Bursar sleepwalks most nights, you know."

"Does he? Tempting . . ."

Rincewind, if that was the creature's name, headed out into Sator Square.

It was crowded. The air shimmered over the braziers of chestnut sellers and hot potato merchants and echoed with the traditional street cries of Old Ankh-Morpork.*

The figure sidled up to a skinny man in a huge overcoat who was frying something over a little oil-heater in a wide tray around his neck.

The possibly-Rincewind grabbed the edge of the tray.

"Got . . . any . . . potatoes?" it growled.

"Potatoes? No, squire. Got some sausages inna bun."

The possibly-Rincewind froze. And then it burst into tears.

"Sausage inna *buuunnnnn!*" it bawled. "Dear old sausage inna inna inna buuunnn! Gimme saussaaage inna *buunnnnn!*"

It grabbed three off the tray and tried to eat them all at once.

"Good grief!" said Ridcully.

The figure half ran, half capered away, fragments of bun and pork-product debris cascading from its unkempt beard.

"I've never seen anyone eat three of Throat Dibbler's sausages inna bun and look so happy," said the Senior Wrangler.

"*I've* never seen someone eat three of Throat Dibbler's sausages inna bun and look so upright," said the Dean.

---

*Such as "Ouch!", "Aargh!", "Give me back my money, you scoundrel!", and "You call these chestnuts? I call them little balls of charcoal, that's what I call them!"

22

"I've never seen anyone eat anything of Dibbler's and get away without paying," said the Lecturer in Recent Runes.

The figure spun happily around the square, tears streaming down its face. The gyrations took it past an alley mouth, whereupon a smaller figure stepped out behind it and with some difficulty hit it on the back of the head.

The sausage-eater fell to his knees, saying, to the world in general, "Ow!"

"No*nononononono*!"

A rather older man stepped out and removed the cosh from the young man's hesitant hands, while the victim knelt and moaned.

"I think you ought to apologize to the poor gentleman," said the older man. "I don't know, what's he going to think? I mean, look at him, he made it so easy for you and what does he get? I mean, what did you think you were doing?"

"Mumblemumble, Mr. Boggis," said the boy, looking at his feet.

"What was that again? Speak up!"

"Overarm Belter, Mr. Boggis."

"*That* was an Overarm Belter? You call that an Overarm Belter? That was an Overarm Belter, was it? *This*—excuse me, sir, we'll just have you up on your feet for a moment, sorry about this—*this* is an Overarm Belter—"

"Ow!" shouted the victim and then, to the surprise of all concerned, he added: "Hahahaha!"

"What *you* did was—sorry to impose again, sir, this won't take a minute—what you did was *this*—"

"Ow! Hahahaha!"

"Now, you lot, you saw that? Come on, gather round . . ."

Half a dozen other youths slouched out of the alleyway and formed a ragged audience around Mr. Boggis, the luckless student and the victim, who was staggering in a circle and making little "oomph oomph" sounds but still, for some reason, apparently enjoying himself immensely.

"Now," said Mr. Boggis, with the air of an old skilled craftsman imparting his professional expertise to an ungrateful posterity, "when inconveniencing a customer from your basic alley entrance, the correct procedure is—Oh, hello, Mr. Ridcully, didn't see you there."

The Archchancellor gave him a friendly nod.

"Don't mind us, Mr. Boggis. Thieves' Guild training, is it?"

Boggis rolled his eyes.

"Dunno what they teaches 'em at school," he said. "It's jus' nothing but reading and writing all the time. When I was a lad school was where you learned somethin' *useful*. Right—you, Wilkins, stop that giggling, you have a go, excuse us just another moment, sir—"

"Ow!"

"No*nonononono!* My old granny could do better than that! Now *look*, you steps up trimly, places one hand on his shoulder here, for control . . . go on, you do it . . . and then smartly—"

"Ow!"

"All right, can anyone tell me what he was doing wrong?"

The figure crawled away unnoticed, except by the wizards, while Mr. Boggis was demonstrating the finer points of head percussion on Wilkins.

It staggered to its feet and plunged on along the road, still moving like one hypnotized.

"He's crying," said the Dean.

"Not surprising," said the Archchancellor. "But why's he grinnin' at the same time?"

"Curiouser and curiouser," said the Senior Wrangler.

Bruised and possibly poisoned, the figure headed back for the University, the wizards still trailing behind.

"You must mean 'curious and more curious,' surely? And even then it doesn't make much sense—"

It entered the gates but, this time, hurried jerkily through the main hall and into the Library.

The Librarian was waiting, holding—with something of a smirk on his face, and an orang-utan can really smirk—the battered hat.

"Amazin'," said Ridcully. "It's true! A wizard *will* always come back for his hat!"

The figure grabbed the hat, evicted some spiders, threw away the sad affair made of leaves and put the hat on his head.

Rincewind blinked at the puzzled faculty. A light came on behind his eyes for the first time, as if up to now he'd merely been operating by reflex action.

"Er. What have I just eaten?"

"Er. Three of Mr. Dibbler's finest sausages," said Ridcully. "Well, when I say finest, I mean 'most typical,' don'tcheknow."

"I see. And who just hit me?"

"Thieves' Guild apprentices out trainin'."

Rincewind blinked. "This is Ankh-Morpork, isn't it?"

"Yes."

"I thought so." Rincewind blinked, slowly. "Well," he said, just as he fell forward, "I'm back."

Lord Hong was flying a kite. It was something he did perfectly.

Lord Hong did everything perfectly. His watercolors were perfect. His poetry was perfect. When he folded paper, every crease was perfect. Imaginative, original, and definitely perfect. Lord Hong had long ago ceased pursuing perfection because he already had it nailed up in a dungeon somewhere.

Lord Hong was twenty-six, and thin, and handsome. He wore very small, very circular steel-rimmed spectacles. When asked to describe him, people often used the word "smooth" or even "lacquered."* And he had risen to the leadership of one of the most influential families in the Empire by relentless application, total focusing of his mental powers, and six well-executed deaths. The last one had been that of his father, who'd died happy in the knowledge that his son was maintaining an old family tradition. The senior families venerated their ancestors, and saw no harm in prematurely adding to their number.

And now his kite, the black kite with the two big eyes, plunged out of the sky. He'd calculated the angle, needless to say, perfectly. Its string, coated with glue and ground glass, sawed through those of his fellow contestants and sent their kites tumbling.

There was genteel applause from the bystanders. People generally found it advisable to applaud Lord Hong.

He handed the string to a servant, nodded curtly at the fellow flyers, and strode towards his tent.

*And often the phrase "a bastard you don't want to cross, and I didn't say that".

Once inside, he sat down and looked at his visitor. "Well?" he said.

"We sent the message," said the visitor. "No one saw us."

"On the contrary," said Lord Hong. "Twenty people saw you. Do you know how hard it is for a guard to look straight ahead and see nothing when people are creeping around making a noise like an army and whispering to one another to be quiet? Frankly, your people do not seem to possess that revolutionary spark. What is the matter with your hand?"

"The albatross bit it."

Lord Hong smiled. It occurred to him that it might have mistaken his visitor for an anchovy, and with some justification. There was the same fishy look about the eyes.

"I don't understand, o lord," said the visitor, whose name was Two Fire Herb.

"Good."

"But they believe in the Great Wizzard and you *want* him to come here?"

"Oh, certainly. I have my . . . people in"—he tried the alien syllables—"Ankh-More-Pork. The one so foolishly called the Great Wizzard *does* exist. But, I might tell you, he is renowned for being incompetent, cowardly, and spineless. Quite proverbially so. So I think the Red Army should have their leader, don't you? It will . . . raise their morale."

He smiled again. "This is politics," he said.

"Ah."

"Now go."

Lord Hong picked up a book as his visitor left. But it was hardly a real book; pieces of paper had simply been fastened together with string, and the text was handwritten.

He'd read it many times before. It still amused him, mainly because the author had managed to be wrong about so many things.

Now, every time he finished a page, he ripped it out and, while reading the next page, carefully folded the paper into the shape of a chrysanthemum.

"Great Wizard," he said, aloud. "Oh, indeed. Very great."

*   *   *

Rincewind awoke. There were clean sheets and no one was saying "Go through his pockets," so he chalked that up as a promising beginning.

He kept his eyes shut, just in case there was anyone around who, once he was seen to be awake, would make life complicated for him.

Elderly male voices were arguing.

"You're all missin' the point. He survives. You keep on tellin' me he's had all these adventures and he's *still* alive."

"What do you mean? He's got scars all over him!"

"My point exactly, Dean. Most of 'em on his back, too. He leaves trouble behind. Someone Up There smiles on him."

Rincewind winced. He had always been aware that Someone Up There was doing *something* on him. He'd never considered it was smiling.

"He's not even a proper wizard! He never got more than two percent in his exams!"

"I think he's awake," said someone.

Rincewind gave in, and opened his eyes. A variety of bearded, overly pink faces looked down upon him.

"How're you feeling, old chap?" said one, extending a hand. "Name's Ridcully. Archchancellor. How're you feeling?"

"It's all going to go wrong," said Rincewind flatly.

"What d'you mean, old fellow?"

"I just know it. It's all going to go wrong. Something dreadful's going to happen. I thought it was too good to last."

"You see?" said the Dean. "Hundreds of little legs. I *told* you. Would you listen?"

Rincewind sat up. "Don't start being nice to me," he said. "Don't start offering me grapes. No one ever wants me for something *nice*." A confused memory of his very recent past floated across his mind and he experienced a brief moment of regret that potatoes, while uppermost in his mind at that point, had not been similarly positioned in the mind of the young lady. No one dressed like that, he was coming to realize, could be thinking of any kind of root vegetable.

He sighed. "All right, what happens now?"

"How do you feel?"

Rincewind shook his head. "It's no good," he said. "I hate it when people are nice to me. It means something bad is going to happen. Do you mind shouting?"

Ridcully had had enough. "Get out of that bed you horrible little man and follow me this minute or it will go very hard for you!"

"Ah, that's better. I feel *right* at home now. *Now* we're cooking with charcoal," said Rincewind, glumly. He swung his legs off the bed and stood up carefully.

Ridcully stopped halfway to the door, where the other wizards had lined up.

"Runes?"

"Yes, Archchancellor?" said the Lecturer in Recent Runes, his voice oozing innocence.

"What is that you've got behind your back?"

"Sorry, Archchancellor?" said the Lecturer in Recent Runes.

"Looks like some kind of tool," said Ridcully.

"Oh, *this,*" said the Lecturer in Recent Runes, as if he'd only just at that moment noticed the eight-pound lump hammer he'd been holding. "My word . . . it's a *hammer,* isn't it? My word. A hammer. I suppose I must just have . . . picked it up somewhere. You know. To keep the place tidy."

"And I can't help noticing," said Ridcully, "that the Dean seems to be tryin' to conceal a battle-axe about his person."

There was a musical twang from the rear of the Chair of Indefinite Studies.

"And that sounded like a saw to me," said Ridcully. "Is there anyone here not concealin' some kind of implement? Right. Would anyone care to explain what the hell you think you're doin'?"

"Hah, you don't know what it was like," muttered the Dean, not meeting the Archchancellor's eye. "A man daren't turn his back for five minutes in those days. You'd hear the patter of those damn feet and—"

Ridcully ignored him. He put an arm around Rincewind's bony shoulders and led the way towards the Great Hall.

"Well, now, Rincewind," he said. "They tell me you're no good at magic."

"That's right."

"Never passed any exams or anything?"

"None, I'm afraid."

"But everyone calls you Rincewind the wizard."

Rincewind looked at his feet. "Well, I kind of worked here as sort of deputy Librarian—"

"—an ape's number two—" said the Dean.

"—and, you know, did odd jobs and things and kind of, you know, helped out—"

"*I say, did anyone notice that? An ape's number two? Rather clever, I thought.*"

"But you have never, in fact, actually been *entitled* to call yourself a wizard?" said Ridcully.

"Not technically, I suppose . . ."

"I *see*. That *is* a problem."

"I've got this hat with the word 'Wizzard' on it," said Rincewind hopefully.

"Not a great help, I'm afraid. Hmm. This presents us with a bit of a difficulty, I'm afraid. Let me see . . . How long can you hold your breath?"

"*I* don't know. A couple of minutes. Is that important?"

"It is in the context of being nailed upside down to one of the supports of the Brass Bridge for two high tides and then being beheaded which, I'm afraid, is the statutory punishment for impersonating a wizard. I looked it up. No one was more sorry than me, I can tell you. But the Lore is the Lore."

"Oh, no!"

"Sorry. No alternative. Otherwise we'd be knee-deep in people in pointy hats they'd no right to. It's a terrible shame. Can't do a thing. Wish I could. Hands tied. The statutes say you can only be a wizard by passing through the University in the normal way or by performing some great service of benefit to magic, and I'm afraid that—"

"Couldn't you just send me back to my island? I *liked* it there. It was dull!"

Ridcully shook his head sadly.

"No can do, I'm afraid. The offence has been committed over a period of many years. And since you haven't passed any exams or performed," Ridcully raised his voice slightly, "*any ser-*

vice of great benefit to magic, I'm afraid I shall have to instruct the bledlows* to fetch some rope and—"

"Er. I think I may have saved the world a couple of times," said Rincewind. "Does that help?"

"Did anyone from the University see you do it?"

"No, I don't think so."

Ridcully shook his head. "Probably doesn't count, then. It's a shame, because *if you had performed any service of great benefit to magic* then I'd be happy to let you keep that hat and, of course, something to wear it on."

Rincewind looked crestfallen. Ridcully sighed, and had one last try.

"So," he said, "since it seems that you haven't actually passed your exams OR PERFORMED A SERVICE OF GREAT BENEFIT TO MAGIC, then—"

"I suppose . . . I could try to perform some great service?" said Rincewind, with the expression of one who knows that the light at the end of the tunnel is an oncoming train.

"Really? Hmm? Well, that's definitely a thought," said Ridcully.

"What sort of services are they?"

"Oh, typically you'd be expected to, for the sake of example, go on a quest, or find the answer to some very ancient and important question—*What the hell is that thing with all the legs?*"

Rincewind didn't even bother to look around. The expression on Ridcully's face, as it stared over his shoulder, was quite familiar.

"Ah," he said, "I think I know that one."

Magic isn't like maths. Like the Discworld itself, it follows common sense rather than logic. And nor is it like cookery. A cake's a cake. Mix the ingredients up right and cook them at the right

*The UU college porters. Renowned among the entire faculty for the hardness of their skulls, their obtuseness in the face of reasonable explanation, and their deeply held conviction that the whole place would collapse without them.

30

temperature and a cake happens. No casserole requires moon-beams. No soufflé ever demanded to be mixed by a virgin.

Nevertheless, those afflicted with an enquiring turn of mind have often wondered whether there are *rules* of magic. There are more than five hundred known spells to secure the love of another person, and they range from messing around with fern seed at midnight to doing something rather unpleasant with a rhino horn at an unspecified time, but probably not just after a meal. Was it possible (the enquiring minds enquired) that an analysis of all these spells might reveal some small powerful common denominator, some meta-spell, some simple little equation which would achieve the required end far more simply, and incidentally come as a great relief to all rhinos?

To answer such questions Hex had been built, although Ponder Stibbons was a bit uneasy about the word "built" in this context. He and a few keen students had put it together, certainly, but . . . well . . . sometimes he thought bits of it, strange though this sounded, *just turned up.*

For example, he was pretty sure no one had designed the Phase of the Moon Generator, but there it was, clearly a part of the whole thing. They *had* built the Unreal Time Clock, although no one seemed to have a very clear idea how it worked.

What he suspected they were dealing with was a specialized case of formative causation, always a risk in a place like Unseen University, where reality was stretched so thin and therefore blown by so many strange breezes. If that was so, then they weren't exactly designing something. They were just putting physical clothes on an idea that was already there, a shadow of something that had been waiting to exist.

He'd explained at length to the Faculty that Hex didn't *think.* It was obvious that it couldn't think. Part of it was clockwork. A lot of it was a giant ant farm (the interface, where the ants rode up and down on a little paternoster that turned a significant cog-wheel was a little masterpiece, he thought) and the intricately controlled rushing of the ants through their maze of glass tubing was the most important part of the whole thing.

But a lot of it had just . . . accumulated, like the aquarium and wind chimes which now seemed to be essential. A mouse had built a nest in the middle of it all and had been allowed to become a fixture, since the thing stopped working when they took it out. Nothing in that assemblage could possibly think, except in fairly limited ways about cheese or sugar. Nevertheless . . . in the middle of the night, when Hex was working hard, and the tubes rustled with the toiling ants, and things suddenly went "clonk" for no obvious reason, and the aquarium had been lowered on its davits so that the operator would have something to watch during the long hours . . . nevertheless, *then* a man might begin to speculate about what a brain was and what thought was and whether things that weren't alive could think and whether a brain was just a more complicated version of Hex (or, around 4 A.M., when bits of the clockwork reversed direction suddenly and the mice squeaked, a *less* complicated version of Hex) and wonder if the whole produced something not apparently inherent in the parts.

In short, Ponder was just a little bit worried.

He sat down at the keyboard. It was almost as big as the rest of Hex, to allow for the necessary levers and armatures. The various keys allowed little boards with holes in them to drop briefly into slots, forcing the ants into new paths.

It took him some time to compose the problem, but at last he braced one foot on the structure and tugged on the Enter lever.

The ants scurried on new paths. The clockwork started to move. A small mechanism which Ponder would be prepared to swear had not been there yesterday, but which looked like a device for measuring wind speed, began to spin.

After several minutes a number of blocks with occult symbols on them dropped into the output hopper.

"Thank you," said Ponder, and then felt extremely silly for saying so.

There was a tension to the thing, a feeling of mute straining and striving towards some distant and incomprehensible goal. As a wizard, it was something that Ponder had only before encountered in acorns: a tiny soundless voice which said, yes, I am but a small, green, simple object—but I dream about forests.

Only the other day Adrian Turnipseed had typed in "Why?"

to see what happened. Some of the students had forecast that Hex would go mad trying to work it out; Ponder had expected Hex to produce the message ?????, which it did with depressing frequency.

Instead, after some unusual activity among the ants, it had laboriously produced: "Because."

With everyone else watching from behind a hastily overturned desk, Turnipseed had volunteered: "Why anything?"

The reply had finally turned up: "Because Everything. ????? Eternal Domain Error. +++++ Redo From Start +++++."

No one knew who Redo From Start was, or why he was sending messages. But there were no more funny questions. No one wanted to risk getting answers.

It was shortly afterwards that the thing like a broken umbrella with herrings on it appeared just behind the thing like a beachball that went "parp" every fourteen minutes.

Of course, books of magic developed a certain . . . *personality,* derived from all that power in their pages. That's why it was unwise to go into the Library without a stick. And now Ponder had helped build an engine for studying magic. Wizards had always known that the act of observation changed the thing that was observed, and sometimes forgot that it also changed the observer, too.

He was beginning to suspect that Hex was redesigning itself.

And he'd just said "Thank you." To a thing that looked like it had been made by a glassblower with hiccups.

He looked at the spell it had produced, hastily wrote it down and hurried out.

Hex clicked to itself in the now empty room. The thing that went "parp" went parp. The Unreal Time Clock ticked sideways.

There was a rattle in the output slot.

"Dont mention it. ++?????++ Out of Cheese Error. Redo From Start."

It was five minutes later.

"Fascinatin'," said Ridcully. "Sapient pearwood, eh?" He knelt down in an effort to see underneath.

The Luggage backed away. It was used to terror, horror, fear, and panic. It had seldom encountered interest before.

The Archchancellor stood up and brushed himself off.

"Ah," he said, as a dwarfish figure approached. "Here's the gardener with the stepladder. The Dean's in the chandelier, Modo."

"I'm quite happy up here, I assure you," said a voice from the ceiling regions. "Perhaps someone would be kind enough to pass me up my tea?"

"And I was amazed the Senior Wrangler could ever *fit* in the sideboard," said Ridcully. "It's amazin' how a man can fold himself up."

"I was just—just inspecting the silverware," said a voice from the depths of a drawer.

The Luggage opened its lid. Several wizards jumped back hurriedly.

Ridcully examined the shark teeth stuck here and there in the woodwork.

"Kills sharks, you say?" he said.

"Oh, yes," said Rincewind. "Sometimes it drags them ashore and jumps up and down on them."

Ridcully was impressed. Sapient pearwood was very rare in the countries between the Ramtops and the Circle Sea. There were probably no living trees left. A few wizards were lucky enough to have inherited staffs made out of it.

Economy of emotion was one of Ridcully's strong points. He had been impressed. He had been fascinated. He'd even, when the thing had landed in the middle of the wizards and caused the Dean's remarkable feat of vertical acceleration, been slightly aghast. But he hadn't been frightened, because he didn't have the imagination.

"My goodness," said a wizard.

The Archchancellor looked up.

"Yes, Bursar?"

"It's this book the Dean loaned me, Mustrum. It's about apes."

"Really."

"It's most fascinating," said the Bursar, who was on the

median part of his mental cycle and therefore vaguely on the right planet even if insulated from it by five miles of mental cotton wool. "It's true what he said. It says here that an adult male orang-utan doesn't grow the large flamboyant cheek pads unless he's the dominant male."

"And that's fascinating, is it?"

"Well, yes, because he hasn't got 'em. I wonder why? He certainly dominates the Library, I should think."

"Ah, yes," said the Senior Wrangler, "but he knows he's a wizard, too. So it's not as though he dominates the whole University."

One by one, as the thought sank in, they grinned at the Archchancellor.

"Don't you look at my cheeks like that!" said Ridcully. "I don't dominate anybody!"

"I was only—"

"So you can all shut up or there will be big trouble!"

"You should read it," said the Bursar, still happily living in the valley of the dried frogs. "It's amazing what you can learn."

"What? Like . . . how to show your bottom to people?" said the Dean, from on high.

"No, Dean. That's baboons," said the Senior Wrangler.

"I beg your pardon, I think you'll find it's gibbons," said the Chair of Indefinite Studies.

"No, gibbons are the ones that hoot. It's baboons if you want to see bottoms."

"Well, he's never shown *me* one," said the Archchancellor.

"Hah, well, he wouldn't, would he?" said a voice from the chandelier. "Not with you being dominant male and everything."

"Two Chairs, you come down here this minute!"

"I seem to be entangled, Mustrum. A candle is giving me some difficulty."

"Hah!"

Rincewind shook his head and wandered away. There had certainly been some changes around the place since he had been there and, if it came to it, he didn't know how long ago that had been . . .

He'd never *asked* for an exciting life. What he really liked, what he sought on every occasion, was boredom. The trouble was that boredom tended to explode in your face. Just when he thought he'd found it he'd be suddenly involved in what he supposed other people—thoughtless, feckless people—would call an adventure. And he'd be forced to visit many strange lands and meet exotic and colorful people, although not for very long because usually he'd be running. He'd seen the creation of the universe, although not from a good seat, and had visited Hell and the afterlife. He'd been captured, imprisoned, rescued, lost, and marooned. Sometimes it had all happened on the same day.

Adventure! People talked about the idea as if it was something worthwhile, rather than a mess of bad food, no sleep, and strange people inexplicably trying to stick pointed objects in bits of you.

The *root* problem, Rincewind had come to believe, was that he suffered from pre-emptive karma. If it even *looked* as though something nice was going to happen to him in the near future, something bad would happen right now. And it went on happening to him right through the part where the good stuff should be happening, so that he never actually experienced it. It was as if he always got the indigestion *before* the meal and felt so dreadful that he never actually managed to eat anything.

Somewhere in the world, he reasoned, there was someone who was on the other end of the see-saw, a kind of mirror Rincewind whose life was a succession of wonderful events. He hoped to meet him one day, preferably while holding some sort of weapon.

Now people were babbling about sending him to the Counterweight Continent. He'd heard that life was dull there. And Rincewind really craved dullness.

He'd really *liked* that island. He'd *enjoyed* Coconut Surprise. You cracked it open and, hey, there was coconut inside. That was the kind of surprise he liked.

He pushed open a door.

The place inside *had* been his room. It was a mess. There was a large and battered wardrobe, and that was about the end of it as far as proper furniture was concerned unless you wanted to broaden the term to include a wicker chair with no bottom and three legs and a mattress so full of the life that inhabits mattresses that it occasionally moved sluggishly around the floor, bumping into things. The rest of the room was a litter of objects dragged in from the street—old crates, bits of planking, sacks . . .

Rincewind felt a lump in his throat. They'd left his room just as it was.

He opened the wardrobe and rummaged through the moth-haunted darkness within, until his questing hand located—

—an ear—

—which was attached to a dwarf.

"Ow!"

"What," said Rincewind, "are you doing in my wardrobe?"

"Wardrobe? Er . . . Er . . . Isn't this the Magic Kingdom of Scrumptiousness?" said the dwarf, trying not to look guilty.

"No, and these shoes you're holding aren't the Golden Jewels of the Queen of the Fairies," said Rincewind, snatching them out of the thief's hands. "And *this* isn't the Wand of Invisibility and *these* aren't Giant Grumblenose's Wonderful Socks but *this* is my boot—"

"Ow!"

"And stay out!"

The dwarf ran for the door and paused, but only briefly, to shout: "I've got a Thieves' Guild card! And you shouldn't hit dwarfs! That's speciesism!"

"Good," said Rincewind, retrieving items of clothing.

He found another robe and put it on. Here and there moths had worked their lacemaking skills and most of the red color had faded to shades of orange and brown, but to his relief it was a proper wizard's robe. It's hard to be an impressive magic-user with bare knees.

Gentle footsteps pattered to a halt behind him. He turned.

"Open."

The Luggage obediently cracked its lid. In theory it should have been full of shark; in fact it was half full of coconuts. Rincewind turfed them out on to the floor and put the rest of the clothes inside.

"Shut."

The lid slammed.

"Now go down to the kitchen and get some potatoes."

The chest did a complicated, many-legged about-turn and trotted away. Rincewind followed it out and headed towards the Archchancellor's study. Behind him he could hear the wizards still arguing.

He'd become familiar with the study through long years at Unseen. Generally he was there to answer quite difficult questions, like "How can *anyone* get a negative mark in Basic Firemaking?" He'd spent a lot of time staring at the fixtures while people harangued him.

There had been changes here, too. Gone were the alembics and bubbling flagons that were the traditional props of wizardry; Ridcully's study was dominated by a full-size snooker table, on which he'd piled papers until there was no room for any more and no sign of green felt. Ridcully assumed that anything people had time to write down couldn't be important.

The stuffed heads of a number of surprised animals stared down at him. From the antlers of one stag hung a pair of corroded boots Ridcully had won as a Rowing Brown for the University in his youth.*

There was a large model of the Discworld on four wooden elephants in a corner of the room. Rincewind was familiar with it. Every student was . . .

The Counterweight Continent was a blob. It was a *shaped* blob; a not very inviting comma shape. Sailors had brought back news of it. They'd said that at one point it broke into a pattern of large islands, stretching around the Disc to the even more mysterious island of Bhangbhangduc and the completely mythical continent known only on the charts as "XXXX."

Not that many sailors went near the Counterweight Continent. The Agatean Empire was known to ignore a very small amount of smuggling; presumably Ankh-Morpork had some things it wanted. But there was nothing official; a boat might

---

*Except during extreme flood conditions it is extremely difficult to make much progress on the Ankh, and the University rowing teams compete by running over the surface of the river. This is generally quite safe provided they don't stand in one place for very long and, of course, it eats the soles off their boots.

come back loaded with silk and rare wood and, these days, a few wild-eyed refugees, or it might come back with its captain riveted upside-down to the mast, or it might not come back.

Rincewind had been very nearly everywhere, but the Counterweight Continent was an unknown land, or *terror incognita*. He couldn't imagine why they'd want any kind of wizard.

Rincewind sighed. He knew what he should do now.

He shouldn't even wait for the return of the Luggage from its argosy to the kitchens, from which the sound of yelling and something being repeatedly hit with a large brass preserving pan suggested it was going about his business.

He should just gather up what he could carry and get the hell out of here. He—

"Ah, Rincewind," said the Archchancellor, who had an amazingly silent walk for such a large man. "Keen to leave, I see."

"Yes, indeed," said Rincewind. "Oh, yes. Very much so."

The Red Army met in secret session. They opened their meeting by singing revolutionary songs and, since disobedience to authority did not come easily to the Agatean character, these had titles like "Steady Progress And Limited Disobedience While Retaining Well-Formulated Good Manners."

Then it was time for the news.

"The Great Wizard *will* come. We sent the message, at great personal risk."

"How will we know when he arrives?"

"If he's the Great Wizard, we'll hear about it. And then—"

"Gently Push Over The Forces Of Repression!" they chorused.

Two Fire Herb looked at the rest of the cadre. "Exactly," he said. "And then, comrades, we must strike at the very heart of the rottenness. We must storm the Winter Palace!"

There was silence from the cadre. Then someone said, "Excuse me, Two Fire Herb, but it is June."

"Then we can storm the Summer Palace!"

* * *

A similar session, although without singing and with rather older participants, was taking place in Unseen University, although one member of the College Council had refused to come down from the chandelier. This was of some considerable annoyance to the Librarian, who usually occupied it.

"All right, if you don't trust my calculations, then what are the alternatives?" said Ponder Stibbons hotly.

"Boat?" said the Chair of Indefinite Studies.

"They sink," said Rincewind.

"It'd get you there in no time at all," said the Senior Wrangler. "We're wizards, after all. We could give you your own bag of wind."

"Ah. Forward the Dean," said Ridcully, pleasantly.

"I heard that," said a voice from above.

"Overland," said the Lecturer in Recent Runes. "Up around the Hub? It's ice practically all the way."

"No," said Rincewind.

"But you don't sink on ice."

"No. You tip up and *then* you sink and *then* the ice hits you on the head. Also killer whales. And great big seals vif teece ike iff."

"This is off the wall, I know," said the Bursar, brightly.

"What is?" said the Lecturer in Recent Runes.

"A hook for hanging pictures on."

There was a brief embarrassed silence.

"Good lord, is it that time already?" said the Archchancellor, taking out his watch. "Ah, so it is. The bottle's in your left-hand pocket, old chap. Take three."

"No, magic is the only way," said Ponder Stibbons. "It worked when we brought him here, didn't it?"

"Oh, yes," said Rincewind. "Just send me thousands of miles with my pants on fire and you don't even know where I'll land? Oh, yes, that's ideal, that is."

"Good," said Ridcully, a man impervious to sarcasm. "It's a big continent; we can't possibly miss it even with Mr. Stibbons' precise calculations."

"Supposing I end up crushed in the middle of a mountain?" said Rincewind.

"Can't. The rock'll be brought back here when we do the spell," said Ponder, who hadn't liked the crack about his maths.

"So I'll still be in the middle of a mountain but in a me-shaped hole," said Rincewind. "Oh, good. Instant fossil."

"Don't *worry*," said Ridcully. "It's just a matter of . . . thingummy, you know, all that stuff about three right angles making a triangle . . . "

"Is it possible you're talking about geometry?" said Rincewind, eyeing the door.

"That kind of thing, yes. And you'll have your amazing Luggage item. Why, it'll practically be a holiday. It'll be easy. They probably just want to . . . to . . . ask you something, or something. And I hear you've got a talent for languages, so no problem there.* You'll probably be away for a couple of hours at the most. Why do you keep sayin' 'hah' under your breath?"

"Was I?"

"And everyone will be so grateful if you come back."

Rincewind looked around—and, in one case, up—at the Council.

"How *will* I get back?" he said.

"Same way you went. We'll find you and bring you out. With surgical precision."

Rincewind groaned. He knew what surgical precision meant in Ankh-Morpork. It meant "to within an inch or two, accompanied by a lot of screaming, and then they pour hot tar on you just where your leg was."

But . . . if you put aside for the moment the certainty that something would definitely go horribly wrong, it looked foolproof. The trouble was that wizards were such ingenious fools.

---

*This at least was true. Rincewind could scream† for mercy in nineteen languages, and just scream in another forty-four.

†This is important. Inexperienced travelers might think that "Aargh!" is universal, but in Betrobi it means "highly enjoyable" and in Howondaland it means, variously, "I would like to eat your foot," "Your wife is a big hippo," and "Hello, Thinks Mr. Purple Cat." One particular tribe has a fearsome reputation for cruelty merely because prisoners appear, to them, to be shouting "Quick! Extra boiling oil!"

"And then I can have my old job back?"

"Certainly."

"And officially call myself a wizard?"

"Of course. With any kind of spelling."

"And never have to go anywhere again as long as I live?"

"Fine. We'll actually ban you leaving the premises, if you like."

"And a new hat?"

"What?"

"A new hat. This one's practically had it."

"Two new hats."

"Sequins?"

"Of course. And those, you know, like glass chandelier things? Lots of those all round the brim. As many as you like. And we'll spell Wizard with three Zs."

Rincewind sighed. "Oh, all right. I'll do it."

Ponder's genius found itself rather cramped when it came to explaining things to people. And this was the case now, as the wizards forgathered to kick some serious magic.

"Yes, but you see, Archchancellor, he's being sent to the opposite side of the Disc, you see—"

Ridcully sighed. "It's *spinnin'*, isn't it," he said. "We're all going the same way. It stands to reason. If people're going the other way just because they're on the Counterweight Continent we'd crash into them once a year. I mean twice."

"Yes, yes, they're *spinning* the same way, of course, but the direction of motion is entirely opposite. I mean," said Ponder, lapsing into logic, "you have to think about vectors, you, you have to ask yourself: what direction would they go in if the Disc wasn't here?"

The wizards stared at him.

"Down," said Ridcully.

"No, no, *no*, Archchancellor," said Ponder. "They wouldn't go down because there'd be nothing to pull them down, they—"

"You don't need anything to *pull* you down. Down's where you go if there's nothing to keep you up."

"They'd keep on going in the same direction!" shouted Ponder.

"Right. Round and round," said Ridcully. He rubbed his hands together. "You've got to maintain a grip if you want to be a wizard, lad. How're we doing, Runes?"

"I . . . I can make out something," said the Lecturer in Recent Runes, squinting into the crystal ball. "There's a *lot* of interference . . ."

The wizards gathered round. White specks filled the crystal. There *were* vague shapes just visible in the mush. Some of them could be human.

"Very peaceful place, the Agatean Empire," said Ridcully. "Very tranquil. Very cultured. They set great store in politeness."

"Well, yes," said the Lecturer in Recent Runes, "I heard it was because people who *aren't* tranquil and quiet get serious bits cut off, don't they? I heard the Empire has a tyrannical and repressive government!"

"What form of government is that?" said Ponder Stibbons.

"A tautology," said the Dean, from above.

"How serious are these bits?" said Rincewind. They ignored him.

"I heard that gold's very common there," said the Dean. "Lying around like dirt, they say. Rincewind could bring back a sackful."

"I'd rather bring back all my bits," said Rincewind.

After all, he thought, I'm only the one who's going to end up in the middle of it all. So please don't anyone bother to listen to me.

"Can't you stop it blurring like that?" said the Archchancellor.

"I'm sorry, Archchancellor—"

"These bits . . . big bits or small bits?" said Rincewind, unheard.

"Just find us an open space with something about the right size and weight."

"It's very hard to—"

"Very serious bits? Are we in arms and legs territory here?"

"They say it's very boring there. Their biggest curse is 'May you live in interesting times', apparently."

"There's a thing . . . it's very blurry. Looks like a wheelbarrow or something. Quite small, I think."

43

"—or toes, ears, that kind of thing?"

"Good, let's get started," said Ridcully.

"Er, I think it'll help if he's a bit heavier than the thing we move here," said Ponder. "He won't arrive at any speed, then. I think—"

"Yes, yes, thank you very much, Mister Stibbons, now get in the circle and let us see that staff crackle, there's a good chap."

"Fingernails? Hair?"

Rincewind tugged at the robe of Ponder Stibbons, who seemed slightly more sensible than the others.

"Er. What's my next move here?" he said.

"Um. About six thousand miles, I hope," said Ponder Stibbons.

"But . . . I mean . . . Have you got any advice?"

Ponder wondered how to put things. He thought: I've done my best with Hex, but the actual business will be undertaken by a bunch of wizards whose idea of experimental procedure is to throw it and then sit down and argue about where it's going to land. We want to change your position with that of something six thousand miles away which, whatever the Archchancellor says, is heading through space in a quite different direction. The key is *precision*. It's no good using any old traveling spell. It'd come apart halfway, and so would you. I'm pretty sure that we'll get you there in one or, at worst, two pieces. But we've no way of knowing the weight of the thing we change you with. If it's pretty much the same weight as you, then it might just all work out provided you don't mind jogging on the spot when you land. But if it's a *lot* heavier than you, then my suspicion is that you'll appear over there traveling at the sort of speed normally only experienced by sleepwalkers in clifftop villages in a very terminal way.

"Er," he said. "Be afraid. Be very afraid."

"Oh, *that*," said Rincewind. "No problem there. I'm good at that."

"We're going to try to put you in the center of the continent, where Hunghung is believed to be," said Ponder.

"The capital city?"

"Yes. Er." Ponder felt guilty. "Look, whatever happens I'm sure you'll get there alive, which is more than would happen if it'd just been left to them. And I'm *pretty* sure you'll end up on the right continent."

"Oh, good."

"Come *along,* Mr. Stibbons. We're all agog to hear how you wish us to do this," said Ridcully.

"Ah, er, yes. Right. Now, you, Mr. Rincewind, if you will go and stand in the center of the octagon . . . thank you. Um. You see, gentlemen, what has always been the problem with teleporting over large distances is Heisenberg's Uncertainty Principle,* since the object teleported, that's from *tele,* 'I see,' and *porte,* 'to go,' the whole meaning 'I see it's gone,' er, the object teleported, er, no matter how large, is reduced to a thaumic particle and is therefore the subject of an eventually fatal dichotomy: it can either know what it is or where it is going, but not both. Er, the tension this creates in the morphic field eventually causes it to disintegrate, leaving the subject as a randomly shaped object, er, smeared across up to eleven dimensions. But I'm sure you all know this."

There was a snore from the Chair of Indefinite Studies, who was suddenly giving a lecture in room 3B.

Rincewind was grinning. At least, his mouth had gaped open and his teeth were showing.

"Er, excuse me," he said. "I don't remember anyone saying anything about being sm—"

"Of course," said Ponder, "the subject would not, er, actually experience this—"

"Oh."

"—as far as we know—"

"What?"

"—although it is theoretically possible for the psyche to remain present—"

"Eh?"

"—to briefly witness the explosive discorporation."

"Hey?"

---

*Named after the wizard Sangrit Heisenberg and not after the more famous Heisenberg who is renowned for inventing what is *possibly* the finest lager in the world.

"Now, we're all familiar with the use of the spell as a fulcrum, er, so that one does not actually move *one* object but simply exchanges the position of two objects of similar mass. It is my aim tonight, er, to demonstrate that by imparting exactly the right amount of spin and the maximum velocity to the object—"

"Me?"

"—from the very first moment, it is virtually certain—"

"Virtually?"

"—to hold together for distances of up to, er, six thousand miles—"

"Up to?"

"—give or take ten percent—"

"Give or take?"

"So if you'd—excuse me, Dean, I'd be obliged if you'd stop dripping wax—if you'd all take up the positions I've marked on the floor . . ."

Rincewind looked longingly towards the door. It was no distance at all for the experienced coward. He could just trot out of here and they could . . . they could . . .

What could they do? They could just take his hat away and stop him ever coming back to the University. Now he came to think about it, they probably wouldn't be bothered about the nailing bit if he was too much bother to find.

And that was the problem. He wouldn't be dead, but then neither would he be a wizard. And, he thought, as the wizards shuffled into position and screwed down the knobs on the end of their staffs, not being able to think of himself as a wizard *was* being dead.

The spell began.

Rincewind the shoemaker? Rincewind the beggar? Rincewind the thief? Just about everything apart from Rincewind the corpse demanded training or aptitudes that he didn't have.

He was no good at anything else. Wizardry was the only refuge. Well, actually he was no good at wizardry either, but at least he was *definitively* no good at it. He'd always felt he had a right to exist as a wizard in the same way that you couldn't do proper maths without the number 0, which wasn't a number at all but, if it went away, would leave a lot of larger numbers looking bloody stupid. It was a vaguely noble thought that had kept him warm during those occasional 3 A.M. awakenings when he had evaluated his life and found it weighed a little less than a puff of warm hydrogen. And he probably *had* saved the world a few times, but it had generally happened accidentally, while he was trying to do something else. So you almost certainly didn't actually get any karmic points for that. It probably only counted if you started out by thinking in a loud way "By criminy, it's jolly well time to save the world, and no two ways about it!" instead of "Oh shit, this time I'm *really* going to die."

The spell continued.

It didn't seem to be going very well.

"Come on, you chaps," said Ridcully. "Put some backbone into it!"

"Are you sure . . . it's . . . just something small?" said the Dean, who'd broken into a sweat.

"Looks like a . . . wheelbarrow . . ." muttered the Lecturer in Recent Runes.

The knob on the end of Ridcully's staff began to smoke.

"Will you look at the magic I'm using!" he said. "What's goin' on, Mr. Stibbons?"

"Er. Of course, size isn't the same as mass . . ."

And then, in the same way that it can take considerable effort to push at a sticking door and no effort at all to fall full length into the room beyond, the spell caught.

Ponder hoped, afterwards, that what he saw was an optical illusion. Certainly no one normally was suddenly stretched to about twelve feet tall and then snapped back into shape so fast that their boots ended up under their chin.

There was a brief cry of "Oooooohhhhshhhhhh—" which ended abruptly, and this was probably just as well.

The first thing that struck Rincewind when he appeared on the Counterweight Continent was a cold sensation.

The next things, in order of the direction of travel, were: a surprised man with a sword, another man with a sword, a third man who'd dropped *his* sword and was trying to run away, two other

Terry Pratchett

men who were less alert and didn't even see him, a small tree, about fifty yards of stunted undergrowth, a snowdrift, a bigger snowdrift, a few rocks, and one more and quite final snowdrift.

Ridcully looked at Ponder Stibbons.

"Well, he's gone," he said. "But aren't we supposed to get something back?"

"I'm not sure the transit time is instantaneous," said Ponder.

"You've got to allow for zooming-through-the-occult-dimensions time?"

"Something like that. According to Hex, we might have to wait several—"

Something appeared in the octagon with a "pop," exactly where Rincewind had been, and rolled a few inches.

It did, at least, have four small wheels such as might carry a cart. But these weren't workmanlike wheels; these were mere discs such as may be put on something heavy for those rare occasions it needs to be moved.

Above the wheels things became rather more interesting.

There was a large round cylinder, like a barrel on its side. A considerable amount of effort had been put into its construction; large amounts of brass had gone into making it look like a very large, fat dog with its mouth open. A minor feature was a length of string, which was smoking and hissing because it was on fire.

It didn't do anything dangerous. It just sat there, while the smoldering string slowly got shorter.

The wizards gathered round.

"Looks pretty heavy," said the Lecturer in Recent Runes.

"A statue of a dog with a big mouth," said the Chair of Indefinite Studies. "That's rather dull."

"Bit of a lap-dog, too," said Ridcully.

"Lot of work gone into it," said the Dean. "Can't imagine why anyone'd want to set fire to it."

Ridcully poked his head into the wide tube.

"Some kind of big round ball in here," he said, his voice echoing a little. "Someone pass me a staff or something. I'll see if I can wiggle it out."

Ponder was staring at the fizzing string.

"Er," he said, "I . . . er . . . think we should all just step away from it, Archchancellor. Er. We should all just step back, yes, step back a little way. Er."

"Hah, yes, really? So much for research," said Ridcully. "You don't mind messing around with cogwheels and ants but when it comes to really trying to find out how things work and—"

"Getting your hands dirty," said the Lecturer in Recent Runes.

"Yes, getting your hands dirty, you come over all shy."

"It's not that, Archchancellor," said Ponder. "But I believe it may be dangerous."

"I think I'm working it loose," said Ridcully, poking in the depths of the tube. "Come on, you fellows, tip the thing up a bit . . ."

Ponder took a few more steps back. "Er, I really don't think—" he began.

"Don't think, eh? Call yourself a wizard and you don't think? Blast! I've got my staff wedged now! That's what comes of listening to you when I should have been paying attention, Mr. Stibbons."

Ponder heard a scuffling behind him. The Librarian, with an animal's instinct for danger and a human's instinct for trouble, had upturned a table and was peering over the top of it with a small cauldron on his head, the handle under one of his chins like a strap.

"Archchancellor, I really *do* think—"

"Oh, you think, do you? Did anyone tell you it's your job to think? Ow! It's got my fingers now, thanks to you!"

It needed all Ponder's courage to say, "I think . . . it might perhaps be some kind of firework, sir."

The wizards turned their attention to the fizzling string.

"What . . . colored lights, stars, that sort of thing?" said Ridcully.

"Possibly, sir."

"Must be planning a hell of a display. Apparently they're very keen on firecrackers, over in the Empire." Ridcully spoke in the tone of voice of a man over whom the thought is slowly stealing that he just might have done something very silly.

"Would you like me to extinguish the string, sir?" said Ponder.

"Yes, dear boy, why not? Good idea. Good thinking, that man."

Ponder stepped forward and pinched the string.

"I do hope we haven't ruined something," he said.

Rincewind opened his eyes.

This was *not* cool sheets. It was white, and it was cold, but it lacked basic sheetness. It made up for this by having vast amounts of snowosity.

And a groove. A *long* groove.

Let's see now . . . He could remember the sensation of movement. And he vaguely remembered something small but incredibly *heavy*-looking roaring past in the opposite direction. And then he was here, moving so fast that his feet left this . . .

. . . groove. Yes, groove, he thought, in the easy-going way of the mildly concussed. With people lying around it groaning.

But they looked like people who, once they'd stopped crawling around groaning, were going to draw the swords they had about their persons and pay detailed attention to serious bits.

He stood up, a little shakily. There didn't seem to be anywhere to run to. There was just this wide, snowy waste with a border of mountains.

The soldiers were definitely looking a lot more conscious. Rincewind sighed. A few hours ago he'd been sitting on a warm beach with young women about to offer him potatoes,* and here he was on a windswept, chilly plain with some large men about to offer him violence.

The soles of his shoes, he noticed, were steaming.

And then someone said, "Hey! Are you . . . you're not, are you . . . are you . . . whatsyername . . . Rincewind, isn't it?"

Rincewind turned.

There was a very old man behind him. Despite the bitter wind he was wearing nothing except a leather loincloth and a grubby beard so long that the loincloth wasn't really necessary, at

---

*There was still a certain amount of confusion on this point.

least from the point of view of decency. His legs were blue from the cold and his nose was red from the wind, giving him overall quite a patriotic look if you were from the right country. He had a patch over one eye but rather more notable than that were his teeth. They glittered.

"Don't stand there gawping like a big gawper! Get these damn things off me!"

There were heavy shackles around his ankles and wrists; a chain led to a group of more or less similarly clad men who were huddling in a crowd and watching Rincewind in terror.

"Heh! They think you're some kind of demon," cackled the old man. "But I knows a wizard when I sees one! That bastard over there's got the keys. Go and give him a good kicking."

Rincewind took a few hesitant steps towards a recumbent guard and snatched at his belt.

"Right," said the old man, "now chuck 'em over here. And then get out of the way."

"Why?"

"'Cos you don't want to get blood all over you."

"But you haven't got a weapon and there's one of you and they've got big swords and there's five of them!"

"I know," said the old man, wrapping the chain around one of his fists in a businesslike manner. "It's unfair, but I can't wait around all day."

He grinned.

Gems glittered in the morning light. Every tooth in the man's head was a diamond. And Rincewind knew of only one man who had the nerve to wear troll teeth.

"Here? Cohen the Barbarian?"

"Ssh! Ingconitar! Now get out of the way, I said." The teeth flashed at the guards, who were now vertical. "Come on, boys. There's five of you, after all. An' I'm an old man. Mumble, mumble, oo me leg, ekcetra . . ."

To their credit, the guards hesitated. It was probably not, to judge from their faces, because there's something reprehensible about five large, heavily be-weaponed men attacking a frail old man. It might have been because there's something odd about a frail old man who keeps on grinning in the face of obvious oblivion.

"Oh, come *on*," said Cohen. The men edged closer, each waiting for one of the others to make the first move.

Cohen took a few steps forward, waving his arms wearily. "Oh, *no*," he said. "It makes me ashamed, honestly it does. This is *not* how you attack someone, all milling around like a lot of millers; when you attack someone the important thing to remember is the element of . . . *surprise—*"

Ten seconds later he turned to Rincewind.

"All right, Mister Wizard. You can open your eyes now."

One guard was upside-down in a tree, one was a pair of feet sticking out of a snowdrift, two were slumped against rocks, and one was . . . generally around the place. Here and there. Certainly hanging out.

Cohen sucked his wrist thoughtfully.

"I reckon that last one came within an inch of getting me," he said. "I must be getting old."

"Why are you h—" Rincewind paused. One packet of curiosity overtook the first one. "How old *are* you, exactly?"

"Is this still the Century of the Fruitbat?"

"Yes."

"Oh, I dunno. Ninety? Could be ninety. Maybe ninety-five?" Cohen fished the keys out of the snow and ambled over to the group of men, who were cowering even more. He unlocked the first set of manacles and handed the shocked prisoner the keys.

"Bugger off, the lot of you," he said, not unkindly. "And don't get caught again."

He strolled back to Rincewind.

"What brings you into this dump, then?"

"Well—"

"Interestin'," said Cohen, and that was that. "But can't stay chatting all day, got work to do. You coming, or what?"

"What?"

"Please yourself." Cohen tied the chain around his waist as a makeshift belt and wedged a couple of swords in it.

"Incidentally," he said, "what did you do with the Barking Dog?"

"What dog?"

"I expect it doesn't matter."

Rincewind scuttled after the retreating figure. It wasn't that he felt safe when Cohen the Barbarian was around. *No one* was safe when Cohen the Barbarian was around. Something seemed to have gone wrong with the ageing process there. Cohen had always been a barbarian hero because barbaric heroing was all he knew how to do. And while he got old he seemed to get harder, like oak.

But he was a known figure, and therefore comforting. He just wasn't in the right place.

"No future in it, back around the Ramtops," said Cohen, as they trudged through the snow. "Fences and farms, fences and farms *everywhere*. You kill a dragon these days, people *complain*. You know what? You know what happened?"

"No. What happened?"

"Man came up to me, said my teeth were offensive to trolls. What about that, eh?"

"Well, they *are* made of—"

"I said they never complained to *me*."

"Er, did you ever give them a cha—"

"I said, I see a troll up in the mountains with a necklace o' human skulls, I say good luck to him. Silicon Anti-Defamation League, my bottom. It's the same all over. So I thought I'd try my luck the other side of the icecap."

"Isn't it dangerous, going around the Hub?" said Rincewind.

"Used to be," said Cohen, grinning horribly.

"Until you left, you mean?"

"'S right. You still got that box on legs?"

"On and off. It hangs around. You know."

Cohen chuckled.

"I'll get the bloody lid off that thing one day, mark my words. Ah. Horses."

There were five, looking depressed in a small depression.

Rincewind looked back at the freed prisoners, who seemed to be milling around aimlessly.

"We're not taking all five horses, are we?" he said.

"Sure. We might need 'em."

"But . . . one for me, one for you . . . What's the rest for?"

"Lunch, dinner, and breakfast?"

"It's a little . . . unfair, isn't it? Those people look a bit . . . bewildered."

Cohen sneered the sneer of a man who has never been truly imprisoned even when he's been locked up.

"I freed 'em," he said. "First time they've ever been free. Comes as a bit of a shock, I expect. They're waiting for someone to tell 'em what to do next."

"Er . . ."

"I could tell 'em to starve to death, if you like."

"Er . . ."

"Oh, all *right*. You lot! Formee uppee right now toot sweet chop chop!"

The small crowd hurried over to Cohen and stood expectantly behind his horse.

"I tell you, I don't regret it. This is the land of opportunity," said Cohen, urging the horse into a trot. The embarrassed free men jogged behind. "Know what? Swords are banned. No one except the army, the nobles and the Imperial Guard are allowed to own weapons. Couldn't believe it! Gods' own truth, though. Swords are outlawed, so only outlaws have swords. And *that*," said Cohen, giving the landscape another glittering grin, "suits me fine."

"But . . . you were in chains . . . " Rincewind ventured.

"Glad you reminded me," said Cohen. "Yeah. We'll find the rest of the lads, then I'd better try and find who did it and talk to them about that."

The tone of his voice suggested very clearly that all they were likely to say would be, "Highly enjoyable! Your wife is a big hippo!"

"Lads?"

"No future in one-man barbarianing," said Cohen. "Got myself a . . . Well, you'll see."

Rincewind turned to look at the trailing party, and at the snow, and at Cohen.

"Er. Do you know where Hunghung is?"

"Yeah. It's the boss city. We're on our way. Sort of. It's under siege right now."

"Siege? You mean like . . . lots of armies outside, everyone inside eating rats, that sort of thing?"

"Yeah, but this is the Counterweight Continent, see, so it's a polite siege. Well, I call it a siege . . . The old Emperor's dying, so the big families are all waiting to move in. That's how it goes in these parts. There's five different top nobs and they're all watching one another, and no one's going to be the first to move. You've got to think sideways to understand anything in this place."

"Cohen?"

"Yes, lad?"

"What the hell's going on?"

Lord Hong was watching the tea ceremony. It took three hours, but you couldn't hurry a good cuppa.

He was also playing chess, against himself. It was the only way he could find an opponent of his calibre but, currently, things were stalemated because both sides were adopting a defensive strategy which was, admittedly, brilliant.

Lord Hong sometimes wished he could have an enemy as clever as himself. Or, because Lord Hong was indeed very clever, he sometimes wished for an enemy *almost* as clever as himself, one perhaps given to flights of strategic genius with nevertheless the occasional fatal flaw. As it was, people were so *stupid*. They seldom thought more than a dozen moves ahead.

Assassination was meat and drink to the Hunghung court; in fact, meat and drink were often the means. It was a game that everyone played. It was just another kind of move. It was not considered good manners to assassinate the Emperor, of course. The correct move was to put the Emperor in a position where you had control. But moves at this level were very dangerous; happy as the warlords were to squabble amongst themselves, they could be relied upon to unite against any who looked in danger of rising above the herd. And Lord Hong had risen like bread, by making everyone else believe that, while *they* were the obvious candidate for the Emperorship, Lord Hong would be better than any of the alternatives.

It amused him to know that they thought he was plotting for the Imperial pearl . . .

He glanced up from the board and caught the eye of the young woman who was busy at the tea table. She blushed and looked away.

The door slid back. One of his men entered, on his knees.

"Yes?" said Lord Hong.

"Er . . . O lord . . ."

Lord Hong sighed. People seldom began like this when the news was good.

"What happened?" he said.

"The one they call the Great Wizard arrived, o lord. Up in the mountains. Riding on a dragon of wind. Or so they say," the messenger added quickly, aware of Lord Hong's views about superstition.

"Good. But? I assume there is a but."

"Er . . . one of the Barking Dogs has been lost. The new batch? That you commanded should be tested? We don't quite . . . that is to say . . . we think Captain Three High Trees was ambushed, perhaps . . . our information is somewhat confused . . . the, um, the informant says the Great Wizard magicked it away . . ." The messenger crouched lower.

Lord Hong merely sighed again. Magic. It had fallen out of favor in the Empire, except for the most mundane purposes. It was *uncultured.* It put power in the hands of people who couldn't write a decent poem to save their lives, and sometimes hadn't.

He believed in coincidence a lot more than he did in magic.

"This is most vexing," said Lord Hong.

He stood up and took his sword off the rack. It was long and curved and had been made by the finest sword-maker in the Empire, who was Lord Hong. He'd heard it took twenty years to learn the art, so he had stretched himself a little. It had taken him three weeks. People never *concentrated,* that was their trouble . . .

The messenger groveled.

"The officer concerned has been executed?" he said.

The messenger tried to scrabble through the floor and decided to let truth stand in for honesty.

"Yes!" he piped.

56

Lord Hong swung. There was a hiss like the fall of silk, a thump and clatter as of a coconut hitting the ground, and the tinkle of crockery.

The messenger opened his eyes. He concentrated on his neck region, fearful that the slightest movement might leave him a good deal shorter. There were dire stories about Lord Hong's swords.

"Oh, do get up," said Lord Hong. He wiped the blade carefully and replaced the sword. Then he reached across and pulled a small black bottle from the robe of the tea girl.

Uncorked, it produced a few drops that hissed when they hit the floor.

"Really," said Lord Hong. "I wonder why people bother." He looked up. "Lord Tang or Lord McSweeney has probably stolen the Dog to vex me. Did the Wizard escape?"

"So it seems, o lord."

"Good. See that harm almost comes to him. And send me another tea girl. One with a head."

There was this to be said about Cohen. If there was no reason for him to kill you, such as you having any large amount of treasure or being between him and somewhere he wanted to get to, then he was good company. Rincewind had met him a few times before, generally while running away from something.

Cohen didn't bother overmuch with questions. As far as Cohen was concerned, people appeared, people disappeared. After a five-year gap he'd just say, "Oh, it's you." He never added, "And how are you?" You were alive, you were upright, and beyond that he didn't give a damn.

It was a lot warmer beyond the mountains. To Rincewind's relief a spare horse didn't have to be eaten because a leopardly sort of creature dropped off a tree branch and tried to disembowel Cohen.

It had a rather strong flavor.

Rincewind *had* eaten horse. Over the years he'd nerved himself to eat anything that couldn't actually wriggle off his fork. But he was feeling shaken enough without eating something you could call Dobbin.

"How did they catch you?" he said, when they were riding again.

"I was busy."

"Cohen the Barbarian? Too busy to *fight?*"

"I didn't want to upset the young lady. Couldn't help meself. Went down to a village to pick up some news, one thing led to another, next thing a load of soldiers were all over the place like cheap armour, and I can't fight that well with my arms shackled behind my back. Real nasty bugger in charge, face I won't forget in a hurry. Half a dozen of us were rounded up, made to push the Barking Dog thing all the way out here, then we were chained to that tree and someone lit the bit of string and they all legged it behind a snowdrift. Except you came along and vanished it."

"I didn't vanish it. Not exactly, anyway."

Cohen leaned across towards Rincewind. "I reckon I know what it was," he said, and sat back looking pleased with himself.

"Yes?"

"I reckon it was some kind of firework. They're very big on fireworks here."

"You mean the sort of things where you light the blue touch paper and stick it up your nose?"*

"They use 'em to drive evil spirits away. There's a lot of evil spirits, see. Because of all the slaughtering."

"Slaughtering?"

Rincewind had always understood that the Agatean Empire was a peaceful place. It was civilized. They *invented* things. In fact, he recalled, he'd been instrumental in introducing a few of their devices to Ankh-Morpork. Simple, innocent things, like clocks worked by demons, and boxes that painted pictures, and extra glass eyes you could wear over the top of your own eyes to help you see better, even if it did mean you made a spectacle of yourself.

---

*KIDS! Only very silly wizards with bad sinus trouble do this. *Sensible* people go off to a roped-off enclosure where they can watch a heavily protected man, in the middle distance, light (with the aid of a very long pole) something that goes "fsst." And then they can shout "Hooray."

It was supposed to be *dull.*

"Oh, yeah. Slaughtering," said Cohen. "Like, supposing the population is being a bit behind with its taxes. You pick some city where people are being troublesome and kill everyone and set fire to it and pull down the walls and plough up the ashes. That way you get rid of the trouble and all the other cities are suddenly really well behaved and polite and all your back taxes turn up in a big rush, which is handy for governments, I understand. Then if they ever give trouble you just have to say 'Remember Nangnang?' or whatever, and they say 'Where's Nangnang?' and you say, 'My point exactly.'"

"Good grief! If that sort of thing was tried back home—"

"Ah, but this place has been going a long time. People think that's how a country is supposed to run. They do what they're told. The people here are treated like slaves."

Cohen scowled. "Now, I've got nothing against slaves, you know, as slaves. Owned a few in my time. *Been* a slave once or twice. But where there's slaves, what'll you expect to find?"

Rincewind thought about this. "Whips?" he said at last.

"Yeah. Got it in one. Whips. There's something *honest* about slaves and whips. Well . . . they ain't got whips here. They got something worse than whips."

"What?" said Rincewind, looking slightly panicky.

"You'll find out."

Rincewind found himself looking around at the half-dozen other prisoners, who had trailed after them and were watching in awe from a distance. He'd given them a bit of leopard, which they'd looked at initially as if it was poison and then eaten as if it was food.

"They're still following us," he said.

"Yeah, well . . . you did give 'em meat," cackled Cohen, starting to roll a post-prandial cigarette. "Shouldn't have done that. Should've let 'em have the whiskers and the claws and you'd've been *amazed* at what they'd cook up. You know their big dish down on the coast?"

"No."

"Pig's ear soup. Now, what's that tell you about a place, eh?"

Rincewind shrugged. "Very provident people?"

59

Terry Pratchett

"Some other bugger pinches the pig."

He turned in the saddle. The group of ex-prisoners shrank back.

"Now, see here," he said. "I *told* you. You're free. Understand?"

One of the braver men spoke up. "Yes, master."

"I ain't your master. You're *free*. You can go wherever you like, excepting if you follow me I'll kill the lot of you. And now—go away!"

"Where, master?"

"Anywhere! Somewhere not here!"

The men gave one another some worried looks and then the whole group, as one man, turned and trotted away along the path.

"Probably go straight back to their village," he said, rolling his eyes. "Worse than whips, I tell you."

He waved a scrawny hand at the landscape as they rode on.

"Strange bloody country," he said. "Did you know there's a wall all round the Empire?"

"That's to keep . . . barbarian invaders . . . out . . ."

"Oh, yes, very defensive," said Cohen sarcastically. "Like, oh my goodness, there's a twenty-foot wall, dear me, I suppose we'd just better ride off back over a thousand miles of steppe and not, e.g., take a look at the ladder possibilities inherent in that pine wood over there. Nah. It's to keep the people in. And rules? They've got rules for everything. No one even goes to the privy without a piece of paper."

"Well, as a matter of fact I myself—"

"A piece of paper saying they can go, is what I meant. Can't leave your village without a chit. Can't get married without a chit. Can't even have a sh—Ah, we're here."

"Yes, indeed," said Rincewind.

Cohen glared at him. "How did you know?" he demanded.

Rincewind tried to think. It had been a long day. In fact it had, because of the thaumic equivalent of jetlag, been several hours longer than most other days he'd experienced and had contained two lunchtimes, neither of which had contained anything worth eating.

60

"Er . . . I thought you were making a general philosophical point," he hazarded. "Er. Like, 'We'd better make the best of it'?"

"I meant we're here at my hideout," said Cohen. Rincewind stared around them. There were scrubby bushes, a few rocks, and a sheer cliff face.

"I can't see anything," he said.

"Yep. That's how you can tell it's mine."

The Art of War was the ultimate basis of diplomacy in the Empire.

Clearly war had to exist. It was a cornerstone of the processes of government. It was the way the Empire got its leaders. The competitive examination system was how it got its bureaucrats and public officials, and warfare was for its leaders, perhaps, only a different kind of competitive examination. Admittedly, if you lost you probably weren't allowed to re-sit next year.

But there had to be rules. Otherwise it was just a barbaric scuffle.

So, hundreds of years ago, the Art of War had been formulated. It was a book of rules. Some were very specific: there was to be no fighting within the Forbidden City, the person of the Emperor was sacrosanct . . . and some were more general guidelines for the good and civilized conduct of warfare. There were the rules of position, of tactics, of the enforcement of discipline, of the correct organization of supply lines. The Art laid down the optimum course to take in every conceivable eventuality. It meant that warfare in the Empire had become far more *sensible*, and generally consisted of short periods of activity followed by long periods of people trying to find things in the index.

No one remembered the author. Some said it was One Tzu Sung, some claimed it was Three Sun Sung. Possibly it was even some unsung genius who had penned, or rather painted, the very first principle: Know the enemy, and know yourself.

Lord Hong felt that he knew himself very well, and seldom had trouble knowing his enemies. And he made a point of keeping his enemies alive and healthy.

Take the Lords Sung, Fang, Tang, and McSweeney. He cherished

Terry Pratchett

them. He cherished their *adequacy*. They had adequate military brains, which was to say that they had memorized the Five Rules and Nine Principles of the Art of War. They wrote adequate poetry, and were cunning enough to counter such coups as were attempted in their own ranks. They occasionally sent against him assassins who were sufficiently competent to keep Lord Hong interested and observant and entertained.

He even admired their adequate treachery. No one could fail to realize that Lord Hong would be the next Emperor, but when it came to it they would nevertheless contest the throne. At least, officially. In fact, each warlord had privately pledged his personal support to Lord Hong, being adequately bright to know what was likely to happen if he didn't. There would still have to be a battle, of course, for custom's sake. But Lord Hong had a place in his heart for any leader who would sell his own men.

Know your enemy. Lord Hong had decided to find a worthwhile one. So Lord Hong had seen to it that he got books and news from Ankh-Morpork. There were ways. He had his spies. At the moment Ankh-Morpork didn't know it was the enemy, and that was the best kind of enemy to have.

And he had been amazed, and then intrigued, and finally lost in admiration for what he saw . . .

I should have been born there, he thought as he watched the other members of the Serene Council. Oh, for a game of chess with someone like Lord Vetinari. No doubt he would carefully watch the board for three hours before he even made his first move . . .

Lord Hong turned to the Serene Council's minutes eunuch.

"Can we get on?" he said.

The man licked his brush nervously. "Nearly finished, o lord," he said.

Lord Hong sighed.

Damn calligraphy! There would be changes! A written language of seven thousand letters and it took all day to write a thirteen-syllable poem about a white pony trotting through wild hyacinths. And that was fine and beautiful, he had to concede, and no one did it better than Lord Hong. But Ankh-Morpork had an alphabet of twenty-six unexpressive, ugly, crude letters, suitable only for peasants and artisans . . . and had produced poems and plays that left white-hot trails across the soul. And you could also use it to write the bloody minutes of a five-minute meeting in less than a day.

"How far have you got?" he said.

The eunuch coughed politely.

"'How softly the bloom of the apric—'" he began.

"Yes, yes, yes," said Lord Hong. "Could we on this occasion dispense with the poetic framework, please."

"Uh. 'The minutes of the last meeting were duly signed.'"

"Is that all?"

"Uh . . . you see, I have to finish painting the petals on—"

"I wish this council to be concluded by this evening. Go away."

The eunuch looked anxiously around the table, grabbed his scrolls and brushes and scuttled out.

"Good," said Lord Hong. He nodded at the other warlords. He saved a special friendly nod for Lord Tang. Lord Hong had prodded the thought with some intrigued interest, but it really did seem that Lord Tang was a man of honor. It was a rather cowed and crabbed honour, but it was definitely in there somewhere, and would have to be dealt with.

"It would be better in any case, my lords, if we spoke in private," he said. "On the matter of the rebels. Disturbing intelligence has reached me of their activities."

Lord McSweeney nodded. "I have seen to it that thirty rebels in Sum Dim have been executed," he said. "As an example."

As an example of the mindlessness of Lord McSweeney, thought Lord Hong. To his certain knowledge, and none had better knowledge than he, there had not even been a cadre of the Red Army in Sum Dim. But, almost certainly, there was one now. It was really too easy.

The other warlords also made small but proud speeches about their efforts to turn barely noticeable unrest into bloody revolution, although they hadn't managed to see it like that.

They were nervous, under the bravado, like sheepdogs who'd had a glimpse of a world where the sheep did not run.

Lord Hong cherished the nervousness. He intended to use it, by and by. He smiled and smiled.

Finally he said: "However, my lords, despite your sterling efforts the situation remains grave. I have information that a very senior wizard from Ankh-Morpork has arrived to assist the rebels here in Hunghung, and that there is a plot to overthrow the good organization of the celestial world and assassinate the Emperor, may he live for ten thousand years. I must naturally assume that the foreign devils are behind this."

"I know nothing of this!" snapped Lord Tang.

"My dear Lord Tang, I was not suggesting that you should," said Lord Hong.

"I meant—" Lord Tang began.

"Your devotion to the Emperor is unquestioned," Lord Hong continued, as smoothly as a knife through warm butter. "It is true that there is almost certainly someone highly placed assisting these people, but not one shred of evidence points to you."

"I should hope not!"

"Indeed."

The Lords Fang and McSweeney moved very slightly away from Lord Tang.

"How can we have let this happen?" said Lord Fang. "Certainly it is true that people, foolish deranged people, have sometimes ventured out beyond the Wall. But to let one come *back*—"

"I am afraid the Grand Vizier at the time was a man of changeable humors," said Lord Hong. "He thought it would be interesting to see what intelligence was brought back."

"Intelligence?" said Lord Fang. "This city of Ank . . . More . . . Pork is an abomination! Mere anarchy! There appear to be no nobles of consequence and the society is that of a termite nest! It would be better for us, my lords, if it was wiped from the face of the world!"

"Your incisive comments are duly noted, Lord Fang," said Lord Hong, while part of him rolled on the floor laughing. "In any event," he went on, "I shall see that extra guards are posted in the Emperor's chambers. However all this trouble began, we must see that it ends here."

He watched them watching him. They think I want to rule the

Empire, he thought. So they're all—except for Lord Tang, rebel fellow traveler as he will undoubtedly prove to be—working out how this will be to their advantage . . .

He dismissed them, and retired to his chambers.

It was a fact that the ghosts and devils who lived beyond the Wall had no grasp of culture and certainly no concept of books, and being in possession of such a patently impossible object was punishable by eventual death. And confiscation.

Lord Hong had built up quite a library. He had even acquired maps.

And more than maps. There was a box he kept locked, in the room with the full-length mirror . . .

Not now. Later on . . .

Ankh-Morpork! Even the name sounded rich.

All he needed was a year. The dreadful scourge of the rebellion would allow him to wield the kind of powers that even the maddest Emperor had not dreamed of. And then it would be unthinkable not to build a vengeful fleet to wreak terror on the foreign devils. Thank you, Lord Fang. Your point is duly noted.

As if it mattered who was Emperor! The Empire was possibly a bonus, to be acquired later, perhaps, in passing. Let him just have Ankh-Morpork, with its busy dwarfs and its grasp, above all, of machinery. Look at the Barking Dogs. Half the time they blew up. They were inaccurate. The principle was sound but the execution was terrible, especially when they blew up.

It had come as a revelation to Lord Hong when he looked at the problem the Ankh-Morpork way and realized that it might just possibly be better to give the job of Auspicious Dog-maker to some peasant with a fair idea about metal and explosive earths than to some clerk who'd got the highest marks in an examination to find the best poem about iron. In Ankh-Morpork people *did* things.

Let him just walk down Broadway as owner, and eat the pies of the famous Mr. Dibbler. Let him play one game of chess against Lord Vetinari. Of course, it would mean leaving the man one arm.

He was shaking with excitement. Not later . . . now. His fingers reached for the secret key on its chain around his neck.

* * *

It was barely a track. Rabbits would have walked right past it. And you'd have sworn there was a sheer, passless rock wall until you found the gap.

Once you *did* find it, it was hardly worth the bother. It led to a long gully with a few natural caves in it, and a bit of grass, and a spring.

And, as it turned out, Cohen's gang. Except that he called it a horde. They were sitting in the sun, complaining about how it wasn't as warm as it used to be.

"I'm back then, lads," said Cohen.

"Been away, have you?"

"Whut? Whut's he say?"

"He said HE'S BACK."

"Black what?"

Cohen beamed at Rincewind. "I brought 'em with me," he said. "Like I said, no future in going it alone these days."

"Er," said Rincewind, after surveying the little scene, "are any of these men under eighty years old?"

"Stand up, Boy Willie," said Cohen.

A dehydrated man only marginally less wrinkled than the others got to his feet. It was his feet that were particularly noticeable. He wore boots with extremely thick soles.

"So's me feet touch the ground," he said.

"Don't they . . . er . . . touch the ground in ordinary boots?"

"Nope. Orthopedic problem, see. Like . . . you know how a lot of people've got one leg shorter than the other? Funny thing, with me it's—"

"Don't tell me," said Rincewind. "Sometimes I get these amazing flashes . . . *Both* legs are shorter than the other, right?"

"Amazing. O' course, I can see you're a wizard," said Boy Willie. "You'd know about this sort of thing."

Rincewind gave the next member of the Horde a bright mad smile. It was almost certainly a human being, because wizened little monkeys didn't usually go around in a wheelchair while wearing a helmet with horns on it. It grimaced at Rincewind.

"This is—"

"Whut? Whut?"

"Mad Hamish," said Cohen.

"Whut? Whozee?"

"I bet that wheelchair *terrifies* them," said Rincewind. "Especially the blades."

"We had the devil of a job getting it over the wall," Cohen conceded. "But you'd be amazed at his turn of speed."

"Whut?"

"And this is Truckle the Uncivil."

"Sod off, wizard."

Rincewind beamed at Exhibit B. "Those walking sticks . . . Fascinating! Very impressive the way you've got LOVE and HATE written on them."

Cohen smiled proprietorially.

"Truckle used to be reckoned one of the biggest badasses in the world," he said.

"Really? Him?"

"But it's amazing what you can do with a herbal suppository."

"Up yours, mister," said Truckle.

Rincewind blinked. "Er. Can I have a word, Cohen?"

He drew the ancient barbarian aside.

"I don't want to seem to be making trouble here," he said, "but it doesn't strike you, does it, that these men are a bit, well, past their sell-by date? A little, not to put too fine a point on it, old?"

"Whut? Whutzeesayin'?"

"He says IT'S COLD."

"Whut?"

"What're you saying? There's nearly five hundred years of concentrated barbarian hero experience in 'em," said Cohen.

"'Five hundred years' experience in a fighting unit is good," said Rincewind. "It's *good*. But it should be spread over more than one person. I mean, what are you expecting them to do? Fall over on people?"

"Nothin' wrong with 'em," said Cohen, indicating a frail man who was staring intently at a large block of teak. "Look at ole Caleb the Ripper over there. See? Killed more'n four hundred men with his bare hands. Eighty-five now and but for the dust he's marvellous."

"What the hell is he *doing?*"

"Ah, see, they're into bare-handed combat here. Very big thing, unarmed combat, on account of most people not being allowed weapons. So Caleb reckons he's on to a good thing. See that big lump of teak? It's amazin'. He just gives this blood-curdlin' shout and—"

"Cohen, they're all very old men."

"They're the cream!"

Rincewind sighed.

"Cohen, they're the cheese. Why've you brought them all the way here?"

"Gonna help me steal something," said Cohen.

"What? A jewel or something?"

"'S something," said Cohen, sulkily. "'S in Hunghung."

"Really? My word," said Rincewind. "And there's a lot of people in Hunghung, I expect?"

"About half a million," said Cohen.

"Lots of guards, no doubt?"

"About forty thousand, I heard. About three-quarters of a million if you count all the armies."

"Right," said Rincewind. "So, with these half-dozen old men—"

"The Silver Horde," said Cohen, with a touch of pride.

"What? Pardon?"

"That's their name. Got to have a name in the horde business. The Silver Horde."

Rincewind turned around. Several of the Horde had fallen asleep.

"The Silver Horde," he said. "Right. Matches the color of their hair. Those that have *got* hair. So . . . with this . . . Silver Horde you're going to rush the city, kill all the guards and steal all the treasure?"

Cohen nodded. "Yeah . . . something like that. Of course, we won't have to kill *all* the guards . . ."

"Oh, no?"

"It'd take too long."

"Yes, and of course you'll want to leave something to do tomorrow."

"I mean they'll be busy, what with the revolution and everything."

"A revolution, too? My word."

"They say it's a time of portents," said Cohen. "They—"

"I'm surprised they've got time to worry about the state of their camping equipment," said Rincewind.

"You'd be well advised to stay along o' us," said Ghenghiz Cohen. "You'll be safer with us."

"Oh, I'm not sure about that," said Rincewind, grinning horribly. "I'm not sure about that at all."

By myself, he thought, only *ordinary* horrible things can happen to me.

Cohen shrugged, and then stared around the clearing until his gaze lighted on a slight figure who was sitting a little apart from the rest, reading a book.

"Look at him," he said, benevolently, like a man pointing out a dog doing a good trick. "Always got his nose in a book." He raised his voice. "Teach? Come and show this wizard the way to Hunghung."

He turned back to Rincewind. "Teach'll tell you anything you want to know, 'cos he knows everything. I'll leave you with him. I've got to go and have a talk with Old Vincent." He waved a hand dismissively. "Not that there's anything wrong with him, at all," he said defiantly. "It's just that his memory's bad. We had a bit of trouble on the way over. I keep telling him, it's rape the *women* and set fire to the *houses*."

"Rape?" said Rincewind. "That's not very—"

"He's eighty-seven," said Cohen. "Don't go and spoil an old man's dreams."

Teach turned out to be a tall, stick-like man with an amiably absentminded expression and a fringe of white hair so that, when viewed from above, he would appear to be a daisy. He certainly did not appear to be a bloodthirsty brigand, even though he was wearing a chain-mail vest slightly too big for him and a huge scabbard strapped across his back, which contained no sword but held a variety of scrolls and brushes. His chain-mail shirt had a breast pocket with three different colored pens in a leather pocket protector.

69

"Ronald Saveloy," he said, shaking Rincewind's hand. "The gentlemen do rather assume considerable knowledge on my part. Let me see . . . You want to go to Hunghung, yes?"

Rincewind had been thinking about this.

"I want to know the *way* to Hunghung," he said guardedly.

"Yes. Well. At this time of year I'd head towards the setting sun until I left the mountains and reached the alluvial plain where you'll see evidence of drumlins and some quite fine examples of obviously erratic boulders. It's about ten miles."

Rincewind stared at him. A brigand's directions were usually more on the lines of "keep straight on past the burning city and turn right when you've passed all the citizens hanging up by their ears."

"Those drumlins sound dangerous," he said.

"They're just a type of post-glacial hill," said Mr. Saveloy.

"What about these erratic boulders? They sound like the kind of thing that'd pounce on—"

"Just boulders dropped a long way from home by a glacier," said Mr. Saveloy. "Nothing to worry about. The landscape is not hostile."

Rincewind didn't believe him. He'd had the ground hit him very hard many times.

"However," said Mr. Saveloy, "Hunghung is a little dangerous at the moment."

"No, really?" said Rincewind wearily.

"It's not *exactly* a siege. Everyone's waiting for the Emperor to die. These are what they call here"—he smiled—"interesting times."

"I *hate* interesting times."

The other Horders had wandered off, fallen asleep again, or were complaining to one another about their feet. The voice of Cohen could be heard somewhere in the distance: "Look, *this* is a match, and *this* is—"

"You know, you sound a very educated man for a barbarian," said Rincewind.

"Oh, dear me, I didn't start out a barbarian. I used to be a school teacher. That's why they call me Teach."

"What did you teach?"

"Geography. And I was very interested in Auriental* studies. But I decided to give it up and make a living by the sword."

"After being a teacher all your life?"

"It did mean a change of perspective, yes."

"But . . . well . . . surely . . . the privation, the terrible hazards, the daily risk of death . . . "

Mr. Saveloy brightened up. "Oh, you've *been* a teacher, have you?"

Rincewind looked around when someone shouted. He turned, to see two of the Horde arguing nose to nose.

Mr. Saveloy sighed.

"I'm trying to teach them chess," he said. "It's vital to the understanding of the Auriental mind. But I am afraid they have no concept of taking turns at moving, and their idea of an opening gambit is for the King and all the pawns to rush up the board together and set fire to the opposing rooks."

Rincewind leaned closer.

"Look, I mean . . . *Ghenghiz* Cohen?" he said. "Has he gone off his head? I mean . . . just killing half a dozen geriatric priests and nicking some paste gems, *yes*. Attacking forty thousand guards all by himself is certain death!"

"Oh, he won't be by himself," said Mr. Saveloy.

Rincewind blinked. There was something about Cohen. People caught optimism off him as though it was the common cold.

"Oh, yes. Of course. Sorry. I'd forgotten that. Seven against forty thousand? I shouldn't think you'll have any problems. I'll just be going. Fairly quickly, I think."

"We have a plan. It's a sort of—" Mr. Saveloy hesitated. His eyes unfocused slightly. "You know? Thing. Bees do it. Wasps, too. Also some jellyfish, I believe . . . Had the word only a moment ago . . . er. It's going to be the biggest one ever, I think."

Rincewind gave him another blank stare. "I'm sure I saw a spare horse," he said.

"Let me give you this," said Mr. Saveloy. "Then perhaps you'll understand. It's what it's all about, really . . ."

*The Ankh-Morpork name for the Counterweight Continent and its nearby islands. It means "place where the gold comes from."

He handed Rincewind a small bundle of papers fastened together by a loop of string through one corner.

Rincewind, shoving it hastily into his pocket, noticed only the title on the first page.

It said:

WHAT I DID ON MY HOLIDAYS

The choices seemed very clear to Rincewind. There was the city of Hunghung, under siege, apparently throbbing with revolution and danger, and there was everywhere else.

Therefore it was important to know where Hunghung was so that he didn't blunder into it by accident. He paid a lot of attention to Mr. Saveloy's instructions, and then rode the other way.

He could get a ship somewhere. Of course, the wizards would be surprised to see him back, but he could always say there'd been no one in.

The hills gave way to scrubland which in turn led down to an apparently endless damp plain which contained, in the misty distance, a river so winding that half the time it must have been flowing backwards.

The land was a checkerboard of cultivation. Rincewind liked the countryside in theory, providing it wasn't rising up to meet him and was for preference happening on the far side of a city wall, but this was hardly countryside. It was more like one big, hedgeless farm. Occasional huge rocks, looking dangerously erratic, rose out of the fields.

Sometimes he'd see people hard at work in the distance. As far as he could tell, their chief activity was moving mud around.

Occasionally he'd see a man standing ankle-deep in a flooded field holding a water buffalo on the end of a length of string. The buffalo grazed and occasionally moved its bowels. The man held the string. It seemed to be his entire goal and occupation in life.

There were a few other people on the road. Usually they were pushing wheelbarrows loaded with water buffalo dung or, possibly, mud. They didn't pay any attention to Rincewind. In fact they made a *point* of not paying attention; they scurried past staring intently at the scenes of mud dynamics or bovine bowel movement happening in the fields.

Rincewind would be the first to admit that he was a slow thinker.* But he'd been around long enough to spot the signs. These people weren't paying him any attention because they didn't *see* people on horseback.

They were probably descended from people who learned that if you look too hard at anyone on horseback you receive a sharp stinging sensation such as might be obtained by a stick around the ear. Not looking up at people on horseback had become hereditary. People who stared at people on horseback in what was considered to be a funny way never survived long enough to breed.

He decided to try an experiment. The next wheelbarrow that trundled past was carrying not mud but people, about half a dozen of them, on seats either side of the huge central wheel. The method of propulsion was secondarily by a small sail erected to catch the wind but primarily by that pre-eminent source of motive power in a peasant community, someone's great-grandfather, or at least someone who looked like someone's great-grandfather.

Cohen had said, "There's men here who can push a wheelbarrow for thirty miles on a bowl of millet with a bit of scum in it. What does that tell you? It tells *me* someone's porking all the beef."

Rincewind decided to explore the social dynamics and also try out the language. It had been years since he'd last used it, but he had to admit that Ridcully had been right. He did have a gift for languages. Agatean was a language of few basic syllables. It was really all in the tone, inflection, and context. Otherwise, the word for military leader was also the word for long-tailed marmot, male sexual organ, and ancient chicken coop.

"Hey there, you!" he shouted. "Er . . . to bend bamboo? An expression of disapproval? Er . . . I mean . . . Stop!"

The barrow slewed to a halt. No one looked at him. They looked past him, or around him, or towards his feet.

---

*In fact, he'd be about the seventy-third to admit it.

Eventually the wheelbarrow-pusher, in the manner of a man who knows he's in for it no matter what he does, mumbled, "Your honor commands?"

Rincewind felt very sorry, later, for what he said next.

He said, "Just give me all your food and . . . unwilling dogs, will you?"

They watched him impassively.

"Damn. I mean . . . arranged beetles? . . . variety of water-fall? . . . Oh, yes . . . *money.*"

There was a general fumbling and shifting among the passengers. Then the wheelbarrow-pusher sidled towards Rincewind, head down, and held up his hat. It contained some rice, some dried fish, a highly dangerous-looking egg. And about a pound of gold, in big round coins.

Rincewind stared at the gold.

Gold was as common as copper on the Counterweight Continent. That was one of the few things everyone knew about the place. There was no *point* in Cohen trying any kind of big robbery. There was a limit to what anyone could carry. He might as well rob one peasant village and live like a king for the rest of his life. It wouldn't be as if he'd need that much . . .

The "later" suddenly caught up with him, and he did indeed feel quite ashamed. These people had hardly anything, apart from loads of gold.

"Er. Thanks. Thank you. Yes. Just checking. Yes. You can all have it back now. I'll . . . er . . . keep . . . the elderly grandmother . . . to run sideways . . . oh, damn . . . *fish.*"

Rincewind had always been on the bottom of the social heap. It didn't matter what size heap it was. The top got higher or lower, but the bottom was always in the same place. But at least it was an Ankh-Morpork heap.

No one bowed to anyone in Ankh-Morpork. And anyone who tried what he'd just tried in Ankh-Morpork would, by now, be scrabbling in the gutter for his teeth and whimpering about the pain in his groin and his horse would already have been repainted twice and sold to a man who'd be swearing he'd owned it for years.

He felt oddly proud of the fact.

Something strange welled up from the sludgy depths of his soul. It was, to his amazement, a generous impulse.

He slid off the horse and held out the reins. A horse was useful, but he was used to doing without one. Besides, over a short distance a man could run faster than a horse, and this was a fact very dear to Rincewind's heart.

"Here," he said. "You can have it. For the fish."

The wheelbarrow-pusher screamed, grabbed the handles of his conveyance, and hurtled desperately away. Several people were thrown off, took one almost-look at Rincewind, also screamed, and ran after him.

Worse than whips, Cohen had said. They've got something here worse than whips. They don't *need* whips anymore. Rincewind hoped he'd never find out what it was, if it had done this to people.

He rode on through an endless panorama of fields. There weren't even any patches of roadside scrub, or taverns. Away among the fields were shapes that might be small towns or villages, but no apparent paths to them, possibly because paths used up valuable agricultural mud.

Finally he sat down on a rock that presumably not even the peasants' most concerted efforts had been able to move, and reached into his pocket for his shameful dried fish lunch.

His hand touched the bundle of papers Mr. Saveloy had given him. He pulled them out, and got crumbs on them.

This is what it's all about, the barbarian teacher had said. He hadn't explained what "it" was.

WHAT I DID ON MY HOLIDAYS, said the title. It was in bad handwriting or, rather, bad painting—the Agateans wrote with paintbrushes, assembling little word pictures out of handy components. One picture wasn't just worth a thousand words, it *was* a thousand words.

Rincewind wasn't much good at reading the language. There were very few Agatean books even in the Unseen University Library. And this one looked as though whoever had written it had been trying to make sense of something unfamiliar.

He turned over a couple of pages. It was a story about a Great City, containing magnificent things—"beer strong like an ox," it said, and "pies containing many many parts of pig." Everyone in the city seemed to be wise, kind, strong or all three, especially some character called the Great Wizard who seemed to feature largely in the text.

And there were mystifying little comments, as in, "I saw a man tread upon the toes of a City Guard who said to him 'Your wife is a big hippo!' to which the man responded 'Place it where the sun does not shed daylight, enormous person,' upon which the Guard [this bit was in red ink and the handwriting was shaky, as if the writer was quite excited] *did not remove the man's head according to ancient custom.*" The statement was followed by a pictogram of a dog passing water, which was for some obscure reason the Agatean equivalent of an exclamation mark. There were five of these.

Rincewind flicked through the pages. They were filled with the same dull stuff, sentences stating the blindingly obvious but often followed by several incontinent dogs. Such as: "The innkeeper said the City had demanded tax but he did not intend to pay, and when I asked if he was not afraid he vouchsafed: '[Complicated pictogram] them all except one and he can [complicated pictogram] himself' [urinating dog, urinating dog]. He went on to say, 'The [pictogram indicating Supreme Ruler] is a [another pictogram which, after some thought and holding up the picture at various angles, Rincewind decided meant "a horse's bottom"] and you can tell him I said so,' *at which point* a Guard in the tavern *did not disembowel him* [urinating dog, urinating dog] but said, 'Tell him from me also' [urinating dog, urinating dog, urinating dog, urinating dog, urinating dog]."

What was so odd about that? People talked like that in Ankh-Morpork all the time, or at least expressed those sentiments. Apart from the dog.

Mind you, a country that'd wipe out a whole city to teach the other cities a lesson was a mad place. Perhaps this was a book of jokes and he just hadn't seen the point. Perhaps comedians here got big laughs with lines like: "I say, I say, I say, I met a man on the way to the theater and *he didn't chop my legs off,* urinating dog, urinating dog—"

He had been aware of the jingle of harness on the road, but

hadn't paid it any attention. He hadn't even looked up at the sound of someone approaching. By the time he did think of looking up it was too late, because someone had their boot on his neck.

"Oh, urinating dog," he said, before passing out.

There was a puff of air and the Luggage appeared, dropping heavily into a snowdrift.

There was a meat cleaver sticking into its lid.

It remained motionless for some time and then, its legs moving in a complicated little dance, it turned around 360 degrees.

The Luggage did not think. It had nothing to think with. Whatever processes went on inside it probably had more to do with the way a tree reacts to sun and rain and sudden storms, but speeded up very fast.

After a while it seemed to get its bearings and ambled off across the melting snow.

The Luggage did not feel, either. It had nothing to feel with. But it reacted, in the same way that a tree reacts to the changing of the seasons.

Its pace quickened.

It was close to home.

Rincewind had to concede that the shouting man was right. Not, that is, about Rincewind's father being the diseased liver of a type of mountain panda and his mother being a bucket of turtle slime; Rincewind had no personal experience of either parent but felt that they were probably at least vaguely humanoid, if only briefly. But on the subject of appearing to own a stolen horse he had Rincewind bang to rights and, also, a foot on his neck. A foot on the neck is nine points of the law.

He felt hands rummaging in his pockets.

Another person—Rincewind was not able to see much beyond a few inches of alluvial soil, but from context it appeared to be an unsympathetic person—joined in the shouting.

Rincewind was hauled upright.

The guards were pretty much like guards as Rincewind had experienced them everywhere. They had exactly the amount of intellect required to hit people and drag them off to the scorpion pit. They were league champions at shouting at people a few inches from their face.

The effect was made surreal by the fact that the guards themselves had no faces, or at least no faces they could call their own. Their ornate, black-enameled helmets had huge moustached visages painted on them, leaving only the owner's mouth uncovered so that he could, for example, call Rincewind's grandfather a box of inferior goldfish droppings.

What I Did On My Holidays was waved in front of his face.

"Bag of rotted fish!"

"I don't know what it means," said Rincewind. "Someone just gave it to—"

"Feet of extreme decayed milk!"

"Could you perhaps not shout quite so loud? I think my eardrum has just exploded."

The guard subsided, possibly only because he had run out of breath. Rincewind had a moment to look at the scenery.

There were two carts on the road. One of them seemed to be a cage on wheels; he made out faces watching him in terror. The other was an ornate palanquin carried by eight peasants; rich curtains covered the sides but he could see where they had been twitched aside so that someone within could look at him.

The guards were aware of this. It seemed to make them awkward.

"If I could just expl—"

"Silence, mouth of—" The guard hesitated.

"You've used turtle, goldfish, and what you probably meant to be cheese," said Rincewind.

"Mouth of chicken gizzards!"

A long, thin hand emerged from the curtains and beckoned, just once.

Rincewind was hustled forward. The hand had the longest fingernails he'd ever seen on something that didn't purr.

"Kowtow!"

"Sorry?" said Rincewind.

"*Kowtow!*"

Swords were produced.

"I don't know what you mean!" Rincewind wailed.

"Kowtow, please," whispered a voice by his ear. It was not a particularly friendly voice but compared to all the other voices it was positively affectionate. It sounded as though it belonged to quite a young man. And it was speaking very good Morporkian.

"*How?*"

"You don't know *that?* Kneel down, press your forehead on the ground. That's if you want to be able to wear a hat again."

Rincewind hesitated. He was a free-born Morporkian, and on the list of things a citizen didn't do was bow down to any, not to put too fine a point on it, *foreigner.*

On the other hand, right at the *top* of the list of things a citizen didn't do was get their head chopped off.

"That's better. That's good. How did you know you ought to tremble?"

"Oh, I thought up that bit myself."

The hand beckoned with a finger.

A guard slapped Rincewind in the face with the mud-encrusted *What I Did* . . . Rincewind clutched it guiltily as the guard scurried towards his master's digit.

"Voice?" said Rincewind.

"Yes?"

"What happens if I claim immunity because I'm a foreigner?"

"There's a special thing they do with a wire-mesh waistcoat and a cheesegrater."

"Oh."

"And there are torturers in Hunghung who can keep a man alive for years."

"I suppose you're not talking about healthy early morning runs and a high-fiber diet?"

"No. So keep quiet and with any luck you'll be sent to be a slave in the palace."

"Luck is my middle name," said Rincewind, indistinctly. "Mind you, my first name is Bad."

"Remember to gibber and grovel."

"I'll do my very best."

The white hand emerged bearing a scrap of paper. The guard took it, turned towards Rincewind, and cleared his throat.

"Harken to the wisdom and justice of District Commissioner Kee, ball of swamp emanations! Not him, I mean you!"

He cleared his throat again and peered closer at the paper in the manner of one who learned to read by saying the name of each letter very carefully to himself.

"'The white pony runs through the . . . the . . .'"

The guard turned and held a whispered conversation with the curtains, and turned back again.

> "'. . . chrysanthemum . . . mumum blossoms,
> The cold wind stirs the
> Apricot trees. Send him to
> The palace to slave
> Until all appendages drop
> Off.'"

Several of the other guards applauded.

"Look up and clap," said the Voice.

"I'm afraid my appendages will drop off."

"It's a *big* cheesegrater."

"Encore! Wow! Superb! That bit about the chrysanthemu-mums? Wonderful!"

"Good. Listen. You're from Bes Pelargic. You've got the right accent, damned if I know why. It's a seaport and people there are a little strange. You were robbed by bandits and escaped on one of their horses. That's why you haven't got your papers. You need pieces of paper for everything here, including being anybody. And pretend you don't know me."

"I *don't* know you."

"Good. Long Live The Changing Things To A More Equitable State While Retaining Due Respect For The Traditions Of Our Forebears And Of Course Not Harming The August Personage Of The Emperor Endeavor!"

"Good. Yes. What?"

A guard kicked Rincewind in the region of the kidneys. This suggested, in the universal language of the boot, that he should get up.

He managed to get up on one knee, and saw the Luggage.
It wasn't his, and there were three of them.

The Luggage trotted to the crest of a low hill and stopped so fast
that it left a lot of little grooves in the dirt.

In addition to not having any equipment with which to think
or feel, the Luggage also had no means of seeing. The manner in
which it perceived events was a complete mystery.

It perceived the other Luggages.

The three of them stood patiently in a line behind the palanquin. They were big. They were black.

The Luggage's legs disappeared inside its body.

After a while it very cautiously opened its lid, just a fraction.

Of the three things that most people know about the horse, the third
is that, over a short distance, it can't run as fast as a man. As
Rincewind had learned to his advantage, it has more legs to sort out.

There are additional advantages if a) the people on horseback
aren't expecting you to run and b) you happen to be, very conveniently, in an athletic starting position.

Rincewind rose like a boomerang curry from a sensitive
stomach.

There was a lot of shouting but the comforting thing, the
important thing, was that it was all behind him. It would soon try
to catch him up but that was a problem for the future. He could
also consider where he was running to as well, but an experienced coward never bothered with the *to* when the *from* held
such fascination.

A less practiced runner would have risked a glance behind, but
Rincewind instinctively knew all about wind drag and the tendency
of inconvenient rocks to position themselves under the unwary
foot. Besides, why look behind? He was already running as fast as
he could. Nothing he could see would make him run any faster.

There was a large shapeless village ahead, a construction
apparently of mud and dung. In the fields in front of it a dozen
peasants looked up from their toil at the accelerating wizard.

Perhaps it was Rincewind's imagination, but as he passed them he could have sworn that he heard the cry:

"Necessarily Extended Duration To The Red Army! Regrettable Decease Without Undue Suffering To The Forces Of Oppression!"

Rincewind dived through the huts as the soldiers charged at the peasants.

Cohen had been right. There seemed to be a revolution. But the Empire had been in unchanged existence for thousands of years, courtesy and a respect for protocol were part of its very fabric, and by the sound of it the revolutionaries had yet to master the art of impolite slogans.

Rincewind preferred running to hiding. Hiding was all very well, but if you were found then you were stuck. But the village was the only cover for miles around, and some of the soldiers had horses. A man might be faster than a horse over a short distance, but over this panorama of flat, open fields a horse had a running man done up like a clam.

So he ducked into a building at random and pushed aside the first door he came to.

It had, pasted on it, the words: Examination. Silence!

Forty expectant and slightly worried faces looked up at him from their writing stools. They weren't children, but full-grown adults.

There was a lectern at the end of the room and, on it, a pile of papers sealed with string and wax.

Rincewind felt the atmosphere was familiar. He'd breathed it before, even if it had been a world away. It was full of those cold sweaty odours created by the sudden realization that it was probably too late to do that revision you'd kept on putting off. Rincewind had faced many horrors in his time, but none held quite the same place in the lexicon of dread as those few seconds after someone said, "Turn over your papers *now.*"

The candidates were watching him.

There was shouting somewhere outside.

He hurried up to the lectern, tore at the string and distributed the papers as fast as he could. Then he dived back to the safety of the lectern, removed his hat, and was bent low when the door opened slowly.

"Go away!" he screamed. "Examination in progress!"

The unseen figure behind the door murmured something to someone else. The door was closed again.

The candidates were still staring at him.

"Er. Very well. Turn over your papers."

There was a rustle, a few moments of that dreadful silence, and then much activity with brushes.

Competitive examinations. Oh, yes. That was another thing people knew about the Empire. They were the only way to get any kind of public post and the security that brought. People had said that this must be a very good system, because it opened up opportunities for people of merit.

Rincewind picked up a spare paper and read it.

It was headed: Examination for the post of Assistant Night-Soil Operative for the District of W'ung.

He read question one. It required candidates to write a sixteen-line poem on evening mist over the reed beds.

Question two seemed to be about the use of metaphor in some book Rincewind had never heard of.

Then there was a question about music . . .

Rincewind turned the paper over a couple of times. There didn't seem to be any mention, anywhere, of words like "compost" or "bucket" or "wheelbarrow." But presumably all this produced a better class of person than the Ankh-Morpork system, which asked just one question: "Got your own shovel, have you?"

The shouting outside seemed to have died away; Rincewind risked poking his head out of the door. There was a commotion near the road but it no longer seemed Rincewind-orientated.

He ran for it.

The students got on with their examination. One of the more enterprising, however, rolled up his trouser leg and copied down a poem about mist he'd composed, at great effort, some time previously. After a while you got to know what kind of questions the examiners asked.

Rincewind trotted onwards, trying to keep to ditches wherever these weren't knee deep in sucking mud. It wasn't a landscape built for concealment. The Agateans grew crops on any piece of ground the seeds wouldn't roll off. Apart from the occasional rocky outcrop there was a distinct lack of places in which to lurk.

No one paid him much attention once he'd left the village far behind. The occasional water buffalo operative would turn to watch him until he was out of sight, but displayed no special curiosity; it was merely that Rincewind was marginally more interesting than watching a water buffalo defecate.

He kept the road just in sight and, by evening, reached a crossroads.

There was an inn.

Rincewind hadn't eaten since the leopard. The inn meant food, but food meant money. He was hungry, and he had no money.

He chided himself for this kind of negative thinking. That was not the right approach. What he should do was go in and order a large, nourishing meal. Then instead of being hungry with no money he'd be well fed with no money, a net gain on his current position. Of course, the world was likely to raise some objections, but in Rincewind's experience there were few problems that couldn't be solved with a scream and a good ten yards' start. And, of course, he would just have had a strengthening meal.

Besides, he liked Hunghungese food. A few refugees had opened restaurants in Ankh-Morpork and Rincewind considered himself something of an expert on the dishes.*

The one huge room was thick with smoke and, insofar as this could be determined through the swirls and coils, quite busy. A couple of old men were sitting in front of a complicated pile of ivory tiles, playing *Shibo Yangcong-san.* He wasn't sure what they were smoking but, by the looks on their faces, they were happy they'd chosen it.

Rincewind made his way to the fireplace, where a skinny man was tending a cauldron.

He gave him a cheery smile. "Good morning! Can I partake of your famous delicacy 'Meal A for two People with extra Prawn Cracker'?"

"Never heard of it."

*Such as Dish of Glistening Brown Stuff, Dish of Glistening Crunchy Orange Stuff, and Dish of Soft White Lumps.

"Um. Then . . . could I see a painful ear . . . a croak of a frog . . . a menu?"

"What's a menu, friend?"

Rincewind nodded. He knew what it meant when a stranger called you "friend" like that. No one who called someone else "friend" was feeling very kindly disposed.

"What is there to eat, I meant."

"Noodles, boiled cabbage, and pork whiskers."

"Is that *all?*"

"Pork whiskers don't grow on trees, san."

"I've been seeing water buffalo all day," Rincewind said. "Don't you people ever eat beef?"

The ladle splashed into the cauldron. Somewhere behind him a *shibo* tile dropped on to the floor. The back of Rincewind's head prickled under the stares.

"We don't serve rebels in this place," said the landlord loudly.

Probably too meaty, Rincewind thought. But it seemed to him that the words had been addressed to the world in general rather than to him.

"Glad to hear it," he said, "because—"

"Yes indeed," said the landlord, a little louder. "No rebels welcome here."

"That's fine by me, because—"

"If I knew of any rebels I would be certain to alert the authorities," the landlord bellowed.

"I'm not a rebel, I'm just hungry," said Rincewind. "I'd, er, like a bowlful, please."

A bowl was filled. Rainbow patterns shimmered on its oily surface.

"That'll be half a *rhinu*," said the landlord.

"You mean you want me to pay before I eat it?" said Rincewind.

"You might not want to afterwards, friend."

A *rhinu* was more gold than Rincewind had ever owned. He patted his pockets theatrically.

"In fact, it seems that—" he began. There was a small thump beside him. *What I Did On My Holidays* had fallen on to the floor.

"Yes, thank you, that will do nicely," said the landlord to the room at large. He pushed the bowl into Rincewind's hand and, in one movement, scooped up the booklet and crammed it back into the wizard's pocket.

"Go and sit down in the corner!" he hissed. "And you'll be told what to do!"

"But I'm sure I *know* what to do. Dip spoon in bowl, raise spoon to mouth—"

"Sit down!"

Rincewind found the darkest corner and sat down. People were still watching him.

To avoid the group gaze he pulled out *What I Did* and opened it at random, in an effort to find out why it had a magical effect on the landlord.

"... sold me a bun containing what was called a [complicated pictogram] made *entirely of the inside of pigs* [urinating dog]" he read. "And such as these could be bought for small coin at any time, and so replete were the citizens that hardly any bought these [complicated pictogram] from the stall of [complicated pictogram, but it seemed to involve a razor]-san."

Sausages filled with pig parts, thought Rincewind. Well, perhaps they *might* be amazing if, up until then, a bowl of dishwater with something congealing on the top of it had been your idea of a hearty meal.

Hah! Mister What-I-Did-On-My-Holidays should try coming to Ankh-Morpork next time, and see how much he liked one of old ... Dibbler's sausages ... full of genuine ... pig product ...

The spoon splashed into the bowl.

Rincewind turned the pages hurriedly.

"... peaceful streets, along which I walked, were quite free of crime and brigandage ..."

"Of course they were, you four-eyed little git!" shouted Rincewind. "That was because it was all happening to me!"

"... a city where all men are free ..."

"Free? *Free?* Well, yes, free to starve, get robbed by the Thieves' Guild ..." said Rincewind to the book.

He fumbled through to another page.

"... my companion was the Great Wizard [complicated

pictogram, but now that Rincewind studied it he realized with a plummeting heart it had a few lines that looked like the Agatean for "wind"], the most prominent and powerful wizard in the entire country . . ."

"I never said that! I—" Rincewind stopped. Memory treacherously dredged up a few phrases, such as *Oh, the Archchancellor listens to everything I say* and *That place would just fall down without me around.* But that was just the sort of thing you said after a few beers, surely no one would be so gullible as to write . . .

A picture focused itself in Rincewind's memory. It was of a happy, smiling little man with huge spectacles and a trusting, innocent approach to life which brought terror and destruction everywhere he wandered. Twoflower had been quite unable to believe that the world was a bad place and that was largely because, to him, it wasn't. It saved it all up for Rincewind.

Rincewind's life had been quite uneventful before he'd met Twoflower. Since then, as far as he could remember, it had contained events in huge amounts.

And the little man had gone back home, hadn't he? To Bes Pelargic—the Empire's only proper seaport.

Surely no one would be so gullible as to write this sort of thing?

Surely no one apart from one person would be so gullible.

Rincewind was not politically minded but there were some things he could work out not because they were to do with politics but because they had a lot to do with human nature. Nasty images moved into place like bad scenery.

The Empire had a wall around it. If you lived in the Empire then you learned how to make soup out of pig squeals and swallow spit because that's how it was done, and you were bullied by soldiers all the time because that was how the world worked.

But if someone wrote a cheerful little book about . . .

. . . what I did on my holidays . . .

. . . in a place where the world worked quite differently . . .

. . . then however fossilized the society there would always be *some* people who asked themselves dangerous questions like "Where's the pork?"

Rincewind stared glumly at the wall. Peasants of the Empire, Rebel! You have nothing to lose but your heads and hands and feet and there's this thing they do with a wire waistcoat and a cheesegrater . . .

He turned the book over. There was no author's name. There was simply a little message: Increased Luck! Make Copies! Extended Duration And Happiness To The Endeavor!

Ankh-Morpork had had the occasional rebellion, too, over the years. But no one went around *organizing* things. They just grabbed themselves a weapon and took to the streets. No one bothered with a formal battlecry, relying instead on the well-tried "There 'e goes! Get 'im! Got 'im? Now *kick* 'im inna fork!"

The point was . . . whatever *caused* that sort of thing wasn't usually the *reason* for it. When Mad Lord Snapcase had been hung up by his figgin* it hadn't *really* been because he'd made poor old Spooner Boggis eat his own nose, it had been because years of inventive nastiness had piled on one another until the grievances reached—

There was a terrible scream from the far side of the room. Rincewind was half out of his seat before he noticed the little stage, and the actors.

A trio of musicians had squatted down on the floor. The inn's customers turned to watch.

It was, in a way, quite enjoyable. Rincewind didn't quite follow the plot, but it went something like: man gets girl, man loses girl to other man, man cuts couple in half, man falls on own sword, all come up front for a bow to what might be the Agatean equivalent of "Happy Days Are Here Again." It was a little hard to make out the fine detail because the actors shouted "Hoorrrrrraa!" a lot and spent much of their time talking to the audience and their masks all looked the same to Rincewind. The musicians were in a world of their own or, by the sound of it, three different worlds.

---

*According to the history books. However, in common with every other young student, Rincewind had hopefully looked up "figgin" in the dictionary and found it was "a small bun with currants in it." This meant that either the language had changed a little over the years, or that there really was some horrifying aspect to suspending a man alongside a teacake.

"Fortune cookie?"

"Huh?"

Rincewind re-emerged from the thickets of thespianism to see the landlord beside him.

A dish of vaguely bivalvular biscuits was thrust under his nose.

"Fortune cookie?"

Rincewind reached out. Just as his fingers were about to close on one, the plate was jerked sideways an inch or two, bringing another under his hand.

Oh, well. He took it.

The thing was—his thoughts resumed, as the play screamed on—at least in Ankh-Morpork you *could* lay your hands on real weapons.

Poor devils. It took more than well-turned slogans and a lot of enthusiasm to run a good rebellion. You needed well-trained fighters and, above all, a good leader. He hoped they found one when he was well away.

He unrolled the fortune and read it idly, oblivious to the landlord walking around behind him.

Instead of the usual "You have just enjoyed an inferior meal" it was quite a complicated pictogram.

Rincewind's fingers traced the brush strokes.

"'Many . . . many . . . apologies . . .' What kind—"

The musician with the cymbals clashed them together sharply.

The wooden cosh bounced off Rincewind's head.

The old men playing *shibo* nodded happily to themselves and turned back to their game.

It was a fine morning. The hideout echoed to the sounds of the Silver Horde getting up, groaning, adjusting various homemade surgical supports, complaining that they couldn't find their spectacles, and mistakenly gumming one another's dentures.

Cohen sat with his feet in a bath of warm water, enjoying the sunshine.

"Teach?"

The former geography teacher concentrated on a map he was making.

"Yes, Ghenghiz?"

"What's Mad Hamish going on about?"

"He says the bread's stale and he can't find his teeth."

"Tell him if things go right for us he can have a dozen young women just to chew his bread for him," said Cohen.

"That is not very hygienic, Ghenghiz," said Mr. Saveloy, without bothering to look up. "Remember, I explained about hygiene."

Cohen didn't bother to answer. He was thinking: six old men. And you can't really count Teach, he's a thinker, not a fighter . . .

Self-doubt was not something regularly entertained within the Cohen cranium. When you're trying to carry a struggling temple maiden and a sack of looted temple goods in one hand and fight off half a dozen angry priests with the other there is little time for reflection. Natural selection saw to it that professional heroes who at a crucial moment tended to ask themselves questions like "What is my purpose in life?" very quickly lacked both.

But: six old men . . . and the Empire had almost a million men under arms.

When you looked at the odds in the cold light of dawn, or even this rather pleasant warm light of dawn, they made you stop and do the arithmetic of death. If the Plan went wrong . . .

Cohen bit his lip thoughtfully. If the Plan went wrong, it'd take *weeks* to kill all of them. Maybe he should have let old Thog the Butcher come along, too, even though he had to stop fighting every ten minutes to go to the lavatory.

Oh, well. He was committed now, so he might as well make the best of it.

Cohen's father had taken him to a mountain top, when he was no more than a lad, and explained to him the hero's creed and told him that there was no greater joy than to die in battle.

Cohen had seen the flaw in this straight away, and a lifetime's experience had reinforced his belief that in fact a greater joy was to kill the *other* bugger in battle and end up sitting on a heap of gold higher than your horse. It was an observation that had served him well.

He stood up and stretched in the sunshine.

"It's a lovely morning, lads," he said. "I feel like a million dollars. Don't you?"

There was a murmur of reluctant agreement.

"Good," said Cohen. "Let's go and get some."

The Great Wall completely surrounds the Agatean Empire. The word is *completely.*

It is usually about twenty-feet high and sheer on its inner side. It is built along beaches and across howling deserts and even on the lip of sheer cliffs where the possibility of attack from outside is remote. On subject islands like Bhangbhangduc and Tingling there are similar walls, all metaphorically the same wall, and that seems strange to those of an unthinking military disposition who do not realize what its function really is.

It is more than just a wall, it is a marker. On one side is the Empire, which in the Agatean language is a word identical with "universe." On the other side is—nothing. After all, the universe is everything there is.

Oh, there may *appear* to be things, like sea, islands, other continents and so on. They may even appear solid, it may be possible to conquer them, walk on them . . . but they are not *ultimately* real. The Agatean word for foreigner is the same as the word for ghost, and only one brush stroke away from the word for victim.

The walls are sheer in order to discourage those boring people who persist in believing that there might be anything interesting on the other side. Amazingly enough there are people who simply won't take the hint, even after thousands of years. The ones near the coast build rafts and head out across lonely seas to lands that are a fable. The ones inland resort to man-carrying kites and chairs propelled by fireworks. Many of them die in the attempt, of course. Most of the others are soon caught, and made to live in interesting times.

But some did make it to the great melting pot called Ankh-Morpork. They arrived with no money—sailors charged what the market would bear, which was everything—but they had a mad gleam in their eye and they opened shops and restaurants and worked twenty-four hours a day. People called this the Ankh-Morpork Dream (of making piles of cash in a place where your death was unlikely to be a matter of public policy). And it was dreamed all the stronger by people who didn't sleep.

Rincewind sometimes thought that his life was punctuated by awakenings. They were not always rude ones. Sometimes they were merely impolite. A very few—one or two, perhaps—had been quite nice, especially on the island. The sun had come up in its humdrum fashion, the waves had washed the beach in quite a boring way, and on several occasions he'd managed to erupt from unconsciousness without his habitual small scream.

This one wasn't just rude. It was downright insolent. He was being bumped about and someone had tied his hands together. It was dark, a fact occasioned by the sack over his head.

Rincewind did some calculation, and reached a conclusion.

"This is the seventeenth worst day of my life so far," he thought.

Being knocked unconscious in pubs was quite common-place. If it happened in Ankh-Morpork then you'd likely as not wake up lying on the Ankh with all your money gone or, if a ship was due out on a long and unpopular voyage, chained up in some scupper somewhere with no option for the next two years but to plough the ocean wave.* But generally the knocker wanted to keep you alive. The Thieves' Guild were punctilious about that. As they said: "Hit a man too hard and you can only rob him once; hit him just hard enough and you can rob him every week."

If he was in what felt like a cart then someone had some purpose in keeping him alive.

He wished he hadn't thought of that.

Someone pulled the sack off. A terrifying visage stared down at him.

"'I would like to eat your foot!'" said Rincewind.

---

*A dismal prospect, especially when the horses keep sinking.

"Don't worry. I am a friend."

The mask was lifted away. There was a young woman behind it—round-faced, snub-nosed, and quite different from any other citizen Rincewind had met hitherto. That was, he realized, because she was looking straight at him. Her clothes, if not her face, had last been seen on the stage.

"Don't cry out," she said.

"Why? What are you going to do?"

"We would have welcomed you properly but there was no time." She sat down among the bundles in the back of the swaying cart and regarded him critically.

"Four Big Sandal said you arrived on a dragon and slaughtered a regiment of soldiers," she said.

"I did?"

"And then you worked magic on a venerable old man and he became a great fighter."

"He did?"

"And you gave him whole meat, even though Four Big Sandal is only of the *pung* class."

"I did?"

"And you have your hat."

"Yes, yes, got my hat."

"And yet," said the girl, "you don't *look* like a Great Wizard."

"Ah. Well, the fact is—"

The girl looked as fragile as a flower. But she had just pulled out, from somewhere in the folds of her costume, a small but perfectly serviceable knife.

Rincewind had picked up an instinct for this sort of thing. This was probably not the time to deny Great Wizardry.

"The fact is . . ." he repeated, "that . . . how do I know I can trust you?"

The girl looked indignant. "Do you not have amazing wizardly powers?"

"Oh, yes. Yes! Certainly! But—"

"Say something in wizard language!"

"Er. *Stercus, stercus, stercus, moriturus sum,*" said Rincewind, his eye on the knife.

"'O excrement, I am about to die?'"

"It's ... er ... a special mantra I say to raise the magical fluxes."

The girl subsided a little.

"But it takes it out of you, wizarding," said Rincewind. "Flying on dragons, magically turning old men into warriors ... I can only do so much of that sort of thing before it's time for a rest. Right now I'm very weak on account of the *tremendous* amounts of magic I've just used, you see."

She looked at him with doubt still in her eyes.

"All the peasants believe in the imminent arrival of the Great Wizard," she said. "But, in the words of the great philosopher Ly Tin Wheedle, 'When many expect a mighty stallion they will find hooves on an ant.'"

She gave him another calculating look.

"When you were on the road," she said, "you grovelled in front of District Commissioner Kee. You could have blasted him with terrible fire."

"Biding my time, spying out the land, not wanting to break my cover," Rincewind gabbled. "Er. No good revealing myself straight away, is there?"

"You are maintaining a disguise?"

"Yes."

"It is a very good one."

"Thank you, because—"

"Only a great wizard would dare to look like such a pathetic piece of humanity."

"Thank you. Er ... how *did* you know I was on the road?"

"They would have killed you there and then if I had not told you what to do."

"You were the *guard?*"

"We had to catch up with you quickly. It was sheer luck you were seen by Four Big Sandal."

"We?"

She ignored the question. "They are only provincial soldiers. I would not have got away with it in Hunghung. But I can play many roles." She put away the knife, but Rincewind had a feeling that he hadn't talked her into believing him, only into not killing him.

94

He groped for a straw.

"I've got a magic box on legs," he said, with a touch of pride. "It follows me around. It seems to have got itself mislaid right now, but it's quite an amazing thing."

The girl gave him a wooden look. Then she reached down with a delicate hand and hauled him upright.

"Is it," she said, "something like this?"

She twitched aside the curtains at the rear of the cart.

Two boxes were trundling along in the dust. They were more battered and cheaper looking than the Luggage, but recognizably the same general species, if you could apply the word to travel accessories.

"Er. Yes."

She let go. Rincewind's head hit the floor.

"Listen to me," she said. "A lot of bad things are happening. I don't believe in great wizards, but other people do, and sometimes people need something to believe in. And if these other people die because we've got a wizard who is not so very great, then he will be a very unlucky wizard indeed. You may be the Great Wizard. If you are not, then I suggest you study very hard to be great. Do I make myself clear?"

"Er. Yes."

Rincewind had been faced with death on numerous occasions. Often there was armour and swords involved. This occasion just involved a pretty girl and a knife, but somehow managed to be among the worst. She sat back.

"We are a traveling theater," she said. "It is convenient. Noh actors are allowed to move around."

"Aren't they?" said Rincewind.

"You do not understand. We *are* Noh actors."

"Oh, you weren't too bad."

"Great Wizard, 'Noh' is a non-realist symbolic form of theater employing archaic language, stylized gestures and an accompaniment of flutes and drums. Your pretence of stupidity is masterly. So much so that I could even believe that you are no actor."

"Excuse me, what is your name?" Rincewind said.

"Pretty Butterfly."

"Er. Yes?"

95

She glared at him and slipped away towards the front of the cart.

It rumbled on. Rincewind lay with his head in a sack smelling of onions and methodically cursed things. He cursed women with knives, and history generally, and the entire faculty of Unseen University, and his absent Luggage, and the population of the Agatean Empire. But right now, at the top of the list, was whoever had designed this cart. By the feel of it, whoever had thought that rough, splintery wood was the right surface for a floor was also the person who thought "triangular" was a nice shape for a wheel.

The Luggage lurked in a ditch, watched without much interest by a man holding a water buffalo on the end of a piece of string.

It was feeling ashamed, and baffled, and lost. It was lost because everywhere around it was . . . familiar. The light, the smells, the feel of the soil . . . But it didn't feel *owned*.

It was made of wood. Wood is sensitive to these things.

One of its many feet idly traced an outline in the mud. It was a random, wretched pattern familiar to anyone who's had to stand in front of the class and be scolded.

Finally, it reached something that was probably as close as timber can get to a decision.

It had been given away. It had spent many years trailing through strange lands, meeting exotic creatures and jumping up and down on them. Now it was back in the country where it had once been a tree. Therefore, it was free.

It was not the most logical chain of thought, but pretty good when all you've got to think with are knotholes.

And there was something it very much wanted to do.

"*When* you're ready, Teach?"

"Sorry, Ghenghiz. I'm just finishing . . ."

Cohen sighed. The Horde were taking advantage of the rest to sit in the shade of a tree and tell one another lies about their exploits, while Mr. Saveloy stood on top of a boulder squinting through some kind of homemade device and doodling on his maps.

Bits of paper ruled the world now, Cohen told himself. It certainly ruled this part of it. And Teach . . . well, Teach ruled bits of paper. He might not be traditional barbarian hero material, despite his deeply held belief that all headmasters should be riveted to a cowshed door, but the man was *amazing* with bits of paper.

And he could speak Agatean. Well, speak it better than Cohen, who'd picked it up in a rough and ready way. He said he'd learned it out of some old book. He said it was amazing how much interesting stuff was in old books.

Cohen struggled up alongside him.

"What exactly you plannin', Teach?" he said.

Mr. Saveloy squinted at Hunghung, just visible on the dusty horizon.

"Do you see that hill behind the city?" he said. "The huge round mound?"

"Looks like my dad's burial mound to me," said Cohen.

"No, it must be a natural formation. It's far too big. There's some kind of pagoda on top, I see. Interesting. Perhaps, later, I shall take a closer look."

Cohen peered at the big round hill. It was a big round hill. It wasn't threatening him and it didn't look valuable. End of saga as far as he was concerned. There were more pressing matters.

"People appear to be entering and leaving the outer city," Mr. Saveloy continued. "The siege is more a threat than a reality. So getting inside should not be a problem. Of course, getting into the Forbidden City itself will be a lot more difficult."

"How about if we kill everyone?" said Cohen.

"A good idea, but impractical," said Mr. Saveloy. "And liable to cause comment. No, my current methodology is predicated on the fact that Hunghung is some considerable way from the river yet has almost a million inhabitants."

"Predicated, yeah," said Cohen.

"And the local geography is quite wrong for artesian wells."

"Yeah, 's what I thought . . ."

"And yet there is no visible aqueduct, you notice."

97

"No aqueduct, right," said Cohen. "Prob'ly flown to the Rim for the summer. Some birds do that."

"Which rather leads me to doubt the saying that not even a mouse can get into the Forbidden City," said Mr. Saveloy, with just a trace of smugness. "I suspect a mouse could get into the Forbidden City *if it could hold its breath.*"

"Or ride on one of them invisible ducks," said Cohen.

"Indeed."

The cart stopped. The sack came off. Instead of the cheesegrater Rincewind was secretly expecting, the view consisted of a couple of young, concerned faces. One of them was female, but Rincewind was relieved to see that she wasn't Pretty Butterfly. This one looked younger, and made Rincewind think a little of potatoes.*

"How you are?" she said, in fractured but recognizable Morporkian. "We are very sorry. All better now? We speak you in language of celestial city of Ankh-More-Pork. Language of freedom and progress. Language of One Man, One Vote!"

"Yes," said Rincewind. A vision of Ankh-Morpork's Patrician floated across his memory. One man, one vote. Yes. "I've met him. He's definitely got the vote. But—"

"Extra Luck To The People's Endeavor!" said the boy. "Advance Judiciously!" He looked as though he'd been built with bricks.

"Excuse me," said Rincewind, "but why did you . . . a paper lantern for ceremonial purposes . . . bale of cotton . . . *rescue* me? Uh, that is, when I say rescue, I suppose I mean: why did you hit me on the head, tie me up, and bring me to wherever this is? Because the worst that could have happened to me in the inn was a ding around the ear for not paying for lunch—"

"The worst that *would* have happened was an agonizing death over several years," said the voice of Butterfly. She appeared around the cart and smiled grimly at Rincewind. Her

---

*When you're on a desert island, your appetites can become a bit confused.

hands were tucked demurely in her kimono, presumably to hide the knives.

"Oh. Hello," he said.

"Great Wizard," said Butterfly, bowing. "I you already know, but these two are Lotus Blossom and Three Yoked Oxen, other members of our cadre. We had to bring you here like this. There are spies everywhere."

"Timely Demise To All Enemies!" said the boy, beaming.

"Good, yes, right," said Rincewind. "All enemies, yes."

The cart was in a courtyard. The general noise level on the other side of the very high walls suggested a large city. Nasty certainty crystallized.

"And you've brought me to Hunghung, haven't you?" he said.

Lotus Blossom's eyes widened.

"Then it are *true*," she said, in Rincewind's own language. "You *are* the Great Wizard!"

"Oh, you'd be amazed at the things I can foresee," said Rincewind despondently.

"You two, go and stable the horses," said Butterfly, not taking her eyes off Rincewind. When they'd hurried away, with several backward glances, she walked up to him.

"They believe," she said. "Personally, I have my doubts. But Ly Tin Wheedle says an ass may do the work of an ox in a time of no horses. One of his less convincing aphorisms, I've always thought."

"Thank you. What is a cadre?"

"Have you heard of the Red Army?"

"No. Well . . . I heard someone shout something . . ."

"According to legend, an unknown person known only as the Great Wizard led the first Red Army to an impossible victory. Of course, that was thousands of years ago. But the people believe that he—that is, *you*—will return to do it again. So . . . there should be a Red Army ready and waiting."

"Well, of course, a man can get a little stiff after several thousand years—"

Her face was suddenly level with his own.

"*Personally* I suspect there has been a misunderstanding," she hissed. "But now you're here you'll be a Great Wizard. If I have to prod you every step of the way!"

The other two returned. Butterfly went from snarling tiger to demure doe in an instant.

"And now you must come and *meet* the Red Army," she said.

"Won't they be a little smelly—" Rincewind began, and stopped when he saw her expression.

"The original Red Army was clearly only a legend," she said, in fast and faultless Ankh-Morporkian. "But legends have their uses. You'd better know the legend . . . Great Wizard. When One Sun Mirror was fighting all the armies of the world the Great Wizard came to his aid and the earth itself rose up and fought for the new Empire. And lightning was involved. The army was made from the earth but in some way driven by the lightning. Now, lightning may kill but I suspect it lacks discipline. And earth cannot fight. But no doubt our army of the earth and sky was nothing more nor less than an uprising of the peasants themselves. Well, now we have a new army, and a name that fires the imagination. And a Great Wizard. I don't believe in legends. But I believe that other people believe."

The younger girl, who had been trying to follow this, stepped forward and gripped his arm.

"You come seeing Red Army *now*," she said.

"Forward Motion With Masses!" said the boy, taking Rincewind's other arm.

"Does he always talk like that?" said Rincewind, as he was propelled gently towards a door.

"Three Yoked Oxen does not study," said the girl.

"Extra Success Attend Our Leaders!"

"'Tuppence A Bucket, Well Stamped Down!'" said Rincewind encouragingly.

"Much Ownership of Means of Production!"

"'How's Your Granny Off For Soap?'"

Three Yoked Oxen beamed.

Butterfly opened the door. That left Rincewind outside with the other two.

"Very useful slogans," he said, moving sideways just a little. "But I would draw your attention to the famous saying of the Great Wizard Rincewind."

"Indeed, I am all ear," said Lotus Blossom politely.

"Rincewind, he say . . . Goodbyeeeeeeeee—"

His sandals skidded on the cobbles but he was already traveling fast when he hit the doors, which turned out to be made of bamboo and smashed apart easily.

There was a street market on the other side. That was something Rincewind remembered later about Hunghung; as soon as there was a space, any kind of space, even the space created by the passage of a cart or a mule, people flowed into it, usually arguing with one another at the tops of their voices over the price of a duck which was being held upside down and quacking.

His foot went through a wicker cage containing several chickens, but he pressed on, scattering people and produce. In an Ankh-Morpork street market something like this would have caused some comment, but since everyone around him already seemed to be screaming into other people's faces Rincewind was merely a momentary and unremarked nuisance as he half ran, half limped with one squawking foot past the stalls.

Behind him, the people flowed back. There may have been some cries of pursuit, but they were lost in the hubbub.

He didn't stop until he found an overlooked alcove between a stall selling songbirds and another purveying something that bubbled in bowls. His foot crowed.

He smashed it against cobbles until the cage broke; the cockerel, maddened by the heady air of freedom, pecked him on the knee and fluttered away.

There were no sounds of pursuit. However, a battalion of trolls in tin boots would have had trouble making themselves heard above a normal Hunghung street market.

He let himself get his breath back.

Well, he was his own man again. So much for the Red Army. Admittedly he was in the capital city, where he didn't want to be, and it was only a matter of time before something else unpleasant happened to him, but it wasn't actually happening at the moment. Let him find his bearings and five minutes' start and they could watch his dust. Or mud. There was a lot of both, here.

So . . . this was Hunghung . . .

There didn't seem to be streets in the sense Rincewind understood the term. Alleys opened on to alleys, all of them narrow and made narrower by the stalls that lined them. There was a large animal population in the marketplace. Most of the stalls had their share of caged chickens, ducks in sacks, and strange wriggling things in bowls. From one stall a tortoise on top of a struggling heap of other tortoises under a sign saying: *3r. each, good for Ying* gave Rincewind a slow, "You think you've got troubles?" look.

But it was hard to tell where the stalls ended and the buildings began in any case. Dried-up things hanging on a string might be merchandise or someone's washing or quite possibly next week's dinner.

The Hunghungese were an outdoor kind of people; from the look of it, they conducted most of their lives on the street and at the top of their voice.

Progress was made by viciously elbowing and shoving people until they got out of the way. Standing still and saying, "Er, excuse me" was a recipe for immobility.

The crowds did part, though, at the banging of a gong and a succession of loud "pops." A group of people in white robes danced past, throwing fireworks around and banging on gongs, saucepans and odd bits of metal. The din contrived to be louder than the street noise, but only by very great effort.

Rincewind had been getting the occasional puzzled glance from people who stopped screaming long enough to notice him. Perhaps it was time to act like a native.

He turned to the nearest person and screamed, "Pretty good, eh?"

The person, a little old lady in a straw hat, stared at him in distaste.

"It's Mr. Whu's funeral," she snapped, and walked off.

There were a couple of soldiers nearby. If this had been Ankh-Morpork, then they'd have been sharing a cigarette and trying not to see anything that might upset them. But these had an alert look.

Rincewind backed into another alley. An untutored visitor could clearly find himself in big trouble here.

This alley was quieter and, at the far end, opened into something much wider and empty looking. On the basis that people also meant trouble, Rincewind headed in that direction.

Here, at last, was an open space. It was very open indeed. It was a paved square, big enough to hold a couple of armies. It had cherry trees growing along the verges. And, given the heaving mob everywhere else, a surprising absence of anyone . . .

"You!"

. . . apart from the soldiers.

They appeared abruptly from behind every tree and statue.

Rincewind tried to back away, but that proved unfortunate since there was a guard behind him.

A terrifying armored mask confronted him.

"Peasant! Do you not know this is the Imperial Square?"

"Was that a capital S on Square, please?" said Rincewind.

"You do not ask questions!"

"Ah. I'll take that as a "yes." So it's important, then. Sorry. I'll just sort of go away, then . . ."

"You stay!"

But what struck Rincewind as amazingly odd was that none of them actually took hold of him. And then he realized that this must be because they hardly ever needed to. People did what they were told.

There's something worse than whips in the Empire, Cohen had said.

At this point, he realized, he should be on his knees. He crouched down, hands placed lightly in front of him.

"I wonder," he said brightly, rising into the starting position, "if this is the time to draw your attention to a famous saying?"

Cohen was familiar with city gates. He'd broken down a number in his time, by battering ram, siege gun, and on one occasion with his head.

But the gates of Hunghung were pretty damn good gates. They weren't like the gates of Ankh-Morpork, which were usually wide open to attract the spending customer and whose concession to defense was the sign "Thank You For Not Attacking Our City. Bonum Diem." *These* things were big and made of metal and there was a guardhouse and a squad of unhelpful men in black armor.

"Teach?"

"Yes, Cohen?"

"Why're we doing this? I thought we were going to use the invisible duck the mice use."

Mr. Saveloy waggled a finger.

"That's for the Forbidden City itself. I hope we'll find that inside. Now, remember your lessons," he said. "It's important that you all learn how to behave in cities."

"I *know* how to bloody well behave in cities," said Truckle the Uncivil. "Pillage, ravish, loot, set fire to the damn place on your way out. Just like towns only it takes longer."

"That's all very well if you're just passing through," said Mr. Saveloy, "but what if you want to come back next day?"

"It ain't bloody well there next day, mister."

"Gentlemen! Bear with me. You will have to learn the ways of civilization!"

People couldn't just walk through. There was a line. And the guards gathered rather offensively around each cowering visitor to examine their papers.

And then it was Cohen's turn.

"Papers, old man?"

Cohen nodded happily, and handed the guard captain a piece of paper on which was written, in Mr. Saveloy's best handwriting:

WE ARE WANDERING MADMEN WHO HAVE NO PAPERS. SORRY.

The guard's gaze lifted from the paper and met Cohen's cheerful grin.

"Indeed," he said nastily. "Can't you speak, grandfather?"

Cohen, still grinning, looked questioningly at Mr. Saveloy. They hadn't rehearsed this part.

"Foolish dummy," said the guard.

Mr. Saveloy looked outraged.

"I thought you were supposed to show special consideration for the insane!" he said.

"You cannot be insane without papers to say you're insane," said the guard.

"Oh, I'm fed up with this," said Cohen. "I *said* it wouldn't work if we came across a thick guard."

"Insolent peasant!"

"I'm not as insolent as my friends here," said Cohen.

The Horde nodded.

"That's us, flatfoot."

"Bum to you."

"Whut?"

"Extremely foolish soldier."

"Whut?"

The captain was taken aback. Deeply ingrained in the Agatean psyche was the habit of obedience. But even stronger was a veneration of one's ancestors and a respect for the elderly, and the captain had never seen anyone so elderly while still vertical. They practically *were* ancestors. The one in the wheelchair certainly smelled like one.

"Take them to the guardhouse!" he shouted.

The Horde let themselves be manhandled, and did it quite well. Mr. Saveloy had spent hours training them in this, since he knew he was dealing with men whose response to a tap on the shoulder was to turn around and hack off someone's arm.

It was crowded in the guardhouse, with the Horde and the guards and with Mad Hamish's wheelchair. One of the guards looked down at Hamish, glowering under his blanket.

"What do you have there, grandfather?"

A sword came up through the cloth and stabbed the guard in the thigh.

"Whut? Whut? Whutzeesay?"

"He said, 'Aargh!,' Hamish," said Cohen, a knife appearing in his hand. With one movement his skinny arms had the captain in a lock, the knife at his throat.

"Whut?"

"He said, 'Aargh!'"

"Whut? I ain't even married!"

Cohen put a little more pressure on the captain's neck.

"Now then, friend," he said. "You can have it the easy way, see, or the hard way. It's up to you."

"Blood-sucking pig! You call this the easy way?"

"Well, *I* ain't sweatin'.".

"May you live in interesting times! I would rather die than betray my Emperor!"

"Fair enough."

It took the captain only a fraction of a second to realize that Cohen, being a man of his word, assumed that other people were too. He might, if he had time, have reflected that the purpose of civilization is to make violence the final resort, while to a barbarian it is the first, preferred, only and above all most enjoyable option. But by then it was too late. He slumped forward.

"I *always* lives in interestin' times," said Cohen, in the satisfied voice of someone who did a lot to keep them interesting.

He pointed his knife at the other guards. Mr. Saveloy's mouth was wide open in horror.

"By rights I should be cleanin' this," said Cohen. "But I ain't goin' to bother if it's only goin' to get dirty again. Now, *person'ly*, I'd as soon kill you as look at you but Teach here says I've got to stop doin' that and become respectable."

One of the guards looked sideways at his fellows and then fell on his knees.

"What is your wish, o master?" he said.

"Ah, officer material," said Cohen. "What's your name, lad?"

"Nine Orange Trees, master."

Cohen looked at Mr. Saveloy.

"What do I do now?"

"Take them prisoner, *please.*"

"How do I do that?"

"Well . . . I suppose you tie them up, that sort of thing."

"Ah. And then cut their throats?"

"No! No. You see, once you've got them at your mercy, you're not allowed to kill them."

The Silver Horde, to a man, stared at the ex-teacher.

"I'm afraid that's civilization for you," he added.

"But you said the sods haven't got any bloody weapons!" said Truckle.

"Yes," said Mr. Saveloy, shuddering a little. "That's why you're not allowed to kill them."

"Are you mad? Got mad papers, have you?"

Cohen scratched his stubbly chin. The remainder of the guard watched him in trepidation. They were used to cruel and unusual punishment, but they were unaccustomed to argument first.

"You haven't had a lot of military experience, have you, Teach?" he said.

"Apart from Form Four? Not a lot. But I'm afraid this is the way it has to be done. I'm sorry. You did say you wanted me—"

"Well, *I* vote we just cuts their throats right now," said Boy Willie. "I can't be having with this prisoner business either. I mean, who's gonna feed them?"

"I'm afraid you have to."

"Who, me? Not likely! I vote we make them eat their own eyeballs. Hands up all in favor."

There was a chorus of assent from the Horde and, among the raised hands, Cohen noticed one belonging to Nine Orange Trees.

"What you voting for, lad?" he said.

"Please, sir, I would like to go to the lavatory."

"You listen to me, you lot," said Cohen. "This slaughtering and butchering business isn't how you do it these days, right? That's what Mr. Saveloy says and he knows how to spell words like 'marmalade' which is more than you do. Now, we know why we're here, and we'd better start as we mean to go on."

"Yeah, but you just killed that guard," said Truckle.

"I'm breaking myself in," said Cohen. "You've got to creep up on civilization a bit at a time."

"I still say we should cut their heads off. That's what I did to the Mad Demon-Sucking Priests of Ee!"

The kneeling guard had cautiously raised his hand again.

"Please, master?"

"Yes, lad?"

"You could lock us up in that cell over there. Then we wouldn't be any trouble to anyone."

"Good thinking," said Cohen. "Good lad. The boy keeps his head in a crisis. Lock 'em up."

Thirty seconds later the Horde had limped off, into the city.

The guards sat in the cramped, hot cell.

Eventually one said, "What were they?"

107

"I think they might have been ancestors."

"I thought you had to be dead to be an ancestor."

"The one in the wheelchair *looked* dead. Right up to the point where he stabbed Four White Fox."

"Should we shout for help?"

"They might hear us."

"Yes, but if we don't get let out we'll be stuck in here. And the walls are very thick and the door is very strong."

"Good."

Rincewind stopped running in some alley somewhere. He hadn't bothered to see if they'd followed him. It was true—here, with one mighty bound, you *could* be free. Provided you realized it was one of your options.

Freedom did, of course, include man's age-old right to starve to death. It seemed a long time since his last proper meal.

The voice erupted further down the alley, as if on cue.

"Rice cakes! Rice cakes! Get chore nice rice cakes! Tea! Hundred-Year-Old Eggs! Eggs! Get them while they're nice and vintage! Get chore—Yeah, what is it?"

An elderly man had approached the salesman.

"Dibhala-san! This egg you sold me—"

"What about it, venerable squire?"

"Would you care to smell it?"

The street vendor took a sniff.

"Ah, yes, lovely," he said.

"Lovely? *Lovely?* This egg," said the customer, "this egg is practically fresh!"

"Hundred years old if it's a day, shogun," said the vendor happily. "Look at the color of that shell, nice and black—"

"It rubs off!"

Rincewind listened. There was, he thought, probably something in the idea that there were only a few people in the world. There were lots of *bodies*, but only a few people. That's why you kept running into the same ones. There was probably some mold somewhere.

"You saying my produce is fresh? May I disembowel myself honorably! Look, I'll tell you what I'll do—"

Yes, there seemed to be something familiar and magical about that trader. Someone had come to complain about a fresh egg, and yet within a couple of minutes he'd somehow been talked into forgetting this and purchasing two rice cakes and something strange wrapped in leaves.

The rice cakes looked nice. Well . . . nicer than the other things.

Rincewind sidled over. The trader was idly jigging from one foot to the other and whistling under his breath, but he stopped and gave Rincewind a big, honest, friendly grin.

"Nice ancient egg, shogun?"

The bowl in the middle of the tray was full of gold coins. Rincewind's heart sank. The price of one of Mr. Dibhala's foul eggs would have bought a street in Ankh-Morpork.

"I suppose you don't give . . . credit?" he suggested.

Dibhala gave him a Look.

"I'll pretend I never heard that, shogun," he said.

"Tell me," said Rincewind. "Do you know if you have any relatives overseas?"

This got him another look—a sideways one, full of sudden appraisal.

"What? There's nothing but evil blood-sucking ghosts beyond the seas. Everyone knows that, shogun. I'm surprised you don't."

"Ghosts?" said Rincewind.

"Trying to get here, do us harm," said Disembowel-Meself-Honorably. "Maybe even steal our merchandise. Give 'em a dose of the old firecracker, that's what *I* say. They don't like a good loud bang, ghosts."

He gave Rincewind another look, even longer and more calculating.

"Where you from, shogun?" he asked, and his voice suddenly had the little barbed edge of suspicion.

"Bes Pelargic," said Rincewind quickly. "That explains my strange accent and mannerisms that might otherwise lead people to think I was some sort of foreigner," he added.

"Oh, Bes Pelargic," said Disembowel-Meself-Honorably.

"Well, in that case, I expect you know my old friend Five Tongs who lives in the Street of Heavens, yes?"

Rincewind was ready for this old trick.

"No," he said. "Never heard of him, never heard of the street."

Disembowel-Meself-Honorably Dibhala grinned happily. "If I yell 'foreign devil' loud enough you won't get three steps," he said in conversational tones. "The guards will drag you off to the Forbidden City where there's this special thing they do with—"

"I've heard about it," said Rincewind.

"Five Tongs has been the district commissioner for three years and the Street of Heavens is the main street," said Disembowel-Meself-Honorably. "I've always wanted to meet a blood-sucking foreign ghost. Have a rice cake."

Rincewind's gaze darted this way and that. But strangely enough the situation didn't seem dangerous, or at least inevitably dangerous. It seemed that danger was negotiable.

"Supposing I was to admit I *was* from behind the Wall?" he said, keeping his voice as low as possible.

Dibhala nodded. One hand reached into his robe and, in a quick movement, revealed and then concealed the corner of something which Rincewind was not entirely surprised to see was entitled WHAT I DID . . .

"Some people say that beyond the Wall there's nothing but deserts and burning wastes and evil ghosts and terrible monsters," said Dibhala, "but *I* say, what about the merchandizing opportunities? A man with the right contacts . . . Know what I mean, shogun? He could go a *long* way in the land of blood-sucking ghosts."

Rincewind nodded. He didn't like to point out that if you turned up in Ankh-Morpork with a handful of gold then about three hundred people would turn up with a handful of steel.

"The way I see it, what with all this uncertainty about the Emperor and talk of rebels and that—Long Live His Excellency The Son Of Heaven, of course—there might just be a nitch for the open-minded trader, am I right?"

"Nitch?"

"Nitch. Like . . . we've got this stuff"—he leaned closer—

"comes out of a caterpillar's [unidentified pictogram]. 'S called . . . *silk*. It's—"

"Yes, I know. We get it from Klatch," said Rincewind.

"Or, well, there's this bush, see, you dry the leaves, but then you put it in hot water and you drin—"

"Tea, yes," said Rincewind. "That comes from Howondaland."

D. M. H. Dibhala looked taken aback.

"Well . . . we've got this powder, you put it in tubes—"

"Fireworks? Got fireworks."

"How about this really fine china, it's so—"

"In Ankh-Morpork we've got dwarfs that can make china you can read a book through," said Rincewind. "Even if it's got tiny footnotes in it."

Dibhala frowned.

"Sounds like you are very clever blood-sucking ghosts," he said, backing away. "Maybe it's true and you *are* dangerous."

"Us? Don't worry about us," said Rincewind. "We hardly ever kill foreigners in Ankh-Morpork. It makes it so hard to sell them things afterwards."

"What've we got that you want, though? Go on, have a rice cake. On the pagoda. Wanna try some pork balls? Onna chopstick?"

Rincewind selected a cake. He didn't like to ask about the other stuff.

"You've got gold," he said.

"Oh, *gold*. It's too soft to do much with," said Dibhala. "It's all right for pipes and putting on roofs, though."

"Oh . . . I daresay people in Ankh-Morpork could find a use for some," said Rincewind. His gaze returned to the coins in Dibhala's tray.

A land where gold was as cheap as lead . . .

"What's that?" he said, pointing to a crumpled rectangle half covered with coins.

D. M. H. Dibhala looked down. "It's this thing we have here," he said, speaking slowly. "Of course, it's probably all new to you. It's called mon-ey. It's a way of carrying around your—"

"I meant the bit of paper," said Rincewind.

111

"So did I," said Dibhala. "That's a ten-*rhinu* note."

"What does that mean?" said Rincewind.

"Means what it says," said Dibhala. "Means it's worth ten of these." He held up a gold coin about the size of a rice cake.

"Why'd you want to buy a piece of paper?" said Rincewind.

"You don't buy it, it's for buying things *with*," said Dibhala. Rincewind looked blank.

"You go to a mark-et stall," said Dibhala, getting back into the slow-voice-for-the-hard-of-thinking, "and you say, 'Good morn-ing, but-cher, how much for those dog noses?' and he says, 'Three *rhinu*, shogun,' and *you* say, 'I've only got a pony, okay?' (look, there's an etch-ing of a pony on it, see, that's what you get on ten-*rhinu* notes) and he gives you the dog noses and seven coins in what we call 'change.' Now, if you had a monkey, that's fifty *rhinu*, he'd say 'Got anything smaller?' and—"

"But it's only a bit of paper!" Rincewind wailed.

"It may be a bit of paper to you but it's ten rice cakes to me," said Dibhala. "What do you foreign blood-suckers use? Big stones with holes in them?"

Rincewind stared at the paper money.

There were dozens of papermills in Ankh-Morpork, and some of the craftsmen in the Engravers' Guild could engrave their name and address on a pinhead.

He suddenly felt immensely proud of his countrymen. They might be venal and greedy, but by heaven they were *good* at it and they never assumed that there wasn't any more to learn.

"I think you'll find," he said, "that there's a lot of buildings in Ankh-Morpork that need new roofs."

"Really?" said Dibhala.

"Oh, yes. The rain's just pouring in."

"And people can pay? Only I heard—"

Rincewind looked at the paper money again. He shook his head. Worth more than gold . . .

"They'll pay with notes at least as good as that," he said. "Probably even better. I'll put in a good word for you. And now," he added hurriedly, "which way is out?"

Dibhala scratched his head.

"Could be a bit tricky," he said. "There's armies outside. You look a bit foreign with that hat. Could be tricky—"

There was a commotion further along the alley or, rather, a general increase in the commotion. The crowd parted in that hurried way common to unarmed crowds in the presence of weaponry, and a group of guards hurried towards Disembowel-Meself-Honorably.

He stepped back and gave them the friendly grin of one happy to sell at a discount to anyone with a knife.

A limp figure was being dragged between two of the guards. As it went past it raised a slightly bloodstained head and said, "Extended Duration to the—" before a gloved fist smacked across its mouth.

And then the guards were heading down the street. The crowd flowed back.

"Tch, tch," said D. M. H. "Seems to be—Hello? Where'd you go?"

Rincewind reappeared from around a corner. D. M. H. looked impressed. There had actually been a small thunderclap when Rincewind moved.

"See they got another of 'em," he said. "Putting up wall posters again, I expect."

"Another one of who?" said Rincewind.

"Red Army. Huh!"

"Oh."

"I don't pay much attention," said D. M. H. "They say some old legend's going to come true about emperors and stuff. Can't see it myself."

"He didn't look very legendary," said Rincewind.

"Ach, some people will believe anything."

"What'll happen to him?"

"Difficult to say, with the Emperor about to die. Hands and feet cut off, probably."

"What? Why?"

"'Cos he's young. That's leniency. A bit older and it's his head on a spike over one of the gates."

"That's punishment for putting up a *poster?*"

"Stops 'em doing it again, see," said D. M. H.

Rincewind backed away.

"Thank you," he said, and hurried off.

"Oh, no," he said, pushing his way through the crowds. "I'm *not* getting mixed up in people's heads getting chopped off—"

And then someone hit him again. But politely.

As he sank to his knees, and then to his chin, he wondered what had happened to the good old-fashioned "Hey, you!"

The Silver Horde wandered through the alleys of Hunghung.

"I don't call *this* bloody well sweeping through a city, slaughtering every bugger," muttered Truckle. "When I was riding with Bruce the Hoon, we *never* walked in through a front gate like a bunch of soppy mother—"

"Mr. Uncivil," said Mr. Saveloy hurriedly, "I wonder if this might be a good time to refer you to that list I drew up for you?"

"What bloody list?" said Truckle, sticking out his jaw belligerently.

"The list of acceptable *civilized* words, yes?" He turned to the others. "Remember I was telling you about civ-il-ized be-hav-ior. Civilized behavior is vital to our long-term strategy."

"What's a long-term strategy?" said Caleb the Ripper.

"It's what we're going to do later," said Cohen.

"And what's that, then?"

"It's the Plan," said Cohen.

"Well, I'll be f—" Truckle began.

"The list, Mr. Uncivil, only the words on the *list*," snapped Mr. Saveloy. "Listen, I bow to your expertise when it comes to crossing wilderness, but this is civilization and you must use the right words. Please?"

"Better do what he says, Truckle," said Cohen.

With bad grace, Truckle fished a grubby piece of paper out of his pocket and unfolded it.

"'Dang'?" he said. "Wassat mean? And what's this 'darn' and 'heck'?"

"They are . . . *civilized* swearwords," said Mr. Saveloy.

"Well, you can take 'em and—"

"Ah?" said Mr. Saveloy, raising a cautionary finger.

"You can shove them up—"

"Ah?"

"You can—"

"Ah?"

Truckle shut his eyes and clenched his fists.

"Dang it all to heck!" he shouted.

"Good," said Mr. Saveloy. "That's much better."

He turned to Cohen, who was grinning happily at Truckle's discomfort.

"Cohen," he said, "there's an apple stall over there. Do you fancy an apple?"

"Yeah, might do," Cohen conceded, in the cautious manner of someone giving a conjuror his watch while remaining aware that the man is grinning and holding a hammer.

"Right. Now, then, cla—I mean, gentlemen. Ghenghiz wants an apple. There's a stall over there selling fruit and nuts. What does he do?" Mr. Saveloy looked hopefully at his charges. "Anyone? Yes?"

"Easy. You kill that little"—there was a rustle of unfolding paper again—"*chap* behind the stall, then—"

"No, Mr. Uncivil. Anyone else?"

"Whut?"

"You set fire to—"

"No, Mr. Vincent. Anyone else. . . ?"

"You rape—"

"No, no, Mr. Ripper," said Mr. Saveloy. "We take out some muh—muh—?" He looked at them expectantly.

"—money—" chorused the Horde.

"—and we . . . What do we do? Now, we've gone through this hundreds of times. We . . ."

This was the difficult bit. The Horde's lined faces creased and puckered still further as they tried to force their minds out of the chasms of habit.

"Gi. . . ?" said Cohen hesitantly. Mr. Saveloy gave him a big smile and a nod of encouragement.

"Give? . . . it . . . to . . ." Cohen's lips tensed around the word ". . . him?"

"Yes! Well done. In *exchange* for the apple. We'll talk about

115

making change and saying 'thank you' later on, when you're
ready for it. Now then, Cohen, here's the coin. Off you go."

Cohen wiped his forehead. He was beginning to sweat.

"How about if I just cut him up a bit—"

"No! This is *civilization*."

Cohen nodded uncomfortably. He threw back his shoulders
and walked over to the stall, where the apple merchant, who had
been eying the group suspiciously, nodded at him.

Cohen's eyes glazed and his lips moved silently, as if he were
rehearsing a script. Then he said:

"Ho, fat merchant, give me all your . . . one apple . . . and I
will give you . . . this coin . . ."

He looked around. Mr. Saveloy had his thumb up.

"You want an apple, is that it?" said the apple merchant.

"Yes!"

The apple merchant selected one. Cohen's sword had been
hidden in the wheelchair again but the merchant, in response to
some buried acknowledgement, made sure it was a *good* apple.
Then he took the coin. This proved a little difficult, since his customer seemed loath to let go of it.

"Come on, hand it over, venerable one," he said.

Seven crowded seconds passed.

Then, when they were safely around the corner, Mr. Saveloy
said, "Now, everyone: who can tell me what Ghenghiz did
wrong?"

"Didn't say please?"

"Whut?"

"No."

"Didn't say thank you?"

"Whut?"

"No."

"Hit the man over the head with a melon and thumped him
into the strawberries and kicked him in the nuts and set fire to
his stall and stole all the money?"

"Whut?"

"Correct!" Mr. Saveloy sighed. "Ghenghiz, you were doing *so*
well up to then."

"He didn't ort to have called me what he did!"

"But 'venerable' means old and wise, Ghenghiz."

"Oh. Does it?"

"Yes."

"We-ell . . . I did leave him the money for the apple."

"Yes, but, you see, I do believe you took all his other money."

"But I *paid* for the apple," said Cohen, rather testily.

Mr. Saveloy sighed. "Ghenghiz, I do rather get the impression that several thousand years of the patient development of fiscal propriety have somewhat passed you by."

"Come again?"

"It is possible sometimes for money to legitimately belong to other people," said Mr. Saveloy patiently.

The Horde paused to wrap their minds around this, too. It was, of course, something they knew to be true in theory. Merchants always had money. But it seemed wrong to think of it as *belonging* to them; it *belonged* to whoever took it off them. Merchants didn't actually *own* it, they were just looking after it until it was needed.

"Now, there is an elderly lady over there selling ducks," said Mr. Saveloy. "I think the next stage—Mr. Willie, I am not over there, I am sure whatever you are looking at is very interesting, but please pay attention—is to practice our grasp of social intercourse."

"Hur, hur, hur," said Caleb the Ripper.

"I mean, Mr. Ripper, that you should go and enquire how much it would be for a duck," said Mr. Saveloy.

"Hur, hur, hur—What?"

"And you are not to rip all her clothes off. That's not civilized."

Caleb scratched his head. Flakes fell out.

"Well, what else am I supposed to do?"

"Er . . . engage her in conversation."

"Eh? What's there to talk about with a woman?"

Mr. Saveloy hesitated again. To some extent this was unknown territory to him as well. His experience with women at his last school had been limited to an occasional chat with the housekeeper, and on one occasion the matron had let him put his hand on her knee. He had been forty before he found out that

117

oral sex didn't mean talking about it. Women had always been to him strange and distant and wonderful creatures rather than, as the Horde to a man believed, something to do. He was struggling a little.

"The weather?" he hazarded. His memory threw in vague recollections of the staple conversation of the maiden aunt who had brought him up. "Her health? The trouble with young people today?"

"And then I rip her clothes off?"

"Possibly. Eventually. If she wants you to. I might draw your attention to the discussion we had the other day about taking regular baths"—or even *a* bath, he added to himself—"and attention to fingernails and hair and changing your clothes more often."

"This is leather," said Caleb. "You don't have to change it, it don't rot for *years.*"

Once again Mr. Saveloy readjusted his sights. He'd thought that Civilization could be overlaid on the Horde like a veneer. He had been mistaken.

But the funny thing—he mused, as the Horde watched Caleb's painful attempts at conversation with a representative of half the world's humanity—was that although they were as far away as possible from the kind of people he normally mixed with in staffrooms, or possibly because they were as far away as possible from the kind of people he normally mixed with in staffrooms, he actually *liked* them. Every one of them saw a book as either a lavatorial accessory or a set of portable fire-fighters and thought that hygiene was a greeting. Yet they were honest (from their specialized point of view) and decent (from their specialized point of view) and saw the world as hugely simple. They stole from rich merchants and temples and kings. They didn't steal from poor people; this was not because there was anything virtuous about poor people, it was simply because poor people had no money.

And although they didn't set out to give the money *away* to the poor, that was nevertheless what they did (if you accepted that the poor consisted of innkeepers, ladies of negotiable virtue, pickpockets, gamblers and general hangers-on), because although they would go to great lengths to steal money they then had as much control over it as a man trying to herd cats. It was there to be spent and lost. So they kept the money in circulation, always a praiseworthy thing in any society.

They never worried about what other people thought. Mr. Saveloy, who'd spent his whole life worrying about what other people thought and had been passed over for promotion and generally treated as a piece of furniture as a result, found this strangely attractive. And they never agonized about anything, or wondered if they were doing the right thing. And they enjoyed themselves immensely. They had a kind of honor. He *liked* the Horde. They weren't his kind of people.

Caleb returned, looking unusually thoughtful.

"Congratulations, Mr. Ripper!" said Mr. Saveloy, a great believer in positive reinforcement. "She still appears to be fully clothed."

"Yeah, what'd she say?" said Boy Willie.

"She smiled at me," said Caleb. He scratched his crusty beard uneasily. "A bit, anyway," he added.

"Good," said Mr. Saveloy.

"She, er . . . she said she'd . . . she wouldn't mind seein' me . . . later . . ."

"Well done!"

"Er . . . Teach? What's a *shave?*"

Saveloy explained.

Caleb listened carefully, grimacing occasionally. He turned round occasionally to look at the duck seller, who gave him a little wave.

"Cor," he said. "Er. I dunno . . . " He looked around again. "Never seen a woman who wasn't running away before."

"Oh, women are like deer," said Cohen loftily. "You can't just charge in, you gotta stalk 'em—"

"Hur, hur, h—Sorry," said Caleb, catching Mr. Saveloy's stern eye.

"I think perhaps we should end the lesson here," said Mr. Saveloy. "We don't want to get you *too* civilized, do we. . . ? I suggest we take a stroll around the Forbidden City, yes?"

Terry Pratchett

They'd all seen it. It dominated the center of Hunghung. Its walls were forty feet high.

"There's a lot of soldiers guarding the gates," said Cohen.

"So they should. A great treasure lies within," said Mr. Saveloy. He didn't raise his eyes, though. He seemed to be staring intently at the ground, as though searching for something he'd lost.

"Why don't we just rush up and kill the guards?" Caleb demanded. He was still feeling a bit shaken.

"Whut?"

"Don't be daft," said Cohen. "It'd take all day. Anyway," he added, feeling a little proud despite himself, "Teach here is goin' to get us in on an invisible duck, ain't that so, Teach?"

Mr. Saveloy stopped.

"Ah. Eureka," he said.

"That's Ephebian, that is," Cohen told the Horde. "It means 'Give me a towel.'"

"Oh yeah," said Caleb, who had been surreptitiously trying to untangle the knots in his beard. "And when were you ever in Ephebe?"

"Went bounty hunting there once."

"Who for?"

"You, I think."

"Hah! Did you find me?"

"Dunno. Nod your head and see if it falls off."

"Ah. Gentlemen . . . behold . . ."

Mr. Saveloy's orthopaedic sandal was prodding an ornamental metal square in the ground.

"Behold what?" said Truckle.

"Whut?"

"We should look for more of these," said Mr. Saveloy. "But I think we have it. All we need to do now is wait until dark."

There was an argument going on. All Rincewind could make out were the voices; another sack had been tied over his head, while he himself was tied to a pillar.

"Does he even *look* like a Great Wizard?"

120

"That's what it says on his hat in the language of ghosts—"

"So you say!"

"What about the testimony of Four Big Sandal, then?"

"He was overtaxed. He could have imagined it!"

"I did not! He came out of thin air, flying like a dragon! He knocked over five soldiers. And Three Maximum Luck saw it also. And the others. And then he freed an ancient man and turned him into a mighty fighting warrior!"

"And he can speak our language, just as it says in the book."

"All right. Supposing he *is* the Great Wizard? Then we should kill him now!"

In the darkness of his sack, Rincewind shook his head furiously.

"Why?"

"He will be on the side of the Emperor."

"But the legend says the Great Wizard led the Red Army!"

"Yes, for Emperor One Sun Mirror. It crushed the people!"

"No, it crushed all the bandit chiefs! Then it built the Empire!"

"So? The Empire is so great? Untimely Demise To The Forces Of Oppression!"

"But *now* the Red Army is on the side of the people! Maximum Advancement With The Great Wizard!"

"The Great Wizard is the Enemy of the People!"

"I saw him, I tell you! A legion of soldiers collapsed with the wind of his passage!"

The wind of his passage was beginning to worry Rincewind as well. It always tended to when he was frightened.

"If he is such a great wizard, why is he still tied up? Why has he not made his bonds disappear in puffs of green smoke?"

"Perhaps he is saving his magic for some even mightier deeds. He wouldn't do firecracker tricks for earthworms."

"Hah!"

"And he had the Book! He was looking for us! It is his destiny to lead the Red Army!"

Shake, shake, shake.

"We can lead ourselves!"

Nod, nod, nod.

"We don't need any suspicious Great Wizards from illusionary places!"

Nod, nod, nod.

"So we should kill him now!"

Nod, no—*Shakeshakeshake.*

"Hah! He laughs at you with scorn! He waits to make your head explode with snakes of fire!"

Shake, shake, shake.

"You do know that while we're arguing Three Yoked Oxen is being tortured?"

"The People's Army is more than just individuals, Lotus Blossom!"

In the fetid sack Rincewind grimaced. He was already beginning to take a dislike to the first speaker, as one naturally does with people urging that you be put to death without delay. But when that sort of person started talking about things being more important than people, you knew you were in big trouble.

"I'm sure the Great Wizard could rescue Three Yoked Oxen," said a voice by his ear. It was Butterfly.

"Yes, he could easily rescue Three Yoked Oxen!" said Lotus Blossom.

"Hah! You say? He could get into the Forbidden City? Impossible! It's certain death!"

Nod, nod, nod.

"Not to the Great Wizard," said the voice of Butterfly.

"*Shut up!*" hissed Rincewind.

"*Would you like to know how big the meat cleaver is that Two Fire Herb is holding in his hand?*" whispered Butterfly.

"*No!*"

"*It's very big.*"

"*He said that going into the Forbidden City is certain death!*"

"*No. It's only* probable *death. I assure you, if you run away from me again that is* certain *death.*"

The sack was pulled away.

The face immediately in front of him was that of Lotus Blossom, and a man could see a lot worse things with his daylight than her face, which made him think of cream and masses of butter and just the right amount of salt.*

One of the things he might see, for example, was the face of Two Fire Herb. This was not a nice face. It was podgy and had tiny little pupils in its eyes, and looked like a living example of the fact that although the people could be oppressed by kings and emperors and mandarins, the job could often be done just as well by the man next door.

"Great Wizard? Hah!" Two Fire Herb said now.

"He can do it!" said Lotus Blossom (and cream cheese, thought Rincewind, and maybe coleslaw on the side). "He *is* the Great Wizard come back to us! Did he not guide the Master through the lands of ghosts and blood-sucking vampires?"

"Oh, I wouldn't say—" Rincewind began.

"Such a great wizard allowed you to bring him here in a sack?" said Two Fire Herb, sneering. "Let us see him do some conjuring . . ."

"A truly *great* wizard would not stoop to doing party tricks!" said Lotus Blossom.

"That's right," said Rincewind. "Not stoop."

"Shame on Herb to suggest such a thing!"

"Shame," Rincewind agreed.

"Besides, he will need all of his power to enter the Forbidden City," said Butterfly. Rincewind found himself hating the sound of her voice.

"Forbidden City," he murmured.

"Everyone knows there are terrible snares and traps and many, many guards."

"Snares, traps . . ."

"Why, if his magic should fail him because he did tricks for Herb, he would find himself in the deepest dungeon, dying by inches."

"Inches . . . er . . . which particular inch—"

"So much shame to Two Fire Herb!"

Rincewind gave her a sickly grin.

---

*Much later, Rincewind had to have therapy for this. It involved a pretty woman, a huge plate of potatoes, and a big stick with a nail in it.

"Actually," he said, "I'm not *that* great. I'm a *bit* great," he added quickly, as Butterfly began to frown, "but not *very* great—"

"The writings of the Master say that you defeated many powerful enchanters and resolutely succeeded in dangerous situations."

Rincewind nodded glumly. It was more or less true. But most of the time he hadn't intended to. Whereas the Forbidden City had looked . . . well . . . forbidden. It didn't look inviting. It didn't look as though it sold postcards. The only souvenir they were likely to give you would be, perhaps, your teeth. In a bag.

"Er . . . I expect this Oxen lad is in some deep dungeon, yes?"

"The deepest," said Two Fire Herb.

"And . . . you've never seen anyone again? Who's been taken prisoner, I mean."

"We have seen *bits* of them," said Lotus Blossom.

"Usually their heads," said Two Fire Herb. "On spikes over the gates."

"But not Three Yoked Oxen," said Lotus Blossom firmly. "The Great Wizard has spoken!"

"Actually, I'm not sure I actually said—"

"You have spoken," said Butterfly firmly.

As Rincewind got accustomed to the gloom he realized that he was in some storeroom or cellar; the noise of the city came, rather muffled, from grilles near the ceiling. It was half full of barrels and bundles, and every one of them was a perch for someone. The room was crowded.

The people were watching him with expressions of rapt attention, but that wasn't the only thing they had in common.

Rincewind turned right around.

"Who are all these children?" he said.

"This," said Lotus Blossom, "is the Hunghung cadre of the Red Army."

Two Fire Herb snorted.

"Why did you tell him that?" he said. "Now we may have to kill him."

"But they're all so young!"

"They may be underprivileged in years," said Two Fire Herb, "but they are ancient in courage and honor."

"And experienced in fighting?" said Rincewind hotly. "The guards I've seen do not look like nice people. I mean, do you even have any weapons?"

"We will wrest the weapons we need from our enemies!" said Two Fire Herb. A cheer went up.

"Really? How do you actually make them let go?" said Rincewind. He pointed to a very small girl, who leaned away from his digit as though it were loaded. She looked about seven and was holding a toy rabbit.

"What's your name?"

"One Favorite Pearl, Great Wizard!"

"And what do you do in the Red Army?"

"I have earned a medal for putting up of wall posters, Great Wizard!"

"What . . . like 'Slightly Bad Things Please Happen To Our Enemies'? That sort of thing?"

"Er . . . " said the girl, looking imploringly at Butterfly.

"Rebellion is not easy for us," said the older girl. "We don't have . . . experience."

"Well, I'm here to tell you that you don't do it by singing songs and putting up posters and fighting bare-handed," said Rincewind. "Not when you're up against real people with real weapons. You . . ." His voice trailed away as he realized that a hundred pairs of eyes were watching him intently, and two hundred ears were carefully listening.

He played back his own words in the echo chamber of his head. He'd said, "I'm here to tell you . . ."

He spread out his hands and waved them frantically.

". . . that is, it's not up to me to tell you anything," he said.

"That is *correct*," said Two Fire Herb. "We will overcome because history is on our side."

"We will overcome because the Great Wizard is on our side," said Butterfly sharply.

"I'll tell you this!" shouted Rincewind. "I'd rather trust me than history! Oh, shit, did I just say that?"

"So you *will* help Three Yoked Oxen," said Butterfly.

"Please!" said Lotus Blossom.

Rincewind looked at her, and the tears in the corners of her eyes, and the bunch of awed teenagers who really thought that you could beat an army by singing rousing songs.

There was only one thing he could do, if he really thought about it.

He could play along for now and then get the hell out of it at the very first opportunity. Butterfly's anger was bad, but a spike was a spike. Of course, he'd feel a bit of a heel for a while, but that was the point. He'd feel a heel, but he wouldn't feel a spike.

The world had too many heroes and didn't need another one. Whereas the world had only one Rincewind and he owed it to the world to keep this one alive for as long as possible.

There was an inn. There was a courtyard. There was a corral, for the Luggages.

There were large traveling trunks, big enough to carry the needs of an entire household for a fortnight. There were merchant's sample cases, mere square boxes on crude legs. There were sleek overnight bags.

They shuffled aimlessly in their pen. Occasionally there was the rattle of a handle or the creak of a hinge, and once or twice the snap of a lid and the bonk-bonk-bonk of boxes trying to get out of the way.

Three of them were big and covered with studded leather. They looked the kind of travelling accessories that hang around outside cheap hotels and make suggestive remarks to handbags.

The object of their attention was a rather smaller trunk with an inlaid lid and dainty feet. It had already backed into a corner as far as it could go.

A large spiked lid creaked open a couple of times as the largest of the boxes edged closer.

The smaller box had retreated so far its back legs were trying to climb the corral fence.

There was the sound of running feet on the other side of the courtyard wall. They got closer, and then stopped abruptly.

Then there was a twang such as would be made by an object landing on the taut roof of a cart.

For a moment, against the rising moon, there was the shape of something somersaulting slowly through the evening air.

It landed heavily in front of the three big chests, bounced upright, and charged.

Eventually various travelers spilled out into the night but by then items of clothing were strewn and trampled around the courtyard. Three black chests, battered and scarred, were discovered on the roof, each one scrabbling on the tiles and butting the others in an effort to be the highest. Others had panicked and broken down the wall and headed out across the country.

Eventually, all but one of them were found.

The Horde were feeling quite proud of themselves when they sat down for dinner. They acted, Mr. Saveloy thought, rather like boys who'd just got their first pair of long trousers.

Which they had done. Each man had one baggy pair of same, plus a long grey robe.

"We've been *shopping*," said Caleb proudly. "Paying for things with *money*. We're dressed up like civilized people."

"Yes indeed," said Mr. Saveloy indulgently. He was hoping that they could all get through this without the Horde finding out what *kind* of civilized people they were dressed up as. As it was, the beards were a problem. The kind of people who wore these kind of clothes in the Forbidden City didn't usually have beards. They were proverbial for not having them. Actually, they were more properly proverbial for not having other things but, as a sort of consequence of this lack, also for not having beards.

Cohen shifted. "Itchy," he said. "This is pants, is it? Never worn 'em before. Same with shirts. What good's a shirt that's not chain mail?"

"We did very well, though," said Caleb. He had even had a shave, obliging the barber, for the first time in his experience, to use a chisel. He kept rubbing his naked, baby-pink chin.

"Yeah, we're really civilized," said Vincent.

"Except for the bit where you set fire to that shopkeeper," said Boy Willie.

"Nah, I only set fire to him a bit."

"Whut?"

"Teach?"

"Yes, Cohen?"

"Why did you tell that firework merchant that everyone you knew had died suddenly?"

Mr. Saveloy's foot tapped gently against the large parcel under the table, alongside a nice new cauldron.

"So he wouldn't get suspicious about what I was buying," he said.

"Five thousand firecrackers?"

"Whut?"

"Well," said Mr. Saveloy. "Did I ever tell you that after I taught geography in the Assassins' Guild and the Plumbers' Guild I did it for a few terms in the Alchemists' Guild?"

"Alchemists? Loonies, the lot of them," said Truckle.

"But they're keen on geography," said Mr. Saveloy. "I suppose they need to know where they've landed. Eat up, gentlemen. It may be a long night."

"What is this stuff?" said Truckle, spearing something with his chopstick.

"Er. Chow," said Mr. Saveloy.

"Yes, but what *is* it?"

"Chow. A kind of . . . er . . . dog."

The Horde looked at him.

"There's nothing *wrong* with it," he said hurriedly, with the sincerity of a man who had ordered bamboo shoots and bean curd for himself.

"I've eaten everything else," said Truckle, "but I ain't eating dog. I had a dog once. Rover."

"Yeah," said Cohen. "The one with the spiked collar? The one who used to eat people?"

"Say what you like, he was a friend to me," said Truckle, pushing the meat to one side.

"Rabid death to everyone else. I'll eat yours. Order him some chicken, Teach."

"Et a man once," mumbled Mad Hamish. "In a siege, it were."

"You ate someone?" said Mr. Saveloy, beckoning to the waiter.

"Just a leg."

"That's terrible!"

"Not with mustard."

Just when I think I know them, Mr. Saveloy mused . . .

He reached for his wine glass. The Horde reached for their glasses, too, while watching him carefully.

"A toast, gentlemen," he said. "And remember what I said about not quaffing. Quaffing just gets your ears wet. Just sip. To Civilization!"

The Horde joined in with their own toasts.

"'Pcharn'kov!'"*

"'Lie down on the floor and no one gets hurt!'"

"'May you live in interesting pants!'"

"'What's the magic word? Gimme!'"

"'Death to most tyrants!'"

"Whut?"

"The walls of the Forbidden City are forty feet high," said Butterfly.

"And the gates are made of brass. There are hundreds of guards. But of course we have the Great Wizard."

"Who?"

"You."

"Sorry, I was forgetting."

"Yes," said Butterfly, giving Rincewind a long, appraising look. Rincewind remembered tutors giving him a look like that when he'd got high marks in some test by simply guessing at the answers.

He looked down hurriedly at the charcoal scrawls Lotus Blossom had made.

Cohen'd know what to do, he thought. *He'd* just slaughter his way through. It'd never cross his mind to be afraid or worried. He's the kind of man you need at a time like this.

"No doubt you have magic spells that can blow down the walls," said Lotus Blossom.

---

*"Your feet shall be cut off and be buried several yards from your body so your ghost won't walk."

Rincewind wondered what they would do to him when it turned out that he couldn't. Not a lot, he thought, if I'm already running. Of course they could curse his memory and call him names, but he was used to that. Sticks and stones may break my bones, he thought. He was vaguely aware that there was a second half to the saying, but he'd never bothered because the first half always occupied all his attention.

Even the Luggage had left him. That was a minor bright spot, but he missed that patter of little feet . . .

"Before we start," he said, "I think you ought to sing a revolutionary song."

The cadre liked the idea. Under cover of their chanting he sidled over to Butterfly, who gave him a knowing smile.

"You know I can't do it!"

"The Master said you were very resourceful."

"I can't magic a hole in a wall!"

"I'm sure you'll think of something. And . . . Great Wizard?"

"Yes, what?"

"Favorite Pearl, the child with the toy rabbit . . ."

"Yes?"

"The cadre is all she has. The same goes for many of the others. When the warlords fight, lots of people die. Parents. Do you understand? I was one of the first to read *What I Did On My Holidays*, Great Wizard, and what *I* saw in there was a foolish man who for some reason is always lucky. Great Wizard . . . I hope for everyone's sake you have a great deal of luck. Especially for yours."

Fountains tinkled in the courts of the Sun Emperor. Peacocks made their call, which sounds like a sound made by something that shouldn't look as beautiful as that. Ornamental trees cast their shade as only they knew how—ornamentally.

The gardens occupied the heart of the city and it was possible to hear the noises from outside, although these were muted because of the straw spread daily on the nearest streets and also because any sound considered too loud would earn its originator a very brief stay in prison.

Of the gardens, the most aesthetically pleasing was the one laid out by the first Emperor, One Sun Mirror. It consisted entirely of gravel and stones, but artfully raked and laid out as it might be by a mountain torrent with a refined artistic sense. It was here that One Sun Mirror, in whose reign the Empire had been unified and the Great Wall built, came to refresh his soul and dwell upon the essential unity of all things, while drinking wine out of the skull of some enemy or possibly a gardener who had been too clumsy with his rake.

At the moment the garden was occupied by Two Little Wang, the Master of Protocol, who came there because he felt it was good for his nerves.

Perhaps it was the number two, he'd always told himself. It was an unlucky birth number. Being called Little Wang was merely a lack-of-courtesy detail, a sort of minor seagull dropping after the great heap of buffalo excrement that Heaven had pasted into his very horoscope. Although he had to admit that he hadn't made things any better by allowing himself to become Master of Protocol.

It had seemed such a good idea at the time. He'd risen gently through the Agatean civil service by mastering those arts essential to the practice of good government and administration (such as calligraphy, origami, flower arranging, and the Five Wonderful Forms of poetry). He'd dutifully got on with the tasks assigned to him and noticed only vaguely that there didn't seem to be quite as many high-ranking members of the civil service as there used to be, and then one day a lot of senior mandarins—most of them a lot more senior than he was, it occurred to him later—had rushed up to him while he was trying to find a rhyme for "orange blossom" and congratulated him on being the new Master.

That had been three months ago.

And of the things that had occurred to him in those intervening three months the most shameful was this: he had come to believe that the Sun Emperor was not, in fact, the Lord of Heaven, the Pillar of the Sky and the Great River of Blessings, but an evil-minded madman whose death had been too long delayed.

It was an awful thought. It was like hating motherhood and

raw fish, or objecting to sunlight. Most people develop their social conscience when young, during that brief period between leaving school and deciding that injustice isn't necessarily all bad, and it was something of a shock to suddenly find one at the age of sixty.

It wasn't that he was against the Golden Rules. It made sense that a man prone to thieving should have his hands cut off. It prevented him from thieving again and thus tarnishing his soul. A peasant who could not pay his taxes *should* be executed, in order to prevent him falling into the temptations of slothfulness and public disorder. And since the Empire was created by Heaven as the only true world of human beings, all else outside being a land of ghosts, it was certainly in order to execute those who questioned this state of affairs.

But he felt that it wasn't right to laugh happily while doing so. It wasn't *pleasant* that these things should happen, it was merely necessary.

From somewhere in the distance came the screams. The Emperor was playing chess again. He preferred to use live pieces.

Two Little Wang felt heavy with knowledge. There had been better times. He knew that now. Things hadn't always been the way they were. Emperors didn't use to be cruel clowns, around whom it was as safe as mudbanks in the crocodile season. There hadn't always been a civil war every time an Emperor died. Warlords hadn't run the country. People had rights as well as duties.

And then one day the succession had been called into question and there was a war and since then it'd never seemed to go right.

Soon, with any luck, the Emperor would die. No doubt a special Hell was being made ready. And there'd be the usual battle, and then there'd be a new Emperor, and if he was very lucky Two Little Wang would be beheaded, which was what tended to happen to people who had risen to high office under a previous incumbent. But that was quite reasonable by modern standards, since it was possible these days to be beheaded for interrupting the Emperor's thoughts or standing in the wrong place.

At which point, Two Little Wang heard ghosts.

They seemed to be right under his feet.

They were talking in a strange language, so to Two Little Wang the speech was merely sounds, which went as follows:

"Where the hell are we?"

"Somewhere under the palace, I'm sure. Look for another manhole in the ceiling . . ."

"Whut?"

"I'm fed up with pushing this damn wheelchair!"

"It's me for a hot footbath after this, I'm telling you."

"You call this a way to enter a city? You call this a way to enter a city? Waist-deep in water? We didn't enter a . . . wretched . . . city like this when I rode with Bruce the Hoon! You enter a . . . lovemaking . . . city by overrunning it with a thousand horsemen, that's how you take a city—!"

"Yeah, but there ain't room for 'em in this pipe."

The sounds had a hollow, booming quality to them. With a kind of fascinated puzzlement Two Little Wang followed them, walking across the manicured gravel in an unthinking way that would have earned him an immediate tongue-extraction from its original lover of peace and tranquility.

"Can we please hurry? I'd like us to be out of here when the cauldron goes off and I didn't really have much time to experiment with the fuses."

"I still don't understand about the cauldron, Teach."

"I hope all those firecrackers will blow a hole in the wall."

"Right! So why ain't we there? Why are we in this pipe?"

"Because all the guards will rush to see what the bang was."

"Right! So we should be there!"

"No! We should be here, Cohen. The word is decoy. It's . . . more civilized this way."

Two Little Wang pressed his ear to the ground.

"What's the penalty for entering the Forbidden City again, Teach?"

"I believe it's a punishment similar to hanging, drawing, and quartering. So, you see, it would be a good idea if—"

There was a very faint splashing.

"How're you drawn, then?"

"I think your innards are cut out and shown to you."

"What for?"

133

"I don't really know. To see if you recognize them, I suppose."

"What . . . like, 'Yep, that's my kidneys, yep, that's my breakfast'?"

"How're you quartered? Is that, like, they give you somewhere to stay?"

"I think not, from context."

For a while there was no sound but the splash of six pairs of feet and the *squeak-squeak* of what sounded like a wheel.

"Well, how're you hung?"

"Excuse me?"

"Hur, hur, hur . . . sorry, sorry."

Two Little Wang tripped over a two-hundred-year-old bonsai tree and hit his head on a rock chosen for its fundamental serenity. When he came round, a few seconds later, the voices had gone. If there had ever been any.

Ghosts. There were a lot of ghosts around these days. Two Little Wang wished he had a few firecrackers to scatter around.

Being Master of Protocol was even worse than trying to find a rhyme for "orange blossom."

Flares lit the alleys of Hunghung. With the Red Army chattering behind him, Rincewind wandered up to the wall of the Forbidden City.

No one knew better than Rincewind that he was totally incapable of proper magic. He'd only ever done it by accident.

So he could be sure that if he waved a hand and said some magic words the wall would in all probability become just a little bit less full of holes than it was now.

It was a shame to disappoint Lotus Blossom, with her body that reminded Rincewind of a plate of crinkle-cut chips, but it was about time she learned that you couldn't rely on wizards.

And then he could be out of here. What could Butterfly do to him if he tried and failed? And, much to his surprise, he found himself hoping that, on the way out, he could poke Herb in the eye. He was amazed the others couldn't spot him for what he was.

This area of wall was between gates. The life of Hunghung lapped against it like a muddy sea; there were stalls and booths everywhere. Rincewind had thought Ankh-Morpork citizens lived out on the streets, but they were agoraphobes compared to the Hunghungese. Funerals (with associated firecrackers) and wedding parties and religious ceremonies went on alongside, and intermingled with, the normal market activities such as free-form livestock slaughter and world-class arguing.

Herb pointed to a clear area of wall stacked with timber.

"Just about there, Great Wizard," he sneered. "Do not exert yourself unduly. A small hole should be sufficient."

"But there's hundreds of people around!"

"Is that a problem to such a great wizard? Perhaps you can't do it with people watching?"

"I have no doubt that the Great Wizard will astonish us," said Butterfly.

"When the people see the power of the Great Wizard they will speak of it for ever!" said Lotus Blossom.

"Probably," muttered Rincewind.

The cadre stopped talking, although it was only possible to notice this by watching their closed mouths. The hole left by their silence was soon filled by the babble of the market.

Rincewind rolled up his sleeves.

He wasn't even certain about a spell for blowing things up . . .

He waved a hand vaguely.

"I should stand well back, everyone," said Herb, grinning unpleasantly.

"Quanti canicula illa in fenestre?" said Rincewind. "Er . . ."

He stared desperately at the wall and, with that heightened perception that comes to those on the edge of terror, noticed a cauldron half hidden in the timber. There seemed to be a little glowing string attached to it.

"Er," he said, "there seems to be—"

"Having problems?" said Herb, nastily.

Rincewind squared his shoulders.

"—" he said.

There was a sound like a marshmallow gently landing on a plate, and everything in front of him went white.

Then the white turned red, streaked with black, and the terrible noise clapped its hands across his ears.

A crescent-shaped piece of something glowing scythed the top off his hat and embedded itself in the nearest house, which caught fire.

There was a strong smell of burning eyebrows.

When the debris settled Rincewind saw quite a large hole in the wall. Around its edge the brickwork, now a red-hot ceramic, started to cool with a noise like *glinka-glinka*.

He looked down at his soot-blackened hands.

"Gosh," he said.

And then he said, "All *right!*"

And then he turned and began to say, "How about that, then?" but his voice faded when it became apparent that everyone was lying flat on the ground.

A duck watched him suspiciously from its cage. Owing to the slight protection afforded by the bars, its feathers were patterned alternately natural and crispy.

He'd always *wanted* to do magic like that. He'd always been able to visualize it perfectly. He'd just never been able to do it . . .

A number of guards appeared in the gap. One, whose ferocity of helmet suggested that he was an officer, glared at the charred hole and then at Rincewind.

"Did you do this?" he demanded.

"Stand back!" shouted Rincewind, drunk with power. "I'm the Great Wizard, I am! You see this finger? Don't make me use it!"

The officer nodded to a couple of his men.

"Get him."

Rincewind took a step back.

"I warn you! Anyone lays a hand on me, he'll be eating flies and hopping for the rest of his life!"

The guards advanced with the determination of those who were prepared to risk the uncertainty of magic against the definite prospect of punishment for disobeying orders.

"Stand back! This could go off! All right, then, since you force—"

He waved his hand. He snapped his fingers a few times.

"Er—"

The guards, after checking that they were still the same shape, each grabbed an arm.

"It may be delayed action," he ventured, as they gripped harder.

"Alternatively, would you be interested in hearing a famous quotation?" he said. His feet were lifted off the ground. "Or perhaps not?"

Rincewind, running absent-mindedly in mid-air, was brought in front of the officer.

"On your knees, rebel!" said the officer.

"I'd like to, but—"

"I saw what you did to Captain Four White Fox!"

"What? Who's he?"

"Take . . . him . . . to . . . the . . . Emperor."

As he was dragged off Rincewind saw, for one brief moment, the guards closing on the Red Army, swords flashing . . .

A metal plate shuddered for a moment, and then dropped on the floor.

"Careful!"

"I ain't used to being careful! Bruce the Hoon wasn't care—"

"Shut up about Bruce the Hoon!"

"Well, dang you, too!"

"Whut?"

"Anyone out there?"

Cohen stuck his head out of the pipe. The room was dark, damp and full of pipes and runnels. Water went off in every direction to feed fountains and cisterns.

"No," he said, in a disappointed voice.

"Very well. Everyone out of the pipe."

There was some echoey swearing and the scrape of metal as Hamish's wheelchair was manoeuvred into the long, low cellar.

Mr. Saveloy lit a match as the Horde spread out and examined their surroundings.

"Congratulations, gentlemen," he said. "I believe we are in the palace."

"Yeah," said Truckle. "We've conquered a f—a *lovemaking* pipe. What good is that?"

"We could rape it," said Caleb hopefully.

"Hey, this wheel thing turns . . ."

"What's a lovemaking pipe?"

"What does this lever do?"

"Whut?"

"How about we find a door, rush out, and kill everyone?"

Mr. Saveloy closed his eyes. There was something familiar about this situation, and now he realized what it was. He'd once taken an entire class on a school trip to the city armory. His right leg still hurt him on wet days.

"No, no, *no!*" he said. "What good would that do? Boy Willie, please don't pull that lever."

"Well, *I'd* feel better, for one," said Cohen. "Ain't killed anyone all day except a guard, and they hardly count."

"Remember that we're here for theft, not murder," said Mr. Saveloy. "Now, please, out of all that wet leather and into your nice new clothes."

"I don't like this part," said Cohen, pulling on a shirt. "I like people to know who I was."

"Yeah," said Boy Willie. "Without our leather and mail people'll just think we're a load of old men."

"Exactly," said Mr. Saveloy. "That is part of the subterfuge."

"Is that like tactics?" said Cohen.

"Yes."

"All right, but *I* don't like it," said Old Vincent. "S'posing we win? What kind of song will the minstrels sing about people who invaded through a pipe?"

"An echoey one," said Boy Willie.

"They won't sing anything like that," said Cohen firmly. "You pay a minstrel enough, he'll sing whatever you want."

A flight of damp steps led to a door. Mr. Saveloy was already at the top, listening.

"That's right," said Caleb. "They say that whoever pays the piper calls the tune."

"But, gentlemen," said Mr. Saveloy, his eyes bright, "whoever holds a knife to the piper's throat writes the symphony."

*　　*　　*

The assassin moved slowly through Lord Hong's chambers.

He was one of the best in Hunghung's small but very select guild, and he certainly was not a rebel. He disliked rebels. They were invariably poor people, and therefore unlikely to be customers.

His mode of movement was unusual and cautious. It avoided the floor; Lord Hong was known to tune his floorboards. It made considerable use of furniture and decorative screens, and occasionally of the ceiling as well.

And the assassin was very good at it. When a messenger entered the room through a distant door he froze for an instant, and then moved in perfect rhythm towards his quarry, letting the newcomer's clumsy footsteps mask his own.

Lord Hong was making another sword. The folding of the metal and all the tedious yet essential bouts of heating and hammering were, he found, conducive to clear thinking. Too much pure cerebration was bad for the mind. Lord Hong liked to use his hands sometimes.

He plunged the sword back into the furnace and pumped the bellows a few times.

"Yes?" he said. The messenger looked up from his prone position near the floor.

"Good news, o lord. We have captured the Red Army!"

"Well, that *is* good news," said Lord Hong, watching the blade carefully for the change of color. "Including the one they call the Great Wizard?"

"Indeed! But he is not that great, o lord!" said the messenger. His cheerfulness faded when Lord Hong raised an eyebrow.

"Really? On the contrary, I suspect him of being in possession of huge and dangerous powers."

"Yes, o lord! I did not mean—"

"See that they are all locked up. And send a message to Captain Five Hong Man to undertake the orders I gave him today."

"Yes, o lord!"

"And now, stand up!"

The messenger stood up, trembling. Lord Hong pulled on a thick glove and reached for the sword handle. The furnace roared.

"Chin up, man!"

"My lord!"

"Now open your eyes wide!"

There was no need for that order. Lord Hong peered into the mask of terror, noted the flicker of movement, nodded, and then in one almost balletic movement pulled the spitting blade from the furnace, turned, thrust . . .

There was a very brief scream, and a rather longer hiss.

Lord Hong let the assassin sag. Then he tugged the sword free and inspected the steaming blade.

"Hmm," he said. "Interesting . . ."

He caught sight of the messenger.

"Are you still here?"

"No, my lord!"

"See to it."

Lord Hong turned the sword so that the light caught it, and examined the edge.

"And, er, shall I send some servants to clear away the, er, body?"

"What?" said Lord Hong, lost in thought.

"The body, Lord Hong?"

"What body? Oh. Yes. See to it."

The walls were beautifully decorated. Even Rincewind noticed this, though they went past in a blur. Some had marvellous birds painted on them, or mountain scenes, or sprays of foliage, every leaf and bud done in exquisite detail with just a couple of brush-strokes.

Ceramic lions reared on marble pedestals. Vases bigger than Rincewind lined the corridors.

Lacquered doors opened ahead of the guards. Rincewind was briefly aware of huge, ornate and empty rooms stretching away on either side.

Finally they passed through yet another set of doors and he was flung down on a wooden floor.

In these circumstances, he always found, it was best not to look up.

Eventually an officious voice said, "What do you have to say for yourself, miserable louse?"

"Well, I—"

"Silence!"

Ah. So it was going to be *that* kind of interview.

A different voice, a cracked, breathless and elderly voice, said, "Where is the Grand . . . Vizier?"

"He has retired to his rooms, O Great One. He said he had a headache."

"Summon him at . . . once."

"Certainly, O Great One."

Rincewind, his nose pressed firmly to the floor, made some further assumptions. Grand Vizier was always a bad sign; it generally meant that people were going to suggest wild horses and red-hot chains. And when people were called things like "O Great One," it was pretty certain that there was no appeal.

"This is a . . . rebel, is it?" The sentence was wheezed rather than spoken.

"Indeed, O Great One."

"I think I would like a clo . . . ser look."

There was a general murmur, suggesting that a number of people had been greatly surprised, and then the sound of furniture being moved.

Rincewind thought he saw a blanket on the edge of his vision. Someone was wheeling a bed across the floor . . .

"Make it . . . stand up." The gurgle in the pause was like the last bathwater going down the plughole. It sucked as wetly as an outgoing wave.

Once again a foot kicked Rincewind in the kidneys, making its usual explicit request in the Esperanto of brutality. He got up.

It *was* a bed, and quite the biggest Rincewind had ever seen. In it, swathed in brocades and almost lost in pillows, was an old man. Rincewind had never seen anyone look so ill. The face was pale, with a greenish pallor; veins showed up under the skin of his hands like worms in a jar.

The Emperor had all the qualifications for a corpse except, as it were, the most vital one.

"So . . . this is the new Great Wizard of . . . whom we have read so much, is . . . it?" he said.

When he spoke, people waited expectantly for the final gurgle in mid-sentence.

"Well, I—" Rincewind began.

"Silence!" screamed a chamberlain.

Rincewind shrugged.

He hadn't known what to expect of an Emperor, but the mental picture had room for a big fat man with lots of rings. Talking to this one was a hair's breadth from necromancy.

"Can you show us some more . . . magic, Great Wizard?"

Rincewind glanced at the chamberlain.

"W—"

"Silence!"

The Emperor waved a hand vaguely, gurgled with the effort, and gave Rincewind another enquiring look. Rincewind decided to chance things.

"I've got a good one," he said. "It's a vanishing trick."

"Can you . . . do it now?"

"Only if everyone opens all the doors and turns their back."

The Emperor's expression did not change. The court fell silent. Then there was a sound like a number of small rabbits being choked to death.

The Emperor was laughing. Once this was established, everyone else laughed too. No one can get a laugh like a man who can have you put to death more easily than he goes to the lavatory.

"What *shall* we do with . . . you?" he said. "Where *is* the . . . Grand . . . Vizier?"

The crowd parted.

Rincewind risked a sideways squint. Once you were in the hands of a Grand Vizier, you were dead. Grand Viziers were *always* scheming megalomaniacs. It was probably in the job description: "Are you a devious, plotting, unreliable madman? Ah, good, then you can be my most trusted minister."

"Ah, Lord . . . Hong," said the Emperor.

"Mercy?" suggested Rincewind.

"Silence!" screamed the chamberlain.

"Tell me, Lord . . . Hong," said the ancient Emperor. "What

would be the punishment for a . . . foreigner . . . entering the Forbidden City?"

"Removal of all limbs, ears, and eyes, and then allowed to go free," said Lord Hong.

Rincewind raised his hand.

"First offense?" he said.

"Silence!"

"We find, generally, that there is no second offence," said Lord Hong. "What is this person?"

"I like him," said the Emperor. "I think I shall . . . keep him. He makes me . . . laugh."

Rincewind opened his mouth.

"Silence!" screamed the chamberlain, perhaps unwisely in view of current thinking.

"Er . . . could you stop him shouting 'Silence!' every time I try to speak?" Rincewind ventured.

"Certainly . . . Great Wizard," said the Emperor. He nodded at some guards. "Take the chamberlain . . . away and cut his . . . lips off."

"Great One, I—!"

"And his ears . . . also."

The wretched man was dragged away. A pair of lacquered doors slammed shut. There was a round of applause from the courtiers.

"Would you . . . like to watch him eat . . . them?" said the Emperor grinning happily. "It's tre . . . mendous fun."

"Ahahaha," said Rincewind.

"A good decision, lord," said Lord Hong. He turned his head towards Rincewind.

To the wizard's immense surprise, and some horror, too, he winked.

"O Great One . . . " said a plump courtier, dropping to his knees, bouncing slightly, and then nervously approaching the Emperor, "I wonder if perhaps it is entirely wise to be so merciful to this foreign dev—"

The Emperor looked down. Rincewind would have sworn that dust fell off him.

There was a gentle movement among the crowd. Without

anyone apparently doing anything so gross as activating their feet, there was nevertheless a widening space around the kneeling man.

Then the Emperor smiled.

"Your concern is well . . . received," he said. The courtier risked a relieved grin. The Emperor added, "However, your presumption is not. Kill him slowly . . . over several . . . days."

"Aaargh!"

"Yes in . . . deed! Lots of boiling . . . oil!"

"An excellent idea, o lord," said Lord Hong.

The Emperor turned back to Rincewind.

"I am sure the . . . Great Wizard is my friend," he suctioned.

"Ahahaha," said Rincewind.

He'd been in this approximate position before, gods knew. But he'd always been facing someone—well, usually someone who looked like Lord Hong, not a near-corpse who was clearly so far round the bend he couldn't poke sanity with a long pole.

"We shall have *such* . . . fun," said the Emperor. "I read . . . all about you."

"Ahahaha," said Rincewind.

The Emperor waved a hand at the court again.

"Now I will retire," he said. There was a general movement and much ostensible yawning. Clearly no one stayed up later than the Emperor.

"Emperor," said Lord Hong wearily, "what will you have us do with this Great Wizard of yours?"

The old man gave Rincewind the look a present gets around the time the batteries have run out.

"Put him in the special . . . dungeon," he said. "For . . . now."

"Yes, Emperor," said Lord Hong. He nodded at a couple of guards.

Rincewind managed a quick look back as he was dragged from the room. The Emperor was lying back in his movable bed, quite oblivious to him.

"Is he mad or what?" he said.

"Silence!"

Rincewind looked up at the guard who'd said that.

"A mouth like that could get a man into big trouble around here," he muttered.

Lord Hong always found himself depressed by the general state of humanity. It often seemed to him to be flawed. There was no *concentration*. Take the Red Army. If *he* had been a rebel the Emperor would have been assassinated months ago and the country would now be aflame, except for those bits too damp to burn. But these? Despite his best efforts, their idea of revolutionary activity was a surreptitious wall poster saying something like "Unpleasantness To Oppressors When Convenient!"

They had tried to set fire to guardhouses. That was good. That was proper revolutionary activity, except for the bit where they tried to make an appointment first. It had taken Lord Hong some considerable effort to see that the Red Army appeared to achieve any victories at all.

Well, he'd given them the Great Wizard they so sincerely believed in. They had no excuse now. And by the look of him, the wretch was as craven and talentless as Lord Hong had hoped. Any army led by him would either flee or be slaughtered, leaving the way open for the counter-revolution.

The counter-revolution would *not* be inefficient. Lord Hong would see to that.

But things had to be done one step at a time. There were enemies everywhere. Suspicious enemies. The path of the ambitious man was a nightingale floor. One wrong step and it would sing out. It was a shame the Great Wizard would turn out to be so good at locks. Lord Tang's men were guarding the prison block tonight. Of course, if the Red Army were to escape, no blame at all could possibly attach to Lord Tang . . .

Lord Hong risked a little chuckle to himself as he strode back to his suite. Proof, that was the thing. There must never be proof. But that wouldn't matter very long. There was nothing like a fearsomely huge war to unite people, and the fact that the Great Wizard—that is, the leader of the terrible rebel army—was an evil foreign troublemaker was just the spark to light the firecracker.

And then . . . Ankh-Morpork [urinating dog].

Hunghung was old. The culture was based on custom, the alimentary tract of the common water buffalo, and base treachery. Lord Hong was in favor of all three, but they did not add up to world domination, and Lord Hong was particularly in favor of that, provided it was achieved by Lord Hong.

If I was the traditional type of Grand Vizier, he thought as he sat down before his tea table, I'd cackle with laughter at this point.

He smiled to himself, instead.

Time for the box again? No. Some things were all the better for the anticipation.

Mad Hamish's wheelchair caused a few heads to turn, but no actual comment. Undue curiosity was not a survival trait in Hunghung. They just got on with their work, which appeared to be the endless carrying of stacks of paper along the corridors.

Cohen looked down at what was in his hand. Over the decades he'd fought with many weapons—swords, of course, and bows and spears and clubs and . . . well, now he came to think of it, just about anything.

Except this . . .

"I *still* don't like it," said Truckle. "Why're we carrying pieces of paper?"

"Because no one looks at you in a place like this if you're carrying a piece of paper," said Mr. Saveloy.

"Why?"

"Whut?"

"It's—a kind of magic."

"I'd feel happier if it was a weapon."

"As a matter of fact, it can be the greatest weapon there is."

"I know, I've just cut myself on my bit," said Boy Willie, sucking his finger.

"Whut?"

"Look at it like this, gentlemen," said Mr. Saveloy. "Here we are, actually *inside* the Forbidden City, and no one is dead!"

"Yes. That's what we're . . . *danging* . . . complaining about," said Truckle.

Mr. Saveloy sighed. There was something in the way Truckle used words. It didn't matter what he actually said, what you heard was in some strange way the word he actually *meant*. He could turn the air blue just by saying "socks".

The door slammed shut behind Rincewind, and there was the sound of a bolt shooting into place.

The Empire's jails were pretty much like the ones at home. When you want to incarcerate such an ingenious creature as the common human being, you tend to rely on the good old-fashioned iron bar and large amounts of stone. It looked as though this well-tried pattern had been established here for a very long time.

Well, he'd definitely scored a hit with the Emperor. For some reason this did not reassure him. The man gave Rincewind the distinct impression of being the kind of person who is at least as dangerous to his friends as to his enemies.

He remembered Noodle Jackson, back in the days when he was a very young student. Everyone wanted to be friends with Noodle but somehow, if you were in his gang, you found yourself being trodden on or chased by the Watch or being hit in fights you didn't start, while Noodle was somewhere on the edge of things, laughing.

Besides, the Emperor wasn't simply at Death's door but well inside the hallway, admiring the carpet and commenting on the hatstand. And you didn't have to be a political genius to know that when someone like that died, scores were being settled before he'd even got cold. Anyone he'd publicly called a friend would have a life expectancy more normally associated with things that hover over trout streams at sunset.

Rincewind moved aside a skull and sat down. There was the possibility of rescue, he supposed, but the Red Army would be hard put to it to rescue a rubber duck from drowning. Anyway, that'd put him back in the clutches of Butterfly, who terrified him almost as much as the Emperor.

He had to believe that the gods didn't intend for Rincewind, after all his adventures, to rot in a dungeon.

No, he added bitterly, they probably had something much more inventive in mind.

What light reached the dungeon came from a very small grille and had a second-hand look. The rest of the furnishing was a pile of what had possibly once been straw. There was—

—a gentle tapping at the wall.

Once, twice, three times.

Rincewind picked up the skull and returned the signal.

One tap came back.

He repeated it.

Then there were two.

He tapped twice.

Well, this was familiar. Communication without meaning . . . it was just like being back at Unseen University.

"Fine," he said, his voice echoing in the cell. "Fine. Très prisoner. But what are we *saying?*"

There was a gentle scraping noise and one of the blocks in the wall very gently slid out of the wall, dropping on to Rincewind's foot.

"Aargh!"

"What big hippo?" said a muffled voice.

"What?"

"Sorry?"

"What?"

"You wanted to know about the tapping code? It's how we communicate between cells, you see. One tap means—"

"Excuse me, but aren't we communicating now?"

"Yes, but not formally. Prisoners are not . . . allowed . . . to talk . . ." The voice slowed down, as if the speaker had suddenly remembered something important.

"Ah, yes," said Rincewind. "I was forgetting. This is . . . Hunghung. Everyone . . . obeys . . . the rules . . ."

Rincewind's voice died away too.

On either side of the wall there was a long, thoughtful silence.

"Rincewind?"

"*Twoflower?*"

"What are *you* doing here?" said Rincewind.

"Rotting in a dungeon!"

"Me, too!"

"Good grief! How long has it been?" said the muffled voice of Twoflower.

"What? How long has what been?"

"But *you* . . . why are . . . "

"You wrote that damn book!"

"I just thought it would be interesting for people!"

"Interesting? *Interesting?*"

"I thought people would find it an interesting account of a foreign culture. I never meant it to cause trouble."

Rincewind leaned against his side of the wall. No, of course, Twoflower never wanted to cause any trouble. Some people never did. Probably the last sound heard before the Universe folded up like a paper hat would be someone saying, "What happens if I do this?"

"It must have been Fate that brought you here," said Twoflower.

"Yes, it's the sort of thing he likes to do," said Rincewind.

"You remember the good times we had?"

"Did we? I must have had my eyes shut."

"The adventures!"

"Oh, *them.* You mean hanging from high places, that sort of thing . . . ?"

"Rincewind?"

"Yes? What?"

"I feel a lot happier about things now *you're* here."

"That's amazing."

Rincewind enjoyed the comfort of the wall. It was just rock. He felt he could rely on it.

"Everyone seems to have a copy of your book," he said. "It's a revolutionary document. And I do mean *copy.* It looks as though they make their own copy and pass it on."

"Yes, it's called *samizdat.*"

"What does that mean?"

"It means each one must be the same as the one before. Oh,

dear. I thought it would just be entertainment. I didn't think people would take it seriously. I do hope it's not causing too much bother."

"Well, your revolutionaries are still at the slogan-and-poster stage, but I shouldn't think that'll count for much if they're caught."

"Oh, dear."

"How come you're still alive?"

"I don't know. I think they may have forgotten about me. That tends to happen, you know. It's the paperwork. Someone makes the wrong stroke with the brush or forgets to copy a line. I believe it happens a lot."

"You mean that there's people in prison and no one can remember why?"

"Oh, yes."

"Then why don't they set them free?"

"I suppose it is felt that they must have done something. All in all, I'm afraid our government does leave something to be desired."

"Like a new government."

"Oh, dear. You could get locked up for saying things like that."

People slept, but the Forbidden City never slept. Torches flickered all night in the great Bureaux as the ceaseless business of Empire went on.

This largely involved, as Mr. Saveloy had said, moving paper.

Six Beneficent Winds was Deputy District Administrator for the Langtang district, and good at a job which he rather enjoyed. He was not a wicked man.

True, he had the same sense of humor as a chicken casserole. True, he played the accordion for amusement, and disliked cats intensely, and had a habit of dabbing his upper lip with his napkin after his tea ceremony in a way that had made Mrs. Beneficent Winds commit murder in her mind on a regular basis over the years. And he kept his money in a small leather shovel purse, and counted it out very thoroughly whenever he made a purchase, especially if there was a queue behind him.

But on the other hand, he was kind to animals and made small but regular contributions to charity. He frequently gave moderate sums to beggars in the street, although he made a note of this in the little notebook he always carried to remind him to visit them in his official capacity later on.

And he never took away from people more money than they actually had.

He was also, unusually for men employed in the Forbidden City after dark, not a eunuch. Guards were not eunuchs, of course, and people had got around this by classifying them officially as furniture. And it had been found that tax officials also needed every faculty at their disposal to combat the wiles of the average peasant, who had this regrettable tendency to avoid paying taxes.

There were much nastier people in the building than Six Beneficent Winds and it was therefore just his inauspicious luck that his paper and bamboo door slid aside to reveal seven strange-looking old eunuchs, one of them in a wheeled contrivance.

They didn't even bow, let alone fall on their knees. And he not only had an official red hat but it had a white button on it!

His brush dropped from his hands when the men wandered into his office as if they owned it. One of them started poking holes in the wall and speaking gibberish.

"Hey, the walls are just made of paper! Hey, look, if you lick your finger it goes right through! See?"

"I will call for the guards and have you all flogged!" shouted Six Beneficent Winds, his temper moderated slightly by the extreme age of the visitors.

"What did he say?"

"He said he'd call for the guards."

"Ooo, yes. Please let him call for the guards!"

"No, we don't want that yet. Act normally."

"You mean cut his throat?"

"I meant a more normal kind of normally."

"It's what I call normal."

One of the old men faced the speechless official and gave him a big grin.

"Excuse us, your supreme . . . *oh dear, what's the word?* . . . pushcart sail? . . . immense rock? . . . *ah, yes* . . . venerableness, but we seem to be a little lost."

A couple of the old men shuffled around behind Six Beneficent Winds and started to read, or at least try to read, what he'd been working on. A sheet of paper was snatched from his hand.

"What's this say, Teach?"

"Let me see . . . 'The first wind of autumn shakes the lotus flower. Seven Lucky Logs to pay one pig and three [*looks like a four-armed man waving a flag*] of rice on pain of having his [*rather a stylized thing here, can't quite make it out*] struck with many blows. By order of Six Beneficent Winds, Collector of Revenues, Langtang.'"

There was a subtle change among the old men. Now they were all grinning, but not in a way that gave him any comfort. One of them, with teeth like diamonds, leaned towards him and said, in bad Agatean:

"You are a tax collector, Mr. Knob on Your Hat?"

Six Beneficent Winds wondered if he'd be able to summon the guard. There was something terrible about these old men. They weren't venerable at all. They were horribly menacing and, although he couldn't see any obvious weapons, he knew for a cold frozen fact that he wouldn't be able to get out more than the first syllable before he'd be killed. Besides, his throat had gone dry and his pants had gone wet.

"Nothing wrong with being a tax collector . . . " he croaked.

"We never said that," said Diamond Teeth. "We always like to meet tax collectors."

"Some of our most favoritest people, tax collectors," said another old man.

"Saves a lot of trouble," said Diamond Teeth.

"Yeah," said a third old man. "Like, it means you don't have to go from house to house killin' everyone for their valuables, you just wait and kill the—"

"Gentlemen, can I have a word?"

The speaker was the slightly goat-faced one that didn't seem quite so unpleasant as the others. The terrible men clustered around him and Six Beneficent Winds heard the strange syllables of a coarse foreign tongue:

"*What? But he's a tax collector! That's what they're for!*"

"*Whut?*"

"*A firm tax base is the foundation of sound governance, gentlemen. Please trust me.*"

"*I understood all of that up to 'A firm tax'.*"

"*Nevertheless, no useful purpose will be served by killing this hardworking tax gatherer.*"

"*He'd be dead. I call that useful.*"

There was some more of the same. Six Beneficent Winds jumped when the group broke up and the goat-faced man gave him a smile.

"My humble friends are overawed by your . . . variety of plum . . . small knife for cutting seaweed . . . *presence*, noble sir," he said, his every word slandered by Truckle's vigorous gesticulations behind his back.

"*How about if we just cut a bit off?*"

"*Whut?*"

"How did you get in here?" said Six Beneficent Winds. "There are many strong guards."

"I *knew* we missed something," said Diamond Teeth.

"We would like you to show us around the Forbidden City," said Goat Face. "My name is . . . Mr. Stuffed Tube, I think you would call it. Yes. Stuffed Tube, I'm pretty sure—"

Six Beneficent Winds glanced hopefully towards the door.

"—and we are here to learn more about your wonderful . . . mountain . . . variety of bamboo . . . sound of running water at evening . . . drat . . . civilization."

Behind him, Truckle was energetically demonstrating to the rest of the Horde what he and Bruce the Hoon's Skeletal Riders once did to a tax gatherer. The sweeping arm movements in particular occupied Six Beneficent Winds' attention. He couldn't understand the words but, somehow, you didn't need to.

"*Why are you talking to him like that?*"

"*Ghenghiz, I'm lost. There are no maps of the Forbidden City. We need a guide.*"

Goat Face turned back to the taxman. "Perhaps you would like to come with us?" he said.

Out, thought Six Beneficent Winds. Yes! There may be guards out there!

"Just a minute," said Diamond Teeth, as he nodded. "Pick up your paintbrush and write down what I say."

A minute later, they'd gone. All that remained in the taxman's office was an amended piece of paper, which read as follows:

"Roses are red, violets are blue. Seven Lucky Logs to be given one pig and all the rice he can carry, because he is now One Lucky Peasant. By order of Six Beneficent Winds, Collector of Revenues, Langtang. Help. Help. If anyone reads this I am being held prisoner by an evil eunuch. Help."

Rincewind and Twoflower lay in their separate cells and talked about the good old days. At least, Twoflower talked about the good old days. Rincewind worked at a crack in the stone with a piece of straw, it being all he had to hand. It would take several thousand years to make any kind of impression, but that was no reason to give up.

"Do we get fed in here?" he said, interrupting the flow of reminiscence.

"Oh, sometimes. But it's not like the marvelous food in Ankh-Morpork."

"Really," murmured Rincewind, scratching away. A tiny piece of mortar seemed ready to move.

"I'll always remember the taste of Mr. Dibbler's sausages."

"People do."

"A once-in-a-lifetime experience."

"Frequently."

The straw broke.

"Damn and blast!" Rincewind sat back. "What's so important about the Red Army?" he said. "I mean, they're just a bunch of kids. Just a nuisance!"

"Yes, I'm afraid things got rather confused," said Twoflower. "Um. Have you ever heard of the theory that History goes in cycles?"

"I saw a drawing in one of Leonard of Quirm's notebooks—" Rincewind began, trying again with another straw.

"No, I mean . . . like a . . . wheel, spinning. If you stand in the same place it all comes round again?"

"Oh, *that*. Blast!"

"Well, a lot of people believe it here. They think History starts again every three thousand years."

"Could be," said Rincewind, who was looking for another straw and wasn't really listening. Then the words sank in: "Three thousand years? That's a bit short, isn't it? The whole thing? Stars and oceans and intelligent life evolving from arts graduates, that sort of thing?"

"Oh, no. That's just . . . stuff. *Proper* history started with the founding of the Empire by One Sun Mirror. The first Emperor. And his servant, the Great Wizard. Just a legend, really. It's the sort of thing peasants believe. They look at something like the Great Wall and say, that's such a marvelous thing it must have been built by magic . . . And the Red Army . . . what it *probably* was was just a well-organized body of trained fighting men. The first real army, you see. All there was before was just undisciplined mobs. That's what it must have been. Not magical at all. The Great Wizard couldn't really have *made* . . . What the peasants believe is silly . . ."

"Why, what do they believe?"

"They say the Great Wizard made the earth come alive. When all the armies on the continent faced One Sun Mirror the Great Wizard . . . flew a kite."

"Sounds sensible to me," said Rincewind. "When there's war around take the day off, that's my motto."

"No, you don't understand. This was a special kite. It trapped the lightning in the sky and the Great Wizard stored it in bottles and then took the mud itself and . . . baked it with the lightning, and made it into an army."

"Never heard of any spells for that."

"And they have funny ideas about reincarnation, too . . ."

Rincewind conceded that they probably would. It probably whiled away those long water-buffaloid hours: hey, after I die I

155

hope I come back as . . . a man holding a water buffalo, but facing a different way.

"Er . . . no," said Twoflower. "They don't think you come *back* at all. Er . . . I'm not using the right words, am I? . . . Bit corroded on this language . . . I mean *pre*incarnation. It's like reincarnation backwards. They think you're born before you die."

"Oh, really?" said Rincewind, scratching at the stones. "Amazing! Born before you die? Life before death? People will get really excited when they hear about that."

"That's not exactly . . . er. It's all tied in with ancestors. You should always venerate ancestors because you might be them one day, and . . . Are you listening?"

The little piece of mortar fell away. Not bad for ten minutes' work, thought Rincewind. Come the next Ice Age, we're out of here . . .

It dawned on him that he was working on the wall that led to Twoflower's cell. Taking several thousand years to break into an adjoining cell could well be thought a waste of time.

He started on a different wall. Scratch . . . scratch . . .

There was a terrible scream.

Scratchscratchscratch—

"Sounds like the Emperor has woken up," said Twoflower's voice from the hole in the wall.

"That's kind of an early morning torture, is it?" said Rincewind. He started to hammer at the huge blocks with a piece of shattered stone.

"It's not really his fault. He just doesn't understand about people."

"Is that so?"

"You know how common kids go through a stage of pulling the wings off flies?"

"*I* never did," said Rincewind. "You can't trust flies. They may look small but they can turn nasty."

"Kids generally, I mean."

"Yes? Well?"

"*He* is an Emperor. No one ever dared tell him it was wrong. It's just a matter of, you know, scaling up. All the five families fight among themselves for the crown. He killed his nephew to become Emperor. No one has ever told him that it's not right to keep killing people for fun. At least, no one who has ever managed to get to the end of the first sentence. And the Hongs and the Fangs and the Tangs and the Sungs and the McSweeneys have been killing one another for thousands of years. It's all part of the royal succession."

"McSweeneys?"

"Very old-established family."

Rincewind nodded gloomily. It was probably like breeding horses. If you have a system where treacherous murderers tend to win, you end up breeding *really* treacherous murderers. You end up with a situation where it's dangerous to lean over a cradle . . .

There was another scream.

Rincewind started kicking at the stones.

A key turned in the lock.

"Oh," said Twoflower.

But the door didn't open.

Finally Rincewind walked over and tried the big iron ring.

The door swung outwards, but not too far because the recumbent body of a guard makes an unusual but efficient doorstop.

There was a whole ring of keys hanging from the one in the door . . .

An inexperienced prisoner would simply have run for it. But Rincewind was a post-graduate student in the art of staying alive, and knew that in circumstances like these much the best thing to do was let out every single prisoner, pat each one hurriedly on the back and say, "Quick! They're coming for you!" and then go and sit somewhere nice and quiet until the pursuit has disappeared in the distance.

He opened the door to Twoflower's cell first.

The little man was skinnier and grubbier than he remembered, and had a wispy beard, but in one very significant way he had the feature that Rincewind remembered so well—the big, beaming, *trusting* smile that suggested that anything bad currently happening to him was just some sort of laughable mistake and would be bound to be sorted out by reasonable people.

"Rincewind! It *is* you! I certainly never thought I'd see *you* again!" he said.

"Yes, I thought something on those lines," said Rincewind.

Twoflower looked past Rincewind at the fallen guard.

"Is he dead?" he said, speaking of a man with a sword half buried in his back.

"Extremely likely."

"Did *you* do that?"

"I was *inside* the cell!"

"Amazing! Good trick!"

Despite several years of exposure to the facts of the matter, Rincewind remembered, Twoflower had never really wanted to grasp the fact that his companion had the magical abilities of the common house fly. It was useless to try to dissuade him. It just meant that modesty was added to the list of non-existent virtues.

He tried some of the keys in other cell doors. Various raggedy people emerged, blinking in the slightly better light. One of them, turning his body slightly in order to get it through the door, was Three Yoked Oxen. From the look of him he'd been beaten up, but this might just have been someone's attempt to attract his attention.

"This is Rincewind," said Twoflower proudly. "The Great Wizard. Did you know he killed the guard from inside the cell?"

They politely inspected the corpse.

"I didn't, really," said Rincewind.

"And he's modest, too!"

"Long Life To The People's Endeavor!" said Three Yoked Oxen through rather swollen lips.

"'Mine's A Pint!'" said Rincewind. "Here's bigfella keys belong door, you go lettee people outee chopchop."

One of the freed prisoners limped to the end of the passage.

"There's a dead guard here," he said.

"It wasn't me," said Rincewind plaintively. "I mean, perhaps I *wished* they were dead, but—"

People edged away. You didn't want to be too close to anyone who could wish like that.

If this had been Ankh-Morpork someone would have said,

"Oh, yeah, sure, he magically stabbed them in the back?" But that was because people in Ankh-Morpork knew Rincewind, and they knew that if a wizard really wanted you dead you'd have no back left to stab.

Three Yoked Oxen had been able to master the technical business of opening doors. More swung open . . .

"Lotus Blossom?" said Rincewind.

She clung to Oxen's arm and smiled at Rincewind. Other members of the cadre trooped out behind her.

Then, to Rincewind's amazement, she looked at Twoflower, screamed, and threw her arms around his neck.

"Extended Continuation To Filial Affection!" chanted Three Yoked Oxen.

"'Close Cover Before Striking!'" said Rincewind. "Er. What exactly is happening?"

A very small Red soldier tugged at his robe.

"He is her daddy," it said.

"You never said you had children!"

"I'm sure I did. Often," said Twoflower, disentangling himself. "Anyway . . . it *is* allowed."

"You're *married?*"

"I was, yes. I'm sure I must have said."

"We were probably running away from something at the time. So there's a Mrs. Twoflower, is there?"

"There was for a while," said Twoflower, and for a moment an expression almost of anger distorted his preternaturally benign countenance. "Not, alas, any more."

Rincewind looked away, because that was better than looking at Twoflower's face.

Butterfly had also emerged. She stood just outside the cell door, with her hands clasped in front of her, looking down demurely at her feet.

Twoflower rushed over to her.

"Butterfly!"

Rincewind looked down at the rabbit clutcher.

"She another daughter, Pearl?"

"Yeth."

The little man came towards Rincewind, dragging the girls.

159

"Have you met my daughters?" he said. "This is Rincewind, who—"

"We have had the pleasure," said Butterfly, gravely.

"How did you all get here?" said Rincewind.

"We fought as hard as we could," said Butterfly. "But there were simply too many of them."

"I hope you didn't try to grab their weapons," said Rincewind, as sarcastically as he dared.

Butterfly glared at him.

"Sorry," said Rincewind.

"Herb says it is the system that is to blame," said Lotus Blossom.

"I bet he's got a better system all worked out." Rincewind looked at the throng of prisoners. "They usually have. Where is he, by the way?"

The girls looked around.

"I don't see him here," said Lotus Blossom. "But I think that when the guards attacked us he laid down his life for the cause."

"Why?"

"Because that's what he said we should do. I am ashamed that I did not. But they seemed to want to capture us, not kill us."

"I did not see him," said Butterfly. She and Rincewind exchanged a glance. "I think perhaps . . . he was not there."

"You mean he had been caught already?" said Lotus Blossom.

Butterfly looked at Rincewind again. It occurred to him that whereas Lotus Blossom had inherited a Twoflower view of the world, Butterfly *must* have taken after her mother. She thought more like Rincewind, i.e., the worst of everyone.

"Perhaps," she said.

"Make Considerable Sacrifice For The Common Good," said Three Yoked Oxen.

"'There's One Born Every Minute,'" said Rincewind, absently.

Butterfly seemed to get a grip on herself.

"However," she said, "we must make the most of this opportunity."

Rincewind, who had been heading for the stairs, froze.

"Exactly what do you mean?" he said.

"Don't you see? We are at large in the Forbidden City!"

"Not me!" said Rincewind. "I've never been at large. I've always been at hunched."

"The enemy brought us in here and now we are free—"

"Thanks to the Great Wizard," said Lotus Blossom.

"—and we must seize the day!"

She picked up a sword from a stricken guard and waved it dramatically.

"We must storm the palace, just as Herb suggested!"

"There's only thirty of you!" said Rincewind. "You're not a storm! You're a shower!"

"There are hardly any guards within the city itself," said Butterfly. "If we can overcome those around the Emperor's apartments—"

"You'll be killed!" said Rincewind.

She turned on him. "Then at least we shall have died for something!"

"Cleanse The State With The Blood Of Martyrs," rumbled Three Yoked Oxen.

Rincewind spun around and waved a finger under Three Yoked Oxen's nose, which was as high as he could reach.

"I'll bloody well thump you if you trot out something like that one more time!" he shouted, and then grimaced at the realization that he had just threatened a man three times heavier than he was.

"Listen to me, will you?" he said, settling down a little. "I know about people who talk about suffering for the common good. It's never bloody them! When you hear a man shouting 'Forward, brave comrades!' you'll see he's the one behind the bloody big rock and wearing the only really arrow-proof helmet! Understand?"

He stopped. The cadre were looking at him as if he was mad. He stared at their young, keen faces, and felt very, very old.

"But there are causes worth dying for," said Butterfly.

"No, there aren't! Because you've only got one life but you can pick up another five causes on any street corner!"

"Good grief, how can you *live* with a philosophy like that?"

Rincewind took a deep breath.

"Continuously!"

* * *

Six Beneficent Winds had thought it was a pretty good plan. The horrible old men were lost in the Forbidden City. Although they had a wiry look, rather like natural bonsai trees that had managed to flourish on a wind-swept cliff, they were nevertheless *very* old and not at all heavily armed.

So he led them in the direction of the gymnasium.

And when they were inside he screamed for help at the top of his voice. To his amazement, they didn't turn and run.

"Can we kill him *now?*" said Truckle.

A couple of dozen muscular men had stopped pounding logs of wood and piles of bricks and were regarding them suspiciously.

"Got any ideas?" said Cohen to Mr. Saveloy.

"Oh, dear. They're so very *tough* looking, aren't they?"

"You can't think of anything civilized?"

"No. It's over to you, I'm afraid."

"Hah! Hah! I bin *waiting* for this," said Caleb, pushing forward. "Bin practicing every day, 'n I? With my big lump o' teak."

"These are ninjas," said Six Beneficent Winds proudly, as a couple of the men wandered towards the door and pulled it shut. "The finest fighters in the world! Yield now!"

"That's interesting," said Cohen. "Here, you, in the black pyjamas . . . Just got out of bed, have you? Who's the best out of all of you?"

One of the men stared fixedly at Cohen and thrust out a hand at the nearest wall. It left a dent.

Then he nodded at the tax gatherer. "What are these old fools you've brought us?"

"I think they're barbarian invaders," said the taxman.

"How'd you—How'd he know that?" said Boy Willie. "We're wearin' itchy trousers and eatin' with forks and *everythin'*—"

The leading ninja sneered. "Heroic eunuchs?" he said. "Old men?"

"Who're you calling a eunuch?" Cohen demanded.

"Can I just show him what I've been practicing with my lump o' teak?" said Caleb, hopping arthritically from one foot to the other.

The ninja eyed the slab of timber.

"You could not make a dent on that, old man," he said.

"You watch," said Caleb. He held out the wood at arm's length. Then he raised his other hand, grunting a little as it got past shoulder height.

"You watching this hand? You watching this hand?" he demanded.

"I am watching," said the ninja, trying not to laugh.

"Good," said Caleb. He kicked the man squarely in the groin and then, as he doubled up, hit him over the head with the teak. "'Cos you should've been watchin' this foot."

And that would have been all there was to it if there had only been one ninja. But there was a clatter of rice flails and an unsheathing of long, curved swords.

The Horde drew closer together. Hamish pushed back his rug to reveal their armoury, although the collection of notched blades looked positively homely compared with the shiny toys ranged against them.

"Teach, why don't you take Mr. Taxman over to the corner out of harm's way?" said Ghenghiz.

"This is madness!" said Six Beneficent Winds. "They're the finest fighters in the world and you're just old men! Give in now and I'll see if I can get you a rebate!"

"Calm down, calm down," said Mr. Saveloy. "No one's going to get hurt. Metaphorically, at least."

Ghenghiz Cohen waved his sword a few times.

"Okay, you lads," he said. "Give us your best ninje."

Six Beneficent Winds looked on in horror as the Horde squared up.

"But it will be terrible slaughter!" he said.

"I'm afraid so," said Mr. Saveloy. He fished in his pockets for a bag of peppermints.

"Who are these mad old men? What do they *do?*"

"Barbarian heroing, generally," said Mr. Saveloy. "Rescuing princesses, robbing temples, fighting monsters, exploring ancient and terror-filled ruins . . . that sort of thing."

"But they look old enough to be dead! Why do they do it?"

Saveloy shrugged. "That's all they've ever done."

A ninja somersaulted down the room, screaming, a sword in

163

either hand; Cohen waited in an attitude rather similar to that of a baseball batter.

"I wonder," said Mr. Saveloy, "if you have ever heard of the term 'evolution'?"

The two met. The air blurred.

"Or 'survival of the fittest'?" said Mr. Saveloy.

The scream continued, but rather more urgently.

"I didn't even see his sword move!" whispered Six Beneficent Winds.

"Yes. People often don't," said Mr. Saveloy.

"But . . . they're so old!"

"Indeed," said the teacher, raising his voice above the screams, "and of course this is true. They are very *old* barbarian heroes."

The taxman stared.

"Would you like a peppermint?" said Mr. Saveloy, as Hamish's wheelchair thundered past in pursuit of a man with a broken sword and a pressing desire to stay alive. "You may find it helps, if you are around the Horde for any length of time."

The aroma from the proffered paper bag hit Six Beneficent Winds like a flamethrower.

"How can you smell anything after eating those?"

"You can't," said Mr. Saveloy happily.

The taxman continued to stare. The fighting was a fast and furious affair but, somehow, only on one side. The Horde fought like you'd expect old men to fight—slowly, and with care. All the activity was on the part of the ninjas, but no matter how well flung the throwing star or speedy the kick, the target was always, without any obvious effort, not there.

"Since we have this moment to chat," said Mr. Saveloy, as something with a lot of blades hit the wall just above the taxman's head, "I wonder: could you tell me about the big hill just outside the city? It is quite a remarkable feature."

"What?" said Six Beneficent Winds distractedly.

"The big hill."

"You want to know about *that? Now?*"

"Geography is a little hobby of mine."

Someone's ear hit Six Beneficent Winds on the ear.

"Er. What? We call it the Big Hill . . . Hey, look at what he's doing with his—"

"It seems remarkably regular. Is it a natural feature?"

"What? Eh? Oh . . . I don't know, they say it turned up thousands of years ago. During a terrible storm. When the first Emperor died. He . . . he's going to be killed! He's going to be killed! He's going to be—How did he do that?"

Six Beneficent Winds suddenly remembered, as a child, playing *Shibo Yangcong-san* with his grandfather. The old man always won. No matter how carefully he'd assembled his strategy, he'd find Grandfather would place a tile quite innocently right in the crucial place just before he could make his big move. The ancestor had spent his whole life playing *shibo*. The fight was just like that.

"Oh, my," he said.

"That's right," said Mr. Saveloy. "They've had a lifetime's experience of not dying. They've become very good at it."

"But . . . why here? Why come here?"

"We're going to undertake a robbery," said Mr. Saveloy.

Six Beneficent Winds nodded sagely. The wealth of the Forbidden City was legendary. Probably even blood-sucking ghosts had heard of it.

"The Talking Vase of Emperor P'gi Su?" he said.

"No."

"The Jade Head of Sung Ts'uit Li?"

"No. Wrong track entirely, I'm afraid."

"Not the secret of how silk is made?"

"Good grief. Silkworms' bottoms. Everyone knows that. No. Something rather more precious than that."

Despite himself, Six Beneficent Winds was impressed. Apart from anything else, only seven ninjas were still standing and Cohen was fencing with one of them while rolling a cigarette in the other hand.

And Mr. Saveloy could see *it* dawning in the fat man's eyes.

The same thing had happened to him.

Cohen came into people's lives like a rogue planet into a peaceful solar system, and you felt yourself being dragged along simply because nothing like that would ever happen to you again.

He himself had been peacefully hunting for fossils during the school holidays when he had, more or less, stumbled into the camp of those particular fossils called the Horde. They'd been quite friendly, because he had neither weapons nor money. And they'd taken to him, because he knew things they didn't. And that had been it.

He'd decided there and then. It must have been something in the air. His past life had suddenly unrolled behind him and he couldn't remember a single day of it that had been any fun. And it had dawned on him that he could join the Horde or go back to school and, pretty soon, a limp handshake, a round of applause and his pension.

It was something about Cohen. Maybe it was what they called charisma. It overpowered even his normal smell of a goat that had just eaten curried asparagus. He did everything wrong. He cursed people and used what Mr. Saveloy considered very offensive language to foreigners. He shouted terms that would have earned anyone else a free slit throat from a variety of interesting ethnic weapons—and he got away with it, partly because it was clear that there was no actual malice there but mainly because he was, well, Cohen, a sort of basic natural force on legs.

It worked on everything. When he wasn't actually fighting them, he got on a lot better with trolls than did people who merely thought that trolls had rights just like everyone else. Even the Horde, bloody-minded individualists to a man, fell for it.

But Mr. Saveloy had also seen the aimlessness in their lives and, one night, he'd brought the conversation round to the opportunities offered in the Aurient . . .

There was a light in Six Beneficent Winds' expression.

"Have you got an accountant?" he said.

"Well, no, as a matter of fact."

"Will this theft be treated as income or capital?"

"I haven't really thought like that. The Horde doesn't pay taxes."

"What? Not to *anyone*?"

"No. It's funny, but they never seem to keep their money for long. It seems to disappear on drink and women and high living.

I suppose, from a heroing point of view, they may count as taxes."

There was a "pop" as Six Beneficent Winds uncorked a small bottle of ink and licked his writing brush.

"But those sort of things probably count as allowable expenses for a barbarian hero," he said. "They are part of the job specification. And then of course there is wear and tear on weaponry, protective clothing . . . They could certainly claim for at least one new loincloth a year—"

"I don't think they've claimed for one per century."

"And there's pensions, of course."

"Ah. Don't use that word. They think it's a dirty word. But in a way *that* is what they're here for. This is their last adventure."

"When they've stolen this very valuable thing that you won't tell me about."

"That's right. You'd be very welcome to join us. You could perhaps be a barbarian . . . to push beans . . . a length of knotted string . . . *ah* . . . accountant. Have you ever killed anyone?"

"Not outright. But I've always thought you can do considerable damage with a well-placed Final Demand."

Mr. Saveloy beamed. "Ah, yes," he said. "Civilization."

The last ninja was upright, but only just; Hamish had run his wheelchair over his foot. Mr. Saveloy patted the taxman's arm. "Excuse me," he said. "I find I often have to intervene at this stage."

He padded over to the surviving man, who was looking around wildly. Six swords had become interlaced around his neck as though he'd taken part in a rather energetic folk dance.

"Good morning," said Mr. Saveloy. "I should just point out that Ghenghiz here is, despite appearances, a remarkably honest man. He finds it hard to understand empty bravura. May I venture to suggest therefore that you refrain from phrases like 'I would rather die than betray my Emperor' or 'Go ahead and do your worst' unless you *really, really* mean them. Should you wish for mercy, a simple hand signal will suffice. I strongly advise you not to attempt to nod."

The young man looked sideways at Cohen, who gave him an encouraging smile.

Then he waved a hand quickly.

The swords unwove. Truckle hit the ninja over the head with a club.

"It's all right, you don't have to go on about it, I didn't kill him," he said sulkily.

"Ow!" Boy Willie had been experimenting with a rice flail and had hit his own ear. "How'd they manage to fight with this rubbish?"

"Whut?"

"These little Hogswatch decoration thingies look the business, though," said Vincent, picking up a throwing star. "Aaargh!" He sucked his fingers. "Useless foreign junk."

"That bit where that lad sprang backwards right across the room with them axes in his hands was impressive, though."

"Yeah."

"You didn't ought to have stuck your sword out like that, I thought."

"He's learned an important lesson."

"It won't do him much good now where he's gone."

"Whut?"

Six Beneficent Winds was half laughing, half shocked.

"But . . . but . . . I've seen these guards fight before!" he said. "They're *invincible!*"

"No one told *us.*"

"But you beat them all!"

"Yep!"

"And you're just eunuchs!"

There was a scrape of steel. Six Beneficent Winds closed his eyes. He could feel metal touching his neck in at least five places.

"There's that word again," said the voice of Cohen the Barbarian.

"But . . . you're . . . *dressed* . . . as . . . eunuchs . . ." murmured Six Beneficent Winds, trying not to swallow.

Mr. Saveloy backed away, chuckling nervously.

"You see," he said, speaking fast, "you're too old to be taken for guards and you don't look like bureaucrats, so I thought it would be, er, a very good disguise to—"

"*Eunuch?*" roared Truckle. "You mean people've been

looking at me and thinking I mince around saying, *Helluo, Saltat?*"

Like many men whose testosterone had always sloshed out of their ears, the Horde had never fine-tuned their approach to the more complex areas of sexuality. A teacher to the core, Mr. Saveloy couldn't help correcting them, even at swordpoint.

"That means, 'the glutton dances,' not, as you seem to think, 'hello, sailor,' which is *heus nauta*," he said. "And eunuchs don't say it. Not as a matter of course. Look, it's an *honor* to be a eunuch in the Forbidden City. Many of them occupy very exalted positions in—"

"Then prepare yourself for high office, teacher!" Truckle shouted.

Cohen knocked the sword out of his hand.

"All right, none of that. I don't like it either," he said, "but it's just a disguise. Shouldn't mean anything to a man who once bit a bear's head off, should it?"

"Yeah, but . . . you know . . . it's not . . . I mean, when we went past those young ladies back there they all giggled . . ."

"Maybe later you can find them and make them laugh," said Cohen. "But you should've told us, Teach."

"Sorry."

"Whut? Whatseesay?"

"He said you're a EUNUCH!" Boy Willie bellowed in Hamish's ear.

"Yep!" said Hamish happily.

"What?"

"That's me! The one an' only!"

"No, he didn't mean—"

"Whut?"

"Oh, never mind. It's all pretty much the same to you, Hamish."

Mr. Saveloy surveyed the wrecked gym. "I wonder what time it is?" he said.

"Ah," gurgled Six Beneficent Winds, happy to lighten things a little. "Here, you know, we have an amazing demon-powered device that tells you what the time is even when the sun isn't—"

"Clocks," said Mr. Saveloy. "We've got them in Ankh-

Morpork. Only demons evaporate eventually so now they work by—" He paused. "Interesting. You don't have a word for it. Er. Shaped metal that does work? Toothed wheels?"

The taxman looked frightened. "Wheels with teeth?"

"What do you call the things that grind corn?"

"Peasants."

"Yes, but what do they grind corn with?"

"I don't know. Why should I know? Only peasants need to know *that*."

"Yes, I suppose that says it all, really," said Mr. Saveloy sadly.

"It's a long way off dawn," said Truckle. "Why don't we go and kill everyone in their beds?"

"No, no, no!" said Mr. Saveloy. "I keep telling you, we've got to do it *properly*."

"I could show you the treasure house," said Six Beneficent Winds helpfully.

"Never a good idea to give a monkey the key to a banana plantation," said Mr. Saveloy. "Can you think of anything else to keep them amused for an hour?"

Down in the basement, there was a man who was talking about the government. At the top of his voice.

"You can't fight for a cause! A cause is just a thing!"

"Then we are fighting for the peasants," said Butterfly. She'd backed away. Rincewind's anger was coming off him like steam.

"Oh? Have you ever met them?"

"I—have seen them."

"Oh, good! And what is it you want to *achieve?*"

"A better life for the people," said Butterfly coldly.

"You think you having some uprising and hanging a few people will do it? Well, I come from Ankh-Morpork and we've had more rebellions and civil wars than you've had . . . lukewarm ducks' feet, and you know what? The rulers are still in charge! They always are!"

They smiled at him in polite and nervous incomprehension.

"Look," he said, rubbing his forehead. "All those people out in the fields, the water buffalo people . . . If you have a revolution it'll all be better for them, will it?"

"Of course," said Butterfly. "They will no longer be subject to the cruel and capricious whims of the Forbidden City."

"Oh, that's good," said Rincewind. "So they'll sort of be in charge of themselves, will they?"

"Indeed," said Lotus Blossom.

"By means of the People's Committee," said Butterfly.

Rincewind pressed both hands to his head.

"My word," he said. "I don't know why, but I had this predictive flash!"

They looked impressed.

"I had this sudden feeling," he went on, "that there won't be all that many water buffalo string holders on the People's Committee. In fact . . . I get this kind of . . . voice telling me that a lot of the People's Committee, correct me if I'm wrong, are standing in front of me right now?"

"*Initially,* of course," said Butterfly. "The peasants can't even read and write."

"I expect they don't even know how to farm properly," said Rincewind, gloomily. "Not after doing it for only three or four thousand years."

"We certainly believe that there are many improvements that could be made, yes," said Butterfly. "If we act collectively."

"I bet they'll be really glad when you show them," said Rincewind.

He stared glumly at the floor. He quite liked the job of a water buffalo string holder. It sounded nearly as good as the profession of castaway. He longed for the kind of life where you could really *concentrate* on the squishiness of the mud underfoot, and make up pictures in the clouds; the kind of life where you could let your mind catch up with you and speculate for hours at a time about when your water buffalo was next going to enrich the loam. But it was probably difficult enough as it was without people trying to *improve* it . . .

He wanted to say: how can you be so nice and yet so dumb? The best thing you can do with the peasants is leave them alone. Let them get on with it. When people who can read and write start fighting on behalf of people who can't, you just end up with another kind of stupidity. If you want to help them, build a big library or something somewhere and leave the door open.

But this is Hunghung. You can't think like that in Hunghung. This is where people have learned to do what they're told. The Horde worked that one out.

The Empire's got something worse than whips all right. It's got obedience. Whips in the soul. They obey anyone who tells them what to do. Freedom just means being told what to do by someone different.

You'll all be killed.

I'm a coward. And even *I* know more about fights than you do. I've run away from some really good ones.

"Oh, let's just get out of here," he said. He gingerly took the sword from a dead guard and held it the right way round on the second attempt. He weighed it for a second, then shook his head and threw it away.

The cadre looked a lot happier.

"But I'm not leading you," said Rincewind. "I'm just showing you the way. And it's the way *out,* do you understand?"

They stood wearing rather bruised looks, as people do who've been subject to several minutes' ranting. No one spoke, until Twoflower whispered:

"He often goes on like this, you know. And then he does something very brave."

Rincewind snorted.

There was another dead guard at the top of the stairs. Sudden death seemed to be catching.

And, leaning against the wall, was a bundle of swords. Tied to it was a scroll.

"The Great Wizard has shown us the way for only two minutes and already we have extra luck," said Lotus Blossom.

"Don't touch the swords," said Rincewind.

"But supposing we see more guards? Should we not resist them with every drop of our life's blood?" said Butterfly.

Rincewind looked blank. "No. Run away."

"Ah, yes," said Twoflower. "And live to fight another day. That is an Ankh-Morpork saying."

Rincewind had always assumed that the purpose of running away was to be able to run away another day.

"However," he said, "people don't usually find themselves mysteriously let out of prison with a bunch of weapons handily close by and all the guards out of action. Ever thought of that?"

"And with a map!" said Butterfly.

Her eyes shone. She flourished the scroll.

"It's a map of the way out?" said Rincewind.

"No! To the Emperor's chambers! Look, it has been marked! That's what Herb used to talk about sometimes! He must be in the palace! We should assassinate the Emperor!"

"More luck!" said Twoflower. "But look, you know, I'm sure if we talked to him—"

"Haven't you been listening? We are *not* going to see the Emperor!" hissed Rincewind. "Does it occur to you that guards don't stab themselves? Cells don't suddenly become unlocked? You don't find swords lying around so conveniently and you don't, you really *don't* find maps saying 'This Way, Folks'! And anyway, you can't talk to someone who's a plate of prawn crackers short of a Set Meal A for Two!"

"No," said Butterfly. "We must make the most of this opportunity."

"There will be lots of guards!"

"Well, Great Wizard, you'll have a lot of wishing to do."

"You think I can snap my fingers like *this,* and all the guards would drop dead? Hah! I wish they would!"

"These two out here have," Lotus Blossom reported, from the entrance to the dungeons. She was already in awe of Rincewind. Now she looked positively terrified.

"Coincidence!"

"Let's be serious," said Butterfly. "We have a sympathizer in the palace. Perhaps it is someone risking their lives every moment! We know some of the eunuchs are on our side."

"They've got nothing left to lose, I suppose."

"You have a better idea, Great Wizard?"

"Yes. Back into the cells."

"What?"

"This smells wrong. Would you *really* kill the Emperor? I mean, *really?*"

Butterfly hesitated.

"We've often talked about it. Two Fire Herb said that if we could assassinate the Emperor we would light the torch of freedom . . ."

"Yes. It'd be you, burning. Look, get back in the cells. It's the safest place. I'll lock you in and . . . scout."

"That's a very brave suggestion," said Twoflower. "And typical of the man," he added proudly.

Butterfly gave Rincewind a look he'd come to dread.

"It *is* a good idea," she said. "And I will accompany you."

"Oh, but it's bound to be . . . very dangerous," said Rincewind quickly.

"No harm can possibly come to me when I'm with the Great Wizard," said Butterfly.

"Very true. Very true," said Twoflower. "No harm ever came to me, I know that."

"Besides," his daughter went on, "I have the map. And it would be dreadful if you lost your way and accidentally strayed out of the Forbidden City, wouldn't it?"

Rincewind gave in. It struck him that Twoflower's late wife must have been a remarkably intelligent woman.

"Oh, all right," he said. "But you're not to get in the way. And you're to do what I tell you, okay?"

Butterfly bowed.

"Lead on, O Great Wizard," she said.

"I *knew* it!" said Truckle. "Poison!"

"No, no. You don't eat it. You rub it on your body," said Mr. Saveloy. "Watch. And you get what we in civilization call *clean.*"

Most of the Horde stood waist-deep in the warm water, every man with his hands chastely wrapped around his body. Hamish had refused to relinquish his wheelchair, so only his head was above the surface.

"It's all prickly," said Cohen. "And my skin's peeling off and dissolving."

"That's *not* skin," said Mr. Saveloy. "Haven't *any* of you seen a bath before?"

"Oh, I *seen* one," said Boy Willie. "I killed the Mad Bishop of Pseudopolis in one. You get"—he furrowed his brow—"bubbles and stuff. And fifteen naked maidens."

"Whut?"

"Definitely. Fifteen. Remember it well."

"That's more *like* it," said Caleb.

"All *we've* got to rub is this soap stuff."

"The Emperor is ritually bathed by twenty-two bath women," said Six Beneficent Winds. "I could go and check with the harem eunuchs and wake them up, if you like. It's probably allowable under Entertaining."

The taxman was warming to his new job. He'd worked out that although the Horde, as individuals, had acquired mountains of cash in their careers as barbarian heroes they'd lost almost all of it engaging in the other activities (he mentally catalogued these as Public Relations) necessary to the profession, and therefore were entitled to quite a considerable rebate.

The fact that they were registered with no revenue collecting authority *anywhere** was entirely a secondary point. It was the principle that counted. And the interest, too, of course.

"No, no young women, I insist," said Mr. Saveloy. "You're having a bath to get clean. Plenty of time for young women later."

"Gotta date when all this is over," said Caleb, a little shyly, thinking wistfully of one of the few women he'd ever had a conversation with. "She's got her own farm, she said. I could be all right for a duck."

"I bet Teach don't want you to say that," said Boy Willie. "I bet he'd say you gotta call it a waterfowl."

"Huh, huh, hur!"

"Whut?"

Six Beneficent Winds sidled over to the teacher as the Horde experimented with the bath oil, initially by drinking it.

"I've worked out what it is you're going to steal," he said.

"Oh, yes?" said Mr. Saveloy politely. He was watching Caleb

---

*Except on posters with legends like "Wanted—Dedd."

who, having had it brought home to him that he might have been adopting the wrong approach all his life, was trying to cut his nails with his sword.

"It's the legendary Diamond Coffin of Schz Yu!" said Six Beneficent Winds.

"No. Wrong again."

"Oh."

"Out of the baths, gentlemen," said the teacher. "I think . . . yes . . . you've mastered commerce, social intercourse—"

"—hur, hur, hur . . . sorry—"

"—and the principles of taxation," Mr. Saveloy went on.

"Have we done that? What *are* they, then?" said Cohen.

"You take away almost all the money that the merchants have got," said Six Beneficent Winds, handing him a towel.

"Oh, is that it? I've been doing that for *years*."

"No, you've been taking away *all* the money," said Mr. Saveloy. "That's where you go wrong. You kill too many of them, and the ones you don't kill you leave too poor."

"Sounds *frightfully* good to me," said Truckle, excavating the cretaceous contents of an ear. "Poor merchants, rich us."

"No, no, no!"

"No, no, no?"

"Yes! That's not *civilized*!"

"It's like with sheep," Six Beneficent Winds explained. "You don't tear their skin off all in one go, you just shear them every year."

The Horde looked blank.

"Hunter-gatherers," said Mr. Saveloy, with a touch of hopelessness. "Wrong metaphor."

"It's the marvelous Singing Sword of Wong, isn't it?" whispered Six Beneficent Winds. "That's what you're going to steal!"

"No. In fact, 'steal' is rather the wrong word. Well, anyway, gentlemen . . . you might not yet be civilized but at least you're nice and clean, and many people think this is identical. Time, I think, for . . . action."

The Horde straightened up. This was back in the area they understood.

"To the Throne Room!" said Ghenghiz Cohen.

Six Beneficent Winds wasn't that fast on the uptake, but at last he put two and two together.

"It's the Emperor!" he said, and raised his hand to his mouth in horror tinged with evil delight. "You're going to kidnap him!"

Diamonds glittered when Cohen grinned.

There were two dead guards in the corridor leading to the private Imperial apartments.

"Look, how come you were all taken alive?" whispered Rincewind. "The guards I saw had big swords. How come you're not dead?"

"I suppose they planned to torture us," said Butterfly. "We did injure ten of them."

"Oh? Pasted posters on them, did you? Sang revolutionary songs until they gave in? Listen, someone *wanted* you alive."

The floors sang in the darkness. Every footstep produced a chorus of squeaks and groans, just like the floorboards at the University. But you didn't expect that sort of thing in a nice shiny palace like this.

"They're called nightingale floors," said Butterfly. "The carpenters put little metal collars around the nails so that no one can creep up unawares."

Rincewind looked down at the corpses. Neither man had drawn his sword. He leaned his weight on his left foot. The floor squeaked. Then he leaned on his right foot. The floor groaned.

"This isn't right, then," he whispered. "You can't creep up on someone on a floor like this. So someone they *knew* killed those guards. Let's get out of here . . ."

"We go on," said Butterfly firmly.

"It's a trap. Someone's using you to do their dirty work."

She shrugged. "Turn left by the big jade statue."

It was four in the morning, an hour before dawn. There were guards in the official staterooms, but not very many. After all, this was well inside the Forbidden City, with its high walls and small gates. It wasn't as though anything was going to happen.

Terry Pratchett

It needed a special type of mind to stand guard over some empty rooms all night. One Big River had such a mind, orbiting gently within the otherwise blissful emptiness of his skull.

They'd happily called him One Big River because he was the same size and moved at the same speed as the Hung. Everyone had expected him to become a *tsimo* wrestler, but he'd failed the intelligence test because he hadn't eaten the table.

It was impossible for him to get bored. He just didn't have the imagination. But, since the visor of his huge helmet registered a permanent expression of metal rage, he'd in any case cultivated the art of going to sleep on his feet.

He was dozing happily now, aware only of an occasional squeaking, like that of a very cautious mouse.

The helmet's visor swung up. A voice said: "Would you rather die than betray your Emperor?"

A second voice said: "This is not a trick question."

One Big River blinked, and then turned his gaze downwards. An apparition in a squeaky-wheeled wheelchair had a very large sword pointing at exactly that inconvenient place where his upper armour didn't quite meet his lower armour.

A third voice said: "I should add that the last twenty-nine people who answered wrong are . . . dried shredded fish . . . sorry, dead."

A fourth voice said: "And we're not eunuchs."

One Big River rumbled with the effort of thought.

"I tink I rather live," he said.

A man with diamonds where his teeth should have been gave him a comradely pat on the shoulder. "Good man," he said. "Join the Horde. We could use a man like you. Maybe as a siege weapon."

"Who you?" he said.

"This is Ghenghiz Cohen," said Mr. Saveloy. "Doer of mighty deeds. Slayer of dragons. Ravager of cities. He once bought an apple."

No one laughed. Mr. Saveloy had found that the Horde had no concept whatsoever of sarcasm. Probably no one had ever tried it on them.

One Big River had been raised to do what he was told. Everyone had told him what to do, all through his life. He fell in behind the man with diamond teeth because he was the sort of man you followed when he said "follow."

"But, you know, there are tens of thousands of men who *would* die rather than betray their Emperor," whispered Six Beneficent Winds, as they filed through the corridors.

"I hope so."

"Some of them will be on guard around the Forbidden City. We've avoided them, but they're still there. We'll have to deal with them eventually."

"Oh, good!" said Cohen.

"Bad," said Mr. Saveloy. "That business with the ninjas was just high spirits—"

"—high spirits—" murmured Six Beneficent Winds.

"—but you don't want a big fight out in the open. It'll get messy."

Cohen walked over to the nearest wall, which had a gorgeous pattern of peacocks, and took out his knife.

"Paper," he said. "Bloody paper. Paper walls." He poked his head through. There was a shrill whimper. "Oops, sorry, ma'am. Official wall inspection." He extracted his head, grinning.

"But you can't go through walls!" said Six Beneficent Winds.

"Why not?"

"They're—well, they're the *walls*. What would happen if everyone walked through walls? What do you think doors are for?"

"I think they're for other people," said Cohen. "Which way's that throne room?"

"Whut?"

"This is lateral thinking," explained Mr. Saveloy, as they followed him. "Ghenghiz is quite good at a certain kind of lateral thinking."

"What a lateral?"

"Er. It's a kind of muscle, I believe."

"Thinking with your muscles . . . Yes. I see," said Six Beneficent Winds.

* * *

Rincewind sidled into a space between the wall and a statue of a rather jolly dog with its tongue hanging out.

"What now?" said Butterfly.

"How big's the Red Army?"

"We number many thousands," said Butterfly, defiantly.

"In Hunghung?"

"Oh, no. There is a cadre in every city."

"You know that, do you? You've met them?"

"That would be dangerous. Only Two Fire Herb knows how to contact them . . ."

"Fancy that. Well, do you know what I think? I think someone *wants* a revolution. And you're all so damn respectful and polite he's having his work cut out trying to organize one! But once you've got rebels you can do *anything*."

"That can't be true . . ."

"The rebels in other cities, they do great revolutionary deeds, do they?"

"We hear reports all the time!"

"From our friend Herb?"

Butterfly frowned.

"Yes . . ."

"You're thinking, aren't you?" said Rincewind. "The old brain cells are finally banging together, yes? Good. Have I convinced you?"

"I . . . don't know."

"Now let's go back."

"No. Now I've got to find out if what you're suggesting is true."

"Dying to find out, eh? Good grief, you people make me so *angry*. Look, watch this . . ."

Rincewind strode to the end of the corridor. There was a pair of wide doors, flanked by a pair of jade dragons.

He flung them back.

The room inside was low-ceilinged but large. In the centre, under a canopy, was a bed. It was hard to make out the figure lying there, but it had that certain stillness that suggests the kind of sleep from which there is unlikely to be any kind of awakening.

"You see?" he said. "He's been . . . killed . . . already . . ."

A dozen soldiers were staring at Rincewind in amazement.

Behind him he heard the creaking of the floor and then some whooshing sounds followed by a noise like wet leather being hit against rock.

Rincewind looked at the nearest soldier. The man was holding a sword.

One drop of blood coursed down the blade and, with a brief pause for dramatic effect, fell on to the floor.

Rincewind looked up and raised his hat.

"I do beg your pardon," he said, brightly. "Isn't this room 3B?" And ran for it.

The floors screamed under him, and behind him someone screamed Rincewind's nickname, which was: "Don't let him get away!"

Let me get away, Rincewind prayed, oh, please, let me get away.

He slipped as he turned the corner, skidded through a paper wall and landed in an ornamental fish pond. But Rincewind in full flight had catlike, even messianic abilities. The water barely rippled under his feet as he bounced off the surface and headed away.

Another wall erupted and he was in what was possibly the same corridor.

Behind him, someone landed heavily on a valuable koi.

Rincewind shot forward again.

From; that was the most important factor in any mindless escape. You were always running *from. To* could look after itself.

He cleared a long flight of shallow stone steps, rolled upright at the bottom and set off at random along another corridor.

His legs had sorted themselves out now. First the mad, wild dash to get you out of immediate danger and then the good solid strides to put as much distance as possible between you and it. That was the trick.

History told of a runner who'd run forty miles after a battle to report its successful outcome to those at home. He was traditionally regarded as the greatest runner of all time, but if he'd been reporting news of an *impending* battle he'd have been overtaken by Rincewind.

And yet . . . someone was gaining.

A knife poked through the wall of the throne room and cut a hole large enough to afford space for an upright man or one wheelchair.

There was muttering from the Horde.

"Bruce the Hoon never went in the back way."

"Shut up."

"Never one for back gates, Bruce the Hoon."

"Shut up."

"When Bruce the Hoon attacked Al Khali, he did it right at the main guard tower, with a thousand screaming men on very small horses."

"Yeah, but . . . last I saw of Bruce the Hoon, his head was on a spike."

"All right, I'll grant you that. But at least it was over the main gate. I mean, at least he got in."

"His head did."

"Oh, my . . ."

Mr. Saveloy was gratified. The room they'd stepped into was enough to silence the Horde, if only briefly. It was large, of course, but that hadn't been its only purpose. One Sun Mirror, as he welded the tribes and countries and little island nations together, had wanted a room built which said to chieftains and ambassadors: this is the biggest space you've ever been in, it is more splendid than anything you could ever imagine, and we've got a lot more rooms like this.

He had wanted it to be impressive. He had very clearly wanted it to intimidate mere barbarians so much that they'd give in there and then. Let there be huge statues, he'd said. And vast decorative hangings. Let there be pillars and carvings. Let the visitor be silenced by the sheer magnificence. Let it say to him, "This is civilization, and you can join it or die. Now drop to your knees or be shortened some other way."

The Horde gave it the benefit of their inspection.

Finally Truckle said, "It's all right, I suppose, but not a patch on our chieftain's longhouse back in Skund. It hasn't even got a fire in the middle of the floor, look."

"Gaudy, to my mind."

"Whut?"

"Typically foreign."

"I'd do away with most of this and get some decent straw on the floor, a few shields round the walls."

"Whut?"

"Mind you, get in a few hundred tables and you could have a helluva carouse in here."

Cohen walked across the huge expanse towards the throne, which was under a vast ornamental canopy.

"'S got 'n umbrella over it, look."

"Probably the roof leaks. You can't trust tiles. A good reed thatch'll give you forty years bone dry."

The throne was lacquered wood, but with many precious gems set in it. Cohen sat down.

"Is this it?" he said. "We've done it, Teach?"

"Yes. Of course, now you have to get away with it," said Mr. Saveloy.

"I'm sorry," said Six Beneficent Winds. "What've you done?"

"You know that thing we were here to steal?" said the teacher.

"Yes?"

"It's the Empire."

The taxman's expression didn't change for a few seconds, and then it flowed into a horrified grin.

"I think some breakfast is called for before we go any further," said Mr. Saveloy. "Mr. Winds, perhaps you would be so good as to summon someone?"

The taxman was still grinning fixedly.

"But . . . but . . . you can't conquer an empire like this!" he managed. "You've got to have an army, like the warlords! Just walking in like this . . . It's against the rules! And . . . and . . . there are thousands of guards!"

"Yes, but they're all out there," said Mr. Saveloy.

"Guarding us," said Cohen.

"But they're guarding the *real* Emperor!"

"That's me," said Cohen.

"Oh yeah?" said Truckle. "Who died and made *you* Emperor?"

"No one has to die," said Mr. Saveloy. "It's called usurping."

"That's right," said Cohen. "You just say, see here, Gunga Din, you're out on your ear, okay? Piss off to some island somewhere or—"

"Ghenghiz," said Mr. Saveloy gently, "do you think you could refrain from referring to foreigners in that rather offensive fashion? It's not civilized."

Cohen shrugged.

"You're still going to have big trouble with the guards and things," said Six Beneficent Winds.

"Maybe not," said Cohen. "Tell 'em, Teach."

"Have you ever *seen* the, er, former Emperor?" said Mr. Saveloy. "Mr. Winds?"

"Of course not. Hardly anyone has seen—"

He stopped.

"There you are, then," said Mr. Saveloy. "Very quick on the uptake, Mr. Winds. As befits the Lord High Chief Tax Gatherer."

"But it won't work because—" Six Beneficent Winds stopped again. Mr. Saveloy's words reached his brain.

"Lord High Chief? Me? The black hat *with* the red ruby button?"

"Yes."

"And a feather in it, if you like," said Cohen munificently.

The taxman looked in rapt consideration.

"So . . . if there was, say, a mere District Administrator who was incredibly cruel to his staff, particularly to a hard-working deputy, and thoroughly deserving of a good sound thrashing—"

"As the Lord High Chief Tax Gatherer, of course, that would be entirely your affair."

Six Beneficent Winds' grin now threatened to remove the top of his head.

"On the subject of new taxation," he said, "I've often had this thought that fresh air is all too readily available at far below the cost of production—"

"We will listen to your ideas with extreme interest," said Mr. Saveloy. "In the meantime, please arrange breakfast."

"And have summoned," said Cohen, "all those buggers who think they know what the Emperor looks like."

The pursuer was closing.

Rincewind skidded around a corner and there, blocking the passageway, were three guards. These were not dead. They were alive, and they had got swords.

Someone cannoned into the back of him, pushed him to the ground, and leapt past.

He shut his eyes.

There were a couple of thumps, a groan, and then a very strange metallic noise.

It was a helmet, spinning round and round on the floor.

He was pulled to his feet.

"Are you going to lie around all day?" said Butterfly. "Come on. They're not far behind!"

Rincewind glanced at the recumbent guards, and then loped after the girl.

"How many of them are there?" he managed.

"Seven now. But two of them are limping and one's having trouble breathing. Come *on*."

"You *hit* them?"

"Do you always waste breath like this?"

"Never found anyone who could keep up with me before!"

They turned a corner and almost ran into another guard.

Butterfly didn't even stop. She took a ladylike step, whirled around on one foot, and kicked the man so hard on his ear that he spun on his own axis and landed on his head.

She paused, panted, and tucked a hair back into place.

"We should split up," she said.

"Oh, no!" said Rincewind. "I mean, I must protect you!"

"I'll head back to the others. You lead the guards away some-where—"

"Can you *all* do that?"

"Of course," said Butterfly, testily. "I *told* you we fought the guards. Now, if we split up one of us is bound to escape. The murderers! We were supposed to take the blame for that!"

"Didn't I try to tell you? I thought you *wanted* him dead!"

"Yes, but we're rebels. They were palace guards!"

"Er—"

"No time. See you in Heaven."

She darted away.

"Oh."

Rincewind looked around. It had all gone quiet.

Guards appeared at the end of the corridor, but cautiously, as befitted people who'd just met Butterfly.

"There!"

"Is it her?"

"No, it's him!"

"Get him!"

He accelerated again, rounded a corner, and found that he was in a cul-de-sac that would undoubtedly, given the sounds behind, become a dead end. But there was a pair of doors. He kicked them open, ran inside, and slowed . . .

The room inside was dark, but the sound and air suggested a large space and a certain flatulent component indicated some kind of stable.

There was some light, though, from a fire. Rincewind trotted towards it and saw that it was under a huge cauldron, man-sized, full of boiling rice.

And now that his eyes were accustomed to the gloom he realized that there were shapes lying on slabs along both walls of an enormous room.

They were snoring gently.

They were, in fact, people. They might even have been humans, or at least had humans in their ancestry before someone, hundreds of years ago, had said, "Let's see how big and fat we can breed people. Let's try for really big bastards."

Each giant frame was dressed in what looked like a nappy to Rincewind's eyes and was dozing happily alongside a bowl holding enough rice to explode twenty people, just in case it woke up in the night and felt like a light snack.

A couple of his pursuers appeared in the doorway, and

stopped. Then they advanced, but very cautiously, carefully watching the gently moving mounds.

"Oi, oi, oi!" shouted Rincewind.

The men stopped and stared at him.

"Wakey wakey! Let's see the rising sons!" He grabbed a mighty ladle and banged it on the rice cauldron.

"Up you get! Hands off-er-whatever you can find and on with socks!"

The sleepers stirred.

"Oooorrrrr?"

"Ooooaaaooooooor!"

The room shook as forty tree-trunk legs swung off the slabs. Flesh rearranged itself so that, in the gloom, Rincewind appeared to be being watched by twenty small pyramids.

"Haaaroooooohhhh?"

"Those men," said Rincewind, pointing desperately at his pursuers, who were slowly backing away, "those men have a pork sandwich!"

"Oorrryorrraaah?"

"Oooorrrr?"

"With mustard!"

"Oooorrrr!"

Twenty very small heads turned. A total of eighty specialized neurons fired into life.

And the floor shook. The wrestlers started to move hopefully towards the men, in a slow but deliberate run designed to be halted only by collision with another wrestler or a continent.

"Oooorrr!"

Rincewind dashed for the far door and burst through it. A couple of men were sitting in a small room drinking tea and playing *shibo,* watched by a third.

"The wrestlers are wrestless!" he shouted. "I think you've got a stampede going on!"

A man threw down his *shibo* tiles. "Blast! And it's been at least an hour since they were fed!"

The men grabbed various nets and prods and items of protective clothing, leaving Rincewind alone.

There was another door. He sashayed through it. He'd never

essayed a sashay before, but he reckoned he was due a sashay for quick thinking.

There was another passage. He ran down it, on the basis that absence of pursuit is no reason to stop running.

Lord Hong was folding paper.

He was an expert at it because when he did it he gave it his full attention. Lord Hong had a mind like a knife, although possibly a knife with a curved blade.

The door slid aside. A guard, red in the face from running, threw himself on to the floor.

"O Lord Hong, who is exalted—"

"Yes, indeed," said Lord Hong distantly, essaying a taxing crease. "What has gone wrong this time?"

"My lord?"

"I asked you what has gone wrong."

"Uh . . . we killed the Emperor as directed—"

"By whom?"

"My lord! You commanded it!"

"Did I?" said Lord Hong, folding the paper lengthwise.

The guard shut his eyes. He had a vision, a very short vision, of the future. There was a spike in it. He carried on.

"But the . . . prisoners can't be found anywhere, lord! We heard someone approach and then . . . well, we saw two people, lord. We're chasing them. But the others have vanished."

"No slogans? No revolutionary posters? No *culprits?*"

"No, lord."

"I see. Remain here."

Lord Hong's hands continued with the folding as he looked at the room's other occupant.

"You have something to say, Two Fire Herb?" he said pleasantly.

The revolutionary leader looked sheepish.

"The Red Army has been quite expensive," said Lord Hong. "The printing costs alone . . . And you cannot say I have not helped you. We unlocked the doors and killed the guards and gave your wretched people swords and a map, did we not?

And now I can hardly claim that they killed the Emperor, may he stay dead for ten thousand years, when there is no sign of them. People will ask too many questions. I can hardly kill *everyone*. And we appear to have some barbarians in the building, too."

"Something must have gone wrong, my lord." Herb was hypnotized by the moving hands as they caressed that paper.

"What a pity. I do not like it when things go wrong. Guard? Redeem your miserable self. Take him away. I will have to try a different plan."

"My lord!"

"Yes, Two Fire Herb?"

"When you . . . when we agreed . . . when it was agreed that the Red Army should be turned over to you, you did promise me indemnity."

Lord Hong smiled.

"Oh, yes. I recall. I said, did I not, that I would neither say nor write any order for your death? And I must keep my word, otherwise what am I?"

He folded the last crease and opened his hands, putting the little paper decoration on the lacquered table beside him.

Herb and the guard stared at it.

"Guard . . . take him away," said Lord Hong.

It was a marvellously constructed paper figure of a man.

But there didn't seem to have been enough paper for a head.

The immediate court turned out to be about eighty men, women, and eunuchs, in various states of sleeplessness.

They were astonished at what sat on the throne.

The Horde were quite astonished at the court.

"Who're all them vinegar-faced old baggages at the front?" whispered Cohen, who was idly tossing a throwing knife into the air and catching it again. "I wouldn't even set fire to them."

"They're the wives of former Emperors," hissed Six Beneficent Winds.

"We don't have to marry them, do we?"

"I don't think so."

"Why're their feet so small?" said Cohen. "I like to see big feet on a woman."

Six Beneficent Winds told him. Cohen's expression hardened.

"I'm learning a lot about civilization, I am," he said. "Long fingernails, crippled feet and servants running around without their family jewels. Huh."

"What is going on here, pray?" said a middle-aged man. "Who are you? Who are these old eunuchs?"

"Who're you?" said Cohen. He drew his sword. "I need to know so's it can be put on your gravestone—"

"I wonder if I might effect some introductions at this point?" said Mr. Saveloy. He stepped forward.

"This," he said, "is Ghenghiz Cohen—put it away, Ghenghiz—who is technically a barbarian, and this is his Horde. They have overrun your city. And you are—?"

"Barbarian invaders?" said the man haughtily, ignoring him. "Barbarian invaders come in their thousands! Big screaming men on little horses!"

"I *told* you," said Truckle. "But would anyone listen?"

"—and there is fire, terror, rapine, looting, and blood in the streets!"

"We haven't had breakfast yet," said Cohen, tossing his knife into the air again.

"Hah! I would rather die than submit to such as you!"

Cohen shrugged. "Why didn't you say earlier?"

"Oops," said Six Beneficent Winds.

It was a very accurate throw.

"Who *was* he, anyway?" said Cohen, as the body folded up. "Anyone know who he was?"

"Ghenghiz," said Mr. Saveloy, "I've kept meaning to tell you: when people say they'd rather die, they don't really *mean* they'd rather die. Not always."

"Why'd they say it, then?"

"It's the done thing."

"Is this civilization again?"

"I'm afraid so."

"Let's settle this once and for all, shall we?" said Cohen. He stood up. "Hands up those who'd rather die than have me as Emperor."

"Anyone?" said Mr. Saveloy.

Rincewind trotted along another passage. Was there no outside to this place? Several times he thought he'd found an exit, but it led only to a courtyard within the huge building, filled with tinkling fountains and willow trees.

And the place was waking up. There were—

—running steps behind him.

A voice shouted, "Hey—"

He dived for the nearest door.

The room beyond was full of steam. It roiled in great billowing clouds. He could dimly make out a figure toiling at the huge wheel and the words "torture chamber" crossed his mind until the smell of soap replaced them with the word "laundry." Rather wan but incredibly clean figures looked up from their vats and watched him with barely a hint of interest.

They did not look like people in close touch with current events.

He half ran, half sauntered between the bubbling cauldrons.

"Keep it up. Good man. That's it, scrub, scrub, scrub. Let me see those wringers wringing. Well done. Is there another door out of here? Good bubbles there, very good bubbles. Ah . . ."

One of the laundry workers, who appeared to be in charge, gave him a suspicious glare and seemed to be about to say something.

Rincewind dodged through a courtyard crisscrossed with washing lines and stopped, panting, with his back to a wall.

Although it was against his general principles, it was perhaps time to stop and think.

People were chasing him. That is to say, they were chasing a running figure in a faded red robe and a very charred pointy hat.

It took a great effort for Rincewind to come to terms with the idea, but it was just possible that if he was *wearing something else* he might not be chased.

On the line in front of him, shirts and trousers flapped in the breeze. Their construction was to tailoring in the same way that woodchopping is to carpentry. Someone had mastered the art of the tube, and left it at that. They looked just like the clothes nearly everyone wore in Hunghung.

The palace was almost a city in its own right, said the voice of reason. It must be full of people on all sorts of errands, it added.

It would mean . . . taking off our hat, it added.

Rincewind hesitated. It would be hard for a non-wizard to grasp the enormity of the suggestion. A wizard would sooner go without his robe and trousers than forgo his hat. Without his hat, people might think he was an *ordinary person*.

There was shouting in the distance.

The voice of reason could see that if it wasn't careful it was going to end up as dead as the rest of Rincewind and added sarcastically: all right, keep our wretched hat. Our damn hat is why we're in this mess in the first place. Perhaps you think you're going to have a head left to wear it on?

Rincewind's hands, also aware that times were going to be extremely interesting and very short unless they took matters into themselves, reached out slowly and removed a pair of pants and a shirt and rammed them inside his robe.

The door burst open. There were *still* guards behind him, and a couple of the *tsimo* herders had joined in the chase. One of them waved a prod in Rincewind's direction.

He plunged towards an archway and out into a garden.

It had a little pagoda. It had willow trees, and a pretty lady on a bridge feeding the birds.

And a man painting a plate.

Cohen rubbed his hands together.

"No one? Good. That's all sorted, then."

"Ahem."

A small man at the front of the crowd made a great play of keeping his hands to himself, but said:

"Excuse me, but . . . what would happen in the hypothetical situation of us calling the guards and denouncing you?"

"We'd kill you all before they were halfway through the

door," said Cohen, matter of factly. "Any more questions?" he added, to a chorus of gasps.

"Er . . . the Emperor . . . that is to say, the *last* Emperor . . . had some very special guards . . ."

There was a tinkling sound. Something small and multi-pointed rolled down the steps and spun round on the floor. It was a throwing star.

"Met them," said Boy Willie.

"Fine, fine," said the little man. "That all seems in order. Ten Thousand Years to the Emperor!"

The shout was taken up, a little raggedly.

"What's your name, young man?" said Mr. Saveloy.

"Four Big Horns, my lord."

"Very good. Very good. I can see that you will go a long way. What is your job?"

"I am Grand Assistant to the Lord Chamberlain, my lord."

"Which one of you is the Lord Chamberlain?"

Four Big Horns pointed to the man who had preferred to die.

"There we are, you see?" said Mr. Saveloy. "Promotion comes fast to adaptable people, Lord Chamberlain. And now, the Emperor will breakfast."

"And what is his pleasure?" said the new Lord Chamberlain, endeavoring to look bright and adaptable.

"All sorts of things. But right now, big lumps of meat and lots of beer. You will find the Emperor very easy to cater for." Mr. Saveloy smiled the knowing little smile he sometimes smiled when he knew he was the only one seeing the joke. "The Emperor doesn't favor what he calls 'fiddly foreign muck full of eyeballs and suchlike' and much prefers simple, wholesome food like sausages, which are made of miscellaneous animal organs minced up in a length of intestine. Ahaha. But if you want to please him, just keep up the big lumps of meat. Isn't that so, my lord?"

Cohen had been gazing at the assembled courtiers. When you've survived for ninety years all the attacks that can be thrown at you by men, women, trolls, dwarfs, giants, green things with lots of legs, and, on one occasion, an enraged lobster, you can learn a lot by looking at faces.

Terry Pratchett

"Eh?" said Cohen. "Oh. Yep. Right enough. Big lumps. Here, Mr. Taxman . . . what do these people *do* all day?"

"What would you like them to do?"

"I'd like them to bugger off."

"Sorry, my lord?"

"[Complicated pictogram]," said Mr. Saveloy. The new Lord Chamberlain looked a little startled.

"What, *here?*"

"It's a figure of speech, lad. He just means he wants everyone to go away quickly."

The court scurried out. A sufficiently complicated pictogram is worth a thousand words.

After the stampede the artist Three Solid Frogs got to his feet, retrieved his brush from his nostril, pulled his easel out of a tree, and tried to think placid thoughts.

The garden was not what it had been.

The willow tree was bent. The pagoda had been demolished by an out-of-control wrestler, who had eaten the roof. The doves had flown. The little bridge had been broken. His model, the concubine Jade Fan, had run off crying after she'd managed to scramble out of the ornamental pond.

And someone had stolen his straw hat.

Three Solid Frogs adjusted what remained of his dress and endeavored to compose himself.

The plate with his sketch on had been smashed, of course.

He pulled another one out of his bag and reached for his palette.

There was a huge footprint in the middle of it . . .

He wanted to cry. He'd had such a *good* feeling about this picture. He just *knew* it would be one that people would remember for a long time. And the colors? Did anyone *understand* how much vermilion cost these days?

He pulled himself together. So there was only blue left. Well, he'd show them . . .

He tried to ignore the devastation in front of him and concentrated on the picture in his mind.

194

"Let me see, now," he thought. "Jade Fan being pursued over a bridge by man waving his arms and screaming, 'Get out of the way!' followed by man with prod, three guards, five laundry men, and a wrestler unable to stop."

He had to simplify it a bit, of course.

The pursuers rounded a corner, except for the wrestler, who wasn't built for such a difficult maneuver.

"Where'd he go?"

They were in a courtyard. There were pigsties on one side, and middens on the other.

And, in the middle of the courtyard, a pointy hat.

One of the guards reached out and grabbed a colleague's arm before the man stepped forward.

"Steady now," he said.

"It's just a hat."

"So where's the rest of him? He couldn't have just . . . disappeared . . . into . . ."

They backed away.

"You heard about him too?"

"They said he blew a hole in the wall just by waving his hands!"

"That's nothing! I heard he appeared on an invisible dragon up in the mountains!"

"What shall we tell Lord Hong?"

"I don't want to be blown to pieces!"

"*I* don't want to tell Lord Hong we lost him. We're in enough trouble already. And I've only just paid for this helmet."

"Well . . . we could take the hat. That'd be evidence."

"Right. You pick it up."

"Me? *You* pick it up!"

"It might be surrounded by terrible spells."

"Really? So it's all right for *me* to touch it? Thank you! Get one of them to pick it up!"

The laundry men backed away, the Hunghungese habit of obedience evaporating like morning dew. The soldiers weren't the only ones to have heard rumors.

"Not us!"

"Got a rush order for socks!"

The guard turned. A peasant was stumbling out of one of the pigsties, carrying a sack, his face covered by his big straw hat.

"Hey, you!"

The man dropped to his knees and banged his head on the ground.

"Don't kill me!"

The guards exchanged a glance.

"We ain't going to kill you," said one of them. "We just want you to try and pick up that hat over there."

"What hat, o mighty warrior?"

"That hat there! Right now!"

The man crawled crabwise across the cobbles.

"This hat, o great lord?"

"Yes!"

The man's fingers crept over the stones and prodded the hat's ragged brim.

Then he screamed.

"Your wife is a big hippo! My face is melting! My face is meltinnnnggg!"

Rincewind waited until the sound of fleeing sandals had quite faded, and then stood up, dusted off his hat, and put it in the sack.

That had gone a lot better than he'd expected. So there was another valuable thing to know about the Empire: no one looked at peasants. It must be the clothes and the hat. No one but the common people dressed like that, so anyone dressed like that must be a common person. It was the advertising principle of a wizard's hat, but in reverse. You were careful and polite around people in a pointy hat, in case they took a very physical offense, whereas someone in a big straw hat was a suitable target for a "Hey, you!" and a—

It was at exactly this point that someone behind him shouted, "Hey, you!" and hit Rincewind across the shoulders with a stick.

The irate face of a servant appeared in front of him. The man waved a finger in front of Rincewind's nose.

"You are late! You are a bad man! Get inside right now!"

"I—"

The stick hit Rincewind again. The servant pointed at a distant doorway.

"Insolence! Shame! Go to work!"

Rincewind's brain prepared the words: Oh, so we think we're Clever-san just because we've got a big stick, do we? Well, I happen to be a great wizard and you know what you can do with your big stick.

Somewhere between the brain and his mouth they became: "Yessir! Right away!"

The Horde were left alone.

"Well, gentlemen, we did it," said Mr. Saveloy eventually. "You have the world on a plate."

"All the treasure we want," said Truckle.

"That's right."

"Let's not hang around, then," said Truckle. "Let's get some sacks."

"There's no *point*," said Mr. Saveloy. "You'd only be stealing from yourselves. This is an *Empire*. You don't just shove it in a bag and divvy it up at the next campfire!"

"How about the ravishing?"

Mr. Saveloy sighed. "There are, I understand, three hundred concubines in the imperial harem. I'm sure they will be very pleased to see you, although matters will be improved if you take your boots off."

The old men wore the puzzled look such as might be worn by fish trying to understand the concept of the bicycle.

"We ought to take just small stuff," said Boy Willie at last. "Rubies and emeralds, for preference."

"And chuck a match on the place as we go out," said Vincent. "These paper walls and all this lacquered wood should go up a treat."

"No, no, no!" said Mr. Saveloy. "The vases in this room alone are priceless!"

"Nah, too big to carry. Can't get 'em onna horse."

"But I've shown you civilization!" said Mr. Saveloy.

"Yeah. It's all right to visit. Ain't that so, Cohen?"

Cohen was hunched down in the throne, glaring at the far wall. "What's that?"

"I'm saying we take everything we can carry and head off back home, right?"

"Home . . . yeah . . ."

"That was the Plan, yeah?"

Cohen didn't look at Mr. Saveloy's face.

"Yeah . . . the Plan . . ." he said.

"It's a good plan," said Truckle. "Great idea. You move in as boss? Fine. Great scam. Saves trouble. None of that fiddling with locks and things. So we'll all be off home, okay? With all the treasure we can carry?"

"What for?" said Cohen.

"What for? It's *treasure.*"

Cohen seemed to reach a decision.

"What did you spend your last haul on, Truckle? You said you got three sacks of gold and gems from that haunted castle."

Truckle looked puzzled, as if Cohen had asked what purple smelled like.

"Spend it on? *I* dunno. You know how it is. What's it matter what you spend it on? It's *loot.* Anyway . . . what do you spend yours on?"

Cohen sighed.

Truckle gaped at him.

"You're not thinking of *really* staying here?" He glared at Mr. Saveloy. "Have you two been cooking up something?"

Cohen drummed his fingers on the arm of the throne. "You said go home," he said. "Where to?"

"Well . . . wherever . . ."

"And Hamish there—"

"Whut? Whut?"

"I mean . . . he's a hundred and five, right? Time to settle down, maybe?"

"Whut?"

"Settle down?" said Truckle. "*You* tried it once. Stole a farm and said you was goin' to raise pigs! Gave it up after . . . What was it? . . . three hours?"

"Whutzeesayin'? Whutzeesayin'?"

"He said IT'S TIME YOU SETTLED DOWN, Hamish."

"Bugrthat!"

The kitchens were in uproar. Half the court had ended up there, in most cases for the first time. The place was as crowded as a street market, through which the servants tried to go about their business as best they could.

The fact that one of them seemed a little unclear as to what his business actually consisted of was quite unnoticed in the turmoil.

"Did you *smell* him?" said Lady Two Streams. "The *stink!*"

"Like a hot day in a pig yard!" said Lady Peach Petal.

"*I'm* pleased to say I have never experienced that," said Lady Two Streams haughtily.

Lady Jade Night, who was rather younger than the other two, and who had been rather attracted to Cohen's smell of unwashed lion, said nothing.

The head cook said: "Just that? Big lumps? Why doesn't he just eat a cow while he's about it?"

"You wait till you hear about this devil food called *sausage*," said the Lord Chamberlain.

"Big lumps." The cook was almost in tears. "Where's the skill in big lumps of meat? Not even sauce? I'd rather die than simply heat up big lumps of meat!"

"Ah," said the new Lord Chamberlain, "I should think very carefully about that. The new Emperor, may he have a bath for ten thousand years, tends to interpret that as a request—"

The babble of voices stopped. The cause of the sudden silence was one small, sharp noise. It was a cork, popping.

Lord Hong had a Grand Vizier's talent for apparently turning up out of nowhere. His gaze swept the kitchens. It was certainly the only housework that he had ever done.

He stepped forward. He'd taken a small black bottle from out of the sleeve of his robe.

"Bring me the meat," he said. "The sauce will take care of itself."

The assembled people watched with horrified interest. Poison was all part of the Hunghungese court etiquette but people generally did it while hidden from sight somewhere, out of good manners.

"Is there anyone," said Lord Hong, "who has anything they would like to say?"

His gaze was like a scythe. As it swung around the room people wavered, and hesitated, and fell.

"Very well," said Lord Hong. "I would rather die than see a . . . *barbarian* on the Imperial throne. Let him have his . . . big lumps. Bring me the meat."

There was movement in the ground, and the sound of shouting and the thump of a stick. A peasant scuttled forward, reluctantly wheeling a huge covered dish on a trolley.

At the sight of Lord Hong he pushed the trolley aside, flung himself forward and grovelled.

"I avert my gaze from your . . . an orchard in a favorable position . . . *damn* . . . countenance, o lord."

Lord Hong prodded the prone figure with his foot.

"It is good to see the arts of respect maintained," he observed. "Remove the lid."

The man got up and, still bowing and ducking, lifted the cover.

Lord Hong upended the bottle and held it there until the last drop had hissed out. His audience was transfixed.

"And now let it be taken to the barbarians," he said.

"Certainly, your celestial . . . ink brush . . . willow frond . . . righteousness."

"Where are you from, peasant?"

"Bes Pelargic, o lord."

"Ah. I thought so."

The big bamboo doors slid back. The new Lord Chamberlain stepped in, followed by a caravan of trolleys.

"Breakfast, o lord of a thousand years," he said. "Big lumps of pig, big lumps of goat, big lumps of ox, and seven fried rice."

One of the servants lifted the lid of a dish. "But take my tip and don't go for this pork," he said. "It's been poisoned."

The Chamberlain spun around.

"Insolent pig! You will die for this."

"It's Rincewind, isn't it?" said Cohen. "*Looks* like Rincewind—"

"Got my hat here somewhere," said Rincewind. "Had to stuff it down my trousers—"

"Poison?" said Cohen. "You sure?"

"Well, okay, it was a black bottle and it had a skull and crossbones on it and when he tipped it out it smoked," said Rincewind, as Mr. Saveloy helped him up. "Was it anchovy essence? I don't *think* so."

"Poison," said Cohen. "I *hate* poisoners. Just about the worst sort, poisoners. Creeping around, putting muck in a man's grub . . ."

He glared at the Chamberlain.

"Was it you?" He looked at Rincewind and jerked a thumb towards the cowering Chamberlain. "Was it him? Because if it was he's going to get done to him what I did to the mad Snake Priests of Start, and this time I'll use both thumbs!"

"No," said Rincewind. "It was someone they called Lord Hong. But they all watched him do it."

A little scream erupted from the Lord Chamberlain. He threw himself to the floor and was about to kiss Cohen's foot until he realized that this would have about the same effect as eating the pork.

"Mercy, o celestial being! We are all pawns in the hands of Lord Hong!"

"What's so special about Lord Hong, then?"

"He's . . . a fine man!" the Chamberlain gibbered. "I won't say a word against Lord Hong! I certainly don't believe it's true that he has spies everywhere! Long life to Lord Hong, that's what I say!"

He risked looking up and found the point of Cohen's sword just in front of his eyes.

"Yeah, but right now who're you more frightened of? Me or this Lord Hong?"

"Uh . . . Lord Hong!"

Cohen raised an eyebrow. "I'm impressed. Spies everywhere, eh?"

He looked around the huge room and his gaze came to rest on a very large vase. He sauntered over to it and raised the lid.

"You okay in there?"

"Er . . . yes?" said a voice from the depths of the vase.

"Got everythin' you want? Spare notebook? Potty?"

"Er . . . yes?"

"Would you like, oh, let's say about sixty gallons of boiling water?"

"Er . . . no?"

"Would you rather die than betray Lord Hong?"

"Er . . . can I have a moment to think about it, please?"

"No problem. It takes a long time to heat the water in any case. As you were, then."

He replaced the lid.

"One Big Mother?" he said.

"That's One Big *River*, Ghenghiz," said Mr. Saveloy.

The guard rumbled into life.

"Just you watch this vase and if it moves again you do to it what I once did to the Green Necromancer of the Night, all right?"

"Don't know what that was you did, lord," said the soldier.

Cohen told him. One Big River beamed. From inside the jar came the noise of someone trying not to be sick.

Cohen strolled back to the throne.

"So tell me a bit more about Lord Hong, then," he said.

"He's the Grand Vizier," said the Chamberlain.

Cohen and Rincewind looked at one another.

"That's right. And everyone knows," said Rincewind, "that Grand Viziers are *always*—"

"—complete and utter bastards," said Cohen. "Dunno why. Give 'em a turban with a point in the middle and their moral wossname just gets eaten away. I always kill 'em soon as I meet 'em. Saves time later on."

"I *thought* there was something fishy about him as soon as I saw him," said Rincewind. "Look, Cohen—"

"That's *Emperor* Cohen to you," said Truckle. "I've never trusted wizards, mister. Never trusted any man in a dress."

"Rincewind's all right—" said Cohen.

"Thank you!" said Rincewind.

"—but a bloody useless wizard."

"I just happened to risk my neck to save you, thank you so very much," said Rincewind. "Look, some friends of mine are in the prison block. Could you . . . *Emperor?*"

"Sort of," said Cohen.

"Temp'ry," said Truckle.

"Technically," said Mr. Saveloy.

"Does that mean you can get my friends somewhere safe? I think Lord Hong has murdered the old Emperor and wants them to take the blame. I'm just hoping he won't believe they'll be hiding in the cells."

"Why in the cells?" said Cohen.

"Because if I had the chance to get away from Lord Hong's cells I would," said Rincewind, fervently. "No one in their right minds'd go back inside if they thought they had a chance to get away."

"Okay," said Cohen. "Boy Willie, One Big Mother, go and round up some of your mates and bring those people here."

"Here?" said Rincewind. "I wanted them to be somewhere safe!"

"Well, *we're* here," said Cohen. "We can protect 'em."

"Who's going to protect you?"

Cohen ignored this. "Lord Chamberlain," he said, "I don't 'spect Lord Hong'll be around but . . . in the court was a guy with a nose like a badger. A fat bugger, he was, with a big pink hat. And a skinny woman with a face like a hatful of pins."

"That would be Lord Nine Mountains and Lady Two Streams," said the Lord Chamberlain. "Er. You are not angry with me, o lord?"

"Gods bless you, no," said Cohen. "In fact, mister, I'm so impressed I'm going to give you extra responsibilities."

"Lord?"

"Food taster, for a start. And now go and fetch them other two. Didn't like the look of them at *all*."

Nine Mountains and Two Streams were ushered in a few moments later. Their merest glance from Cohen to the untouched

203

food would have passed entirely unnoticed by those who weren't watching for it.

Cohen nodded cheerfully at them. "Eat it," he said.

"My lord! I had a large breakfast! I am entirely full!" said Nine Mountains.

"That's a pity," said Cohen. "One Big Mother, before you go off just see Mr. Nine Mountains over there and make some room in him so he can have another breakfast. The same goes for the lady, too, if I don't hear chomping in the next five seconds. A good mouthful of everything, understand? With lots of sauce."

One Big River drew his sword.

The two nobles stared fixedly at the glistening mounds.

"Looks good to me," said Cohen conversationally. "The way *you're* looking at it, anyone'd think there was something wrong with it."

Nine Mountains gingerly put a piece of pork into his mouth.

"Extremely good," he said, indistinctly.

"Now *swallow*," said Cohen.

The mandarin gulped.

"Marvelous," he said. "And now, if your excellency will excuse me, I—"

"Don't rush off," said Cohen. "We don't want you accidentally sticking your fingers down your throat or anything like that, do we?"

Nine Mountains hiccuped.

Then he hiccupped again.

Smoke appeared to be rising from the bottom of his robe.

The Horde dived for cover just as the explosion removed an area of floorboards, a circular part of the ceiling and all of Lord Nine Mountains.

A black hat with a ruby button on it spun around on the floor for a moment.

"That's just like me and pickled onions," said Vincent.

Lady Two Streams was standing with her eyes shut.

"Not hungry?" said Cohen.

She nodded.

Cohen leaned back.

"One Big Mother?"

"It's 'River,' Cohen," said Mr. Saveloy, as the guard lumbered forward.

"Take her with you and put her in one of the dungeons. See that she has plenty to eat, if you know what I mean."

"Yes, excellency."

"And Mr. Chamberlain here can push off down to the kitchen again and tell the chef *he's* going to share what we eat this time, and he's gonna eat it *first,* all right?"

"Yes indeed, excellency."

"Call this living?" Caleb burst out, as the Lord Chamberlain scuttled away. "This is being Emperor, is it? Can't even trust the food? We'll probably be murdered in our beds!"

"Can't see *you* being murdered in your bed," said Truckle.

"Yeah, 'cos you're never in it," said Cohen.

He walked over to the big jar and gave it a kick.

"You getting all this?"

"Yessir," said the jar.

There was some laughter. But it had an edge of nervousness. Mr. Saveloy realized that the Horde weren't used to this. If a true barbarian wanted to kill someone during a meal, he'd invite him in with all his henchmen, sit them down, get them drunk and sleepy and then summon his own men from hiding places to massacre them instantly in a straight-forward, no-nonsense and honorable manner. It was completely fair. The "get them drunk and butcher the lot of them" stratagem was the oldest trick in the book, or would have been if barbarians bothered with books. Anyone falling for it would be doing the world a favor by being slaughtered over the pudding. But at least you could trust the *food.* Barbarians didn't poison food. You never knew when you might be short of a mouthful yourself.

"Excuse me, your excellency," said Six Beneficent Winds, who had been hovering, "I think Lord Truckle is right. Er. I know a little history. The correct method of succession is to wade to the throne through seas of blood. That is what Lord Hong is planning to do."

"You say? Seas of blood, right?"

"Or over a mountain of skulls. That's an option, too."

"But . . . but . . . I thought the Imperial crown was handed down from father to son," said Mr. Saveloy.

"Well, yes," said Six Beneficent Winds. "I suppose that could happen in theory."

"You said once we were at the top of the pyramid everyone'd do what we said," said Cohen to Mr. Saveloy.

Truckle looked from one to the other. "You two *planned* this?" he said accusingly. "This is what it's all been about, isn't it? All that learnin' to be civilized? And right at the start you just said it was going to be a really big theft! Eh? I thought we were just going to nick a load of stuff and push off! Loot and pillage, that's the way—"

"Oh, loot and pillage, loot and pillage, I've had it up to here with loot and pillage!" said Mr. Saveloy. "Is that all you can think of, looting and pillaging?"

"Well, there used to be ravishing, too," said Vincent wistfully.

"I hate to tell you, but they've got a point, Teach," said Cohen. "Fightin' and lootin' . . . that's what we do. I ain't happy with all this bowing and scraping business. I ain't sure if I was cut out for civilization."

Mr. Saveloy rolled his eyes. "Even you, Cohen? You're all so . . . *dim-witted!*" he snapped. "I don't know why I bother! I mean, look at you! You know what you are? You're legends!"

The Horde stepped back. No one had ever seen Teach lose his temper before.

"From *legendum*, which means 'something written down'," said Mr. Saveloy. "Books, you know. Reading and writing. Which incidentally is as alien to you as the Lost City of Ee—"

Truckle's hand went up, a little nervously.

"Actually, I once discovered the Lost City of—"

"Shut up! I'm saying . . . What was I saying? . . . yes . . . you don't read, do you? You never learned to read? Then you've wasted half your life. You could have been accumulating pearls of wisdom instead of rather shoddy gems. It's just as well people read about you and don't meet you face to face because, gentlemen, you are a big disappointment!"

Rincewind watched, fascinated, waiting for Mr. Saveloy to

have his head cut off. But this didn't seem about to happen. He was possibly too angry to be beheaded.

"What have you actually *done,* gentlemen? And don't tell me about stolen jewels and demon lords. What have you done that's *real?*"

Truckle raised a hand again.

"Well, I once killed all four of the—"

"Yes, yes, yes," said Mr. Saveloy. "You killed *this* and you stole *that* and you defeated the giant man-eating avocados of somewhere else, but . . . it's all . . . *stuff.* It's just wallpaper, gentlemen! It never changes anything! No one *cares!* Back in Ankh-Morpork I've taught boys who think you are myths. That's what you've achieved. They don't believe you ever really existed. They think someone made you up. You're *stories,* gentlemen. When you die no one will know, because they think you're already dead."

He paused for breath, and then continued more slowly. "But here . . . here you *could* be real. You could stop playing at your lives. You could take this ancient and somewhat rotten Empire back into the world. At least . . ." he trailed off. "That's what I'd hoped. I really thought that, perhaps, we might actually achieve something . . ."

He sat down.

The Horde stood staring at its various feet or wheels.

"Um. Can I say something? The warlords will all be against you," said Six Beneficent Winds. "They're out there now, with their armies. Normally they'd fight amongst themselves, but they'll *all* fight you."

"They'd rather have some poisoner like this Hong instead of me?" said Cohen. "But he's a bastard!"

"Yes, but . . . he's *their* bastard, you see."

"We could hold out here. This place has got thick walls," said Vincent. "The ones not made of paper, that is."

"Don't think about that," said Truckle. "Not a siege. Sieges are messy. I hate eating boots and rats."

"Whut?"

"He said WE DON'T WANT A SIEGE WHERE WE HAVE TO EAT BOOTS AND RATS, Hamish."

"Run outa legs, have we?"

"How many soldiers have they got?" said Cohen.

"I think . . . six or seven hundred thousand," said the taxman.

"Excuse us," said Cohen, getting off the throne. "I have to join my Horde."

The Horde went into a huddle. There was an occasional "Whut?" in the hoarse whispered interchanges. Then Cohen turned round.

"Seas of blood, wasn't it?" he said.

"Er. Yes," said the taxman.

The huddle resumed.

After some further exchanges Truckle's head poked up.

"Did you say *mountain* of skulls?" he said.

"Yes. Yes, I think that's what I said," said the taxman. He glanced nervously at Rincewind and Mr. Saveloy, who shrugged.

Whisper, whisper, Whut . . .

"Excuse me?"

"Yes?"

"About how big a mountain? Skulls don't pile up that well."

"I don't know how big a mountain! A lot of skulls!"

"Just checking."

The Horde seemed to reach a decision. They turned to face the other men.

"We're going to fight," said Cohen.

"Yes, you should have said all that about skulls and blood before," said Truckle.

"We'll show ye whether we'm dead or not!" cackled Hamish.

Mr. Saveloy shook his head.

"I think you must have misheard. The odds are a hundred thousand to one!" he said.

"I reckon *that*'ll show people we're still alive," said Caleb.

"Yes, but the whole point of my plan was to show you that you could get to the top of the pyramid without having to fight your way up," said Mr. Saveloy. "It really is possible in such a stale society. But if you try to fight hundreds of thousands of men you'll *die*."

And then, to his surprise, he found himself adding: "Probably."

The Horde grinned at him.

"Big odds don't frighten us," said Truckle.

"We *like* big odds," said Caleb.

"Y'see, Teach, odds of a thousand to one ain't a lot worse than ten to one," said Cohen. "The reasons bein'—" He counted on his fingers. "One, your basic soldier who's fightin' for pay rather than his life ain't goin' to stick *his* neck out when there's all these other blokes around who might as well do the business, and, two, not very many of 'em are goin' to be able to get near us at one time and they'll all be pushin' and shovin', and . . ." He looked at his fingers with an expression of terminal calculation.

". . . Three . . ." said Mr. Saveloy, hypnotized by this logic.

". . . three, right . . . Half the time when they swings their swords they'll hit one of their mates, savin' us a bit of effort. See?"

"But even if that were true it'd only work for a little while," Mr. Saveloy protested. "Even if you killed as many as two hundred you'd be tired and there'd be fresh troops attacking you."

"Oh, they'd be tired, too," said Cohen cheerfully.

"Why?"

"Because by then, to get to us, they'd have to be running uphill."

"That's logic, that is," said Truckle, approvingly.

Cohen slapped the shaken teacher on the back.

"Don't you worry about a thing," he said. "If we've got the Empire by your kind of plan, we'll keep it by *our* kind of plan. You've shown us civilization, so we'll show you barbarism."

He walked a few steps and then turned, an evil glint in his eye. "Barbarism? Hah! When we kills people we do it there and then, lookin' 'em in the eye, and we'd be happy to buy 'em a drink in the next world, no harm done. I never knew a barbarian who cut up people slowly in little rooms, or tortured women to make 'em look pretty, or put poison in people's grub. Civilization? If that's civilization, you can shove it where the sun don't shine!"

"Whut?"

"He said SHOVE IT WHERE THE SUN DOESN'T SHINE, Hamish."

"Ah? Bin there."

"But there is more to civilization than that!" said Mr. Saveloy. "There's . . . music, and literature, and the concept of justice, and the ideals of—"

The bamboo doors slid aside. As one man, joints creaking, the Horde turned with weapons raised.

The men in the doorway were taller and much more richly dressed than the peasants, and they moved in the manner of people who are used to there being no one in the way. Ahead of them, though, was a trembling peasant holding a red flag on a stick. He was prodded into the room at swordpoint.

"Red flag?" whispered Cohen.

"It means they want to parley," said Six Beneficent Winds.

"You know . . . it's like our white flag of surrender," said Mr. Saveloy.

"Never heard of it," said Cohen.

"It means you mustn't kill anyone until they're ready."

Mr. Saveloy tried to shut out the whispers behind him.

"Why don't we just invite them to dinner and massacre them all when they're drunk?"

"You heard the man. There's seven hundred thousand of them."

"Ah? So it'd have to be something simple with pasta, then."

A couple of the lords strode into the middle of the room. Cohen and Mr. Saveloy went to meet them.

"And you, too," said Cohen, grabbing Rincewind as he tried to back away. "You're a weasely man with words in a tight spot, so come on."

Lord Hong regarded them with the expression of a man whose ancestry had bequeathed to him the ability to look down on everything.

"My name is Lord Hong. I am the Emperor's Grand Vizier. I order you to quit these premises immediately and submit to judgment."

Mr. Saveloy turned to Cohen.

"Ain't gonna," said Cohen.

Mr. Saveloy tried to think.

"Um, how shall I phrase this? Ghenghiz Cohen, leader of

the Silver Horde, presents his compliments to Lord Hong but—"

"Tell him he can stuff it," said Cohen.

"I think, Lord Hong, that perhaps you may have perceived the general flow of opinion here," said Mr. Saveloy.

"Where are the rest of your barbarians, peasant?" he demanded.

Rincewind watched Mr. Saveloy. The old teacher seemed at a loss for words this time.

The wizard wanted to run away. But Cohen had been right. Mad as it sounded, it was probably safer to be near him. Running away would put him closer, sooner or later, to Lord Hong.

Who believed that there were a lot of *other* barbarians somewhere . . .

"I tell you this, and this only," said Lord Hong. "If you quit the Forbidden City now, your deaths, at least, will be quick. And then your heads and significant parts will be paraded through the cities of the Empire so that people will know of the terrible punishment."

"Punishment?" said Mr. Saveloy.

"For killing the Emperor."

"We ain't killed no Emperor," said Cohen. "I've got nothing *against* killing Emperors, but we ain't killed one."

"He was killed in his bed an hour ago," said Lord Hong.

"Not by us," said Mr. Saveloy.

"By you," said Rincewind. "Only it's against the rules to kill the Emperor so you wanted it to look as though the Red Army did it."

Lord Hong looked at him as if seeing him for the first time and less than happy about doing so.

"In the circumstances," said Lord Hong, "I doubt that anyone will believe you."

"What will happen if we yield now?" said Mr. Saveloy. "I like to know these things."

"Then you will die very slowly in . . . interesting ways."

"That's the saga of my life," said Cohen. "I've *always* been dying very slowly in interesting ways. What's it to be? Street fighting? House to house? Free for all or what?"

"In the real world," said one of the other lords, "we *battle*. We do not scuffle like barbarians. Our armies will meet on the plain before the city."

"Before the city what?"

"He means in front of the city, Cohen."

"Ah. Civilized talk again. When?"

"Dawn tomorrow!"

"Okay," said Cohen. "It'll give us an appetite for our breakfast. Anything else we can do for you?"

"How big is your army, barbarian?"

"You would not believe how big," said Cohen, which was probably true. "We have overrun countries. We have wiped whole cities off the map. Where my army passes, nothing grows."

"That's true, at least," said Mr. Saveloy.

"We have not heard of you!" said the warlord.

"Yeah," said Cohen. "*That's* how good we are."

"There is one other thing about his army, actually," said someone.

They all turned to Rincewind, who'd been almost as surprised as they were to hear his voice. But a train of thought had just reached the terminus . . .

"Yes?"

"You may have been wondering why you have only seen the . . . generals," Rincewind went on, slowly, as if working it out as he went along. "That is because, you see, the men themselves are . . . invisible. Er. Yes. Ghosts, in fact. Everyone knows this, don't they?"

Cohen gaped at him in astonishment.

"Blood-sucking ghosts, as a matter of fact," said Rincewind. "After all, everyone knows that's what you get beyond the Wall, don't they?"

Lord Hong sneered. But the warlords stared at Rincewind with the expressions of people who strongly suspected that the people beyond the Wall were flesh and blood but who also relied on millions of people not believing that this was so.

"Ridiculous! *You* are not invisible blood-sucking ghosts," said one of them.

Cohen opened his mouth so that the diamond teeth glinted.

"'S right," he said. "Fact is . . . we're the *visible* sort."

"Hah! A pathetic attempt!" said Lord Hong. "Ghosts or no ghosts, we will beat you!"

"Well, that went better than I expected," Mr. Saveloy remarked as the warlords strode out. "Was that an attempt at a little bit of psychological warfare there, Mr. Rincewind?"

"Is that what it was? I know about that kind of stuff," said Cohen. "It's where you bang your shield all night before the fight so's the enemy can't get any sleep and you sing, 'We're gonna *cut* yer *tonkers* off,' and stuff like that."

"Similar," said Mr. Saveloy, diplomatically. "But it failed to work, I'm afraid. Lord Hong and his generals are rather too sophisticated. It's a great shame you couldn't try it on the common soldiers."

There was a faint squeak of rabbit behind them. They turned, and looked at the somewhat under-age cadre of the Red Army that was being ushered in. Butterfly was with them. She even gave Rincewind a very faint smile.

Rincewind had always relied on running away. But sometimes, perhaps, you had to stand and fight, if only because there was nowhere left to run.

But he was no good at all with weapons.

At least, the normal sort.

"Um," he said, "if we leave the palace now, we'll be killed, right?"

"I doubt it," said Mr. Saveloy. "It's become a matter of the Art of War now. Someone like Hong would probably slit our throats, but now war is declared things have to be done according to custom."

Rincewind took a deep breath.

"It's a million-to-one chance," he said, "but it might just work . . ."

The Four Horsemen whose Ride presages the end of the world are known to be Death, War, Famine, and Pestilence. But even less significant events have their own Horsemen. For example, the Four Horsemen of the Common Cold are Sniffles, Chesty,

Nostril, and Lack of Tissues; the Four Horsemen whose appearance foreshadows any public holiday are Storm, Gales, Sleet, and Contra-flow.

Among the armies encamped in the broad alluvial plain around Hunghung, the invisible horsemen known as Misinformation, Rumor, and Gossip saddled up . . .

A large army encamped has all the tedious problems of a city without any of the advantages. Its watchfires and picket lines are, after a while, open to local civilians, especially if they have anything to sell and even more so if they are women whose virtue has a certain commercial element and even, sometimes, if they appear to be selling food which is a break from the monotonous army diet. The food currently on sale was certainly such a break.

"Pork balls! Pork balls! Get them while they're . . ." There was a pause as the vendor mentally tried out ways of ending the sentence, and gave up. "Pork balls! Onna stick! How about you, shogun, you look like—Here, aren't you the—?"

"Shutupshutupshutup!"

Rincewind pulled D. M. H. Dibhala into the shadows by a tent.

The trader looked at the anguished face framed between a eunuch outfit and a big straw hat.

"It's the Wizard, isn't it? How are—?"

"You know how you seriously wanted to become very rich in international trade?" Rincewind said.

"Yes? Can we start?"

"Soon. Soon. But there's something you must do. You know this rumor about the army of invisible vampire ghosts that's heading this way?"

D. M. H. Dibhala's eyes swivelled nervously. But it was part of his stock in trade never to appear to be ignorant of anything except, perhaps, how to give correct change.

"Yes?" he said.

"The one about there being millions of them?" said Rincewind. "And very hungry on account of not having eaten on the way? And made specially fierce by the Great Wizard?"

"Um . . . yes?"

214

"Well, it's *not true*."

"It's not?"

"You don't believe me? After all, I ought to know."

"Good point."

"And we don't want people to panic, do we?"

"Very bad for business, panic," said D. M. H., nodding uncomfortably.

"So make sure you tell people there's no truth in this rumor, will you? Set their minds at rest."

"Good idea. Er. These invisible vampire ghosts . . . Do they carry money of any sort?"

"No. Because they don't exist."

"Ah, yes. I forgot."

"And there are not 2,300,009 of them," said Rincewind. He was rather proud of this little detail.

"Not 2,300,009 of them . . ." said D. M. H., a little glassy-eyed.

"Absolutely not. There are *not* 2,300,009 of them, no matter what anyone says. Nor has the Great Wizard made them twice as big as normal. Good man. Now I'd better be off—"

Rincewind hurried away.

The trader stood in thought for a while. It stole over him that he'd probably sold enough things for now, and he might as well go home and spend a quiet night in a barrel in the root cellar with a sack over his head.

His route led him through quite a large part of the camp. He made sure that soldiers he met knew there was no truth in the rumor, even though this invariably meant that, first of all, he had to tell them what the rumor actually *was*.

A toy rabbit squeaked nervously.

"And I'm afraid of the big invisible wampire ghosts!" sobbed Favorite Pearl.

The soldiers around this particular campfire tried to comfort her but, unfortunately, there was no one to comfort them.

"An' I heard they alweady et some men!"

One or two soldiers looked over their shoulders. There was

215

nothing to be seen in the darkness. This wasn't, however, a reassuring sign.

The Red Army moved obliquely from campfire to campfire.

Rincewind had been very specific. He'd spent all his adult life—at least, those parts of it where he wasn't being chased by things with more legs than teeth—in Unseen University, and he felt he knew what he was talking about here. Don't tell people anything, he said. Don't *tell* them. You didn't get to survive as a wizard in UU by believing what people told you. You believed what you were *not* told.

Don't tell them. *Ask* them. Ask them if it's true. You can beg them to tell you it's *not* true. Or you can even tell them you've been told to tell them it's not true, and that is the best of all.

Because Rincewind knew very well that when the Four rather small and nasty Horsemen of Panic ride out there is a good job done by Misinformation, Rumor, and Gossip, but they are as nothing compared to the fourth horseman, whose name is Denial.

After an hour Rincewind felt quite unnecessary.

There were conversations breaking out everywhere, particularly in those areas on the edge of the camps, where the night stretched away so big and dark and, so very obviously, empty.

"All right, so how come they're saying there's not 2,300,009 of them, eh? If there's none of them, then why's there a number?"

"Look, there's no such thing as invisible vampire ghosts, all right?"

"Oh yeah? How do you know? Have you ever seen any?"

"Listen, I went and asked the captain and he says he's certain there's no invisible ghosts out there."

"How can he be certain if he can't see them?"

"He says there's no such things as invisible vampire ghosts at all."

"Oh? How come he's saying that all of a sudden? My grandfather told me there's millions of them outside the—"

"Hold on . . . What's that out there. . . ?"

"What?"

"Could've sworn I heard something . . ."

"*I* can't see anything."

"Oh, *no!*"

Things must have filtered through to High Command because, getting on towards midnight, trumpets were sounded around the camps and a special proclamation was read out.

It confirmed the reality of vampire ghosts in general but denied their existence in any specific, here-and-now sense. It was a masterpiece of its type, particularly since it brought the whole subject to the ears of soldiers the Red Army hadn't been able to reach yet.

An hour later the situation had reached the point of criticality and Rincewind was hearing things he personally hadn't made up and, on the whole, would much rather not hear.

He'd chat with a couple of soldiers and say: "I'm sure there's no huge hungry army of vampire ghosts" and get told, "No, there's seven old men."

"Just seven old men?"

"I heard they're *very* old," said a soldier. "Like, too old to die. I heard from someone at the palace that they can walk through walls and make themselves invisible."

"Oh, come *on,*" said Rincewind. "Seven old men fighting this whole army?"

"Makes you think, eh? Corporal Toshi says the Great Wizard is helping them. Stands to reason. I wouldn't be fighting a whole army if I didn't have a lot of magic on my side."

"Er. Anyone know what the Great Wizard looks like?" said Rincewind.

"They say he's taller than a house and got three heads."

Rincewind nodded encouragingly.

"I heard," said a soldier, "that the Red Army is going to fight on their side, too."

"So what? Corporal Toshi says they're just a bunch of kids."

"No, I heard . . . the *real* Red Army . . . you know . . ."

"The Red Army ain't gonna side with barbarian invaders! Anyway, there's no such thing as the Red Army. That's just a myth."

"Like the invisible vampire ghosts," said Rincewind, giving the clockwork of anxiety another little turn.

"Er . . . yeah."

He left them arguing.

No one was deserting. Running off into a night full of non-specific terrors was worse than staying in camp. But that was all to the good, he decided. It meant that the really frightened people were staying put and seeking reassurance from their comrades. And there was nothing like someone repeating "I'm *sure* there's no vampire wizards" and going to the latrine four times an hour to put backbone into a platoon.

Rincewind crept back towards the city, rounded a tent in the shadows, and collided with a horse, which trod heavily on his foot.

"Your wife is a big hippo!"

SORRY.

Rincewind froze, both hands clutching his aching foot. He knew only one person with a voice like a cemetery in midwinter.

He tried to hop backwards, and collided with another horse.

RINCEWIND, ISN'T IT? said Death. YES. GOOD EVENING. I DON'T BELIEVE YOU HAVE MET WAR. RINCEWIND, WAR. WAR, RINCEWIND.

War touched his helmet in salute.

"Pleasure's all mine," he said. He indicated the other three riders. "Like to introduce you to m'sons, Terror and Panic. And m'daughter, Clancy."

The children chorused a "hello." Clancy was scowling, looked about seven years old and was wearing a hard hat and a Pony Club badge.

I WASN'T EXPECTING TO SEE *YOU* HERE, RINCEWIND.

"Oh. Good."

Death pulled an hourglass out of his robe, held it up to the moonlight, and sighed. Rincewind craned to see how much sand was left.

HOWEVER, I COULD—

"Don't you make any special arrangement just on my account," said Rincewind hurriedly. "I, er . . . I expect you're all here for the battle?"

YES. IT PROMISES TO BE EXTREMELY—SHORT.

"Who's going to win?"

NOW, YOU KNOW I WOULDN'T TELL YOU THAT, EVEN IF I KNEW.

"Even if you knew?" said Rincewind. "I thought you were supposed to know everything!"

Death held up a finger. Something fluttered down through the night. Rincewind thought it was a moth, although it looked less fluffy and had a strange speckled pattern on its wings.

It settled on the extended digit for a moment, and then flew up and away again.

ON A NIGHT LIKE THIS, said Death, THE ONLY CERTAIN THING IS UNCERTAINTY. TRITE, I KNOW, BUT TRUE.

Somewhere on the horizon, thunder rumbled.

"I'll, er, just be sort of going, then," said Rincewind.

DON'T BE A STRANGER, said Death, as the wizard hurried off.

"Odd person," said War.

WITH HIM HERE, EVEN UNCERTAINTY IS UNCERTAIN. AND I'M NOT SURE EVEN ABOUT THAT.

War pulled a large paper-wrapped package out of his saddlebag.

"We've got . . . let's see now . . . Egg and Cress, Chicken Tikka, and Mature Cheese with Crunchy Pickle, I think."

THEY DO SUCH MARVELOUS THINGS WITH SANDWICHES THESE DAYS.

"Oh . . . and Bacon Surprise."

REALLY? WHAT IS SO SURPRISING ABOUT BACON?

"I don't know. I suppose it comes as something of a shock to the pig."

Ridcully had been having a long wrestle with himself, and had won.

"We're going to bring him back," he said. "It's been four days. And then we can send them back their bloody tube thing. It gives me the willies."

The senior wizards looked at one another. No one was very keen on a university with a Rincewind component, but the metal dog *did* give them the willies. No one had wanted to go near it. They'd piled some tables around it and tried to pretend it wasn't there.

"All right," said the Dean. "But Stibbons kept going on about things weighing the same, right? If we send that back, won't it mean Rincewind arrives here going very fast?"

"Mr. Stibbons says he's working on the spell," said Ridcully. "Or we could pile some mattresses up at one end of the hall or something."

The Bursar raised a hand.

"Yes, Bursar?" said Ridcully encouragingly.

"Ho, landlord, a pint of your finest ale!" said the Bursar.

"Good," said Ridcully. "That's settled, then. I've already told Mr. Stibbons to start looking . . ."

"On that demonic device?"

"Yes."

"Then nothing can *possibly* go wrong," said the Dean sourly.

"A trumpet of lobsters, if you would be so good."

"And the Bursar agrees."

The warlords had gathered in Lord Hong's chambers. They carefully kept a distance from one another, as befitted enemies who were in the most shaky of alliances. Once the barbarians were dealt with, the battle might still continue. But they wanted assurance on one particular point.

"No!" said Lord Hong. "Let me make this absolutely clear! There is *no* invisible army of blood-sucking ghosts, do you understand? The people beyond the Wall are just like us—except vastly inferior in every respect, of course. But totally visible."

One or two of the lords did not look convinced.

"And all this talk about the Red Army?" said one of them.

"The Red Army, Lord Tang, is an undisciplined rabble that shall be put down with resolute force!"

"You know what Red Army the peasants are talking about," said Lord Tang. "They say that thousands of years ago it—"

"They say that thousands of years ago a wizard who did not exist took mud and lightning and made soldiers that couldn't die," said Lord Hong. "Yes. It's a *story*, Lord Tang. A story made up by peasants who did not understand what really happened. One Sun Mirror's army just had"—Lord Hong waved a hand vaguely—"better armor, better discipline. I am not frightened of ghosts and I am *certainly* not afraid of a legend that probably never existed."

"Yes, but—"

"Soothsayer!" snapped Lord Hong. The soothsayer, who hadn't been expecting it, gave a start.

"Yes, my lord?"

"How're those entrails coming along?"

"Er—they're about ready, my lord," said the soothsayer.

The soothsayer was rather worried. This must have been the wrong kind of bird, he told himself. About the only thing the entrails were telling him was that if he got out of this alive he, the soothsayer, might be lucky enough to enjoy a nice chicken dinner. But Lord Hong sounded like a man with the most dangerous kind of impatience.

"And what do they tell you?"

"Er—the future is . . . the future is . . ."

Chicken entrails had never looked like this. For a moment he thought they were moving.

"Er . . . it is uncertain," he hazarded.

"*Be* certain," said Lord Hong. "Who will win in the morning?"

Shadows flickered across the table.

Something was fluttering around the light.

It looked like an undistinguished yellow moth, with black patterns on its wings.

The soothsayer's precognitive abilities, which were considerably more powerful than he believed, told him: this is not a good time to be a clairvoyant.

On the other hand, there was never a good time to be horribly executed, so . . .

"Without a shadow of doubt," he said, "the enemy will be most emphatically beaten."

"How can you be so certain?" said Lord McSweeney.

The soothsayer bridled.

"You see this wobbly bit near the kidneys? You want to argue with this green trickly thing? You know all about liver suddenly? All right?"

"So there you are," said Lord Hong. "Fate smiles upon us."

"Even so—" Lord Tang began. "The men are very—"

"You can tell the men—" Lord Hong began. He stopped. He smiled.

"You can tell the men," he said, "that there *is* a huge army of invisible vampire ghosts."

"What?"

"Yes!" Lord Hong began to stride up and down, snapping his fingers. "Yes, there is a terrible army of foreign ghosts. And this has so enraged our *own* ghosts . . . yes, a thousand generations of our ancestors are riding on the wind to repel this barbaric invasion! The ghosts of the Empire are arising! Millions and millions of them! Even our demons are furious at this intrusion! They will descend like a mist of claws and teeth to—Yes, Lord Sung?"

The warlords were looking at one another nervously.

"Are you *sure*, Lord Hong?"

Lord Hong's eyes gleamed behind his tiny spectacles.

"Make the necessary proclamations," he said.

"But only a few hours ago we told the men there were no—"

"Tell them differently!"

"But will they believe that there—"

"They will believe what they are told!" shouted Lord Hong. "If the enemy thinks his strength lies in deceit, then we will use their deceit against them. Tell the men that behind them will be a billion ghosts of the Empire!"

The other warlords tried to avoid his gaze. No one was actually going to suggest that your average soldier would not be totally happy with ghosts front and rear, especially given the capriciousness of ghosts.

"Good," said Lord Hong. He looked down.

"Are you *still* here?" he said.

"Just clearing up my giblets, my lord!" squealed the soothsayer.

He picked up the remains of his stricken chicken and ran for it.

After all, he told himself as he pelted back home, it's not as though I said *whose* enemy.

Lord Hong was left alone.

He realized he was shaking. It was probably fury. But perhaps

... perhaps things could be turned to his advantage, even so. Barbarians came from outside, and to most people everywhere outside was the same. Yes. The barbarians were a minute detail, easily disposed of, but carefully managed, perhaps, might figure in his overall strategy.

He was breathing heavily, too.

He walked into his private study and shut the door.

He pulled out the key.

He opened the box.

There was a few minutes' silence, except for the rustle of cloth.

Then Lord Hong looked at himself in the mirror.

He'd gone to great lengths to achieve this. He had used several agents, none of whom knew the whole plan. But the Ankh-Morpork tailor had been good at his work and the measurements had been followed exactly. From pointy boots to hose to doublet, cloak, and hat with a feather in it, Lord Hong knew he was a perfect Ankh-Morpork gentleman. The cloak was lined with silk.

The clothes felt uncomfortable and touched him in unfamiliar ways, but those were minor details. This was how a man looked in a society that breathed, that moved, that could really go somewhere . . .

He'd walk through the city on that first great day and the people would be silent when they saw their natural leader.

It never crossed his mind that anyone would say, "'Ere, wot a toff! 'Eave 'arf a brick at 'im!"

The ants scurried. The thing that went "parp" went parp.

The wizards stood back. There wasn't much else to do when Hex was working at full speed, except watch the fish and oil the wheels from time to time. There were occasional flashes of octarine from the tubes.

Hex was spelling several hundred times a minute. It was as simple as that. It would take a human more than an hour to do an ordinary finding spell. But Hex could do them faster. Over and over again. It was netting the whole occult sea in the search for one slippery fish.

It achieved, after ninety-three minutes, what would otherwise have taken the faculty several months.

"You see?" said Ponder, his voice shaking a little as he took the line of blocks out of the hopper. "I *said* he could do it."

"Who's he?" said Ridcully.

"Hex."

"Oh, you mean *it*."

"That's what I said, sir . . . er . . . yes."

Another thing about the Horde, Mr. Saveloy had noticed, was their ability to relax. The old men had the catlike ability to do nothing when there was nothing to do.

They'd sharpened their swords. They'd had a meal—big lumps of meat for most of them, and some kind of gruel for Mad Hamish, who'd dribbled most of it down his beard—and assured its wholesomeness by dragging the cook in, nailing him to the floor by his apron, and suspending a large axe on a rope that crossed a beam in the roof and was held at the other end by Cohen, while he ate.

Then they'd sharpened their swords again, out of habit, and . . . stopped.

Occasionally one of them would whistle a snatch of a tune, through what remained of his teeth, or search a bodily crevice for a particularly fretful louse. Mainly, though, they just sat and stared at nothing.

After a long while, Caleb said, "Y'know, I've never been to XXXX. Been everywhere else. Often wondered what it's like."

"Got shipwrecked there once," said Vincent. "Weird place. Lousy with magic. There's beavers with beaks and giant rats with long tails that hops around the place and boxes with one another. Black fellas wanderin' around all over the place. They say they're in a dream. Bright, though. Show 'em a bit of desert with one dead tree in it, next minute they've found a three-course meal with fruits and nuts to follow. Beer's good, too."

"Sounds like it."

There was another long pause.

Then:

"I suppose they've *got* minstrels here? Be a bit of a bloody waste, wouldn't it, if we all got killed and no one made up any songs about it."

"Bound to have loads of minstrels, a city like this."

"No problem there, then."

"No."

"No."

There was another lengthy pause.

"Not that we're going to get killed."

"Right. I don't intend to start getting killed at my time of life, haha."

Another pause.

"Cohen?"

"Yep?"

"You a religious man at all?"

"Well, I've robbed loads of temples and killed a few mad priests in my time. Don't know if that counts."

"What do your tribe believe happens to you when you die in battle?"

"Oh, these big fat women in horned helmets take you off to the halls of Io where there is fighting and carousing and quaffing for ever."

Another pause.

"You mean, like, *really* for ever?"

"S'pose so."

"'Cos generally you get fed up even with turkey by about day four."

"All right, what do *your* lot believe?"

"I think we go off to Hell in a boat made of toenail clippings. Something like that, anyway."

Another pause.

"But it's not worth talking about 'cos we're not going to get killed today."

"You said it."

"Hah, it's not worth dying if all you've got to look forward to is leftover meat and floating around in a boat smelling of your socks, is it, eh?"

"Haha."

Another pause.

"Down in Klatch they believe if you lead a good life you're rewarded by being sent to a paradise with lots of young women."

"That's your reward, is it?"

"Dunno. Maybe it's their punishment. But I do remember you eat sherbet all day."

"Hah. When I was a lad we had proper sherbet, in little tube things and a liquorice straw to suck it up with. You don't get that sort of thing today. People're too busy rushin' about."

"Sounds a lot better than quaffing toenails, though."

Another pause.

"Did you ever believe that business about every enemy you killed becoming your servant in the next world?"

"Dunno."

"How many you killed?"

"What? Oh. Maybe two, three thousand. Not counting dwarfs and trolls, o' course."

"Definitely not going to be short of a hairbrush or someone to open doors for you after you're dead, then."

A pause.

"We're definitely not going to die, right?"

"Right."

"I mean, odds of 100,000 to one . . . hah. The difference is just a lot of zeroes, right?"

"Right."

"I mean, stout comrades at our side, a strong right arm . . . What more could we want?"

Pause.

"A volcano'd be favorite."

Pause.

"We're going to die, aren't we?"

"Yep."

The Horde looked at one another.

"Still, to look on the bright side, I recall I still owe Fafa the dwarf fifty dollars for this sword," said Boy Willie. "Looks as though I could end up ahead of the game."

Mr. Saveloy put his head in his hands.

"I'm really sorry," he said.

"Don't worry about it," said Cohen.

The grey light of dawn was just visible in the high windows.

"Look," said Mr. Saveloy, "you don't *have* to die. We could ... well, we could sneak out. Back along the pipe, maybe. Perhaps we could carry Hamish. People are coming and going all the time. I'm sure we could get out of ... the city ... without ... any ..."

His voice faded away. No voice could keep going under the pressure of those stares. Even Hamish, whose gaze was generally focused on some point about eighty years away, was glaring at him.

"Ain't gonna run," said Hamish.

"It's not running away," he managed. "It's a sensible withdrawal. Tactics. Good grief, it's common sense!"

"Ain't gonna run."

"Look, even barbarians can count! And you've admitted you're going to die!"

"Ain't gonna run."

Cohen leaned forward and patted Mr. Saveloy on the hand.

"It's the heroing, see," he said. "Who's ever heard of a hero running away? All them kids you was telling us about ... you know, the ones who think we're stories ... you reckon they'd believe we ran away? Well, then. No, it's not part of the whole deal, running away. Let someone else do the running."

"Besides," said Truckle, "where'd we get another chance like this? Six against five armies! That's bl—that's fantastic! We're not talking legends here, I reckon we've got a good crack at some mythology as well."

"But ... you'll ... *die.*"

"Oh, that's part of it, I'll grant you, that's part of it. But what a way to go, eh?"

Mr. Saveloy looked at them and realized that they were speaking another language in another world. It was one he had no key to, no map for. You could teach them to wear interesting pants and handle money but something in their soul stayed exactly the same.

"Do teachers go anywhere special when they die?" said Cohen.

"I don't think so," said Mr. Saveloy gloomily. He wondered for a moment whether there really *was* a great Free Period in the sky. It didn't sound very likely. Probably there would be some marking to do.

"Well, whatever happens, when you're dead, if you ever feel like a good quaff, you're welcome to drop in at any time," said Cohen. "It's been *fun*. That's the important thing. And it's been an education, hasn't it, boys?"

There was a general murmur of assent.

"Amazing, all those long words."

"And learnin' to buy things."

"And social intercourse, hur, hur . . . sorry."

"Whut?"

"Shame it didn't work out, but I've never been one for plans," said Cohen.

Mr. Saveloy stood up.

"I'm going to join you," he said grimly.

"What, to fight?"

"Yes."

"Do you know how to handle a sword?" said Truckle.

"Er. No."

"Then you've wasted *all* your life."

Mr. Saveloy looked offended at this.

"I expect I'll get the hang of it as we go along," he said.

"Get the hang of it? It's a *sword!*"

"Yes, but . . . when you're a teacher, you have to pick things up fast." Mr. Saveloy smiled nervously. "I once taught practical alchemy for a whole term when Mr. Schism was off sick after blowing himself up, and up until then I'd never seen a crucible."

"Here." Boy Willie handed the teacher a spare sword. He hefted it.

"Er. I expect there's a manual, or something?"

"Manual? No. You hold the blunt end and poke the other end at people."

"Ah? Really? Well, that seems quite straightforward. I thought there was rather more to it than that."

"You *sure* you want to come with us?" said Cohen.

Mr. Saveloy looked firm. "Absolutely. I very much doubt if I'll survive if you lose and ... well, it seems that you heroes get a better class of Heaven. I must say I rather suspect you get a better class of life, too. And I really don't know where teachers go when they're dead, but I've got a horrible suspicion it'll be full of sports masters."

"It's just that I don't know if you could really go properly berserk," said Cohen. "Have you ever had the red mist come down and woke up to find you'd bitten twenty people to death?"

"I used to be reckoned a pretty ratty man if people made too much noise in class," said Mr. Saveloy. "And something of a dead shot with a piece of chalk, too."

"How about you, taxman?"

Six Beneficent Winds backed away hurriedly.

"I ... I think I'm probably more cut out for undermining the system from within," he said.

"Fair enough." Cohen looked at the others. "I've never done this official sort of warring before," he said. "How's it supposed to go?"

"I think you just line up in front of one another and then charge," said Mr. Saveloy.

"Seems straightforward enough. All right, let's go."

They strode, or in one case wheeled and in another case moved at Mr. Saveloy's gentle trot, down the hall. The taxman trailed after them.

"Mr. Saveloy!" he shouted. "You know what's going to happen! Have you lost your senses?"

"Yes," said the teacher, "but I may have found some better ones."

He grinned to himself. The whole of his life, so far, had been complicated. There had been timetables and lists and a whole basket of things he must do and things he shouldn't do, and the life of Mr. Saveloy had been this little wriggly thing trying to survive in the middle of it all. But now it had suddenly all become very simple. You held one end and you poked the other into people. A man could live his whole life by a maxim like that. And, afterwards, get a very interesting afterlife—

"Here, you'll need this, too," said Caleb, poking something round at him as they stepped into the grey light. "It's a shield."

"Ah. It's to protect myself, yes?"

"If you really need to, bite the edge."

"Oh, I know about that," said Mr. Saveloy. "That's when you go berserk, right?"

"Could be, could be," said Caleb. "That's why a lot of fighters do it. But personally *I* do it 'cos it's made of chocolate."

"Chocolate?"

"You can never get a proper meal in these battles."

And this is me, thought Mr. Saveloy, marching down the street with *heroes*. They are the great fi—

"And when in doubt, take all your clothes off," said Caleb.

"What for?"

"Sign of a good berserk, taking all your clothes off. Frightens the hell out of the enemy. If anyone starts laughing, stab 'em one."

There was a movement among the blankets in the wheelchair.

"Whut?"

"I said, STAB 'EM ONE, Hamish."

Hamish waved an arm that looked like bone with skin on it, and apparently far too thin to hold the axe it was in fact holding.

"That's right! Right in the nadgers!"

Mr. Saveloy nudged Caleb.

"I ought to be writing this down," he said. "Where exactly are the nadgers?"

"Small range of mountains near the Hub."

"Fascinating."

The citizens of Hunghung were ranged along the city walls. It was not every day you saw a fight like this.

Rincewind elbowed and kicked his way through the people until he reached the cadre, who'd managed to occupy a prime position over the main gate.

"What're you hanging around here for?" he said. "You could be miles away!"

"We want to see what happens, of course," said Twoflower, his spectacles gleaming.

"I know what happens! The Horde will be instantly slaughtered!" said Rincewind. "What did you *expect* to happen?"

"Ah, but you're forgetting the invisible vampire ghosts," said Twoflower.

Rincewind looked at him.

"What?"

"Their secret army. I heard that *we've* got some, too. Should be interesting to watch."

"Twoflower, there are *no* invisible vampire ghosts."

"Ah, yes, everyone's going round denying it," said Lotus Blossom. "So there must be some truth in it."

"But I made it up!"

"Ah, you may *think* you made it up," said Twoflower. "But perhaps you are a pawn of Fate."

"Listen, there's no—"

"Same old Rincewind," said Twoflower, in a jolly way. "You always were so pessimistic about everything, but it always worked out all right in the end."

"There are no ghosts, there are no magic armies," said Rincewind. "There's just—"

"When seven men go out to fight an army 100,000 times bigger there's only one way it can end," said Twoflower.

"Right. I'm glad you see sense."

"They'll win," said Twoflower. "They've got to. Otherwise the world's just not working properly."

"You look educated," said Rincewind to Butterfly. "Explain to him why he's wrong. It's because of a little thing we have in our country. I don't know if you've ever heard of it—it's called *mathematics.*"

The girl smiled at him.

"You don't believe me, do you?" said Rincewind flatly. "You're just like him. What d'you think this is, homeopathic warfare? The smaller your side the more likely you are to win? Well, it's not like that. I wish it *was* like that, but it isn't. Nothing is. There are no amazing strokes of luck, no magic solutions, and the good people don't win because they're small and plucky!" He waved his hand irritably at something.

"*You* always survived," said Twoflower. "We had amazing adventures and you always survived."

"That was just coincidence."

"You kept *on* surviving."

"And you got us safely out of prison," said Lotus Blossom.

"There were just a lot of coinci—*Will you go away!*"

A butterfly skittered away from his flailing hand.

"Damn things," he mumbled. And added: "Well, that's it. I'm off. I can't watch. I've got things to do. Besides, afterwards I think nasty people are going to be looking for me."

And then he realized there were tears in Lotus Blossom's eyes.

"We . . . we thought you would do something," she said.

"Me? I can't do anything! Especially not magic! I'm famous for it! Don't go around believing that Great Wizards solve all your problems, because there aren't any and they don't and I should know because I'm not one!"

He backed away. "This is always happening to me! I'm just minding my own business and everything goes wrong and suddenly everyone's relying on me and saying, 'Oh, Rincewind, what are you going to do about it?' Well, what Mrs. Rincewind's little boy, if she was a Mrs. Rincewind of course, what he's going to do about it is nothing, right? You have to sort it all out yourselves! No mysterious magical armies are going to—Will you stop looking at me like that? I don't see why it's *my* fault! I've got other things to do! It's not my business!"

And then he turned and ran.

The crowds didn't take much notice of him.

The streets were deserted by Hunghung standards, which meant you could quite often see the cobbles. Rincewind pushed and shoved his way along the alleys nearest the Wall, looking for another gateway with guards too busy to ask questions.

There were footsteps behind him.

"Look," he said, spinning round, "I told you, you can all—"

It was the Luggage. It contrived to look a little ashamed of itself.

"Oh, turned up at last, have we?" said Rincewind savagely. "What happened to the following-master-everywhere thing?"

The Luggage shuffled its feet. From out of an alleyway came a slightly larger and far more ornate version of itself. Its lid was inset with decorative wood and, it seemed to Rincewind, its feet were rather more dainty than the horny-nailed, calloused ones of the Luggage. Besides, the toenails had been painted.

"Oh," he said. "Well. Good grief. Fair enough, I suppose. Really? I mean . . . yes. Well. Come on, then."

He reached the end of the alley and turned round. The Luggage was gently bumping the larger chest, urging it to follow him.

Rincewind's own sexual experiences were not excessive although he had seen diagrams. He hadn't the faintest idea about how it applied to travel accessories. Did they say things like "What a chest!" or "Get a load of the hinges on that one!"?

If it came to that, he had no real reason for considering that the Luggage was male. Admittedly it had a homicidal nature, but so had a lot of the women that Rincewind had met, and they had often become a little more homicidal as a result of meeting him. Capacity for violence, Rincewind had heard, was unisexual. He wasn't certain what unisex was, but expected that it was what he normally experienced.

There was a small gate ahead. It seemed to be unguarded.

Despite his fear he walked through it, and refrained from running. Authority always noticed a running man. The time to start running was around about the "e" in "Hey, you!"

No one paid him any attention. The attention of the people along the Wall was all on the armies.

"Look at them," he said bitterly, to the generality of the universe. "*Stupid.* If it was seven against seventy, everyone'd *know* who'd lose. Just because it's seven against 700,000, everyone's not sure. As though suddenly numbers don't mean anything any more. Huh! Why should *I* do anything? It's not as if I even know the guy all that well. Admittedly he saved my life a couple of times, but that's no reason to die horribly just because he can't count. So you can stop looking at me like that!"

The Luggage backed away a little. The *other* Luggage . . .

. . . Rincewind supposed it just *looked* female. Women had bigger luggage than men, didn't they? Because of the—he moved into unknown territory—extra frills and stuff. It was just one of those things, like the fact that they had smaller handkerchiefs than men even though their noses were generally the same size. The Luggage had always been *the* Luggage. Rincewind wasn't mentally prepared for there to be more than one. There was the Luggage and . . . the *other* Luggage.

"Come on, both of you," he said. "We're getting out of here. I've done what I can. I just don't care any more. It's nothing to do with me. I don't see why everyone depends on me. I'm not dependable. Even *I* don't depend on me, and I'm me."

Cohen looked at the horizon. Gray-blue clouds were piling up.

"There's a storm coming," he said.

"It's a mercy that we won't be alive to get wet, then," said Boy Willie, cheerfully.

"Funny thing, though. It looks like it's coming from every direction at once."

"Filthy foreign weather. You can't trust it."

Cohen turned his attention to the armies of the five warlords.

There seemed to have been some agreement.

They'd arranged themselves around the position that Cohen had taken up. The tactic seemed quite clear. It was simply to advance. The Horde could see the commanders riding up and down in front of their legions.

"How's it supposed to start?" said Cohen, the rising wind whipping at what remained of his hair. "Does someone blow a whistle or something? Or do we just scream and charge?"

"Commencement is generally by agreement," said Mr. Saveloy.

"Oh."

Cohen looked at the forest of lances and pennants. Hundreds of thousands of men looked like quite a lot of men when you saw them close to.

"I suppose," he said, slowly, "that none of you has got some amazing plan you've been keeping quiet about?"

"We thought *you* had one," said Truckle.

Several riders had now left each army and approached the Horde in a group. They stopped a little more than a spear's throw away, and sat and watched.

"All right, then," said Cohen. "I hate to say this, but perhaps we should talk about surrender."

"No!" said Mr. Saveloy, and then stopped in embarrassment at the loudness of his own voice. "No," he repeated, a little more quietly. "You won't live if you surrender. You just won't die immediately."

Cohen scratched his nose. "What's that flag . . . you know . . . when you want to talk to them without them killing you?"

"It's got to be red," said Mr. Saveloy. "But look, it's no good you—"

"I don't know, red for surrender, white for funerals . . ." muttered Cohen. "All right. Anyone got something red?"

"I've got a handkerchief," said Mr. Saveloy, "but it's white and anyway—"

"Give it here."

The barbarian teacher very reluctantly handed it over.

Cohen pulled a small, worn knife from his belt.

"I don't believe this!" said Mr. Saveloy. He was nearly in tears. "Cohen the Barbarian talking surrender with people like that!"

"Influence of civilization," said Cohen. "'S probably made me go soft in the head."

He pulled the knife over his arm, and then clamped the handkerchief over the cut.

"There we are," he said. "Soon have a nice red flag."

The Horde nodded approvingly. It was an amazingly symbolic, dramatic and above all stupid gesture, in the finest traditions of barbarian heroing. It didn't seem to be lost on some of the nearer soldiers, either.

"Now," Cohen went on, "I reckon you, Teach, and you, Truckle . . . you two come with me and we'll go and talk to these people."

"They'll drag you off to their dungeons!" said Mr. Saveloy. "They've got torturers that can keep you alive for *years!*"

"Whut? Whutzeesay?"

"He said THEY CAN KEEP YOU ALIVE FOR YEARS IN THEIR DUNGEONS, Hamish."

"Good! Fine by me!"

"Oh, dear," said Mr. Saveloy.

He trailed after the other two towards the warlords.

Lord Hong raised his visor and stared down his nose at them as they approached.

"Red flag, look," said Cohen, waving the rather damp object on the end of his sword.

"Yes," said Lord Hong. "We saw that little show. It may impress the common soldiers but it does not impress me, barbarian."

"Please yourself," said Cohen. "We've come to talk about surrender."

Mr. Saveloy noticed some of the lesser lords relax a little. Then he thought: a real soldier probably doesn't like this sort of thing. You don't want to go to soldier Heaven or wherever you go and say, I once led an army against seven old men. It wasn't medal-winning material.

"Ah. Of course. So much for bravado," said Lord Hong. "Then lay down your arms and you will be escorted back to the palace."

Cohen and Truckle looked at one another.

"Sorry?" said Cohen.

"Lay down your arms." Lord Hong snorted. "That means put down your weapons."

Cohen gave him a puzzled look. "Why should we put down our weapons?"

"Are we not talking about your surrender?"

"*Our* surrender?"

Mr. Saveloy's mouth opened in a mad, slow grin.

Lord Hong stared at Cohen.

"Hah! You can hardly expect me to believe that you have come to ask *us* . . ."

He leaned from the saddle and glared at them.

"You do, don't you?" he said. "You mindless little barbarians. Is it true that you can only count up to five?"

"We just thought that it might save people getting hurt," said Cohen.

"You thought it would save *you* getting hurt," said the warlord.

"I daresay a few of yours might get hurt, too."

"They're peasants," said the warlord.

"Oh, yes. I was forgetting that," said Cohen. "And you're their chief, right? It's like your game of chess, right?"

"I am their lord," said Lord Hong. "They will die at my bidding, if necessary."

Cohen gave him a big, dangerous grin.

"When do we start?" he said.

"Return to your . . . band," said Lord Hong. "And then I think we shall start . . . shortly."

He glared at Truckle, who was unfolding his bit of paper. The barbarian's lips moved awkwardly and he ran a horny finger across the page.

"Misbegotten . . . wretch, so you are," he said.

"My word," said Mr. Saveloy, who'd created the look-up table.

As the three returned to the Horde Mr. Saveloy was aware of a grinding sound. Cohen was wearing several carats off his teeth.

"'Die at my bidding'," he said. "The bugger doesn't even know what a chief is meant to *be*, the bastard! Him and his horse!"

Mr. Saveloy looked around. There seemed to be some arguing among the warlords.

"You know," he said, "they probably will try to take us alive. I used to have a headmaster like him. He liked to make people's lives a misery."

"You mean they'll be trying not to kill us?" said Truckle.

"Yes."

"Does that mean we have to try not to kill them?"

"No, I don't think so."

"Sounds okay to me."

"What do we do now?" said Mr. Saveloy. "Do we do a battle chant or something?"

"We just wait," said Cohen.

"There's a lot of waiting in warfare," said Boy Willie.

"Ah, yes," said Mr. Saveloy. "I've heard people say that. They say there's long periods of boredom followed by short periods of excitement."

Terry Pratchett

"Not really," said Cohen. "It's more like short periods of waiting followed by long periods of being dead."

"Blast."

The fields were crisscrossed with drainage ditches. There seemed to be no straight path anywhere. And the ditches were too wide to jump; they *looked* shallow enough to wade, but only because eighteen inches of water overlay a suffocating depth of rich thick mud. Mr. Saveloy said that the Empire owed its prosperity to the mud of the plains, and right now Rincewind was feeling extremely rich.

He was also quite close to the big hill that dominated the city. It really was rounded, with a precision apparently far too accurate for mere natural causes; Saveloy had said that hills like that were drumlins, great piles of topsoil left behind by glaciers. Trees covered the lower slopes of this one, and there was a small building on the top.

Cover. Now, *that* was a good word. It was a big plain and the armies weren't too far away. The hill looked curiously peaceful, as if it belonged to a different world. It was strange that the Agateans, who otherwise seemed to farm absolutely everywhere a water buffalo could stand, had left it alone.

Someone was watching him.

It *was* a water buffalo.

It would be wrong to say it watched him with interest. It just watched him, because its eyes were open and had to be facing in some direction, and it had randomly chosen one which included Rincewind.

Its face held the completely serene expression of a creature that had long ago realized that it was, fundamentally, a tube on legs and had been installed in the universe to, broadly speaking, achieve throughput.

At the other end of the string was a man, ankle-deep in the mud of the field. He had a broad straw hat, like every other buffalo holder. He had the basic pyjama suit of the Agatean man-in-the-field. And he had an expression not of idiocy, but of preoccupation. He was looking at Rincewind. As with the

238

buffalo, this was only because his eyes had to be doing something.

Despite the pressing dangers, Rincewind found himself overcome by a sudden curiosity.

"Er. Good morning," he said.

The man gave him a nod. The water buffalo made the sound of regurgitating cud.

"Er. Sorry if this is a personal question," said Rincewind, "but . . . I can't help wondering . . . why do you stand out in the fields all day with the water buffalo?"

The man thought about it.

"Good for soil," he said eventually.

"But doesn't it waste a lot of time?" said Rincewind.

The man gave this due appraisal also.

"What's time to a cow?" he said.

Rincewind reversed back on to the highway of reality.

"You see those armies over there?" he said.

The buffalo holder concentrated his gaze.

"Yes," he decided.

"They're fighting for you."

The man did not appear moved by this. The water buffalo burped gently.

"Some want to see you enslaved and some want you to run the country, or at least to let them run the country while telling you it's you doing it really," said Rincewind. "There's going to be a terrible battle. I can't help wondering . . . What do *you* want?"

The buffalo holder absorbed this one for consideration, too. And it seemed to Rincewind that the slowness of the thought process wasn't due to native stupidity, but more to do with the sheer size of the question. He could feel it spreading out so that it incorporated the soil and the grass and the sun and headed on out into the universe.

Finally the man said:

"A longer piece of string would be nice."

"Ah. Really? Well, well. There's a thing," said Rincewind. "Talking to you has been an education. Goodbye."

The man watched him go. Beside him, the buffalo relaxed

some muscles and contracted others and lifted its tail and made the world, in a very small way, a better place.

Rincewind headed on towards the hill. Random as the animal tracks and occasional plank bridges were, they seemed to head right for it. If Rincewind had been thinking clearly, an activity he last remembered doing around the age of twelve, he might have wondered about that.

The trees of the lower slopes were sapient pears, and he didn't even think about *that*. Their leaves turned to watch him as he scrambled past. What he needed now was a cave or a handy—

He paused.

"Oh, no," he said. "No, no, no. You don't catch *me* like that. I'll go into a handy cave and there'll be a little door or some wise old man or something and I'll be dragged back into events. Right. Stay out in the open, that's the style."

He half climbed, half walked to the rounded top of the hill, which rose above the trees like a dome. Now he was closer he could see that it wasn't as smooth as it looked from below. Weather had worn gullies and channels in the soil, and bushes had colonized every sheltered slope.

The building on the top was, to Rincewind's surprise, rusty. It had been made of iron—pointed iron roof, iron walls, iron doorway. There were a few old nests and some debris on the floor, but it was otherwise empty. And not a good place to hide. It'd be the first place anyone would look.

There was a cloud wall around the world now. Lightning crackled in its heart, and there was the sound of thunder—not the gentle rumble of summer thunder but the crackackack of splitting sky.

And yet the heat wrapped the plain like a blanket. The air felt thick. In a minute it was going to rain cats and food.

"Find somewhere where I won't be noticed," he muttered. "Keep head down. Only way. Why should I care? Other people's problem."

Panting in the oppressive heat, he wandered on.

* * *

Lord Hong was enraged. Those who knew him could tell, by the way he spoke more slowly and smiled continuously.

"And how do the men know the lightning dragons are *angry?*" he said. "It may be mere high spirits."

"Not with a sky that color," said Lord Tang. "That is not an auspicious color for a sky. It looks like a bruise. A sky like that is portentous."

"And what, pray, do you think it portends?"

"It's just *generally* portentous."

"I know what's behind this," Lord Hong snarled. "You're too frightened to fight seven old men, is that it?"

"The men say they're the legendary Seven Indestructible Sages," said Lord Fang. He tried to smile. "You know how superstitious they are . . . "

"What Seven Sages?" said Lord Hong. "I am extremely familiar with the history of the world and there are no legendary Seven Indestructible Sages."

"Er . . . not *yet,*" said Lord Fang. "Uh. But . . . a day like this . . . Perhaps legends have to *start* somewhere . . ."

"They're barbarians! Oh, gods! Seven men! Can I believe we're afraid of seven men?"

"It feels wrong," said Lord McSweeney. He added, quickly, "That's what the men say."

"You have made the proclamation about our celestial army of ghosts? All of you?"

The warlords tried to avoid his gaze.

"Er . . . yes," said Lord Fang.

"That must have improved morale."

"Uh. Not . . . entirely . . . "

"What do you mean, man?"

"Uh. Many men have deserted. Uh. They've been saying that foreign ghosts were bad enough, but . . . ."

"But what?"

"They are *soldiers,* Lord Hong," said Lord Tang sharply. "They all have people they do not want to meet. Don't you?"

Just for a second, there was the suggestion of a twitch on Lord Hong's cheek. It was only for a second, but those who saw it took note. Lord Hong's renowned glaze had shown a crack.

"What would you do, Lord Tang? Let these insolent barbarians go?"

"Of course not. But . . . you don't need an army against seven men. Seven ancient old men. The peasants say . . . they say . . ."

Lord Hong's voice was slightly higher.

"Come on, man who talks to peasants. I'm sure you're going to tell us what they say about these foolish and foolhardy old men?"

"Well, that's it, you see. They say, if they're so foolish and foolhardy . . . how did they manage to become so old?"

"Luck!"

It was the wrong word. Even Lord Hong realized it. He'd never believed in luck. He'd always taken pains, usually those of other people, to fill life with certainties. But he knew that others believed in luck. It was a foible he'd always been happy to make use of. And now it was turning and stinging him on the hand.

"There is nothing in the Art of War to tell us how five armies attack seven old men," said Lord Tang. "Ghosts or no ghosts. And this, Lord Hong, is because no one ever thought such a thing would be done."

"If you feel so frightened I'll ride out against them with my mere 250,000 men," he said.

"I am not frightened," said Lord Tang. "I am ashamed."

"Each man armed with two swords," Lord Hong went on, ignoring him. "And I shall see how lucky these . . . sages . . . are. Because, my lords, I will only have to be lucky once. They will have to be lucky a quarter of a million times."

He lowered his visor.

"How lucky do you feel, my lords?"

The other four warlords avoided one another's gaze.

Lord Hong noticed their resigned silence.

"Very well, then," he said. "Let the gongs be sounded and the firecrackers lit—to ensure good luck, of course."

There were a large number of ranks in the armies of the Empire, and many of them were untranslatable. Three Pink Pig and Five

White Fang were, loosely speaking, privates, and not just because they were pale, vulnerable and inclined to curl up and hide when danger threatened.

In fact they were so private as to be downright secretive. Even the army's mules ranked higher than them, because good mules were hard to come by whereas men like Pink Pig and White Fang are found in every army, somewhere where a latrine is in need of cleaning.

They were so insignificant that they had, privately, decided that it would be a waste of an invisible foreign blood-sucking ghost's valuable time to attack them. They felt it only fair, after it had come all this way, to give it the chance of fiendishly killing someone superior.

They had therefore hospitably decamped just before dawn and were now hiding out. Of course, if victory threatened they could always *re*camp. It was unlikely that they'd be missed in all the excitement, and both men were somewhat expert at turning up on battlefields in time to join in the victory celebrations. They lay in the long grass, watching the armies maneuver.

From this height, it looked like an impressive war. The army on one side was so small as to be invisible. Of course, if you accepted the very strong denials of last night, it was so *invisible* as to be invisible.

It was also their elevation which meant that they were the first to notice the ring around the sky.

It was just above the thunderous wall on the horizon. Where stray shafts of sunlight hit it, it glowed golden. Elsewhere it was merely yellow. But it was continuous, and thin as a thread.

"Funny-looking cloud," said White Fang.

"Yeah," said Pink Pig. "So what?"

It was while they were thus engaged, and sharing a small bottle of rice wine liberated by Pink Pig from an unsuspecting comrade the previous evening, that they heard a groan.

"Ooooooohhhhhh . . ."

Their drinks froze in their throats.

"Did you hear that?" said Pink Pig.

"You mean the—"

"Ooooohhhh . . ."

"That's it!"

They turned, very slowly.

Something had pulled itself out of a gully behind them. It was humanoid, more or less. Red mud dripped from it. Strange noises issued from its mouth.

"Oooooohhhhshit!"

Pink Pig grabbed White Fang's arm.

"It's an invisible blood-sucking ghost!"

"But I can see it!"

Pink Pig squinted.

"It's the Red Army! They've come up outa the earth like everybody says!"

White Fang, who had several brain cells more than Pink Pig, and more importantly was only on his second cup of wine, took a closer look.

"It could be just one ordinary man with mud all over him," he suggested. He raised his voice. "Hey, you!"

The figure turned and tried to run.

Pink Pig nudged his friend.

"Is he one of ours?"

"Looking like that?"

"Let's get him!"

"Why?"

"'Cos he's running away!"

"Let him run."

"Maybe he's got money. Anyway, what's he running away for?"

Rincewind slid down into another gully. Of all the luck! Soldiers should be where they were expected to be. What had happened to duty and honor and stuff like that?

The gully had dead grass and moss in the bottom.

He stood still and listened to the voices of the two men.

The air was stifling. It was as if the oncoming storm was pushing all the hot air in front of it, turning the plain into a pressure cooker.

And then the ground creaked, and sagged suddenly.

The faces of the absentee soldiers appeared over the edge of the gully.

There was another creak and the ground sank another inch or two. Rincewind didn't dare breathe in, in case the extra weight of air made him too heavy. And it was very clear that the least activity, such as jumping, was going to make things worse . . .

Very carefully, he looked down.

The dead moss had given way. He seemed to be standing on a baulk of timber buried in the ground, but dirt pouring around it suggested that there was a hole beneath.

It was going to give way any second n—

Rincewind threw himself forward. The ground fell away underneath so that, instead of standing on a slowly breaking piece of timber, he was hanging with his arms over what felt like another concealed log and, by the feel of it, one which was as riddled with rot as the first one.

This one, possibly out of a desire to conform, began to sag.

And then jolted to a stop.

The faces of the soldiers vanished backwards as the sides of the gully began to slide. Dry earth and small stones slid past Rincewind. He could feel them rattle on his boots and drop away.

He felt, as an expert in these things, that he was over a depth. From his point of view, it was also a height.

The log began to shift again.

This left Rincewind with, as he saw it, two options. He could let go and plunge to an uncertain fate in the darkness, or he could hang on until the timber gave way, and then plunge to an uncertain fate in the darkness.

And then, to his delight, there was a third option. The toe of his boot touched something, a root, a protruding rock. It didn't matter. It took some of his weight. It took at least enough to put him in precarious equilibrium—not exactly safe, not exactly falling. Of course, it was only a temporary measure, but Rincewind had always considered that life was no more than a series of temporary measures strung together.

A pale yellow butterfly with interesting patterns on its wings fluttered along the gully and settled on the only bit of color available, which turned out to be Rincewind's hat.

The wood sagged slightly.

"Push off!" said Rincewind, trying not to use heavy language. "Go away!"

The butterfly flattened its wings and sunned itself.

Rincewind pursed his lips and tried to blow up his own nostrils.

Startled, the creature skittered into the air . . .

"Hah!" said Rincewind.

. . . and, in response to its instincts in the face of a threat, moved its wings like *this* and *this*.

The bushes shivered. And around the sky, the towering clouds curved into unusual patterns.

Another cloud formed. It was about the size of an angry gray balloon. And it started to rain. Not rain generally, but specifically. Specifically on about a square foot of ground which contained Rincewind; specifically, on his hat.

A very small bolt of lightning stung Rincewind on the nose.

"Ah! So we have"—Pink Pig, appearing around the curve of the gully, hesitated a bit before continuing slightly more thoughtfully—"a head in a hole . . . with a very small thunderstorm above it."

And then it dawned on him that, storm or no storm, nothing was preventing him from cutting off significant parts. The only significant part available was a head, but that was fine by him.

At which point, Rincewind's hat having absorbed enough moisture, the ancient wood gave way under the strain and plunged him to an uncertain fate in the darkness.

It was utterly dark.

There had been a painful confusion of tunnels and sliding dirt. Rincewind assumed—or the small part of him that was not sobbing with fear assumed—that the earth had caved in after him. Cave. That was a significant word. He was in a cave. Reaching out carefully, in case he felt something, he felt for something to feel.

There was a straight edge. It led to three more straight edges, going off at right angles. So . . . this meant slab.

The darkness was still a choking velvet shroud.

Slab meant that there was some other entrance, some proper entrance. Even now guards were probably hurrying towards him.

Perhaps the Luggage was hurrying towards *them*. It had been acting very funny lately, that was for certain. He was probably better off without it. Probably.

He patted his pockets, saying the mantra that even non-wizards invoke in order to find matches; that is, he said, "Matches, matches, matches," madly to himself, under his breath.

He found some, and scratched one desperately with his thumbnail.

"Ow!"

The smoky yellow flame lit nothing except Rincewind's hand and part of his sleeve.

He ventured a few steps before it burned his fingers, and when it died it left a blue afterglow in the darkness of his vision.

There were no sounds of vengeful feet. There were no sounds at all. In theory there should be the drip of water, but the air felt quite dry.

He tried another match, and this time raised it as high as he could and peered ahead.

A seven-foot warrior smiled at him.

Cohen looked up again.

"It's going to piss down in a minute," he said. "Will you look at that sky?"

There were hints of purple and red in the mass, and the occasional momentary glow of lightning somewhere inside the clouds.

"Teach?"

"Yes?"

"You know everything. Why's that cloud looking like that?"

Mr. Saveloy looked where Cohen was pointing. There was a yellowish cloud low on the horizon. Right around the horizon—

one thin streak, as though the sun was trying to find a way through.

"Could be the lining?" said Boy Willie.

"What lining?"

"Every cloud's supposed to have a silver one."

"Yeah, but that's more like gold."

"Well, gold's cheaper here."

"Is it me," said Mr. Saveloy, "or is it getting wider?"

Caleb was staring at the enemy lines.

"There's been a lot of blokes galloping about on their little horses," he said. "I hope they get a move on. We don't want to be here all day."

"I vote we rushes 'em while they're not expectin' it," said Hamish.

"Hold on . . . hold on . . ." said Truckle. There was the sound of many gongs being beaten, and the crackling of fireworks. "Looks like the bas—the lovechilds are moving."

"Thank goodness for that," said Cohen. He stood up and stubbed out his cigarette.

Mr. Saveloy trembled with excitement.

"Do we sing a song for the gods before we go into battle?" he said.

"You can if you like," said Cohen.

"Well, do we say any heathen chants or prayers?"

"Shouldn't think so," said Cohen. He glanced up at the horizon-girdling band. It was unsettling him far more than the approaching enemy. It was wider now, but slightly paler. For just a moment he found himself wishing that there was one god or goddess somewhere whose temple he hadn't violated, robbed, or burned down.

"Don't we bang our swords on our shields and utter defiance?" said the teacher hopefully.

"Too late for that, really," said Cohen.

Mr. Saveloy looked so crestfallen at the lack of pagan splendor that the ancient barbarian was, to his own surprise, moved to add: "But feel free, if that's what you want."

The Horde drew their various swords. In Hamish's case, another axe was produced from under his rug.

"See you in Heaven!" said Mr. Saveloy excitedly.

"Yeah, right," said Caleb, eyeing the line of approaching soldiers.

"Where there's feasting and young ladies and so forth!"

"Yeah, yeah," said Boy Willie, testing the blade of his sword.

"And carousing and quaffing, I believe!"

"Could be," said Vincent, trying to ease the tendonitis in his arm.

"And we'll do that thing, you know, where you throw the axes and cut ladies' plaits off!"

"Yeah, if you like."

"But—"

"Whut?"

"The actual feasting . . . Do they do anything vegetarian?"

And the advancing army screamed and charged.

They rushed at the Horde, almost as fast as the clouds boiling in from every direction.

Rincewind's brain unfroze slowly, in the darkness and silence of the hill.

It's a statue, he told himself. That's all it is. No problem there. Not even a particularly good one. Just a big statue of a man in armor. Look, there's a couple more, you can just see them at the edge of the light . . .

"Ow!"

He dropped the match and sucked his fingers.

What he needed now was a wall. Walls had exits. True, they could also be entrances, but now there did not seem much danger of any guards hurrying in here. The air had an ancient smell, with a hint of fox and a slight trace of thunderstorms, but above all it tasted unused.

He crept forward, testing each step with his foot.

Then there *was* light. A small blue spark jumped off Rincewind's finger.

Cohen grabbed at his beard. It was straining away from his face.

Mr. Saveloy's fringe of hair stood out from his head and sparked at the ends.

"Static discharges!" he shouted, above the crackle.

Ahead of them the spears of the enemy glowed at the tips. The charge faltered. There was the occasional shriek as sparks leaped from man to man.

Cohen looked up.

"Oh, my," he said. "Will you look at *that!*"

Tiny sparks flickered around Rincewind as he eased himself over the unseen floor.

The word *tomb* had presented itself for his consideration, and one thing Rincewind knew about large tombs was that their builders were often jolly inventive in the traps and spikes department. They also put in things like paintings and statues, possibly so that the dead had something to look at if they became bored.

Rincewind's hand touched stone, and he moved carefully sideways. Now and again his feet touched something yielding and soft. He very much hoped it was mud.

And then, right at hand height, was a lever. It stuck out fully two feet.

Now . . . it *could* be a trap. But traps were generally, well, traps. The first you knew about them was when your head was rolling along the corridor several yards away. And trap builders tended to be straightforwardly homicidal and seldom required victims to actively participate in their own destruction.

Rincewind pulled it.

The yellow cloud sailed overhead in its millions, moving much faster on the wind they'd created than the slow beating of their wings would suggest. Behind them came the storm.

Mr. Saveloy blinked.

"Butterflies?"

Both sides stopped as the creatures sleeted past. It was even possible to hear the rustle of their wings.

"All right, Teach," said Cohen. "Explain *this* one."

"It, it, it could be a natural phenomenon," said Mr. Saveloy.

"Er . . . Monarch butterflies, for example, have been known to . . . er . . . to tell you the truth, I don't know . . ."

The cloud swarmed on towards the hill.

"Not some kind of sign?" said Cohen. "There must have been *some* temple I didn't rob."

"The trouble with signs and portents," said Boy Willie, "is you never know who they're for. This'n could be a nice one for Hong and his pals."

"Then I'm nicking it," said Cohen.

"You can't steal a message from the gods!" said Mr. Saveloy.

"Can you see it nailed down anywhere? No? Sure? Right. So it's mine."

He raised his sword as the stragglers fluttered past overhead.

"The gods smile on us!" he bellowed. "Hahaha!"

"Hahaha?" whispered Mr. Saveloy.

"Just to worry 'em," said Cohen.

He glanced at the other members of the Horde. Each man nodded, very slightly.

"All right, lads," he said quietly. "This is it."

"Er . . . what do I do?" said Mr. Saveloy.

"Think of something to make yourself good and angry. That gets the ole blood boiling. Imagine the enemy is everything you hate."

"Head teachers," said Mr. Saveloy.

"Good."

"Sports masters!" shouted Mr. Saveloy.

"Yep."

"Boys who chew gum!" screamed Mr. Saveloy.

"Look at him, steam coming out of his ears already," said Cohen. "First one to the afterlife gets 'em in. Charge!"

The yellow cloud thronged up the slopes of the hill and then, carried on the uprising wind, rose.

Above it the storm rose, too, piling up and up and spreading into a shape something like a hammer—

It struck.

Lightning hit the iron pagoda so hard that it exploded into white-hot fragments.

*   *   *

It is confusing for an entire army to be attacked by seven old men. No book of tactics is up to the task of offering advice. There is a tendency towards bafflement.

The soldiers backed away in the face of the rush and then, driven by currents in the great mass of men, closed in behind.

A solid circle of shields surrounded the Horde. It buckled and swayed under the press of men, and also under the blows rained on it by Mr. Saveloy's sword.

"Come on, fight!" he shouted. "Smoke pipes at me, would you? You! That boy there! Answer me back, eh! Take that!"

Cohen looked at Caleb, who shrugged. He'd seen berserk rages in his time, but nothing quite so incandescent as Mr. Saveloy.

The circle broke as a couple of men tried to dart backwards and cannoned into the rank behind and then rebounded on to the swords of the Horde. One of Hamish's wheels caught a soldier a vicious blow on the knee and, as he bent over, one of Hamish's axes met him coming the other way.

It wasn't speed. The Horde couldn't move very fast. But it *was* economy. Mr. Saveloy had remarked on it. They were simply always where they wanted to be, which was never where someone's sword was. They let everyone else do the running around. A soldier would risk a slash in the direction of Truckle and find Cohen rising in front of him, grinning and swinging, or Boy Willie giving him a nod of acknowledgement and a stab. Occasionally one of the Horde took time to parry a blow aimed at Mr. Saveloy, who was far too excited to defend himself.

"Pull back, you bloody fools!"

Lord Hong appeared behind the throng, his horse rearing, his helmet visor flung back.

The soldiers tried to obey. Finally, the press eased a little, and then opened. The Horde were left in a widening ring of shields. There was something like silence, broken only by the endless thunder and the crackle of lightning on the hill.

And then, pushing their way angrily through the soldiers, came an altogether different breed of warrior. They were taller, and heavier armored, with splendid helmets and moustaches that looked like a declaration of war in themselves.

One of them glared at Cohen.

"Orrrrr! Itiyorshu! Yutimishu!"

"Wassat?" said Cohen.

"He's a samurai," said Mr. Saveloy, wiping his forehead. "The warrior caste. I think that's their formal challenge. Er. Would you like me to fight him?"

One samurai glared at Cohen. He pulled a scrap of silk out of his armor and tossed it into the air. His other hand grabbed the hilt of his long, thin sword . . .

There was hardly even a hiss, but three shreds of silk tumbled gently to the ground.

"Get back, Teach," said Cohen slowly. "I reckon this one's mine. Got another hanky? Thanks."

The samurai looked at Cohen's sword. It was long, heavy and had so many notches it could have been used as a saw.

"You'll never do it," he said. "With that sword? Never."

Cohen blew his nose noisily.

"You say?" he said. "Watch this."

The handkerchief soared into the air. Cohen gripped his sword . . .

He'd beheaded three upward-staring samurai before the handkerchief started to tumble. Other members of the Horde, who tended to think in much the same way as their leader, had accounted for half a dozen more.

"Got the idea from Caleb," said Cohen. "And the message is: either fight or muck about, it's up to you."

"Have you no honor?" screamed Lord Hong. "Are you just a ruffian?"

"I'm a barbarian," shouted Cohen. "And the honor I got, see, is mine. I didn't steal it off'f someone else."

"I had wanted to take you alive," said Lord Hong. "However, I see no reason to stick to this policy."

He drew his sword.

"Back, you scum!" he screamed. "Right back! Let the bombardiers come forward!" He looked back at Cohen. His face was flushed. His spectacles were askew.

Lord Hong had lost his temper. And, as is always the case when a dam bursts, it engulfs whole countries.

The soldiers pulled back.

The Horde were, once again, in a widening circle.

"What's a bombardier?" said Boy Willie.

"Er, I believe it must mean people who fire some sort of projectile," said Mr. Saveloy. "The word derives from—"

"Oh, archers," said Boy Willie, and spat.

"Whut?"

"He said THEY'RE GOING TO USE ARCHERS, Hamish!"

"Heheh, we never let archers stop us at the Battle of Koom Valley!" cackled the antique barbarian.

Boy Willie sighed.

"That was between dwarfs and trolls, Hamish," he said. "And you ain't either. So whose side were you on?"

"Whut?"

"I said WHOSE SIDE WERE YOU ON?"

"I were on the side of being paid money to fight," said Hamish.

"Best side there is."

Rincewind lay on the floor with his hands over his ears.

The sound of thunder filled the underground chamber. Blue and purple light shone so brightly that he could see it through his eyelids.

Finally the cacophony subsided. There were still the sounds of the storm outside, but the light had faded to a blue-white glow, and the sound into a steady humming.

Rincewind risked rolling over and opening his eyes.

Hanging from rusted chains in the roof were big glass globes. Each one was the size of a man, and lightning crackled and sizzled inside, stabbing at the glass, seeking a way out.

At one time there must have been many more. But dozens of the big globes had fallen down over the years, and lay in pieces on the floor. There were still scores up there, swaying gently on their chains as the imprisoned thunderstorms fought for their freedom.

The air felt greasy. Sparks crawled over the floor and crackled on each angle.

Rincewind stood up. His beard streamed out as a mass of individual hairs.

The lightning globes shone down on a round lake of, to judge from the ripples, pure quicksilver. In the centre was a low, five-sided island. As Rincewind stared, a boat came drifting gently around to his side of the pool, making little *slupslup* noises as it moved through the mercury.

It was not a lot larger than a rowing boat and, lying on its tiny deck, was a figure in armor. Or possibly just the armor. If it *was* just empty armor, then it was lying in the arms-folded position of a suit of armor that has passed away.

Rincewind sidled around the silver lake until he reached a slab of what looked very much like gold, set in the floor in front of a statue.

He knew you got inscriptions in tombs, although he was never sure who it was who was supposed to read them. The gods, possibly, although surely they knew everything already? He'd never considered that they'd cluster round and say things like, "Gosh, 'Dearly Beloved' was he? I never knew that."

This one simply said, in pictograms: One Sun Mirror.

There wasn't anything about mighty conquests. There was no list of his tremendous achievements. There was nothing down there about wisdom or being the father of his people. There was no *explanation*. Whoever knows this name, it seemed to say, knows everything. And there was no admitting the possibility that anyone getting this far would not have heard the name of One Sun Mirror.

The statue looked like porcelain. It had been painted quite realistically. One Sun Mirror seemed an ordinary sort of man. You would not have pointed him out in a crowd as Emperor material. But this man, with his little round hat and little round shield and little round men on little round ponies, had glued together a thousand warring factions into one great Empire, often using their own blood to do it.

Rincewind looked closer. Of course, it was just an impression, but around the set of the mouth and the look of the eyes there was an expression he'd last seen on the face of Ghenghiz Cohen.

It was the expression of someone who was absolutely and totally unafraid of anything.

The little boat headed towards the far side of the lake.

One of the globes flickered a little and then faded to red. It winked out. Another followed it.

He had to get out.

There was something else, though. At the foot of the statue, lying as if they'd just been dropped there, were a helmet, a pair of gauntlets, and two heavy-looking boots.

Rincewind picked up the helmet. It didn't look very strong, but it did look quite light. Normally he didn't bother with protective clothing, reasoning that the best defense against threatening danger was to be on another continent, but right now the idea of armor had its attractions.

He removed his hat, put the helmet on, pulled down the visor, and then wedged the hat on top of the helmet.

There was a flicker in front of his eyes and Rincewind was staring at the back of his own head. It was a grainy picture, and it was in shades of green rather than proper colors, but it was definitely the back of his own head he was looking at. People had told him what it looked like.

He raised the visor and blinked.

The pool was still in front of him.

He lowered the visor.

There he was, about fifty feet away, with this helmet on his head.

He waved a hand up and down.

The figure in the visor waved a hand up and down.

He turned around and faced himself. Yep. That was him.

Okay, he thought. A magic helmet. It lets you see yourself a long way away. Great. You can have fun watching yourself fall into holes you can't see because they're right up close.

He turned around again, raised the visor and inspected the gloves. They seemed as light as the helmet but quite clumsy. You could hold a sword, but not much else.

He tried one on. Immediately, with a faint sizzling noise, a row of little pictures lit up on the wide cuff. They showed soldiers. Soldiers digging, soldiers fighting, soldiers climbing . . .

Ah. So . . . *magic* armor. Perfectly normal magic armor. It had never been very popular in Ankh-Morpork. Of course, it was light. You could make it as thin as cloth. But it tended to lose its magic without warning. Many an ancient lord's last words had been, "You can't kill me because I've got magic aaargh."

Rincewind looked at the boots, with suspicious recollection of the trouble there had been with the University's prototype Seven League Boots. Footwear which tried to make you take steps twenty-one miles long imposed unfortunate groinal strains; they'd got the things off the student just in time, but he'd still had to wear a special device for several months, and ate standing up.

All right, but even *old* magic armor would be useful now. It wasn't as if it weighed much, and the mud of Hunghung hadn't improved what was left of his own boots. He put his feet into them.

He thought: Well, so what is supposed to happen now?

He straightened up.

And behind him, with the sound of seven thousand flower pots smashing together, the lightning still crackling over them, the Red Army came to attention.

Hex had grown a bit during the night. Adrian Turnipseed, who had been on duty to feed the mice and rewind the clockwork and clean out the dead ants, had sworn that he'd done nothing else and that no one had come in.

But now, where there had been the big clumsy arrangement of blocks so that the results could be read, was a quill pen in the middle of a network of pulleys and levers.

"Watch," said Adrian, nervously tapping out a very simple problem. "It's come up with this after doing all those spells at suppertime . . ."

The ants scuttled. The clockwork spun. The springs and levers jerked so sharply that Ponder took a step back.

The quill pen wobbled over to an inkwell, dipped, returned to the sheet of paper Adrian had put under the levers, and began to write.

"It blots a bit," he said, in a helpless tone of voice. "What's *happening?*"

Ponder had been thinking further about this. The latest conclusions hadn't been comforting.

"Well . . . we know that books containing magic become a little bit . . . sapient . . ." he began. "And we've made a *machine* for . . ."

"You mean it's *alive?*"

"Come on, let's not get all occult about this," said Ponder, trying to sound jovial. "We're wizards, after all."

"Listen, you know that long problem in thaumic fields you wanted me to put in?"

"Yes. Well?"

"It gave me the answer at midnight," said Adrian, his face pale.

"Good."

"Yes, good, except that I didn't actually *give* it the problem until half past one, Ponder."

"You're telling me you got the answer before you asked the question?"

"Yes!"

"Why *did* you ask the question, then?"

"I thought about it, and I thought maybe I had to. I mean, it couldn't have known what the answer was going to be if I didn't give it the problem, yes?"

"Good point. Er. You waited ninety minutes, though."

Adrian looked at his pointy boots.

"I . . . was hiding in the privy. Well, Redo from Start could—"

"All right, all right. Go and have something to eat."

"Are we meddling with things we don't understand, Ponder?"

Ponder looked up at the gnomic bulk of the machine. It didn't seem threatening, merely . . . *other.*

He thought: meddle first, understand later. You had to meddle a *bit* before you had anything to try to understand. And the thing was never, ever, to go back and hide in the Lavatory of

Unreason. You have to try to get your mind around the Universe before you can give it a twist.

Perhaps we shouldn't have given you a name. We didn't think about that. It was a joke. But we should have remembered that names are important. A thing with a name is a bit more than a thing.

"Off you go, Adrian," he said firmly.

He sat down and carefully typed:

Hello.

Things whirred.

The quill wrote:

+++ ?????? +++ Hello +++ Redo From Start +++

Far above, a butterfly—its wings an undistinguished yellow, with black markings—fluttered through an open window.

Ponder began the calculations for the transfer between Hunghung and Ankh-Morpork.

The butterfly alighted for a moment on the maze of glass pipes. When it rose again, it left behind a very small blob of nectar.

Ponder typed carefully, far below.

A small but significant ant, one of the scurrying thousands, emerged from a break in the tube and spent a few seconds sucking at the sweet liquid before going back to work.

After a while, Hex gave an answer. Apart from one small but significant point, it was entirely correct.

Rincewind turned around.

With an echoing chorus of creaks and groans, the Red Army turned around, too.

And it *was* red. It was the same color, Rincewind realized, as the soil.

He'd bumped into a few statues in the darkness. He hadn't realized that there were *this* many. They stretched, rank on rank, into the distant shadows.

Experimentally, he turned around. Behind him, there was another chorus of stampings.

After a few false starts he found that the only way to end up facing them was to take off the boots, turn, and put the boots on again.

He lowered the visor for a moment, and saw himself lowering the visor for a moment.

He stuck up an arm. They stuck out their arms. He jumped up and down. They jumped up and down, with a crash that made the globes swing. Lightning sizzled from their boots.

He felt a sudden hysterical urge to laugh.

He touched his nose. They touched their noses. He made, with terrible glee, the traditional gesture for the dismissal of demons. Seven thousand terracotta middle fingers stabbed towards the ceiling.

He tried to calm down.

The word his mind had been groping for finally surfaced, and it was *golem.*

There were one or two of them, even in Ankh-Morpork. You were bound to get them in any area where you had wizards or priests of an experimental turn of mind. They were usually just figures made out of clay and animated with some suitable spell or prayer. They pottered about doing simple odd jobs, but they were not very fashionable these days. The problem was not putting them to work but stopping them from working; if you set a golem to digging the garden and then forgot about it, you'd come back to find it'd planted a row of beans 1500 miles long.

Rincewind looked down at one of the gloves.

He cautiously touched the little picture of a fighting soldier.

The sound of seven thousand swords being simultaneously unsheathed was like the tearing of a thick sheet of steel. Seven thousand points were pointed right at Rincewind.

He took a step back. So did the army.

He was in a place with thousands of artificial soldiers wearing swords. The fact that he appeared to have control of them was no great comfort. He'd theoretically had control of Rincewind for the whole of his life, and look what had happened to him.

He looked at the little pictures again. One of them showed a soldier with two heads. When he touched it, the army turned about smartly. Ah.

Now to get out of here . . .

* * *

The Horde watched the bustle among Lord Hong's men. Objects were being dragged to the front line.

"They don't look like archers to me," said Boy Willie.

"Those things are Barking Dogs," said Cohen. "I should know. Seen 'em before. They're like a barrel full of fireworks, and when the fireworks are lit a big stone comes rushing out of the other end."

"Why?"

"Well, would you hang around if someone had just lit a firework by your arse?"

"Here, Teach, he said 'arse'," complained Truckle. "Look, on my bit of paper here it says you mustn't say—"

"We've got shields, haven't we?" said Mr. Saveloy. "I'm sure if we keep close together and put the shields over our heads we'll be as right as rain."

"The stone's about a foot across and going very fast and it's red hot."

"Not shields, then?"

"No," said Cohen. "Truckle, you push Hamish—"

"We won't get fifty yards, Ghenghiz," said Caleb.

"Better fifty yards now than six feet in a minute, yes?" said Cohen.

"Bravo!" said Mr. Saveloy.

"Whut?"

Lord Hong watched them. He saw the Horde hang their shields around the wheelchair to form a crude traveling wall, and saw the wheels begin to turn.

He raised his sword.

"Fire!"

"Still tamping the charges, o lord!"

"I said *fire!*"

"Got to prime the Dogs, o lord!"

The bombardiers worked feverishly, spurred on less by terror of Lord Hong than by the onrushing Horde.

Mr. Saveloy's hair streamed in the wind. He bounded through the dust, waving his sword and screaming.

He'd never been so happy in all his life.

So this was the secret at the heart of it all: to look death right in the face and charge . . . It made everything so utterly simple.

Lord Hong threw down his helmet. "Fire, you wretched peasants! You scum of the earth! Why must I ask twice! Give me that torch!"

He pushed a bombardier aside, crouched down beside a Dog, heaved on it so that the barrel was pointing at the oncoming Cohen, lifted the torch—

The earth heaved. The Dog reared and rolled sideways.

A round red head, smiling faintly, rose out of the ground.

There were screams in the ranks as the soldiers looked down at the moving dirt under their boots, tried to run on a surface that was just shifting soil, and disappeared in the rising cloud of dust.

The ground caved in.

Then it caved out again as stricken soldiers climbed up one another to escape because, rising gently through the turmoil, was the soil in human shape.

The Horde skidded to a halt.

"What're they? Trolls?" said Cohen. Ten of the figures were visible now, industriously digging at the air.

Then they stopped. One of them turned its gently smiling head this way and that.

A sergeant must have screamed a handful of archers into line, because a few arrows shattered on the terracotta armor, with absolutely no effect.

Other red warriors were climbing up behind the former diggers. They collided with them, with a sound of crockery. Then, as one man—or troll, or demon—they drew their swords, turned around, and headed towards Lord Hong's army.

A few soldiers tried to fight them simply because there was too great a crowd behind them to run away. They died.

It wasn't that the red guards were good fighters. They were very mechanical, each one performing the same thrust, parry, slash, regardless of what their opponent was doing. But they were simply unstoppable. If their opponent escaped one of the blows but didn't get out of the way then he was just trodden on—and by the looks of things, the warriors were extremely heavy.

And it was the way the things *smiled* all the time that added to the terror.

"Well, now, there's a thing," Cohen said, feeling for his tobacco pouch.

"Never seen trolls fight like that," said Truckle. Rank after rank was walking up out of the hole, stabbing happily at the air.

The front row were moving in a cloud of dust and screams. It is hard for a big army to do anything quickly, and divisions trying to move forward to see what the trouble was were getting in the way of fleeing individuals seeking a hole to hide in and permanent civilian status. Gongs were banging and men were trying to shout orders, but no one knew what the gongs were meant to mean or how the orders should be obeyed, because there didn't seem to be enough time.

Cohen finished rolling his cigarette, and struck a match on his chin.

"Right," he said, to the world in general. "Let's get that bloody Hong."

The clouds overhead were less fearsome now. There was less lightning. But there were still a lot of them, greeny-black, heavy with rain.

"But this is *amazing!*" said Mr. Saveloy.

A few drops hit the ground, leaving wide craters in the dirt.

"Yeah, right," said Cohen.

"A most strange phenomenon! Warriors rising out of the ground!"

The craters joined up. It felt as though the drops were joining up as well. The rain began to pour down.

"Dunno," said Cohen, watching a ragged platoon flee past. "Never been here before. P'raps this happens a lot."

"I mean, it's just like that myth about the man who sowed dragons' teeth and terrible fighting skeletons came up!"

"I don't believe *that*," said Caleb, as they jogged after Cohen.

"Why not?"

"If you sow dragons' teeth, you should get dragons. Not fighting skeletons. What did it say on the packet?"

"I don't know! The myth never said anything about them coming in a packet!"

"Should've said 'Comes up Dragons' on the packet."

"You can't believe myths," said Cohen. "I should know. Right . . . there he is . . . " he added, pointing to a distant horseman.

The whole plain was in turmoil now. The red warriors were only the start. The alliance of the five warlords was glass fragile in any case, and panicky flight was instantly interpreted as sneak attack. No one paid any attention to the Horde. They didn't have any colored pennants or gongs. They weren't traditional enemies. And, besides, the soil was now mud, and the mud flew, and everyone from the waist down was the same color and this was rising.

"What're we doing, Ghenghiz?" said Mr. Saveloy.

"We're heading back for the palace."

"Why?"

"'Cos that's where Hong's gone."

"But there's this astonishing—"

"Look, Teach, I've seen walking trees and spider gods and big green things with teeth," said Cohen. "It's no good goin' around saying 'astonishing' all the time, ain't that so, Truckle?"

"Right. D'you know, when I went after that Five-Headed Vampire Goat over in Skund they said I shouldn't on account of it being an endangered species? I said, yes, that was down to me. Were they grateful?"

"Huh," said Caleb. "Should've thanked you, giving them all those endangered species to worry about. Turn around and go home right now, soldier boy!"

A group of soldiers, fighting to get away from the red warriors, skidded in the mud, stared in terror at the Horde, and headed off in a new direction.

Truckle stopped for breath, rain streaming off his beard.

"I can't be having with this running, though," he said. "Not and push Hamish's wheelchair in all this mud. Let's have a breather."

"Whut?"

"Stopping for a breather?" said Cohen. "My gods! I never thought I'd see the day! A *hero* having a rest? Did Voltan the Indestructible have a bit of a rest?"

"He's having one now. He's dead, Ghenghiz," said Caleb.

Cohen hesitated.

"What, old Voltan?"

"Didn't you know? And the Immortal Jenkins."

"Jenkins isn't dead, I saw him only last year."

"But he's dead now. All the heroes are dead, 'cept us. And I ain't too sure about me, too."

Cohen splashed forward and snatched Caleb upright by his shirt.

"What about Hrun? He can't be dead. He's half our age!"

"Last I heard he got a job. Sergeant of the Guard somewhere."

"Sergeant of the *Guard?*" said Cohen. "What, for *pay?*"

"Yep."

"But . . . what, like, for *pay?*"

"He told me he might make Captain next year. He said . . . he said it's a job with a pension."

Cohen released his grip.

"There's not many of us now, Cohen," said Truckle.

Cohen spun around.

"All right, but there's never been many of us! And I ain't dyin'"! Not if it means the world's taken over by bastards like Hong, who don't know what a chieftain is. Scum. That's what he called his soldiers. Scum. It's like that bloody civilized game you showed us, Teach!"

"Chess?"

"Right. The prawns are just there to be slaughtered by the other side! While the king just hangs around at the back."

"Yeah, but the other side's *you,* Cohen."

"Right! Right . . . well, *yes,* that's fine when I'm the *enemy.* But I don't shove men in front of me to get killed instead of me. And I never use bows and them dog things. When I kill someone it's up close and personal. Armies? Bloody tactics? There's only one way to fight, and that's everyone charging all at once, waving their swords and shouting! Now on your feet and let's get after him!"

"It's been a long morning, Ghenghiz," said Boy Willie.

"Don't give me that!"

"I could do with the lavatory. It's all this rain."

Terry Pratchett

"Let's get Hong first."

"If he's hiding in the privy that's fine by me."

They reached the city gates. They had been shut. Hundreds of people, citizens as well as guards, watched them from the walls.

Cohen waved a finger at them.

"Now I ain't gonna say this twice," he said. "I'm coming in, okay? It can be the easy way, or it can be the hard way."

Impassive faces looked down at the skinny old man, and up at the plain, where the armies of the warlords fought one another and, in terror, the terracotta warriors. Down. Up. Down. Up.

"Right," said Cohen. "Don't say afterwards I didn't *warn* youse."

He raised his sword and prepared to charge.

"Wait," said Mr. Saveloy. "Listen . . ."

There was shouting behind the walls, and some confused orders, and then more shouting. And then a couple of screams.

The gates swung open, pulled by dozens of citizens.

Cohen lowered his sword.

"Ah," he said, "they've seen reason, have they?"

Wheezing a little, the Horde limped through the gates. The crowd watched them in silence. Several guards lay dead. Rather more had removed their helmets and decided to opt for a bright new future in Civvy Street, where you were less likely to get beaten to death by an angry mob.

Every face watched Cohen, turning to follow him as flowers follow the sun.

He ignored them.

"Crowdie the Strong?" he said to Caleb.

"Dead."

"Can't be. He was a picture of health when I saw him a coupla months ago. Going on a new quest and everything."

"Dead."

"What happened?"

"You know the Terrible Man-eating Sloth of Clup?"

"The one they say guards the giant ruby of the mad snake god?"

"The very same. Well . . . it was."

The crowd parted to let the Horde through. One or two

people tried a cheer, but were shushed into silence. It was a silence that Mr. Saveloy had only heard before in the most devout of temples.*

There was a whispering, though, growing out of that watchful silence like bubbles in a pot of water on a hot fire.

It went like this.

The Red Army. The Red Army.

"How about Organdy Sloggo? Still going strong down in Howondaland, last I heard."

"Dead. Metal poisoning."

"How?"

"Three swords through the stomach."

The Red Army!

"Slasher Mungo?"

"Presumed dead in Skund."

"Presumed?"

"Well, they only found his head."

The Red Army!

The Horde approached the inner gates of the Forbidden City. The crowd followed them at a distance.

These gates were shut, too. A couple of heavy-set guards were standing in front of them. They wore the expressions of men who'd been told to guard the gates and were going to guard the gates come what may. The military depends on people who will guard gates or bridges or passes come what may and there are often heroic poems written in their honor, invariably posthumously.

"Gosbar the Wake?"

"Died in bed, I heard."

"Not old Gosbar!"

"Everyone's got to sleep some time."

"That's not the only thing they've got to do, mister," said Boy Willie. "I *really* need the wossname."

"Well, there's the Wall."

"Not with everyone watching! That ain't . . . civilized."

---

*The only sound the Horde had ever heard in temples was people shouting "Infidel! He has stolen the Jeweled Eye of—your wife is a big hippo!"

Cohen strode up to the guards.

"I'm not mucking about," he said. "Okay? Would you rather die than betray your Emperor?"

The guards stared ahead.

"Right, fair enough." Cohen drew his sword. A thought seemed to strike him.

"Nurker?" he said. "Big Nurker? Tough as old boots, him."

"Fishbone," said Caleb.

"Nurker? He once killed six trolls with a—"

"Choked on a fishbone in his gruel. I thought you knew. Sorry."

Cohen stared at him. And then at his sword. And then at the guards. For a moment there was silence, broken only by the sound of the rain.

"Y'know, lads," he said, in a voice so suddenly full of weariness that Mr. Saveloy felt a pit opening up, here, at the moment of triumph, "I was goin' to chop your heads off. But . . . what's the point, eh? I mean, when you get right down to it, why bother? What sort of difference does it make?"

The guards still stared straight ahead. But their eyes were widening.

Mr. Saveloy turned.

"You'll end up dead anyway, sooner or later," Cohen went on. "Well, that's about it. You live your life best way you can and then it don't actually matter, 'cos you're dead—"

"Er. Cohen?" said Mr. Saveloy.

"I mean, look at me. Been chopping heads off my whole life and what've I got to show for it?"

"Cohen . . ."

The guards weren't just staring now. Their faces were dragging themselves into very creditable grimaces of fear.

"Cohen?"

"Yeah, what?"

"I think you should look round, Cohen."

Cohen turned.

Half a dozen red warriors were advancing up the street. The crowd had pulled right back and were watching in silent terror.

Then a voice shouted: "Extended Duration To The Red Army!"

Cries rose up here and there in the crowd. A young woman raised her hand in a clenched fist.

"Advance Necessarily With The People While Retaining Due Regard For Traditions!"

Others joined her.

"Deserved Correction To Enemies!"

"I've lost Mr. Bunny!"

The red giants clonked to a halt.

"Look at them!" said Mr. Saveloy. "They're not trolls! They move like some kind of engine! Doesn't that interest you?"

"No," said Cohen, vacantly. "Abstract thinking is not a major aspect of the barbarian mental process. Now then, where was I?" He sighed. "Oh, yes. You two . . . you'd rather die than betray your Emperor, would you?"

The two men were rigid with fear now.

Cohen raised his sword.

Mr. Saveloy took a deep breath, grabbed Cohen's sword arm and shouted:

"Then open the gates and let him through!"

There was a moment of utter silence.

Mr. Saveloy nudged Cohen.

"Go on," he hissed. "Act like an Emperor!"

"What . . . you mean giggle, have people tortured, that sort of thing? Blow that!"

"No! Act like an Emperor ought to act!"

Cohen glared at Saveloy. Then he turned to the guards.

"Well done," he said. "Your loyalty does you . . . wossname . . . credit. Keep on like this and I can see it's promotion for both of you. Now let us all go inside or I will have my flowerpot men chop off your feet so you'll have to kneel in the gutter while you're looking for your head."

The men looked at one another, threw down their swords and tried to kowtow.

"And you can bloody well get up, too," said Cohen, in a slightly nicer tone of voice. "Mr. Saveloy?"

"Yes?"

"I'm Emperor now, am I?"

"The . . . earth soldiers seem to be on our side. The *people* think you've won. We're all alive. I'd say we've won, yes."

"If I'm Emperor, I can tell everyone what to do, right?"

"Oh, indeed."

"Properly. You know. Scrolls and stuff. Buggers in uniform blowing trumpets and saying, 'This is what he wants you to do.'"

"Ah. You want to make a proclamation."

"Yeah. No more of this bloody kowtowing. It makes me squirm. No kowtowing by anyone to anyone, all right? If anyone sees me they can salute, or maybe give me some money. But none of this banging your head on the ground stuff. It gives me the willies. Now, dress that up in proper writing."

"Right away. And—"

"Hang on, haven't finished yet." Cohen bit his lip in unaccustomed cogitation, as the red warriors lurched to a stop. "Yeah. You can add that I'm letting all prisoners go free, unless they've done something really bad. Like attempted poisoning, for a start. You can work out the details. All torturers to have their heads cut off. And every peasant can have a free pig, something like that. I'll leave you to put in all the proper curly bits about 'by order' and stuff."

Cohen looked down at the guards.

"Get *up*, I said. I swear, the next bastard that kisses the ground in front of me is gonna get kicked in the antique chicken coops. Okay? Now open the gates."

The crowd cheered. As the Horde stepped inside the Forbidden City they followed, in a sort of cross between a revolutionary charge and a respectful walk.

The red warriors stood outside. One of them raised a terracotta foot, which groaned a little, and walked towards the wall until it bumped into it.

The warrior staggered drunkenly for a while and then managed to get within a yard or two of the wall without colliding with it.

It raised a finger and wrote, shakily, in red dust that turned to a kind of paint on the wet plaster:

HELP HELP ITS ME IM OUT HERE ON THEE PLAIN HELP I CANT GET THIS BLODY ARMER OFF.

The crowd surged along behind Cohen, shouting and singing. If he'd had a surfboard, he could have ridden on it. The rain drummed heavily on the roof and poured into the courtyards.

"Why're they all so excited?" he said.

"They think you're going to sack the palace," said Mr. Saveloy. "They've heard about barbarians, you see. They want some of it. Anyway, they like the idea about the pig."

"Hey, you!" shouted Cohen to a boy struggling past under the weight of a huge vase. "Get your thieving paws off my stuff! That's valuable, that is! It's a . . . a . . ."

"It's S'ang Dynasty," said Mr. Saveloy.

"That's right," said the vase.

"That's a S'ang Dynasty, that is! Put it back! And you lot back there—" He turned and waved his sword. "Get those shoes off! You're scratching the floor! Look at the state of it already!"

"You never bothered about the floor yesterday," Truckle grumbled.

"'Tweren't my floor then."

"Yes, it was," said Mr. Saveloy.

"Not properly," said Cohen. "*Rite* of conquest, that's the thing. Blood. People understand blood. You just walk in and take over and no one takes it seriously. But seas of blood . . . Everyone understands that."

"Mountains of skulls," said Truckle approvingly.

"Look at history," said Cohen. "Whenever you—Hey, you, the man with the hat, that's my . . ."

"Inlaid mahogany *Shibo Yangcong-san* table," murmured Mr. Saveloy.

"—so put it back, d'you hear? Yes, whenever you comes across a king where everyone says, 'Oo, he was a good king all right,' you can bet your sandals he was a great big bearded bastard who broke heads a lot and laughed about it. Hey? But some king who just passed decent little laws and read books and tried to look intelligent . . . 'Oh,' they say, 'oh, he was all right, a bit wet, not what I'd call a proper king.' That's people for you."

Mr. Saveloy sighed.

Cohen grinned at him and slapped him on the back so hard

he stumbled into two women trying to carry off a bronze statue of Ly Tin Wheedle.

"Can't quite face it, Teach, can you? Can't get your mind round it? Don't worry about it. Basically, you ain't a barbarian. *Put the damn statue back, missus, or you'll feel the flat of my sword, so you will!*"

"But I thought we could do it without anyone getting hurt. By using our brains."

"Can't. History don't work like that. Blood first, then brains."

"Mountains of skulls," said Truckle.

"There's got to be a better way than fighting," said Mr. Saveloy.

"Yep. Lots of 'em. Only none of 'em work. Caleb, take those . . . those . . ."

"—fine Bhong jade miniatures—" muttered Mr. Saveloy.

"—take them off that feller. He's got one under his hat."

Another set of carved doors was swung open. This room was already crowded, but the people shuffled backwards as the doors parted and tried to look keen while avoiding catching Cohen's eye.

As they pulled away they left Six Beneficent Winds standing all alone. The court had become very good at this maneuver.

"Mountains of skulls," said Truckle, not a man to let go in a hurry.

"Er. We saw the Red Army rise out of the ground, er, just as the legend foretold. Er. Truly you are the preincarnation of One Sun Mirror."

The little taxman had the decency to look embarrassed. As speeches went it was on a dramatic level with the one that traditionally began, "As you know, your father—the king—" Besides, he'd never believed in legends up to now—not even the one about the peasant who every year filed a scrupulously honest tax return.

"Yeah, right," said Cohen.

He strode to the throne and stuck his sword in the floor, where it vibrated.

"Some of you are going to get your heads cut off for your own good," he said. "But I haven't decided who yet. And someone show Boy Willie where the privy is."

"No need," said Boy Willie. "Not after them big red statues turned up behind me so sudden."

"Mountains of—" Truckle began.

"Dunno about mountains," said Cohen.

"And where," said Six Beneficent Winds tremulously, "is the Great Wizard?"

"Great Wizard," said Cohen.

"Yes, the Great Wizard who summoned the Red Army from the earth," said the taxman.

"Don't know anything about *him*," said Cohen.

The crowd staggered forward as more people piled into the room.

"They're coming!"

A terracotta warrior clomped its way into the room, its face still wearing a very faint smile.

It stopped, rocking a little, while water dripped off it.

People had crouched back in terror. Except the Horde, Mr. Saveloy noticed. Faced with unknown yet terrible dangers, the Horde were either angry or puzzled.

Then he cheered up. They weren't better, just different. They're all right facing huge terrible creatures, he told himself, but ask them to go down the street and buy a bag of rice and they go all to pieces . . .

"What's my move now, Teach?" Cohen whispered.

"Well, you're Emperor," said Mr. Saveloy. "I think you talk to it."

"Okay."

Cohen stood up and nodded cheerfully at the terracotta giant.

"'Morning," he said. "Nice bit of work out there. You and the rest of your lads can have the day off to plant geraniums in yourselves or whatever you do. Er. You got a Number One giant I ought to speak to?"

The terracotta warrior creaked as it raised one finger.

Then it pressed two fingers against one forearm, then raised a finger again.

Everyone in the crowd started talking at once.

The giant tugged one vestigial ear with two fingers.

"What can this mean?" said Six Beneficent Winds.

"I find this a little hard to credit," said Mr. Saveloy, "but it is an ancient method of communication used in the land of blood-sucking vampire ghosts."

"You can understand it?"

"Oh, yes. I think so. You have to try to guess the word or phrase. It's trying to tell us . . . er . . . one word, two syllables. First syllable sounds like . . ."

The giant cupped one hand and made circular, handle-turning motions with the other alongside it.

"Turning," said Mr. Saveloy. "Winding? Reeling? Revolve? Grind? Grind? Chop? Mince—"

The giant tapped its nose hurriedly and did a very heavy, noisy dance, bits of terracotta armor clanking.

"Sounds like mince," said Mr. Saveloy. "First syllable sounds like mince."

"Er . . ."

A ragged figure pushed its way through the crowd. It wore glasses, one lens of which was cracked.

"Er," it said, "I've got an idea about that . . ."

Lord Fang and some of his more trusted warriors had clustered on the side of the hill. A good general always knows when to leave the battlefield, and as far as Lord Fang was concerned, it was when he saw the enemy coming towards him.

The men were shaken. They hadn't tried to face the Red Army. Those who had were dead.

"We . . . regroup," panted Lord Fang. "And then we'll wait until nightfall and—What's that?"

There was a rhythmic noise coming from the bushes further up the slope, where sliding earth had left another bush-filled ravine.

"Sounds like a carpenter, m'lord," said one of the soldiers.

"Up here? In the middle of a war? Go and see what it is!"

The man scrambled away. After a while there was a pause in the sawing noise. Then it started again.

Lord Fang had been trying to work out a fresh battle plan according to the Nine Useful Principles. He threw down his map.

"Why is that still going on? Where is Captain Nong?"

"Hasn't come back, m'lord."

"Then go and see what has happened to him!"

Lord Fang tried to remember if the great military sage had ever had anything to say about fighting giant invulnerable statues. He—

The sawing paused. Then it was replaced by the sound of hammering.

Lord Fang looked around.

"Can I have an order obeyed around here?" he bellowed.

He picked up his sword and scrambled up the muddy slope. The bushes parted ahead of him. There was a clearing. There was a rushing shape, on hundreds of little le—

There was a snap.

The rain was coming down so fast that the drops were having to queue.

The red earth was hundreds of feet deep in places. It produced two or three crops a year. It was rich. It was fecund. It was, when wet, extremely sticky.

The surviving armies had squelched from the field of battle, as red from head to toe as the terracotta men. Not counting those merely trodden on, the Red Army had not in fact killed very many people. Terror had done most of *their* work. Rather more soldiers had been killed in the brief inter-army battles and, in the scramble to escape, by their own sides.*

The terracotta army had the field to itself. It was celebrating victory in various ways. Many guards were walking around in circles, wading through the clinging mud as if it was so much dirty air. A number were digging a trench, the sides of which were washing in on them in the thundering rain. A few were trying to climb walls that weren't there. Several, possibly as a result of the exertion following centuries of zero maintenance, had spontaneously exploded in a shower of blue sparks, the red-hot clay shrapnel being a major factor in the opposition's death count.

---

*"Friendly stab", as it is formally known.

And all the time the rain fell, a solid curtain of water. It didn't look natural. It was as though the sea had decided to reclaim the land by air drop.

Rincewind shut his eyes. Mud covered the armor. He couldn't make out the pictures any more, and that was something of a relief because he was pretty certain he was messing things up. You could see what any warrior was seeing—at least, presumably you could, if you knew what some of the odder pictures actually did and how to press them in the right order. Rincewind didn't, and in any case whoever had made the magic armor hadn't assumed it would be used in knee-deep mud during a vertical river. Every now and again it sizzled. One of the boots was getting hot.

It had started out so well! But there had been what he was coming to think of as the Rincewind factor. Probably some other wizard would have marched the army out and wouldn't have been rained on and even now would be parading through the streets of Hunghung while people threw flowers and said, "My word, there's a Great Wizard and no mistake."

Some *other* wizard wouldn't have pressed the wrong picture and started the things digging.

He realized he was wallowing in self-pity. Rather more pertinently, he was also wallowing in mud. And he was sinking. Trying to pull a foot out was no use—it didn't work, and the other foot only went deeper, and got hotter.

Lightning struck the ground nearby. He heard it sizzle, saw the steam, felt the tingle of electricity and tasted the taste of burning tin.

Another bolt hit a warrior. Its torso exploded, raining a sticky black tar. The legs kept going for a few steps, and then stopped.

Water poured past him, thick and red now that the river Hung was overflowing. And the mud continued to suck on his feet like a hollow tooth.

Something swirled past on the muddy water. It looked like a scrap of paper.

Rincewind hesitated, then reached out awkwardly with a gloved hand and scooped it up.

It was, as he'd expected, a butterfly.

"Thank you very much," he said, bitterly.

The water drained through his fingers.

He half closed his hand and then sighed and, as gently as he could, maneuvered the creature on to a finger. Its wings hung damply.

He shielded it with his other hand and blew on the wings a few times.

"Go on, push off."

The butterfly turned. Its multi-faceted eyes glinted green for a moment and then it flapped its wings experimentally.

It stopped raining.

It started to snow, but only where Rincewind was.

"Oh, yes," said Rincewind. "Yes indeed. Oh, thank you so very much."

Life was, he had heard, like a bird which flies out of the darkness and across a crowded hall and then through another window into the endless night again. In Rincewind's case it had managed to do something incontinent in his dinner.

The snow stopped. The clouds pulled back from the dome of the sky with astonishing speed, letting in hot sunlight which almost immediately made the mud steam.

"There you are! We've been looking everywhere!"

Rincewind tried to turn, but the mud made that impossible. There was a wooden thump, as of a plank being laid down on wet ooze.

"Snow on his head? In bright sunshine? I said to myself, that's him all right."

There was the thump of another plank.

A small avalanche slid off the helmet and slid down Rincewind's neck.

Another thump, and a plank squelched into the mud beside him.

"It's me, Twoflower. Are you all right, old friend?"

"I think my foot is being cooked, but apart from that I'm as happy as anything."

"I knew it would be you doing the charades," said Twoflower, sticking his hands under the wizard's shoulders and hauling.

"You got the 'Wind' syllable?" said Rincewind. "That was very hard to do, by remote control."

"Oh, none of us got that," said Twoflower, "but when it did

'ohshitohshitohshit I'm going to die' everyone got *that* first go. Very inventive. Er. You seem to be stuck."

"I think it's the magic boots."

"Can't you wiggle them off? This mud dries like—well, like terracotta in the sun. Someone can come along and dig them out afterwards."

Rincewind tried to move his feet. There was some sub-mud bubblings and he felt his feet come free, with a muffled slurping noise.

Finally, with considerable effort, he was sitting on the plank.

"Sorry about the warriors," he said. "It looked so simple when I started out, and then I got confused with all the pictures and it was impossible to stop some of them doing things—"

"But it was a famous victory!" said Twoflower.

"Was it?"

"Mr. Cohen's been made Emperor!"

"He has?"

"Well, not made, no one made him, he just came along and took it. And everyone says he's the preincarnation of the first Emperor and he says if you want to be the Great Wizard that's fine by him."

"Sorry? You lost me there . . ."

"You led the Red Army, didn't you? You made them rise up in the Empire's hour of need?"

"Well, I wouldn't exactly say that I—"

"So the Emperor wants to reward you. Isn't that nice?"

"How do you mean, reward?" said Rincewind, with deep suspicion.

"Not sure, really. Actually, what he said was . . ." Twoflower's eyes glazed as he tried to recall. "He said, 'You go and find Rincewind and say he might be a bit of a pillock but at least he's straight so he can be Chief Wizard of the Empire or whatever he wants to call it, 'cos I don't trust you foreign . . .'" Twoflower squinted upwards as he tried to remember Cohen's precise words "'. . . house of auspicious aspect . . . scent of pine trees . . . buggers.'"

The words trickled into Rincewind's ear, slid up into his brain, and started to bang on the walls.

"Chief Wizard?" he said.

"That's what he said. Well . . . actually what he said was he
wanted you to be a blob of swallow's vomit, but that was because
he used the low sad tone rather than the high questioning one.
He definitely *meant* wizard."

"Of the whole Empire?"

Rincewind stood up.

"Something very bad is about to happen," he said flatly.

The sky was quite blue now. A few citizens had ventured on
to the battlefield to tend the wounded and retrieve the dead. Terracotta warriors stood at various angles, motionless as rocks.

"Any minute now," said Rincewind.

"Shouldn't we get back?"

"Probably a meteorite strike," said Rincewind.

Twoflower looked up at the peaceful sky.

"You know me," said Rincewind. "Just when I'm getting a
grip on something Fate comes along and jumps on my fingers."

"I don't *see* any meteorites," said Twoflower. "How long do
we wait?"

"It'll be something else, then," said Rincewind. "Someone
will come leaping out, or there'll be an earthquake, or
something."

"If you insist," said Twoflower, politely. "Um. Do you want to
wait for something horrible here or would you like to go back to
the palace and have a bath and change your clothes and then see
what happens?"

Rincewind conceded that he might as well await a dreadful
fate in comfort.

"There's going to be a feast," said Twoflower. "The Emperor
says he's going to teach everyone how to quaff."

They made their way, plank by plank, back towards the city.

"You know, I swear you never told me that you were married."

"I'm sure I did."

"I was, er, I was sorry to hear that your wife, er—"

"Things happen in war. I have two dutiful daughters."

Rincewind opened his mouth to say something but
Twoflower's bright, brittle smile froze the words in his throat.

They worked without speaking, picking up the planks behind them and extending the walkway in front.

"Looking on the bright side," said Twoflower, breaking the silence, "the Emperor said you could start your own University, if you wanted."

"No! No! Someone hit me with an iron bar, please!"

"He said he's well in favor of education provided no one makes him have one. He's been making proclamations like mad. The eunuchs have threatened to go on strike."

Rincewind's plank dropped on to the mud.

"What is it that eunuchs do," he said, "that they stop doing when they go on strike?"

"Serve food, make the beds, things like that."

"Oh."

"They run the Forbidden City, really. But the Emperor talked them round to his point of view."

"Really?"

"He said if they didn't get cracking right now he'd cut off everything else. Um, I think the ground's firm enough now."

His own University. That'd make him . . . Archchancellor. Rincewind the Archchancellor pictured himself visiting Unseen University. He could have a hat with a really big point. He'd be able to be rude to everyone. He'd—

He tried to stop himself from thinking like that. It'd all go wrong.

"Of course," said Twoflower, "it might be that the bad things have already happened to you. Have you considered that? Perhaps you're due something nice?"

"Don't give me any of that karma stuff," said Rincewind. "The wheel of fortune has lost a few spokes where I'm concerned."

"It's worth considering, though," said Twoflower.

"What, that the rest of my life will be peaceful and enjoyable? Sorry. No. You wait. When my back's turned and—bang!"

Twoflower looked around with some interest.

"I don't know why you think your life has been so bad," he said. "We had a lot of fun when we were younger. Hey, do you remember the time when we went over the edge of the world?"

"Often," said Rincewind. "Usually around 3 A.M."

"And that time we were on a dragon and it disappeared in mid-air?"

"You know," said Rincewind, "sometimes a whole hour will go by when I *don't* remember that."

"And that time we were attacked by those people who wanted to kill us?"

"Which of those one hundred and forty-nine occasions are you referring to?"

"Character building, that sort of thing," said Twoflower, happily. "Made me what I am today."

"Oh, yes," said Rincewind. It was no effort, talking to Twoflower. The little man's trusting nature had no concept of sarcasm and a keen ability not to hear things that might upset him. "Yes, I can definitely say it was that sort of thing that made me what I am today, too."

They stepped inside the city. The streets were practically empty. Most people had flocked to the huge square in front of the palace. New Emperors tended towards displays of generosity. Besides, the news had got around that this one was different and was giving away free pigs.

"I heard him talking about sending envoys to Ankh-Morpork," said Twoflower, as they dripped up the street. "I expect there's going to be a bit of a fuss about that."

"Was that man Disembowel-Meself-Honorably present at the time?" said Rincewind.

"Yes, as a matter of fact."

"When you visited Ankh-Morpork, did you ever meet a man called Dibbler?"

"Oh, yes."

"If those two ever shake hands I think there might be some sort of explosion."

"But you could go back, I'm sure," said Twoflower. "I mean, your new University will need all sorts of things and, well, I seem to recall that people in Ankh-Morpork were very keen on gold."

Rincewind gritted his teeth. The image wouldn't go away—of Archchancellor Rincewind buying the Tower of Art and getting them to number all the stones and send it back to Hunghung, of

Archchancellor Rincewind hiring all the faculty as college porters, of Archchancellor Rincewi . . .

"No!"

"Pardon?"

"Don't encourage me to think like that! The moment I think that it's all going to be worthwhile something dreadful will happen!"

There was a movement behind him, and a knife suddenly pressed against his throat.

"The Great Blob of Swallow's Vomit?" said a voice by his ear.

"There," said Rincewind. "You see? Run away! Don't stand there, you bloody idiot! *Run!*"

Twoflower stared for a moment and then turned and scampered away.

"Let him go," said the voice. "He doesn't matter."

Hands pulled him into the alley. He had a vague impression of armor, and mud; his captors were skilled in the way of dragging a prisoner so that he had no chance to get a foothold anywhere.

Then he was flung on to the cobbles.

"He does not look so great to me," said an imperious voice. "Look up, Great Wizard!"

There was some nervous laughter from the soldiers.

"You fools!" raged Lord Hong. "He is just a man! Look at him! Does he look so powerful? He is just a man who has found some old trickery! And we will find out how great he is without his arms and legs."

"Oh," said Rincewind.

Lord Hong leaned down. There was mud on his face and a wild glint in his eyes. "We shall see what your barbarian Emperor can do *then*, won't we?" He indicated the sullen group of mud-encrusted soldiers. "You know, they half believe you really *are* a great wizard? That's superstition, I'm afraid. Very useful most of the time, damn inconvenient on occasion. But when we march you into the square and show them how great you really are, I think your barbarian will not have so very long left. What are these?"

He snatched the gloves off Rincewind's hands.

"Toys," he said. "Made things. The Red Army are just machines, like mills and pumps. There's no magic there."

He tossed them aside and nodded at one of the guards.

"And now," said Lord Hong, "let us go to the Imperial Square."

"How'd you like to be governor of Bhangbhangduc and all these islands around here?" said Cohen, as the Horde pored over a map of the Empire. "You like the seaside, Hamish?"

"Whut?"

The doors of the Throne Room were flung open. Twoflower scuttled in, trailed by One Big River.

"Lord Hong's got Rincewind! He's going to kill him!"

Cohen looked up.

"He can wizard himself out of it, can't he?"

"No! He hasn't got the Red Army any more! He's going to *kill* him! You've got to *do* something!"

"Ach, well, you know how it is with wizards," said Truckle. "There's too many of 'em as it is—"

"No." Cohen picked up his sword and sighed.

"Come on," he said.

"But, Cohen—"

"I said *come on*. We ain't like Hong. Rincewind's a weasel, but he's *our* weasel. So are you coming or what?"

Lord Hong and his group of soldiers had almost reached the bottom of the wide steps to the palace when the Horde emerged. The crowd surrounded them, held back by the soldiers.

Lord Hong held Rincewind tightly, a knife at his throat.

"Ah, Emperor," he said, in Ankh-Morporkian. "We meet again. Check, I think."

"What's he mean?" Cohen whispered.

"He thinks he has you cornered," said Mr. Saveloy.

"How's he know I won't just let the wizard die?"

"Psychology of the individual, I'm afraid."

"It doesn't make any sense!" Cohen shouted. "If you kill him, you'll be dead yourself in seconds. I shall see to it pers'nally!"

"Indeed, no," said Lord Hong. "When your . . . Great Wizard . . . is dead, when people see how easily he dies . . . how long will you be Emperor? You won by trickery!"

"What are your terms?" said Mr. Saveloy.

"There are none. You can give me nothing I cannot take myself." Lord Hong grabbed Rincewind's hat from one of the guards and rammed it on to Rincewind's head.

"This is yours," he hissed. "'Wizzard' hah! You can't even spell! Well, *wizzard?* Aren't you going to say something?"

"Oh, no!"

Lord Hong smiled. "Ah, that's better," he said.

"Oh, noooooo!"

"Very good!"

"Aarrgh!"

Lord Hong blinked. For a moment the figure in front of him appeared to stretch to twice its height and then have its feet snap up under its chin.

And then it disappeared, with a small thunderclap.

There was silence in the square, except for the sound of several thousand people being astonished.

Lord Hong waved his hand vaguely in the air.

"Lord Hong?"

He turned. There was a short man behind him, covered in grime and mud. He wore a pair of spectacles, one lens of which was cracked.

Lord Hong hardly glanced at him. He prodded the air again, unwilling to believe his own senses.

"Excuse me, Lord Hong," said the apparition, "but do you by any chance remember Bes Pelargic? About six years ago? I think you were quarreling with Lord Tang? There was something of a skirmish. A few streets destroyed. Nothing very major."

Lord Hong blinked.

"How dare you address me!" he managed.

"It doesn't really matter," said Twoflower. "But it's just that I'd have liked you to have remembered. I got . . . quite angry about it. Er. I want to fight you."

"*You* want to fight *me?* Do you know who you are talking to? Have you any *idea?*"

"Er. Yes. Oh, yes," said Twoflower.

Lord Hong's attention finally focused. It had not been a good day.

"You foolish, stupid little man! You don't even have a sword!"

"Oi! Four-eyes!"

They both turned. Cohen threw his sword. Twoflower caught it clumsily and was almost knocked over by the weight.

"Why did you do that?" said Mr. Saveloy.

"Man wants to be a hero. That's fine by me," said Cohen.

"He'll be slaughtered!"

"Might do. Might do. Might do. He might do that, certainly," Cohen conceded. "That's not up to me."

"Father!"

Lotus Blossom grabbed Twoflower's arm.

"He *will* kill you! Come away!"

"No."

Butterfly took her father's other arm.

"No good purpose will be served," she said. "Come on. We can find a better time—"

"He killed your mother," said Twoflower flatly.

"His soldiers did."

"That makes it worse. He didn't even know. Please get back, both of you."

"Look, Father—"

"If you don't both do what you're told I shall get angry."

Lord Hong drew his long sword. The blade gleamed.

"Do you know *anything* about fighting, clerk?"

"No, not really," said Twoflower. "But the important thing is that someone should stand up to you. Whatever happens to them afterwards."

The Horde were watching with considerable interest. Hardened as they were, they had a soft spot for pointless bravery.

"Yes," said Lord Hong, looking around at the silent crowd. "Let *everyone* see what happens."

He raised his sword.

The air crackled.

The Barking Dog dropped on to the flagstones in front of him.

It was very hot. Its string was alight.

There was a brief sizzle.

Then the world went white.

After some time, Twoflower picked himself up. He seemed to be the first one upright; those people who hadn't flung themselves to the ground had fled.

All that remained of Lord Hong was one shoe, which was smouldering. But there was a smoking trail all the way up the steps behind it.

Staggering a little, Twoflower followed the trail.

A wheelchair was on its side, one wheel spinning.

He peered over it.

"You all right, Mr. Hamish?"

"Whut?"

"Good."

The rest of the Horde were crouched in a circle at the top of the steps. Smoke billowed around them. In its continuing passage, the ball had set fire to part of the palace.

"Can you hear me, Teach?" Cohen was saying.

"'Course he can't hear you! How can he hear you, looking like that?" said Truckle.

"He could still be alive," said Cohen defiantly.

"He is *dead*, Cohen. Really, really *dead*. Alive people have more *body*."

"But you're all alive?" said Twoflower. "I saw it bark straight at you!"

"We got out of the way," said Boy Willie. "We're good at getting out of the way."

"Poor ole Teach didn't have our experience of not dyin'," said Caleb.

Cohen stood up.

"Where's Hong?" he said grimly. "I'm going to—"

"He's dead, too, Mr. Cohen," said Twoflower.

Cohen nodded, as if this was all perfectly normal.

"We *owe* it to ole Teach," he said.

"He was a good sort," Truckle conceded. "Funny ideas about swearing, mind you."

"He had brains. He cared about stuff! And he might not have lived like a barbarian, but he's bloody well going to be buried like one, all right?"

"In a longship, set on fire," suggested Boy Willie.

"My word," said Mr. Saveloy.

"In a big pit, on top of the bodies of his enemies," suggested Caleb.

"Good heavens, all of 4B?" said Mr. Saveloy.

"In a burial mound," suggested Vincent.

"Really, I wouldn't put you to the trouble," said Mr. Saveloy.

"*In* a longship set on fire, *on top* of a heap of the bodies of his enemies, *under* a burial mound," said Cohen flatly. "Nothing's too good for ole Teach."

"But I assure you, I feel fine," said Mr. Saveloy. "Really, I—er . . . Oh . . ."

RONALD SAVELOY?

Mr. Saveloy turned.

"Ah," he said. "Yes. I see."

IF YOU WOULD CARE TO STEP THIS WAY?

The palace and the Horde froze and faded gently, like a dream.

"It's funny," said Mr. Saveloy, as he followed Death. "I didn't expect it to be this way."

FEW PEOPLE EVER EXPECT IT TO BE *ANY* WAY.

Gritty black sand crunched under what Mr. Saveloy supposed he should still call his feet.

"Where is this?"

THE DESERT.

It was brilliantly lit, and yet the sky was midnight-black. He stared at the horizon.

"How big is it?"

FOR SOME, VERY BIG. FOR LORD HONG, FOR INSTANCE, IT CONTAINS A LOT OF IMPATIENT GHOSTS.

"I thought Lord Hong didn't believe in ghosts."

HE MAY DO SO NOW. A LOT OF GHOSTS BELIEVE IN LORD HONG.

"Oh. Er. What happens now?"

Terry Pratchett

"Come on, come on, haven't got all day! Step lively, man!"

Mr. Saveloy turned around and looked up at the woman on the horse. It was a big horse but, then, it was a big woman. She had plaits, a hat with horns on it, and a breastplate that must have been a week's work for an experienced panelbeater. She gave him a look that was not unkind but had impatience in every line.

"I'm sorry?" he said.

"Says here Ronald Saveloy," she said. "The what?"

"The what?"

"Everyone I pick up," said the woman, leaning down, "is called 'Someone *the* Something.' What *the* are you?"

"I'm sorry, I—"

"I'll put you down as Ronald the Apologetic, then. Come on, hop up, there's a war on, got to be going."

"Where to?"

"Says here quaffing, carousing, throwing axes at young women's hair?"

"Ah, er, I think perhaps there's been a bit of a—"

"Look, old chap, are you coming or what?"

Mr. Saveloy looked around at the black desert. He was totally alone. Death had gone about his essential business.

He let her pull him up behind her.

"Have they got a library, perhaps?" he asked hopefully, as the horse rose into the dark sky.

"Don't know. No one's ever asked."

"Evening classes, perhaps. I could start evening classes?"

"What in?"

"Um. Anything, really. Table manners, perhaps. Is that allowed?"

"I suppose so. I don't think anyone's ever asked that, either." The Valkyrie turned in the saddle.

"You *sure* you're coming to the right afterlife?"

Mr. Saveloy considered the possibilities.

"On the whole," he said, "I think it's worth a try."

*   *   *

288

The crowd in the square were getting to their feet.

They looked at all that remained of Lord Hong, and at the Horde.

Butterfly and Lotus Blossom joined their father. Butterfly ran her hand over the cannon, looking for the trick.

"You see," said Twoflower, a little indistinctly because he couldn't quite hear the sound of his own voice yet, "I *told* you he was the Great Wizard."

Butterfly tapped him on the shoulder.

"What about those?" she said.

A small procession was picking its way through the square. In front, Twoflower recognized, was something he'd once owned.

"It was a very cheap one," he said, to no one in particular. "I always thought there was something a little warped about it, to tell you the truth."

It was followed by a slightly larger Luggage. And then, in descending order of size, four little chests, the smallest being about the size of a lady's handbag. As it passed a prone Hunghungese who'd been too stunned to flee, it paused to kick him in the ear before hurrying after the others.

Twoflower looked at his daughters.

"Can they do that?" he said. "Make new ones? I thought it needed carpenters."

"I suppose it learned many things in Ankh-More-Pork," said Butterfly.

The Luggages clustered together in front of the steps. Then *the* Luggage turned around and, after one or two sad backward glances, or what might have been glances if it had eyes, cantered away. By the time it reached the far side of the square it was a blur.

"Hey, you! Four-eyes!"

Twoflower turned. Cohen was advancing down the steps.

"I remember you," he said. "D'you know anything about Grand Viziering?"

"Not a thing, Mr. Emperor Cohen."

"Good. The job's yours. Get cracking. First thing, I want a cup of tea. Thick enough to float a horseshoe. Three sugars. In five minutes. Right?"

"A cup of tea in *five minutes?*" said Twoflower. "But that's not long enough for even a short ceremony!"

Cohen put a companionable arm around the little man's shoulders.

"There's a *new* ceremony," he said. "It goes: 'Tea up, luv. Milk? Sugar? Doughnut? Want another one?' And you could tell the eunuchs," he added, "that the Emperor is a lit'ral-minded man and used the phrase 'heads will roll'."

Twoflower's eyes gleamed behind his cracked glasses. Somehow, he liked the sound of that.

It looked as though he was living in interesting times—

The Luggages sat quietly, and waited.

Fate sat back.

The gods relaxed.

"A draw," he announced. "Oh, yes. You have appeared to win in Hunghung *but* you have had to lose your most valuable piece, is that not so?"

"I'm sorry?" said the Lady. "I don't quite follow you."

"Insofar as I understand this . . . physics . . ." said Fate, "I cannot believe that anything could be materialized in the University without dying almost instantly. It is one thing to hit a snowdrift, but quite another to hit a wall."

"I never sacrifice a pawn," said the Lady.

"How can you hope to win without sacrificing the occasional pawn?"

"Oh, I never play to win." She smiled. "But I do play not to lose. Watch . . ."

The Council of Wizards gathered in front of the wall at the far end of the Great Hall and stared up at the thing which now covered half of it.

"Interesting effect," said Ridcully, eventually. "How fast do you think it was going?"

"About five hundred miles an hour," said Ponder. "I think perhaps we were a little enthusiastic. Hex says—"

"From a standing start to five hundred miles an hour?" said the Lecturer in Recent Runes. "That must have come as a shock."

"Yes," said Ridcully, "but I suppose it's a mercy for the poor creature that it was such a brief one."

"And, of course, we must all be thankful that it wasn't Rincewind."

A couple of the wizards coughed.

The Dean stood back.

"But what *is* it?" he said.

"Was," said Ponder Stibbons.

"We could have a look in the Bestiaries," said Ridcully. "Shouldn't be hard to find. Gray. Long hind feet like a clown's boots. Rabbit ears. Tail long and pointy. And, of course, not many creatures are twenty feet across, one inch thick and deep fried, so that narrows it down a bit."

"I don't want to cast a shadow on things," said the Dean, "but if this isn't Rincewind, then where is he?"

"I'm sure Mr. Stibbons can give us an explanation as to why his calculations went wrong," said Ridcully.

Ponder's mouth dropped open.

Then he said, as sourly as he dared, "I probably forgot to take into account that there's three right angles in a triangle, didn't I? Er. I'll have to try and work everything back, but I think that somehow a lateral component was introduced into what should have been a bidirectional sortilegic transfer. It's probably that this was most pronounced at the effective median point, causing an extra node to appear in the transfers at a point equidistant to the other two as prediction in Flume's Third Equation, and Turffe's Law would see to it that the distortion would stabilize in such a way as to create three separate points, each moving a roughly equal mass one jump around the triangle. I'm not sure why the third mass arrived here at such speed, but I think the increased velocity might have been caused by the sudden creation of the node. Of course, it might have been going quite fast anyway. But I shouldn't think it is cooked in its natural state."

"Do you know," said Ridcully, "I think I actually understood some of that? Certainly some of the shorter words."

"Oh, it's perfectly simple," said the Bursar brightly. "We sent the . . . dog thing to Hunghung. Rincewind was sent to some other place. And this creature was sent here. Just like Pass the Parcel."

"You see?" said Ridcully to Stibbons. "You're using language the *Bursar* can understand. And *he's* been chasing the dried frog all morning."

The Librarian staggered into the hall under the weight of a large atlas.

"Oook."

"At least you can show us where you think our man is," said Ridcully.

Ponder took a ruler and a pair of compasses out of his hat.

"Well, if we assume Rincewind was in the middle of the Counterweight Continent," he said, "then all we need do is draw—"

"Oook!"

"I assure you, I was only going to use pencil—"

"*Eeek.*"

"All we have to do is *imagine,* all right, a third point equidistant from the other two . . . er . . . that looks like somewhere in the Rim Ocean to me, or probably over the Edge."

"Can't see that thing in the sea," said Ridcully, glancing up at the recently laminated corpse.

"In that case, it must have been in the other direction—"

The wizards crowded round.

There *was* something there.

"'S not even properly drawn in," said the Dean.

"That's because no one's sure it really exists," said the Senior Wrangler.

It floated in the middle of the sea, a tiny continent by Discworld standards.

"'XXXX,'" Ponder read.

"They only put that on the map because no one knows what it's really called," said Ridcully.

"And we've sent him there," said Ponder. "A place that we're not even certain *exists?*"

"Oh, we know it exists now," said Ridcully. "Must do. Must do. Must be a pretty rich land, too, if the rats grow that big."

"I'll go and see if we can bring—" Ponder began.

"Oh, no," said Ridcully firmly. "No, thank you very much. Next time it might be an elephant whizzing over our heads, and those things make a splash. No. Give the poor chap a rest. We'll have to think of something else . . ."

He rubbed his hands together. "Time for dinner, I feel," he said.

"Um," said the Senior Wrangler. "Do you think we were wise to light that string when we sent the thing back?"

"Certainly," said Ridcully, as they strolled away. "No one could say we didn't return it in exactly the same state as it arrived . . ."

Hex dreamed gently in its room.

The wizards were right. Hex couldn't think.

There weren't words, yet, for what it could do.

Even Hex didn't know what it could do.

But it was going to find out.

The quill pen scritched and blotted its way over a fresh sheet of paper and drew, for no good reason, a calendar for the year surmounted by a rather angular picture of a beagle, standing on its hind legs.

The ground was red, just like at Hunghung. But whereas that was a kind of clay so rich that leaving a chair on the lawn meant that you had four small trees by nightfall, this ground was sand that looked as if it had got red by being baked in a million-year summer.

There were occasional clumps of yellowed grass and low stands of gray-green trees. But what there was everywhere was heat.

This was especially noticeable in the pond under the ghost gums. It was steaming.

A figure emerged from the clouds, absentmindedly picking the burnt bits off his beard.

Rincewind waited until his own personal world had stopped

spinning and concentrated on the four men who were watching him.

They were black with lines and whorls painted on their faces and had, between them, about two square feet of clothing.

There were three reasons why Rincewind was no racist. He'd ended up in too many places too suddenly to develop that kind of mind. Besides, if he'd thought about it much, most of the really dreadful things that had happened to him had been done by quite pale people with big wardrobes. Those were two of the reasons.

The third was that these men, who were just rising from a half-crouching position, were all holding spears pointing at Rincewind and there is something about the sight of four spears aimed at your throat that causes no end of respect and the word "sir" to arise spontaneously in the mind.

One of the men shrugged, and lowered his spear.

"G'day, bloke," he said.

This meant only three spears, which was an improvement.

"Er. This isn't Unseen University, is it, sir?" said Rincewind.

The other spears stopped pointing at him. The men grinned. They had very white teeth.

"Klatch? Howondaland? It looks like Howondaland," said Rincewind hopefully.

"Don't know them blokes, bloke," said one of the men.

The other three clustered around him.

"What'll we call him?"

"He's Kangaroo Bloke. No worries there. One minute a kangaroo, next minute a bloke. The old blokes say that sort of thing used to happen all the time, back in the Dream."

"I reckoned he'd look better than that."

"Yeah."

"One way to tell."

The man who was apparently the leader of the group advanced on Rincewind with the kind of grin reserved for imbeciles and people holding guns, and held out a stick.

It was flat, and had a bend in the middle. Someone had spent a long time making rather nice designs on it in little colored dots. Somehow, Rincewind wasn't at all surprised to see a butterfly among them.

The hunters watched him expectantly.

"Er, yes," he said. "Very good. Very good workmanship, yes. Interesting pointillistic effect. Shame you couldn't find a straighter bit of wood."

One of the men laid down his spear, and squatted down and picked up a long wooden tube, covered with the same designs. He blew into it. The effect was not unpleasant. It sounded like bees would sound if they'd invented full orchestration.

"Um," said Rincewind. "Yes."

It was a test, obviously. They'd given him this bent piece of wood. He had to do something with it. It was clearly very important. He'd—

Oh, no. He'd say something or do something, wouldn't he, and then they'd say, yes, you are the Great Bloke or something, and they'd drag him off and it'd be the start of another Adventure, i.e., a period of horror and unpleasantness. Life was full of tricks like that.

Well, this time Rincewind wasn't going to fall for it.

"I want to go home," he said. "I want to go back home to the Library where it was nice and quiet. And I don't know where I am. And I don't care what you do to me, right? I'm not going to have any kind of adventure or start saving the world again and you can't trick me into it with mysterious bits of wood."

He gripped the stick and flung it away from him with all the force he could still muster.

They stared at him as he folded his arms.

"I'm not playing," he said. "I'm stopping right here."

They were still staring. And now they were grinning, too, at something behind him.

He felt himself getting quite annoyed.

"Do you understand? Are you listening?" he said. "That's the last time the universe is going to trick Rincewi—"